"I THOUGHT I'D FIND YOU HERE."

Kurt leaned on the railing next to Julia.

"You must be psychic."

"I just know you."

"Oh, really?" Julia turned sideways against the railing to face him, a small smile of disbelief curving her mouth.

He eyed her. "You have a low tolerance for crowds. And you've been avoiding me ever since we got back from our little outing this afternoon, although I'm not certain if it's the kiss or that I saw you cry that bothers you the most."

"Not bad," she said lightly and waited for him to make his next move. It didn't take long.

"So which is it?"

"Both," she admitted with uncharacteristic candor.

Unlike this afternoon when he had caught her by surprise, this time she knew he was going to kiss her.

"I've been wanting to do this all evening," he murmured, cupping her face in his hands. "You are rare . . . beautiful . . ."

From the first gentle contact and the accompanying zing through her bloodstream, the kiss went beyond the mere epidermal. This was not the brief, friendly peck of this afternoon. Julia's shocked gasp of recognition was smothered under the increasing demand of Kurt's mouth as he gathered her more tightly in his arms. It all came back to her—passion so intense it swept away caution, hunger so urgent it was both pleasure and pain. . . .

PLAYING BY HEART

Jacquelyn Ross

ZEBRA BOOKS
KENSINGTON PUBLISHING CORP.

http://www.kensingtonbooks.com

ZEBRA BOOKS are published by

Kensington Publishing Corp.
850 Third Avenue
New York, NY 10022

All Kensington titles, imprints and distributed lines are available at special quantity discounts for bulk purchases for sales promotion, premiums, fund-raising, educational or institutional use.

Special book excerpts or customized printings can also be created to fit specific needs. For details, write or phone the office of the Kensington Special Sales Manager: Kensington Publishing Corp., 850 Third Avenue, New York, NY 10022. Attn. Special Sales Department. Phone: 1-800-221-2647.

First Printing: September 2002
10 9 8 7 6 5 4 3 2 1

Printed in the United States of America

A Weekend in the Country

Chapter 1

"Alex—over here!" A week after her grandfather's funeral, Julia Griffin waved to catch her friend's attention through the throng of noisy travelers crowding the busy little airport. Alex finally spied her and plowed her way through like a queen, tawny hair flying behind, carry-on bag casually thrown over one shoulder of her sleek suit. As if for royalty, the crowd parted before her. She always had that effect on people; the sheer force of a nuclear-powered personality swept aside life's annoying obstacles.

"God, I've missed you!" Alex exclaimed, coming to a full stop in front of Julia and enfolding her in an enthusiastic embrace. "I'm sorry about your grandfather, but I'm glad something finally pried you loose from those dreary Brits."

"Hello to you, too." Julia smiled. "How was your flight?"

"Awful! Let's go grab my bags before someone else does. They cost me an arm."

Their unlikely friendship had its roots at Briarwood Academy for Girls, an exclusive Connecticut boarding school where Julia was sent after her maternal grandmother wrested control of her away from her recently departed paternal grandfather. A few weeks after Julia's arrival, Alexandra Chase was banished there by her Beacon Hill family to atone for a lengthy list of transgressions. As the new girls, they were assigned the same room. By then, in that alien world of wealth and privilege, Julia was already labeled an outcast. From the first, Alex mistook Julia's indifference to her classmates, and her artistic bent, as evidence of a kindred rebel spirit. Supremely confident in her assessment, she simply ignored all Julia's attempts to keep her at arm's length and pulled her along in her powerful wake. Eventually, Julia had stopped resisting the inevitable. Their friendship had outlasted Briarwood and, later, Wesleyan University.

After five years in London, Julia had to concentrate to stay on the right side of the road. Ignoring scenic vistas of vineyards and orchards rising on hillsides from Lake Michigan, she coaxed her grandfather's ancient Jeep up Leelanau Peninsula toward Cherry Beach.

"Tell me everything." Alex gingerly settled her expensively clad back against the Jeep's tatty upholstery. "Is Hugo in a snit that you left?"

"He's coping." Julia smiled, thinking of the cross-Atlantic earful her partner and accompanist had given her last night over her replacement. She figured he'd earned the right. They'd been in the middle of a rehearsal at the club when the call came through about her grandfather's death. Hugo had been a brick. While she stumbled along in shock at the news, he'd booked tickets, helped pack her kit, and gently delivered her to the British Airways departure gate.

"How long will you stay?"

"I'm not sure. It's taking longer than I expected to go through all his things. Alex, he kept everything!" Julia glanced across the front seat. "It's hard to even imagine selling the place."

"Why not keep it? Come back for vacations."

"I've thought about it. Evidently that was my grandfather's hope, according to the neighbors." That bit of news had hit hard. Now she felt guilty every time she thought about selling it. But she wasn't sure she wanted to keep it, with all its ties to the past. Or could afford to.

"My brother, Kip, is taking a few days off from that sweatshop law firm he works for and wants us to go with him to Rob Weston's summer place," Alex was saying. "How about it? It's only an hour or two north of here."

"When?"

"Next weekend."

"I don't know." Julia shook her head doubtfully. "There's so much I need to do."

"Oh, come on. I have to go Sunday and I never get to see you. It would be like old times."

"You don't still fancy Rob do you?" Julia glanced suspiciously at Alex.

Kip Chase and Rob Weston had been classmates at Yale Law during the same years Julia and Alex had attended nearby Wesleyan. The four had occasionally gone out together, mostly because Alex had a hopeless crush on Rob. A steady stream of colorful men had passed through Alex's orbit since then, but Rob was the one who got away.

Alex waved a dismissive hand. "It's been five years. No way I would humiliate myself by throwing myself at his feet again." But then her mouth curved up into a naughty smirk. "I guess I wouldn't mind though if he groveled at *my* feet, or better yet, someplace higher up."

She glanced over at Julia. "Stop looking at me in that tone of voice. I was *joking*."

Julia rolled her eyes. "I'll think about it."

"Waiting is not exactly my strong suit."

"Okay, fine. *If* I'm still here."

Satisfied, Alex launched into an account of her unpromising new boyfriend and her promising new art gallery. When Alex graduated from college, her mother passed over the reins of a sleepy little Boston art gallery of no particular note, a suitable avocation for a young woman from a prominent Boston family until such time as she married a young man of similar background. Unexpectedly, Alex discovered she had an eye for selecting marketable art and a knack for sales. Five years later, she was poised to expand into the Chicago market.

"So tell me about your grandfather," Alex eventually got around to asking.

During the rest of the drive, Julia filled her in on Seth Griffin's death, the investigation, and her lingering doubts about the sheriff's finding of suicide. Morphine overdose, the coroner had concluded, mixed into his favorite beer. His dog, Murphy, had died of the same combination.

From Dr. Susan Cleary, her grandfather's nearest neighbor on Gull Inlet, Julia had learned that he'd had terminal cancer. He hadn't told her. The thought of that made the backpack full of guilt she'd been dragging around for the past week feel a few rocks heavier. She'd repeatedly put off coming to visit because it was easier to turn her back on the past. She'd always assumed there would be time. But time had run out, and his death severed her last connection to family.

"The cancer would explain why he did it," Alex said gently, her eyes sympathetic. "What other explanation could there be?"

Julia shook her head. There had been no evidence of foul play, and no one—except her—stood to gain a thing. "I don't know. It just doesn't fit. My grandfather was a crusty old curmudgeon." She smiled faintly at a memory. "I once heard him called the John McEnroe of wooden-boat builders by an irritated customer. He was a survivor, Alex." After a time, she added, "Even if I could accept that he would take his own life, why would he kill his dog?"

But the sheriff had his tidy chain of evidence and a motive. Seth was dying. The dog was old. And really, Julia acknowledged, she didn't have anything to dispute the sheriff's findings except a nagging feeling that the Seth Griffin she knew would not have taken his own life.

Thirty miles up the peninsula they passed through Cherry Beach. Still early for the tide of summer visitors, the village streets were nearly deserted. A few miles farther, Julia turned onto a dirt track that wound beneath a high canopy of beech trees leading into Gull Inlet. The dense canopy formed by the loosely spaced giants inhibited understory growth, creating an enormous living cathedral. The giant beech gave way to smaller mixed hardwoods, mostly sugar maple and birch, which in turn gave way to a wide rim of dazzling sugar-sand beach, barren but for sparse patches of windswept dune grass.

The Jeep bumped along the two-track, following the curve of the inlet. Julia pointed out the lodge as they drove past, explaining its history as a guesthouse turned private residence. "The Clearys bought it from my grandfather a few years ago when they decided to leave the city. I'd never met them before last week, but they're distant cousins." A quarter-mile farther, Julia pulled the Jeep to a stop at the end of the road, next to the small pole barn her grandfather had used as a boat shop for smaller projects.

"This is it," she announced.

The rear of the cottage nestled up against a few stunted trees; its front yard consisted mainly of low dunes and the clear blue of the inlet. The cedar-shake exterior was painted gray with peeling white trim. A rough-hewn porch spanned the front. The cottage itself was modest, a tad run down, at best quaint. Here the panoramic view of surf, sand, and sky took center stage.

Alex gaped at the view. "Good Lord, the land must be worth a fortune."

"And unfortunately has the property taxes to match," Julia said, following her up onto the porch. Uncharacteristically, Alex fell silent, appearing mesmerized by the sight and sounds of the waves and windswept dunes. The place had that effect on people.

Julia stared unseeingly out over the barren dunes and endless blue beyond, remembering when her grandfather had brought her here—a broken sixteen-year-old orphan just released from a Nassau hospital. She had never been north of the Bahamas before. For a few critical months he had provided the safe haven she'd desperately needed. And he'd been there, a solid human presence she could depend on while she first disintegrated and then, because there had been no other choice, rebuilt herself piece by piece. By the end of the summer, she'd filled the sketchbooks he'd given her and stopped thinking about the past. If she didn't let it in, it couldn't hurt her. And if she didn't let other people in, they couldn't hurt her either.

Alex was regarding her quizzically. Julia forced a smile. "Come see the rest."

Inside, a wood-burning stove separated a small living area from an even smaller dining area. A large fieldstone fireplace and an open stairway to the second floor took up the opposite wall. Worn area rugs covered the wide plank floor.

"Bedrooms upstairs?" Alex wandered past mismatched furniture toward the kitchen.

"Two bedrooms, one bath."

"This is not bad at all," Alex mused. "Some fresh paint, slipcovers, and curtains. Lose the moose." She grimaced at the deer head mounted over the fireplace. "It's charming."

"Before you get carried away, remember that I'm probably going to sell it."

"But how can you resist keeping it?" Alex protested. "This place is perfect for you. You've always been a sort of hermit, and this would be a perfect place to come and be a hermit once in awhile. Look, if it's a matter of money, why don't we try to sell some of your paintings?"

Julia shook her head. "I haven't been painting much lately."

"In a slump?"

"Something like that." Now, there was an understatement. She was still taking classes at the art institute—supporting herself by playing the clubs at night with Hugo—but her work lately seemed uninspired. She'd lost her spark. "Someday, though, I'll dump them in your lap and then you'll regret your offer." Julia grimaced. "But thanks."

"What are old friends for, anyway? They can give advice—"

"And not get upset when it's not taken," Julia countered with a grin. "I've missed you, Alex."

After dinner, they wandered down to the beach. The last

color was fading from the sky behind the cottage as the first stars blinked on in the darker sky over the water.

"Now I want to hear all about you," Alex insisted, settling down on the cold sand. "I've spilled my guts all day and you haven't told me anything."

"I told you about my grandfather."

"I want to hear about you—your life. So . . ." Alex eyed her. "Are you seeing anyone?"

Julia groaned, used to the drill. "Sadly, no. Just Hugo."

"Gay guys don't count. Even if you almost live together."

Julia shrugged. "He's a good friend."

"They usually are." Alex blew out a frustrated breath. "I could just shake you. Look at you. . . ." Through the dark, Julia could feel Alex mentally cataloging the mop of reddish-brown hair and string-bean build she'd inherited from her father and—her best feature—turquoise eyes she got from her mother. "You have a face that could make a fortune, a body men would like to drool over given half a chance. But it's wasted on you. When are you going to let go and live?"

"Maybe you're right."

Alex stopped midbreath. "What did you say?"

"I said, *maybe you're right.*"

Alex raised two perfectly shaped eyebrows. "We've been having this conversation since we were sixteen years old—ten years!—and you've always blown me off. Has something happened?"

"No. Nothing." Julia looked out over the water. "I just—I don't know. Maybe I am missing something. You're right, I don't feel alive. I feel . . ." *Empty? Frozen?* She shook her head. "But I don't think I can change. I'm not sure I want to."

But something inside her already had, she recognized. She was restless. Even before Seth's death, her solitary life had begun to feel arid and empty, the years ahead a barren desert. Sometimes she found herself yearning for physical love, any connection to another person. Sometimes she dreamed about what it would be like to feel a man's body heavy on hers. But she was afraid to risk it, afraid of the inevitable loss that went with it.

Alex had been watching her closely. "Oh, dear. I had no idea you were unhappy."

"Not unhappy really, just . . . restless, I guess."

"Ah. I think I'm beginning to understand. Sometimes you're as cryptic as a sine wave," Alex complained. "What you need is a man in your life."

Julia pulled a face. "I don't want that sort of commitment."

"Who said anything about commitment?" Alex laughed. "That would be rich coming from me. I'm simply suggesting you test the water, wade around some, get used to it. Then if you like it, you can go deeper." Alex's voice took on a more serious note. "I don't want to say anything that would make you duck for cover, but you're wrong, you know—about changing. You can. You are a strong woman. You can climb over that wall you've built up."

"Thanks. Who knows? Maybe this time I will take your advice."

"That would be a first," Alex laughed.

"Come on. It's getting cold." Julia stood and brushed sand off her jeans. "Let's go back and open that bottle of wine you brought."

A week later Julia drove back to the Traverse City airport to meet Alex and her brother, Kip. She left the Jeep in long-term parking. They made the rest of the two-hour trip to Harbor Springs in a rented sedan. Kip liked to sing and inevitably coaxed Julia into his fun. His baritone wasn't half bad, but he couldn't harmonize for anything.

"I think I've got it this time," he insisted.

Julia groaned.

Alex complained, "We've already done it five times and you keep singing my part."

Julia compromised. "Let's take a break first." Kip's enthusiasm was hard to resist. It, and the fact that he'd always treated her like another sister, made him fun to be around.

Julia watched the passing scenery and reflected on all she'd learned during the week. In addition to the twenty-acre parcel on which the cottage sat, it turned out her grandfather had owned a larger adjoining piece of prime undeveloped waterfront to the north known as Deer Cove. Both parcels had passed to her as joint owner, but the Deer Cove tract was heavily mortgaged with a balloon due in six years. Seth's bank accounts and stock funds would cover taxes and payments on both parcels for several years at least, but not the balloon payment on Deer Cove. She'd decided to hang on to both parcels for the time being and face that problem later.

Eventually, Kip broke the reflective silence that had settled over the trio. "So, what are you going to do with the cottage now that you've decided to keep it, Julia?"

"I'm going to come back and spend time every summer. It feels like home." It had been a long time since any place felt like more than a temporary abode. "Ted Cleary is the principal of the high school in Cherry Beach. He knows of a teacher who might be interested in letting it for the school year."

"I'm just glad you're staying awhile," Alex said.

"Me, too. Hugo's not grumbling too much anymore, which means my replacement must be working out, although he would never admit it. We knock off soon for the summer anyway."

She'd gradually taken to the idea of having the entire summer to spend sketching and painting around the inlet. Everywhere she hiked—in the woods, along the beach, in the village—she encountered people and scenes that cried out to be captured. For the first time in ages she wanted to paint. Everything was working out better than expected: the finances, a possible renter. The only dark cloud was the lingering question she had about her grandfather's death. And her guilt. She was beginning to wonder if her guilt wasn't fueling her questions.

She glanced across the seat at Kip. Wind from the open window ruffled his sandy hair. It had thinned in the five years since she'd moved across the Atlantic. He looked tired, too.

Julia smiled at him and began singing his favorite Dylan tune, "*I was so much older then, I'm younger than that now. . . .*"

The rest of the drive passed in a blur of high spirits. A mile past Harbor Springs, they turned down a scenic road lined with stately rows of elms leading up to a security gate. Kip stopped and gave his name to the uniformed guard. After checking a list, the guard welcomed them to Breakers and pushed a button that sent the gate rolling smoothly along its track.

Julia sat in surprised silence until finally she said, "Why didn't you warn me? You let me think that Rob's *cottage* was really just a cottage."

Old summer mansions drifted by on both sides, set well back from the winding road. Mature trees, gardens, and an occasional tennis court dotted vast expanses of manicured lawn. Glimpses of Lake Michigan could be caught behind the houses and trees on one side, while an inland lake formed the backdrop for the houses on the other. This was plainly old money.

Kip and Alex exchanged a guilty look. "I didn't know either until yesterday," Alex said.

"You should have warned me then." Julia leveled an exasperated look on her. "You know how I feel about places like this. I loathe making endless small talk with people I don't know, much less have anything in common with."

"You're right and I'm sorry. I should have told you." Alex's apology flowed easily, too easily. Julia gave her another irritated look. "But it's not going to be like that," Alex hastily went on. "It's barely June. The summer season isn't in full swing for at least another couple weeks."

"Rob said he had the place to himself," Kip put in. "The rest of the family don't come up until later in the summer."

Julia recalled that Rob Weston came from a big-time

industrial family. This place was probably the family's summer compound, like the Kennedy compound on Martha's Vineyard.

"It's not going to be like visiting your grandmother," Alex assured her.

Mary March died shortly after Julia started college. She still shuddered at the memory of the uncomfortable school vacations she had endured in the stiffly formal March home in Chicago.

As Kip turned onto a long drive that ended in a circle in front of a cedar-sided beauty, Julia resigned herself to making the best of it. She didn't want to cast a pall over Kip's vacation. He needed a break. And if the summer residents had not yet arrived—she speculatively eyed lush grounds sweeping down to the beach—they would have this beautiful spot all to themselves.

"Are you okay with this, Julia?"

She caught the gratifying hint of anxiety in Alex's voice.

"I know it's not what you were expecting. If you want to leave at any time, just say the word and I'll run you back."

"It's okay." Julia gave her a grudging smile, letting her off the hook. "I should be able to tolerate spending a few days in paradise with my best friends."

Kip let out a whoop and ran around the car to open their doors. "Ladies," he said, with a mock bow, "allow me the pleasure of escorting you to your destinies."

Julia faltered at his glib choice of words, even though she knew they were aimed at Alex and her mad quest to see Rob again. Still, they heightened the uneasy feeling she'd had since returning to Gull Inlet of standing at a crossroads with the known in one direction and the unknown in the other. Dismissing her unease as silly, she placed her hand in Kip's. Real or imagined, perhaps it was time to meet more of life's challenges head on.

The housekeeper escorted them to adjacent rooms on the second floor, which opened out onto a gallery running across the rear of the house. That's where Julia headed after unpacking the small selection of casual clothes she'd brought in anticipation of a much different weekend.

This was definitely not what she'd envisioned. Her gaze slid over immaculate lawns and clay tennis courts to zero in on the half-dozen sleek and tan-looking twenty- and thirty-somethings swigging cocktails around a multilevel pool set off to one side of the grounds. So much for a quiet weekend in the country.

Chapter 2

Kurt Weston anticipated spending a quiet weekend at Belle House before the rest of the family descended for the summer. He needed a refuge. A place to work free of the noisy clutter that perpetually surrounded him at Westco's headquarters in Chicago. A place to step back and analyze where his teetering young company was headed before embarking on a critical round of meetings that would likely determine Westco's future, or lack thereof.

But his expectation of a quiet respite fizzled when he pulled into the drive and spotted his cousin Rob's car, among others, parked near the front entrance. He quickly revised his planned accommodation in favor of the small guest cottage located near the beach, a good distance away from the main house. He could have told Alfred Livingston to close the estate to guests this weekend. He owned it, bore the hefty cost of maintaining it. But Belle House had always been the family's summer home. He wasn't going to change that simply because he had the dubious distinction of temporarily holding title to it until the next generation's turn.

Tamping down his irritation at the inconvenience, Kurt parked the loaner car in front, where an airline employee could collect it later. Then he hoisted his duffel over one shoulder, grabbed his laptop, and set off across the grounds toward the cottage.

When he rounded the corner of the main house, he spied the cars' owners lounging around the pool. Most he recognized as pool lizards from other families in Breakers. Rob wasn't present, but Rob's cousin, Marcus Fuller, was there in full glory playing host.

The whole lot of them looked tanned and fit and bored. Kurt grimaced. He'd be willing to bet that not one of them held down a legitimate, full-time job. They made up the soft underbelly of Breakers. The ones with nothing better to do than hang around a pool on a Friday afternoon sipping martinis and calculating the odds of getting laid tonight. The guys, at least. The women were probably wondering which body part to nip, tuck, or pump up next.

Kurt's hope of passing unnoticed was dashed when one of the women spotted him and squealed his name. Fresh from a second divorce and a tune-up that threatened to overflow her bikini top with every bouncing step she took, Vanessa Chambers scampered across the lawn at him. With mixed fascination and reluctance, Kurt changed course and met her halfway, averting a potential accident that would not have particularly embarrassed either one, because once upon a time they had been more than friends.

"Oh, Kurt," she purred against his neck, "I'm so glad you're here."

"You're looking well, Vanessa."

She continued to cling to his arm after he eased away.

"I guess you've probably heard," she said in a more subdued tone.

"Yeah." For a moment she looked like the lost little girl he remembered from childhood. Impulsively, he reached out and tucked a lock of blond hair behind her ear. "I'm sorry it didn't work out, Nessa," he murmured, reverting to her childhood nickname.

But the little girl instantly disappeared behind a petulant mask.

"Everything had to revolve around his company and his kids' stupid soccer games," she complained. "It got old fast."

About ten months fast, by Kurt's calculation. What a waste. She was a bright, well-educated, beautiful woman. But for Vanessa, like so many pampered offspring of the rich, boredom and discontent had become a lifestyle.

From her discreet vantage point on the upper gallery, Julia observed the little drama being played out on the lawn below.

"That didn't take you long." Alex dropped down in a wicker chair next to her.

"I didn't have much to unpack," Julia reminded her pointedly.

"You look fine." Alex flicked a glance at Julia's shorts and T-shirt before noticing the couple below. "Well, well. I didn't know Kurt Weston would be here."

"Rob's brother?" Julia asked, studying the man. He was tall, lean, nice-looking in a rugged, Mad Max sort of way.

"Rob's cousin."

"The woman looks familiar." Julia shifted her focus to the very tall, very blond, very built woman in a tiny bikini, sticking to the man like superglue.

"She should. She was a senior when we were freshmen in college. Vanessa Chambers. Homecoming queen, Kappa sorority . . ."

"Oh, right."

A slow grin lit Alex's face with unholy amusement. "Honey, I'd pay big money to see those babies pop their rigging right under Kurt Weston's nose."

"Do you think she had them . . . ?"

Alex rolled her eyes. "Of course she did. Word is she's between husbands, and I bet she's angling for number three."

The show soon ended with the woman going back to the pool and the man striding off across the lawn toward the lake, battered duffel slung over one shoulder. Soon after that, their host arrived and Julia promptly forgot about the interesting tableau on the lawn.

Nearing thirty, Rob Weston looked much the same as she remembered with his lanky frame, brown hair, and serious brown eyes. As expected, he'd joined Weston Industrial, the family empire, fresh out of law school. Privately, Julia had never understood Alex's attraction to him. She liked Rob well enough, as little as she knew him, but he and Alex seemed complete opposites. Rob Weston might as well have had the word *tradition* rather than his initials embroidered on the pocket of the buttoned-down oxford cloth shirt he wore.

After lunch, Rob took them on a tour of the grounds, eventually leading them toward the beach. "That's the guest house." He waved in the direction of a charming little cottage set in a grove of hardwoods. "We used it as a playhouse when I was a kid."

He pointed out a tree house perched overhead in the gnarled branches of an old oak. "When I was about eight, my cousin Kurt designed the tree house and let me help build it. It was one of the greatest adventures of my youth. We used to play pirates and murder our sisters with squirt guns." Rob's eyes sparkled.

Julia and Alex laughed at this unexpectedly bloodthirsty childhood picture of him.

"Every summer Kurt had new plans for it. Some of the other guys didn't want to include me because I was the youngest, but Kurt insisted it was all the Weston men or none."

"That's because you were a top first mate, laddie," a low voice drawled from the cottage stoop. Julia recognized the man from the lawn leaning casually against a porch column.

"Kurt!" Rob eagerly crossed the clearing to shake the other man's hand. "Livingston said you'd come up. I didn't know you planned to be here this weekend."

"It was a spur-of-the-moment thing."

"I was reminiscing about our wayward youth."

"So I heard." He grinned. "At least you left out that part about taking our sisters hostage."

Rob performed the introductions, although it turned out Kurt had met both Alex and Kip before in passing. While they sorted out when and where, Julia had a chance to study Rob's cousin. His physical characteristics—tall, athletic build, wavy brown hair, gray eyes—she noted with only passing interest. Her artist's eye, though, was caught by the aura of self-assurance he wore like a second skin. Not an unexpected trait under the circumstances. Men of his class were bred from birth for leadership. Kip and Rob aside, Julia ordinarily steered clear of men like him—rich, entitled men, smooth and charming on the surface. Too often in her experience, they were greedy and arrogant below.

This one liked to dress down. His khaki trousers were comfortably worn, his polo shirt faded. An insignia on the shirt identified a long-ago sailing regatta.

"And this is Julia Griffin." Rob had turned to her. "My cousin, Kurt Weston."

His interested eyes inevitably lingered on her face as they exchanged the usual pleasantries. She was aware of the size and heat of the hand enveloping hers and pulled free.

Rob's cousin continued with them toward the lake. Julia wandered along the water's edge looking for Petosky stones, a coral fossil much sought after in the area. She hadn't gone far when Kurt Weston fell into step with her.

"I gather you have all been friends for some time?" he asked after a moment.

"Yes." She briefly explained the connection.

"Are you summering in the area?" he then asked.

Which, Julia knew, was rich-speak for "Are you one of us?" She hid her irritation and answered lightly, "No, Mr. Weston. Unfortunately, I'm not one of the lucky rich. I have a pesky job and an employer who insists on my actual presence." *Unlike you and your indolent friends,* Julia implied but left unspoken.

He seemed about to say something, then apparently reconsidered. But the corners of his mouth tugged up in amusement. "My condolences. Just what does this pesky job consist of?"

Julia hesitated. Some men had preconceived notions about her line of work that could be a nuisance. She kept her answer vague. "I work in a club."

Before he could ask the inevitable next question she took the offensive. Giving him a cool smile, she pointed out, "I've answered three of your questions, now it's my turn."

"Okay. But just for the record, you don't get full credit for that last answer."

"Your point," she conceded, without elaborating on her own answer. "First question: Was your tree house inspired by *The Swiss Family Robinson?"*

"Absolutely." He grinned at the unexpected direction of her question. "It was one of my favorite stories. Along with *Robinson Crusoe.*"

"Did you continue your life of crime?"

"Life of crime?" He looked perplexed.

"After the abduction of your sister."

"Oh." He chuckled. "No. It came to an abrupt end. Alas, our captives escaped when Rob and I went for a swim. They told and we were grounded for a week." He sighed and raised his hands palms up in mock defeat. "After that I lost the taste for forcing girls to play games. Anyway, I soon figured out it was more fun if they cooperated."

By then they were almost back to the others, and Julia was saved from a response to that.

"Join us for dinner," Rob urged as Kurt was about to leave. "Mrs. Livingston is probably whipping up something special for you. She'll hold me responsible if you don't show."

Kurt's unreadable gaze flicked to Julia. "I'll try to make it."

When Kurt was out of earshot, Kip teased Rob, "I guess we know which one of you is Mrs. Livingston's favorite."

"I don't know about that." Rob glanced up the path after Kurt. "Every family has a leader. Kurt's ours. Ida knows that. She also knows who pays her salary."

Julia's startled gaze fixed on Rob. "Then Belle House is his?" She winced when he nodded. *Oh, sod.* Technically that would make them the guests of the man she'd just now practically insulted with her crack about the lucky rich. She didn't know whether to laugh or strangle Alex.

Dinner turned out to be a more casual affair than Julia expected. The early arrivals pitched in to help with last-minute preparations. When they finally sat down, there were seven people gathered around the dining room table. In addition to Kurt, another of Rob's cousins, Marcus Fuller, was there, and Vanessa, too, had dropped by and stayed. Kurt sat at the head of the table, Rob directed Julia to Kurt's left, and Marcus was next to her. The others were arrayed along the opposite sides. Conversation flowed easily from Alex's gallery opening to a building renovation project in Chicago that Kurt had something to do with. For the most part Julia simply listened, enjoying the lively exchange, yet aware of Kurt's presence next to her and of his gaze often touching on her. Others also noticed the direction of his gaze. Julia saw it in the looks of speculation and, on Vanessa's face, irritation.

Puzzled about how the renovation of an opera house fit into Weston Industrial's business scheme, Julia finally asked, "Is Westco part of Weston Industrial?"

"No," Kurt answered. "Westco is my own company. It's a historic renovation firm."

Julia was still confused. "I assumed Weston Industrial was your company."

Dense silence fell over the table in the wake of her statement. Rob frowned. Alex looked uncomfortable. Vanessa looked faintly excited. Kurt, though, appeared unfazed.

"No. I no longer have any connection to the family business."

Rob jumped in. "Kurt built Westco from the ground up. It's his baby."

Realizing she must have stumbled smack into the middle of a family briar patch, Julia was more than happy to let the subject drop, but Kurt evidently was not.

"There's no reason for any of you to feel uncomfortable. I made my choices and I can live with them." His glance included everyone at the table before he turned back to Julia. "It's a long story. I'll give you the short version. My father and I didn't exactly see eye to eye on what I should do with my life. I was interested in architecture and he was interested in having me take over Weston Industrial. Finally, in college, I changed my major from business to engineering and architecture. He retaliated by cutting me off without a cent. When he died a few years ago, I was included in his will, but the entire bequest was conditioned on my returning to Weston Industrial. That I declined to do."

"But this house . . ."

"Came to me from my grandmother. My father couldn't change that."

Julia didn't know what to say, now mortified by her smug crack on the beach.

As if reading her thoughts, Kurt murmured, "Maybe we're not so different after all."

This time, Rob succeeded in turning the conversation in a cheerier direction: the imminent start of the J-24 class sailboat-racing season, his passion. When the conversation gained momentum, Marcus Fuller leaned over to Julia and said in a lowered voice, "Don't lose any sleep over it. Poor Kurt landed on his feet. Always does."

Startled by the ill-concealed venom in his voice, Julia silently regarded this non-Weston shirttail relative. Marcus Fuller had the debauched beauty of a Calvin Klein model. Tonight, wearing a Cosa Nostra French blue shirt with black slacks, he looked like the unlucky lead in a mob thriller. She'd gleaned from the conversation that he was, in fact, a lawyer.

They'd met earlier at the pool during Rob's tour. Julia would have given his dark Valentino looks no more than passing notice had it not been for the strange way he'd reacted when they were introduced. For a moment, he'd looked at her in horror—even Rob had noticed and looked perplexed. But he'd quickly recovered and been all smooth charm after that. Evidently, he thought his odd reaction required explanation.

"Sorry if I looked at you strangely when we met." He flashed a self-effacing grin that probably turned women of all ages to mush. "The sun was in my eyes. For a moment you reminded me of an old girlfriend."

"Not a happy reminder, I assume."

"Was it that obvious?"

Julia returned his smile. "Only because you looked at me like I was the bloody ghost of Mata Hari."

"Sorry," he repeated, his little-boy grin growing. And then, "Rob said you were visiting from London. How long do you have?"

Her indefinite answer ended the interlude, and they both turned their attention back to the larger conversation. Rob was describing the work he'd had done on his boat over the winter, and Vanessa objected to his choice of hull color.

"White!" she protested. "How dull."

Rob shrugged. "It's necessary if you race."

"Why?" Vanessa asked.

Kurt stepped in before Rob could answer. "Guess," he invited, his glance including the others at the table.

"Because it's faster?" Vanessa shrugged.

"Nope." Rob shook his head.

After another short silence, the puzzled expression on Julia's face gave way to a faint smile.

"What are you thinking, Julia?" Kip demanded.

"My guess is that it has to do with blending in. Are all the boats white?" At Rob's nod, she continued, "If you have the only orange boat in a sea of white, the referees would have no trouble nailing you for any infraction."

Kurt raised his drink to Julia in salute. "Well done."

Vanessa looked annoyed to be upstaged. "You must sail," she said.

They all turned to Julia, interested to hear her answer, except for Alex, who looked uneasy. Although they had never openly discussed it, Julia suspected that Alex knew something about her life prior to Briarwood. Alex was resourceful. She wouldn't have needed Julia to satisfy her curiosity about an event that had been widely reported at the time.

"No," Julia denied evenly.

"You've never been?" Vanessa persisted.

"I have. But I don't care for it."

"You don't like to sail?" Vanesssa looked incredulous, and her blue eyes took on a hard glitter of triumph.

No doubt everyone in Breakers sailed. It was an obsession of old money. And those who didn't care for it kept their mouths shut.

"Well, maybe we can remedy that." Rob's voice was mild, but the back-off warning in the glance he sent Vanessa came through loud and clear. "Kip and I were talking about sailing the Flying Finn out to Fox Island and back while you're all here. How about giving it another chance, Julia? The scenery is fabulous." Rob looked expectantly at her.

"It sounds great. You should go, but—"

"Julia gets seasick," Alex lied blithely.

Julia arched a quizzical brow at Alex but didn't deny it. "Please, don't let me stop you. I would enjoy a quiet day on the beach." Actually, a day alone hiking along the beach and maybe sketching sounded perfect.

"Well, we'll see how the weather shapes up," Rob said.

Julia only half listened to Vanessa alternately press Rob to proceed with the plan and Kurt to participate in it. Her attention was caught by the gradual appearance of dozens of prisms of light in all colors of the rainbow dancing on the walls.

"Beautiful, isn't it?" Kurt said softly, just to her.

"Yes, it is."

"The low sun hits the quartz crystals hung outside the window behind us."

"What a charming idea. Who put them there?"

"At the end of every summer, my grandmother gave a crystal to each grandchild to hang."

"It sounds like in some ways at least you led a charmed childhood."

"I have been fortunate," he agreed. "What about you? Did you lead a charmed childhood?" His voice was casual, but his eyes were interested.

"About average, I expect," she answered, surprised that her voice could sound normal when her throat felt so tight.

"I can't place that charming hint of foreign accent you have. Not quite British, but not American either . . ."

A discerning man, Julia thought. Americans usually heard an English accent while most British heard an American one. In fact, her accent reflected a blend of Caribbean island influences, mostly British, tempered by that of her expatriate American parents. But Julia wasn't about to tell him any of that.

"We moved around a lot."

"A word of advice," Alex said to Julia later that night from the open door of their connecting bath.

"What?" Julia glanced up over the top of Alex's *ArtNews* that she was reading in bed.

"Be careful of Kurt."

Julia tossed the magazine aside. The very idea that she might be interested in a man like Kurt Weston was so absurd that she couldn't resist toying with Alex. "Why, Alex, I do declare," she drawled in her best Scarlet accent, "you are the most contradictory person alive. First, you practically advise me to fling myself at the feet of the first available man, and now you warn me away from him in a way that positively sends chills down my lil'ol' spine."

"You were supposed to start a little lower on the food chain." Alex padded over and plunked down on the bed next to Julia.

"Oh, for heaven's sake. He's hardly my type."

"I didn't know you even had a type," Alex muttered. "Seriously, Julia, I see the way he looks at you. Kurt Weston is the kind of man who usually gets what he wants."

"You're overreacting. You know I've always been able to handle myself." Julia laughed dismissively. "Besides, what would he want with me when Vanessa Chambers is his for the asking?''

Alex stared at Julia in amazement, then shook her head. ''You're clueless.''

The next morning, Julia stretched lazily in bed, delighting in the sweet fragrance of country air and lilac that drifted through the open window. Only 6:00 A.M., but sunlight already streamed into the room. The day promised to be glorious, the kind of crisp country day she pined for most of the year in London.

Minutes later, clad in a tatty T-shirt, purple Suplex running shorts, and running shoes, she slipped out a back door of the silent house and set off at a moderate run. Usually she ran hard, almost to the point of exhaustion, so that she would sleep soundly at night. She welcomed the burn, enjoyed her triumph over it. But today she ran for the sheer joy of being alive on such a day.

She followed the sun-dappled road north. Half an hour later, she retraced her steps to Belle House. At a picnic table on the lawn, she stopped to stretch out her legs, absently humming a tune. After a few bars, her voice faded as a picture surfaced of her mother singing the same tune. The bittersweet memory caught her off guard. Since her grandfather's death and her return to Gull Inlet, old memories like this kept ambushing her at odd moments.

She closed her eyes, drew in a deep breath, and continued to mechanically stretch out each leg. Not for the first time, she doubted the wisdom of her plan to spend the summer at Gull Inlet surrounded by reminders of the past.

Lost in her ruminations, she didn't notice Kurt sitting at a table in the shadows of the screened veranda, his breakfast and newspaper ignored in front of him. But he'd followed her every move from the moment she jogged into view. Last night, he'd wondered what she would look like in an unguarded moment. Now, he watched as one surprising layer after another was revealed. The joy and the pain. He watched her finish working the kinks out of her legs and start for the back door. Rob was coming out when she got there and held it open for her.

"Morning, Julia." Taking in her attire, he asked, "Did you meet up with Kurt on your run?"

"No. Haven't seen him."

"Come back when you're ready for breakfast. We eat here on the porch when it's nice." Then he spotted Kurt at the table. "Oh! Morning, Kurt," he called out over her shoulder. "I see you got the jump on us all."

Kurt noticed the barely perceptible break in Julia's stride before she disappeared into the house without a backward glance. Rob sat down at the table across from his cousin. His gaze followed Kurt's to the door. "Don't waste your time, pal."

"Okay. I'll bite. Why not?"

"For starters, she lives in London. She only came back to attend her grandfather's funeral, and I gather she's not staying long." Rob lowered his voice confidentially. "Look, Kurt, I don't know that much about Julia—she doesn't exactly invite confidences—"

"I've noticed."

"But she's always struck me as the permanently unavailable type."

Before Kurt could question Rob further, Ida Livingston's gray head poked out around the kitchen door. "Telephone, Kurt. It's your secretary."

"Got to go," Kurt said to Rob. "We'll finish this later."

Julia and Alex spent a leisurely morning in town browsing through tourist shops. In a kids' store, Julia picked out small gifts for the Cleary kids—a few art supplies for ten-year-old Annie Cleary and, on impulse, a stuffed frog for the baby, Dustin. By the time they returned to Belle House, the others had already gone over to the inland lake to windsurf.

Julia was critically examining the fit of her bathing suit in the mirror when Alex went next door to collect her.

"Is it okay?" Julia frowned at her reflection, fiddling with the straps on the modest suit.

The question, Alex knew, had nothing to do with vanity and everything to do with hiding the dark horror of her past. A past Alex knew more about than Julia probably suspected. She circled her friend, examining the one-piece suit to ensure that it covered the scars Julia kept hidden from the world. It did, and Alex pronounced it "perfect."

The warm afternoon lived up to the day's earlier promise. A moderate breeze buffeted the windsurfer sail when Rob demonstrated to Julia and Alex how to use the uphaul to raise the sail out of the water. After pulling the sail into a vertical position over the board, he grabbed the waist-high bar that acted as both the sail's boom and sheet. The brightly colored sail immediately filled with air and the board began to glide forward. He rode it out a few yards, then turned it around and sailed back to where the two women regarded him dubiously, up to their knees in chilly water. When he let go of the bar, the sail flopped into the water like a dead tuna.

Rob hopped off the board and eyed them expectantly. "Which one of you ladies would like to go first?"

Alex yawned. "This looks like a lot of work. You go, Julia."

Julia gazed consideringly out to where Kip and Vanessa were already skimming across the clear blue lake. They made it look easy.

"I'll give it a whack."

Gamely Julia waded forward and climbed onto the tippy board. To her chagrin, she almost fell off before she could do anything. She stood a moment, letting the board steady, before pulling on the uphaul. When the sail finally broke free of the suction of the water, she went flying backward into water that felt colder than the North Sea. Shivering but determined, she tried with similar results several more times before Rob took pity and held the sail upright for her.

"Sorry about the water. It's usually just this side of iced tea until July. The big lake is even worse." Rob eyed her goosebumps. "Sure you want to try again?"

"Yes." She grasped the proffered bar and the board began to glide forward.

"Stay close to shore!" he yelled after her.

Tentatively she twisted the soles of her feet against the board's gritty surface. It responded, turning to run parallel to shore. Encouraged, she cautiously straightened aching arms and let her body act as a counterweight to the pull of the sail. For a few minutes she enjoyed the feel of the wind driving the sail under her hands and the beat of the water against the board under her bare feet. Then a gust of wind tore the sail from her hands and sent her plunging into water that was even colder than it had been near shore. The shock brought her sputtering to the surface and racing for the board.

Three times she tried to haul the sail up into position, and each time she splashed back into the water. Freezing cold and aching from the effort, she climbed on and stretched out full length on her stomach, letting the sun warm her back before making another attempt. She almost had it. On her last try she'd had the sail almost into its vertical position but had been too eager and grabbed for the bar too soon.

At the sound of a splash, Julia opened her eyes to see Kurt Weston's head surfacing inches away. He rested his arms on the edge of the board. Rivulets of sparkling water streamed down the angular planes of his face. A crooked smile revealed white teeth in marked contrast against bronzed skin and dark hair.

Julia stared, mesmerized. He was a vision of raw male sexuality—straight out of one of her dreams. A rush of warmth quivered through her, raising even more goosebumps on her wet skin. For a moment, she had the craziest urge to reach out and touch him just to see if he was real.

His eyes changed, and Julia knew he was going to kiss her. "I didn't think you'd ever ask," she heard him murmur.

His words jolted her from the moment of insanity. Appalled, she jerked away at the first brush of his lips. "No!" she croaked. "Sorry. Not interested."

He looked at her a long moment. "Oh, yes, you are," he disagreed. "Or were. I've never seen a clearer invitation on a woman's face."

He was probably right. Shaken, she looked away. What on earth had come over her?

"We can discuss it later," he said. "Right now, we'd better get back before we both freeze. Scoot forward."

Irritated as much by the way he automatically took control as by her own lapse, she foolishly objected, "Thank you, but I don't need to be rescued. I've almost got it."

He seemed about to argue the point, then shrugged. "Fine. But I'm about to turn into an iceberg down here. Mind giving me a ride back?"

"Fine. Sit in back," she ordered.

"Aye, aye, captain." He gave her a grinning salute.

When he was set, Julia carefully stood and began the difficult task of breaking the suction between water and sail. Muscles in her arms and shoulders screamed in protest as she hauled on the line. This time when she felt the sail break loose, she eased off a bit, then drew it up gingerly before grabbing for the bar. Success! But momentary. The wind had come up. The sail strained against her arms. She wouldn't be able to hold on for long. A glance at Kurt's serene face told her that if she wanted help from that quarter she would have to ask.

Cold and tired, she gave in and muttered, "Uncle."

"Did you say something?" Kurt looked at her, all innocence.

"I could use a bit of help. *Please*," she added through gritted teeth,

Seconds later he was behind her, hands and feet straddling hers on the bar and board. She relaxed some as he took over most of the strain of the sail, but as she did, her backside came into contact with the length of his body, separated only by her life vest. She stiffened and automatically pulled forward, almost unbalancing the board before he drew her firmly back against his chest.

"I won't bite," he mocked softly against her ear. "We'll both be warmer, and we just might make it in without any more unscheduled dips."

They did. But awareness of their intimate proximity, and the unfamiliar feeling of a man's bare arms and legs moving against hers, screamed along her nerves. The man was too big, too masculine, too clever, too inquisitive, and a few other things she didn't even want to think about.

After what seemed an eternity, the windsurfer glided to shore. She shot a quick thank-you at him, ignoring his outstretched hand as she stepped hastily off the board, and scurried up the beach for her towel.

"Thanks," she said, stripping off the vest and wrapping up in the beach towel Alex handed her from her chaise longue. Without Kurt's warmth against her back, she was so cold her teeth were chattering. "I'm going to head back. Are you ready?"

"Not yet." Alex's calculating gaze was focused on Rob and Kurt, standing together next to the windsurfer at the water's edge. She waved Julia off. "You go on ahead. This windsurfer thing suddenly looks more intriguing than I realized at first. I think maybe I need a lesson, too."

Uh-oh. Julia silently eyed her friend. Alex was showing all the signs of revving up for another go at Rob. The smartest thing for both of them would be to pack up and leave now. But that wasn't going to happen. They were committed to going to Breakers' clubhouse for dinner tonight. The summer season was kicking off with a Saturday-night dance afterward. And the following day, their last, the others—minus Julia—were to make the trip to Fox Island aboard Rob's Flying Finn.

Alex glanced up at her. "I won't be long. I want you to try on that dress."

Julia had hoped to pass on the evening's activities with

the excuse that she didn't have an appropriate dress. Unfortunately, Alex had preempted that excuse.

"Be careful, Alex. It's freezing out there."

"Oh really?" Alex quirked a sardonic eye at her. "It looked quite warm from here."

Chapter 3

"Sex on a hanger." Julia doubtfully eyed the low-cut midnight blue dinner dress Alex held up for her approval.

"It's a drop-dead gorgeous dress," Alex happily agreed. "I saw it in a little boutique in Chicago and thought of you. And since it's almost your birthday . . ."

"Oh, Alex, it's lovely. Thank you. But I can't wear something cut this low."

"Just try it on," she cajoled.

The dress, Julia saw a moment later as she turned slowly in front of the mirror, was cut full enough at the shoulder to cover the scars. The bodice dipped low to skim along the beginning swell of her chest, but otherwise the dress covered her to her ankles. It reminded her of a tip a London diva had once given her: for maximum impact, uncover only one body part at a time.

"It's incredible! You've got to wear it."

Julia studied it uncertainly. "Who's going with us?"

"Just the four of us. If you're asking about Kurt, he said he may drop by the dance later." Her mouth curved impishly. "You could make like Cinderella and disappear at midnight."

Alex picked up a gold locket from the dresser top and held it dangling from a forefinger. "This is beautiful. I've never seen you wear it."

"I found it in my grandfather's safe-deposit box."

"Whose was it?" Alex started to open it.

Julia snatched it from her hands, then was embarrassed. "Sorry. It's just that . . ."

"Whose was it, Julia?" Alex asked again, more gently.

"My mother's." At her surprised look, Julia added, "Well, I did have one."

"But you've never talked about her."

"I don't like to think about the past." Julia stared at the locket in her hand. "The awful thing is, sometimes I can't seem to help it. Even after all these years."

Alex's face scrunched in concern. "Still have nightmares?"

"Not often. More since I've been back here."

"Maybe you should talk about it."

Julia shook her head. "No, thanks."

"With a pro," Alex pressed.

"I'd rather be rolfed."

"They're not all like that old bat at Briarwood, you know."

Julia shrugged.

Alex sighed and returned her attention to the locket clutched in Julia's hand. "Why don't you wear it tonight? It would be dynamite with the dress."

The garden room was beginning to hum with activity when the four made their entrance after dinner. Residents had supplemented their thin preseason ranks with a generous helping of guests, and all mingled comfortably in small, constantly shifting groups. The chatter of voices flowed under an occasional riff of notes from a jazz combo warming up on a raised dais at the edge of the dance floor. On the far side of the room, people spilled out elegant French doors onto a flower-bedecked veranda overlooking both the inland lake and Lake Michigan a bit farther off. Rob steered their little group around intimate clusters of well-heeled friends, often stopping along the way to make introductions.

Julia gave up trying to remember names after the first half dozen, so she was thrilled and surprised to have a face from her own world materialize before her after the band's first set. Sammy Rose, the combo's leader, had shared the bill with Julia and Hugo, among others, in a staged cabaret review the previous fall.

"Sammy was touring with a different band then," Julia explained to Alex and Rob. Which explained why she hadn't recognized him earlier.

Sammy grinned. "Small world, especially in the music biz."

They caught up on mutual acquaintances until Sammy went back to work.

By the time Kurt arrived at nine-thirty, the party was in full swing. He waded through the crowd of old familiars to the bar, returning greetings called out along the way. "Scotch," he ordered before turning to scan the room. He spotted Marcus Fuller schmoozing his way across the floor, but saw none of the others.

For a lawyer who'd recently been handed the reins of his daddy's law practice, Marcus certainly seemed to have a lot of leisure time, Kurt reflected, watching him work the crowd. Maybe he saw himself as a rainmaker, generating clients in rich playgrounds while others toiled away back at the office. Kurt wouldn't care what Marcus did if he weren't doing it on Kurt's dime. He tolerated Marcus, even threw a few legal tidbits his way from time to time, because he was Rob's cousin. But that didn't mean he had to like the guy.

"Looking for me?" The seductively pitched voice interrupted his search.

Kurt's glance slid briefly to the woman at his side. "Hello, Vanessa."

"Rob said you would be here, but I didn't really believe him. I haven't seen you at one of these parties in years."

"Is Rob still around?"

''Right here,'' Rob called out, already making his way over to them from the other side of the bar. He placed his drink order before saying to Vanessa, ''Marcus was looking for you.''

''I'd better see what he wants. Don't leave before I get back,'' Vanessa purred to Kurt.

''Persistent woman.'' Kurt aimed a pained look at her back.

''She likes you.''

''Her itch is not one I want to scratch.''

''But I suspect you wouldn't mind if it were *hers*.'' Rob nodded across the room to where Julia stood cornered by two men old enough and married enough to know better.

Kurt smiled faintly when he caught sight of her. ''Not a bit.''

''What about Amanda?'' Rob asked.

''We've moved on.'' Kurt contemplated the woman whose presence had distracted him from his work the past two days. It annoyed him that he could get this hot over a woman he knew squat about. He watched Kip extract her from her admirers and escort her onto the dance floor.

A few minutes later, after Julia lost Kip to another partner, Kurt followed her outside. She'd found a quiet spot to watch the sun set over Lake Michigan, her arms resting on the wooden railing as the giant orb slid to its watery death. Its reflection paved a beckoning golden path across the water.

She was magnificent standing there at the railing, her face lifted to the setting sun. Her hair brushed against her shoulders and face, on fire with the colors of the sunset. She had an expectant, waiting quality—one alone among the scattered couples—that fired his imagination.

''It looks like the yellow brick road,'' he said, walking up to her. He saw her start and draw in before the shutters snapped closed. Her hand fell away from a gold locket around her neck.

''I was thinking that, too.'' She greeted him with a polite smile that didn't erase the guarded look in her eyes. ''Like you could walk right over the water all the way to the sun.''

''And what would you want to find waiting for you over there in Oz?'' He saw a flash of pain cross her face before she shrugged.

''Well, this isn't Kansas, but a hot-fudge sundae with lots of whipped cream and nuts would do for starters,'' she replied lightly. ''What about you?''

''Let's see . . . the people I love. Answers to a lot of questions. A bottle of my favorite Scotch. For starters.''

They watched in companionable silence as the water consumed the last fiery crest of flame. Color began to fade from the sky, replaced by the twinkling lights of Breakers dotting the shoreline and reflected on the inky surface of the water.

Julia studied the boats moored in the harbor below them. ''Rob mentioned that you have a sailboat here.''

Kurt pointed through the twilight to a wooden sailboat roughly forty feet in length. ''Her name is *Witchcraft.*''

''The ketch?'' He nodded. ''She's lovely.'' Julia surveyed the classic lines of the two-masted boat with the eye of experience.

''Unfortunately, I have little time to sail her these days. I should probably sell her, but I haven't been able to bring myself to do it.''

''Why?''

''It's sentimental. My grandfather had a hand in her design and construction.''

''She looks like a Herreshoff design,'' Julia said before she thought better of it.

''She is.'' Kurt studied her. ''Now, how would someone who doesn't like to sail know that?''

Under his scrutiny, she hesitated and finally shrugged. ''My grandfather loved classic wooden sailboats.''

''The grandfather who just died?'' She nodded. ''Griffin,'' he mused. ''Seth Griffin was your grandfather?'' He looked at her in surprise.

''Yes.''

''The man was considered a boat-building genius. He was a guru to a generation of sailors in these parts.''

''That he was,'' she said softly.

"I was sorry to hear of his death."

"Thank you."

"You said you moved around a lot. Did that include Cherry Beach?"

"Very little." Julia paused. "It's a long, dull story. You should thank me for not getting started." She said it in a humorous voice that nevertheless held a note that firmly closed the door on any further personal revelations.

"Tell you what," Kurt said after a moment. "I'll stop asking you questions about your mysterious past if you agree to dance with me in exchange."

"Well . . ." She glanced over his shoulder toward the doors to the ballroom. "I don't . . ."

"Dance with me, Julia. *Please*." His eyes held hers with a quietly compelling intensity.

The vulnerable "please" got to her. But, as they crossed the deck, she wondered if he often used the technique to get what he wanted.

Heads turned when they came in together and threaded their way to the dance floor. He danced with the same easy, athletic grace with which he seemed to do everything else—a cotillion legacy, no doubt. "What happened to the lights?" She said the first thing that came to her.

"They're turned down at ten. It's the signal for children to leave."

At length the music ended and Julia automatically drew back a step, but the crowd and Kurt's hand at her waist prevented her from withdrawing farther. Without pause, the band swung into another piece. Wordlessly they began moving. Kurt pulled her closer. His hand moved over the small of her back. Julia stiffened. But when he stopped, she forced herself to relax, then was caught unprepared for the wave of desire that hit her in the wake of her small surrender. As if sensing her response, Kurt tipped her face up. For a suspended moment, searching gray eyes stared into her soul. Then a camera flashed nearby and broke the connection.

"Don't worry," Kurt assured her, "the prints aren't released to the press."

Drifting in an unfamiliar current, Julia had no idea what he was talking about.

He pulled her closer. "Are you feeling what I'm feeling?" he murmured against her ear.

"I don't know what you're feeling." How could she when she wasn't even sure what *she* was feeling? She knew only that there was this awareness that hummed between them. She wasn't entirely sure she even liked the feeling, but found it impossible to ignore.

Kurt laughed, low and warm. "Then maybe I'd better tell you."

Julia grew dimly aware that the music had stopped and Sammy Rose was introducing the next number.

"Julia . . . *Julia!*" Alex squeezed her arm, jerking her back to reality.

She looked blankly at Alex, then blinked in confusion when she saw that they had become a small center of focus. Kurt slid a steadying hand under her elbow, looking as baffled as she was.

". . . if I can prevail upon her to join us . . ." The amplified voice cut across the chatter.

"The price of fame, old girl." Alex nodded toward the dais.

Julia's gaze shot to the band. With understanding came a modicum of composure. "At least he could have warned me," she grumbled, even as she mentally prepared to do what was expected of professionals in these circumstances. She excused herself to Kurt without bothering to enlighten him. He would understand soon enough. The cat was out of the bag, and there wasn't the slimmest chance of shoving it back in now.

On her way across the dance floor, Julia smiled and her stage persona slipped automatically into place. The crowd eagerly anticipated a novelty. She could read it on faces that were focused on the unscripted drama being played out in their midst.

Sammy reached out to assist her onto the dais. "Ladies and gentlemen, I am honored to be able to introduce to you a friend of mine who is visiting from London. She has one of the loveliest and most versatile sets of pipes in the London club scene today. Please welcome Miss Julia Griffin.''

During the ensuing applause, Julia hissed at Sammy though her smile, ''This better be something I know.''

''Oh. You'll recognize this one.'' On his signal the band played the opening notes to a familiar piece. Her sole claim to fame, the one everyone always requested. She'd recorded it for the soundtrack of a low-budget British movie that had become a surprise success. The title song had later been nominated for a Grammy. It was a slow, romantic song about a woman declaring her love for her man.

The audience ate it up and wanted more. Sammy obligingly directed the band into a second number, an old Jerome Kern piece in the same smoldering groove as the first. She needed the sheet music to remember the words, but no one seemed to care. With the ease of long practice, she donned the mantle of a passionate woman struggling with an impossible love, creating the spell more by a certain restraint, a feeling of passion barely controlled, than by melodrama. Her voice floated clear and rich one minute, low and sexy the next.

''She's good, isn't she?'' Alex said to Kurt.

''That's an understatement,'' Kurt answered without taking his eyes off Julia.

''Go easy with her,'' Alex warned.

Kurt flicked her an irritated glance. ''And just what do you think I'm going to do to her?''

Alex gave him a knowing look. ''I can guess what you want to do.'' She forged on before he could respond. ''Julia's going through a tough time right now. I don't want to see her hurt.''

''She's a grown woman. She can make her own decisions.''

Alex studied him closely while he watched Julia, saw his determination. ''Be careful with her. She's an innocent.''

Kurt looked at her in disbelief. ''That woman,'' he said, pointing at Julia, ''can handle herself just fine.''

"It's an act. A role. Nothing more." As the final earthy note drew out, Alex opened her mouth to say more, but Rob pulled her away.

"He's right, Alex." Rob calmly held up a hand to forestall an indignant outburst. "Julia has managed for what—five years now?—without your protection. She's not exactly a babe in the woods."

"Your cousin is giving her the full-court press, and she's too polite to tell him to get lost."

Rob laughed at that. "She knows how to get rid of him. She's had plenty of practice. Maybe she just doesn't want to."

Alex bit off a retort when Julia made her way through the crowd to them.

"You were a hit," Rob congratulated her.

Julia smiled and gave a little shrug. "They weren't expecting much, so it would have been hard to disappoint them." Her world lurched sickeningly when she spotted Kurt wending his way toward them. She was perplexed by her reaction to him, this unwanted attraction to a man from this sort of life and virtually a stranger.

"I'm going to go find my bed," she announced abruptly.

Alex summed up the situation in a glance. "Want me to run interference?"

"Thanks," Julia said gratefully, and promptly disappeared into the crowd.

"Where is she going?" Kurt asked moments later, catching sight of Julia's retreating back.

"I think she's going to the powder room," Alex lied with aplomb. Rob sent her a disapproving look but said nothing.

"Come in," Julia called out half an hour later, expecting Alex. Her back was to the door as she turned down the bedding. "Thanks for helping me escape."

"I rather thought that's what you were doing."

Julia spun around at the sound of Kurt's low voice to discover him lounging in a chair by the door. His suit coat was gone. So was his necktie. His shirtsleeves were casually rolled up.

"What are you doing here?"

"You invited me in." His gaze slid over her.

"I did not," she snapped, before remembering that technically, she had.

"Why didn't you tell me you're a singer?"

"You didn't ask."

"You didn't let me."

"What do you want?" She tightened the sash that held her knee-length silky robe closed, feeling at a distinct disadvantage in her lack of clothing and irritated with him for barging in on her like this. "I'm tired. It's been a long day and I want to go to bed." Oh, Lord, she thought, seeing the glimmer of amusement light his gray eyes at her last pronouncement, she really was losing her timing.

"My first concern was to see that you got back in one piece."

"Thank you. As you see, I did. It's hardly an urban jungle out there, so—"

"I also came to show you something you won't want to miss."

"What?" she asked suspiciously. She stepped warily out of his way when he crossed the room to the door opening out onto the gallery.

"It's okay. Come out a minute." He held the door open. She hesitated. "I don't bite."

"Said the spider to the fly," she muttered under her breath. But she walked out past him, figuring it would at least get him out of her bedroom.

"I heard that." Taking her reluctant hand, he pulled her through the dark to the railing. "There, look," he said, pointing into the night sky.

Colorful bands of light snaked across the northern sky in a slowly moving dance.

Julia went perfectly still. "The northern lights." She breathed the words reverently, awed by the pure beauty and mystery of the shimmering lights. "I've never seen them before."

"I thought you'd want to see this." He stood behind her, gripping the railing on one side, loosely caging her, but she was too engrossed in the divine drama being played out in the heavens to take much notice.

"It's a sight I will always remember," she said simply. "How long will it last?"

"Hard to say. Usually not long."

They stood a while in silence, absorbing the sight, until soon the colors began to fade.

A breeze lifted Julia's hair off her shoulders. Behind her Kurt's breath sighed through his teeth. "I guess the show is about over," he whispered.

His warm breath tickled her ear, sending tingles down her spine. Turning, she started to thank him. "I'm glad you . . ." His close proximity registered. The railing dug into her back when she took an automatic step backward.

Whatever she had been about to say died a silent death when she met his gaze and saw the hunger there, a hunger that sent an answering note shivering through her. She found herself staring into his eyes.

"Kurt . . ." Julia protested, a perfunctory attempt to stop the inevitable.

"Later," he murmured, closing the distance between them.

At the first touch of his mouth, her stomach felt as if it dropped to her knees. He kissed her gently, tenderly at first, only deepening the kiss when she began to respond. She shivered and sighed her reluctant pleasure into his mouth. His tongue twined with hers in a lazy, hot salsa number that turned her legs to mush. Tentatively her hands came up to rest on his shoulders, the only steady object in a suddenly gyrating world.

His mouth left hers and made a hot foray down along her throat. Her head sagged back into his hands. The husky sound of his voice filled her head, but the meaning of the words was lost. His voice and touch seduced her, silencing her better judgment. *Oh, yes,* she thought with her last thread of semicoherent brain activity. She wanted this. She needed this. Needed to satisfy the deep, empty ache that troubled her sleep. A physical need—like exercise—that she had tried too long to ignore, she reasoned before giving over entirely to the dark pleasure.

Her heated response fed Kurt's hunger. Frustrated by the limitations imposed by their position, he maneuvered her through the dark to a settee and pulled her onto his lap.

He stared at her, forcing himself to slow down, wanting to prolong this thrilling, unexpected pleasure. He ran his fingers through her hair, lifting it and letting it float down against his supporting arm. He stroked along the side of her shadowed face, over her forehead, temple, past closed eyes with their graceful fan of dark lashes, over a cheek, down to her chin. Gently now, loving, memorizing. He slid his thumb across her wide mouth. Exploring lips followed his hands, lingering at the racing pulse at the base of her throat.

In a dim corner of Julia's consciousness, a whisper of alarm grew louder. Through a muddled haze she tried to push it away. But it wouldn't stop. She was practically naked under her flimsy robe, lying on her back in Kurt's arms, completely within his control while he skillfully rendered her senseless. Suddenly, it all felt unbearably intimate. Beyond physical. When had he become so gentle? His hands and mouth were loving, worshipping her body, suggesting a level of emotional involvement she was unwilling to accept, even for one night.

A large hand slipped between the overlapping folds of her robe to cup a breast. Julia gasped at the intimate contact. Pleasure hummed through her.

She opened her eyes in time to see Kurt part the robe over her chest, see the hard passion on his face. "So beautiful," he murmured.

Beautiful? *Not the scars.* With clumsy hands she belatedly tried to cover herself. *Please don't see the scars!*

"Kurt, no!" She managed to clutch the robe closed. "I

can't." She struggled to regain her feet, but he held her easily, forcing her to meet his probing gaze.

"Yes, you can." Determination set his face in a rigid line.

Recognizing the futility of a struggle, Julia went perfectly still.

Kurt silently cursed when he felt her withdraw into herself. That damned armor had reappeared and he didn't have a clue why. He sucked in a deep, steadying breath. Without saying a word, he raised his arm and released her.

"Thank you," Julia felt compelled to say once she regained her wobbly legs. She fumbled with the front of her wrap. A breeze cooled her heated face.

She stood uneasily, studying the dark outline of his profile. His silence was oppressive.

"Well—I—it's late." Julia stumbled through unfamiliar territory. She had never let things go this far before and didn't know how best to end it. A part of her didn't want to end it. But whatever this was between them felt too risky, too intimate. The demands probably excessive. She turned away and took a step toward her room.

"I can wait until you're ready." His voice sounded loud in the dark silence. He hadn't moved from the settee.

"That's not going to happen." She tried to keep her voice under control. "I'm sorry about what happened here. I shouldn't have led you on."

"You were not 'leading me on.' You wanted me probably as much as I wanted you. But something happened. Something scared you."

She looked out into the night, away from the pull of his eyes.

"Tell me. Maybe I can help."

"Don't," she whispered, holding up a hand to stop him. "I'm sorry. I can't." Again she started to leave, but was pulled up short when a long arm shot out and snagged her hand.

Julia stiffened and turned, eyeing him warily in the dark.

He stood, stubbornly refusing to release the hand that

bridged the gulf between them. "This isn't over." He raised her hand to his lips in a brief caress, then released it and walked off down the gallery.

Julia sagged against the cedar shakes on the side of the cottage, letting the night breeze and night sounds steady her. Eventually, she went inside to bed, only to lie awake long into the night.

Chapter 4

Kurt was thankfully absent the next morning when the rest of the party gathered for an early breakfast before setting off for Fox Island. Julia resisted Rob's last-ditch appeal to get her on board. The weather forecast promised another blue-sky day with a steady breeze made to fill sails, but Julia stood firm and, in this instance at least, had Alex's support. It was one thing to windsurf on an enclosed lake, quite another entirely to set sail over open water. That, Julia intended never to do again.

And so, when the others left for the harbor, Julia set off alone on a hike several miles down the coast to state forest land. Intending to make a day of it, she carried a small pack loaded with sketch paper, a book, and a snack to tide her over until dinner.

While she plodded along through the warm sand, she replayed her alarming encounter with Kurt Weston the night before. It shocked her to realize how close she had come to ending up in bed with him, how tempting it had been just to let go.

Lately, she had thought that perhaps she could have a casual physical relationship with a man without becoming overly involved emotionally. No strings. No future. No risk. She knew women who did just that, entering and exiting short-term relationships, exhibiting less mental anguish than they did when shopping for a new bathing suit. She was not naive enough to think that a man like Kurt wanted a commitment from someone he barely knew. Yet he did seem to expect a certain emotional closeness, even if only for the short term, that made her uncomfortable.

Yes, Julia told herself, she had made the right decision. She'd pulled back in the nick of time, before all the inevitable questions and turmoil. It was safer this way. Safer to surround herself with the art and music she loved. She understood their demands, accepted their risks.

Deliberately she turned her thoughts to her grandfather and something Mrs. Livingston had said about her son being a private detective. It got her to thinking that perhaps she should hire someone to investigate Seth's death—not the Livingstons' son with his connections to the Westons, but there must be someone who could take another look at the matter. Maybe the sheriff had overlooked something.

When she reached the spot Rob had described to her earlier, she found a vantage point atop a dune from which she could sketch several different scenes without having to move. A tranquil creek meandered out from behind the dunes, through a sandy beach, to empty into a small bay. According to a sign, there were campsites tucked in along the creek. For now, though, the beach was empty.

Later, a family of campers trooped down to the beach: mother, father, boy, girl, and dog. A family. They reminded her of the Clearys. The little girl splashed back and forth through the creek. Her excited shrieks carried up to where Julia sat. An older boy, about eight or nine, threw a tennis ball to the dog. The perfection of the scene, its poignancy, made her feel empty.

Shortly after noon, a runabout nosed onto the beach along the semiprotected leeward side of the bay. Julia watched a lone figure climb out and start up the beach in her direction. He was too far away to see clearly, but she recognized Kurt's long, easy stride. She was not really surprised to see him. The Livingstons knew her destination.

"Hi," Kurt said when he reached her. He took in her little camp in a glance before turning unreadable eyes back to her. "Mrs. Livingston was worried that with all the commotion this morning you might have gone off without a lunch." He held up a canvas bag.

"I grabbed an apple and one of those delicious muffins of hers."

"Not much for a hike like this." He handed her one end of a red-checked tablecloth to spread out. She politely protested that they shouldn't have gone to all the trouble. He ignored her and proceeded to pull containers from the bag, ticking off their contents as he went. "Homegrown strawberries, smoked turkey on sourdough with fresh vegetables and mango chutney, dill pickles, lemonade, and last, the best rhubarb custard pie you will ever have."

"I hope you're planning to help eat it."

Kurt handed her a plate and kept another for himself. "That's the plan. If you don't mind."

"No. Of course not."

They were like fencers, cautiously circling, each trying to determine the other's intentions. On the surface they were friendly acquaintances having lunch together, nothing more. Their conversation was polite and impersonal. They watched the children frolicking on the beach. They commented on the landscape and the weather. The wind had picked up throughout the day, so that now waves were crashing onto the shore. Julia was concerned about the boaters. Kurt assured her that Rob was used to sailing in rough conditions.

"What is that?" She pointed to a narrow channel of tan water extending out from shore a couple hundred feet. The oddly colored plume was surrounded by wind-whipped blue.

"A rip current. Maybe an undertow as well. Sand picked up by the current gives it that cloudy tan color. It happens when there's a strong northwest wind because of the curve of the bay," he explained. "The waves pile water up against the shore and it dissipates toward the middle of the curve from both sides. When the two currents meet in the center, the water has no place to go except back out.'' With his hands, he demonstrated the convergence of the currents along shore and the rip current running back out to sea. ''It's concentrated in a small area.''

Julia squinted at the ominous column of water. ''It looks dangerous.''

''It is. The park service posts signs in the summer when the water warms up. Even so there was a drowning a few years back.'' He squinted out at it. ''When I was a teenager, we used to ride it out. If you're a strong swimmer and know to swim to the side, it's not too risky.''

After lunch Kurt seemed in no hurry to leave. Julia waited to see what his next move would be. But as he continued to talk or simply sit in silence on the other side of the blanket, she began to relax. To her surprise, she discovered she was enjoying his company.

She ventured again to ask about his work and learned that Westco specialized in renovation and reproduction projects. Interested, she asked why he'd chosen to go in that direction.

''Generally, I prefer older styles of architecture to modern. I do like modernism if it's done well. What I object to are anonymous boxes that contractors call 'modern' as an excuse to do it on the cheap. The last thing I want to do is slap up freeway architecture.''

As he warmed to the topic, Julia took up her sketch pad. Quickly, economically, she captured his likeness, leaving the details for later. Partially reclining on the sand, seeming to enjoy himself, he had a relaxed and unpretentious masculine ease that she liked. But she wasn't duped by it. She knew full well that just beneath the surface lurked a dangerous intensity, an almost gravitational pull, that put her in peril.

''So your talent takes multiple forms.'' He watched her sketch.

''I hope so. I'd like to make it my second career. Singers tend to have short shelf lives.'' Her hand paused in midair. ''You don't mind, do you? I should have asked first.'' Her questioning eyes met his.

"Not as long as you give me the pick of the litter—signed, of course."

"Fair enough."

"May I see them?" Kurt nodded to the folder containing her sketches.

Most were landscapes. A few were of young Annie Cleary, who'd taken to popping in after school. Julia handed them over without comment and picked up where she'd left off.

After a few minutes, he put them aside. "You are a woman of extraordinary gifts."

Julia looked up from her work, saw his sincerity, and was touched by the simple compliment. "Thank you." Turning away from the warmth in his eyes, she gazed absently out over the water.

She didn't think of herself as a gifted artist. Talented maybe, but not gifted. A gift implied something that was given to you. It required no real effort on the recipient's part. Her voice was a gift. She'd had to work to develop it, to make a career out of it, but the basic raw material was a gift. That was not the case with art. She had struggled and sweated every inch of the way down that road.

She turned back to her drawing. But something wasn't right. A vague uneasiness stilled her hand.

Kurt was talking, asking about the sketches, but broke off when he saw her face. "Julia?"

She looked past him and saw what had failed to register fully before: the little girl from the family of campers, alone, playing cat and mouse with the brown-water waves at the center of the bay. As she watched, the little girl danced further in, up to her thighs.

"No! My God, no!" Julia breathed, coming to her feet.

She was barely aware of her desperate dash to the water. She ignored Kurt's shouted warning. Her entire focus was on the little girl.

Helplessly, still yards away, she saw the girl stumble in waist-deep water. The next wave crashed over her before she could regain her feet. When the wave retreated, the child was gone.

Julia fought sickening panic as she covered the last few yards, peeling off her sweatshirt on the run.

Kurt angled off toward the runabout. "Julia, no! Go to the boat!" he shouted.

But she was caught in her own nightmare. The past rushed over her, filled with choking fear and adrenaline and a fierce determination to fight back no matter what the cost. She had to reach the child.

At a dead run she forged into the middle of the rip current and dove cleanly over the next swell. The strong current eagerly swallowed her up and dragged her along its path. The shock of the frigid water knocked the air from her lungs. She struggled, trying to reach the surface, but the current slammed her down against the bottom. Instinct told her to swim to the side, out of the current.

But the current would take her to the child. She had to save this child.

The world began to dissolve into black fuzz. Her lungs felt close to bursting before she clawed her way to the surface. She floundered, gasping air, searching, willing the child to appear. At the back of her mind she knew that neither of them would survive long in the cold water.

So cold. Stop! Think! But her thoughts became more sluggish. Everything looked muddy. She was tiring. Vaguely she realized that the current was pulling her farther out. She couldn't fight it. Her arms felt like numb lead. *Ah, the current.* It would take her to . . .

Something warm brushed her leg. She grabbed. Held. *Jack.* She smiled. So sleepy. They would sleep together. Drift in the warm currents. So peaceful.

"No." Julia fought the strong arms pulling her up from her soft bed. She retched water onto the hard surface under her face. Something was thrown over her. The next instant, the surface beneath her cheek began to vibrate as the boat roared to life.

She felt the bottom of the boat bump up onto shore and

pushed herself into a sitting position, looking about in confusion. Big, blurry figures were racing around. Why couldn't she focus her eyes? Someone was crying. *Jack!* she thought on a quick intake of breath. No, not Jack. The little girl.

Then Kurt was there, wrapping her in a blanket and lifting her to shore. Her whole body shook uncontrollably.

"You scared me half to death. Are you all right?" The warm sand felt heavenly when he put her down on it.

A man bustled up. "How is she?" He was dressed in green. Probably a park ranger, Julia thought dully.

"That's what I'm trying to find out."

"I'm fine," she said. "Is she okay?"

The man answered. "The girl? We think she'll be fine. It took some work to get her breathing again, but she's holding her own now." Then to Kurt, he said, "The medevac copter will be here any second. They'll be able to take them both at once."

"No. I don't need to go," Julia said, teeth chattering.

The man leaned over her. "You may be suffering from hypothermia."

"No. Kurt, please. I'm okay." She just wanted to be left alone. From above, the deafening *thwap, thwap, thwap* of helicopter blades drowned her out. Her nightmare. Only this time she was awake. The past all over again.

"It's just routine," Kurt shouted. "We want to make sure you're okay."

"I am," she insisted.

"We've got to get her out of these wet clothes," Kurt shouted.

Julia pulled away and climbed unsteadily to her feet. Two fuzzy shapes loomed up in front of her.

"She's acting disoriented," a woman said, helping her back to the sand.

"Julia, this is the paramedic." Kurt sounded worried.

"I'm fine. Just cold." Suddenly the logical explanation for why she couldn't see occurred to her. "I lost my contact lenses."

The paramedic exchanged a few words with Kurt before moving off. Moments later the doctor bustled over and took control of the situation in a businesslike manner that brooked no objection. In short order, behind a blanket Kurt held up, he helped her out of her wet clothes and into her sweatshirt and donated sweatpants. The only break in the doctor's professional demeanor was a momentary pause during his quick survey of her for signs of injury. An ER doctor would recognize gunshot wounds for what they were.

"I do not want to go to the hospital," she told him through chattering teeth.

"I'll see what I can do." After taking her temperature, he pulled Kurt aside.

A minute later, Kurt came back and hunched down beside her. "You're all set. The doctor said your temperature is low, but if I agree to follow his instructions I can take you home." He looked at her closely. "The question is, will *you* follow his instructions?"

"Yes," Julia agreed readily, and then said, "I want to see her."

Kurt picked her up, carrying her in his arms like a baby, and she was too cold and drained to be anything but grateful. The group surrounding the child made room for them, and Kurt put her down next to the stretcher. Only a pale little face showed through the swath of blankets. Her eyes were closed.

"She'll be fine," the doctor said. "The two of you saved her life."

They were about to move the girl onto the helicopter. Julia bent over the child's face one last time. *Not Jack.* She turned abruptly away, racked by violently conflicting emotions: profound relief that this child's life was spared, and heart-piercing anguish that the one she loved dearly was lost to her. The unwanted memories flooded out through the reopened wound. The present was a blur, but the hated past pressed in on her in stark detail.

Great shudders shook her body. Would it never end? Would she be forever dragged back into the horror? Wordlessly, Kurt put an arm around her, drawing her against his side.

A woman blocked their path. "Thank you for saving my baby. It seems so inadequate. If you hadn't gone in after her . . ." Tears began streaming down her face.

Julia reached out and clasped her hand. "It's a horror no parent should ever experience."

The whine of the outboard engine prevented conversation on the ride down the shoreline. Kurt motored slowly, keeping one eye on the waves tossing the runabout and the other on Julia. She sat huddled under a blanket in the bow. She hadn't minded his ministrations, had hardly seemed to notice them. All energy drained out of her after seeing the child. She was still, all drawn into herself. Her dull eyes gazed unseeingly across the water. The curtain of cool reserve had disintegrated, and he glimpsed pain and vulnerability behind it. The source of that pain was a mystery, but his instinct told him it had been firmly set well before this afternoon's events.

She closed her eyes and rested her head against the hull, exposing a long, graceful column of neck. Kurt looked his fill. He found it odd that she hadn't asked a single question about her near-drowning, other than whether the girl was okay. He knew from experience that survivors of disasters predictably reacted by asking endless questions about their brush with death, as if they could only come to grips with it by reliving it over and over. Julia, though, acted as if she were oblivious to the danger she'd been in. Or didn't care.

He did. He was still shaken from seeing her plunge headlong into the frigid water. It had taken enormous control to resist the impulse to plunge in after her. But he'd known the best chance for all of them—likely the only chance—was for him to intercept them in the boat. Sheer desperation had chased him up the beach to the runabout.

At least ten heart-stopping minutes had elapsed before the boat intercepted the current, and endless more before he spotted her farther out. At first, he'd seen no sign of the child. By the time he pulled the boat alongside her, she was barely treading water, but she had the child clutched tightly to her chest, and a strangely content smile curved her mouth. He'd filed the image away for later analysis and moved quickly, lifting both out together and speeding back to shore.

Kurt pondered that odd smile as he beached the boat at Belle House and hopped over the side into ankle-deep water. Julia unwound her long legs and slowly stood. She didn't say a word when he scooped her up in his arms and set off along the path.

He paused on the threshold of the cottage to explain the doctor's instructions. But her eyes were closed, abdicating responsibility for her immediate future as if she held it out to him on a platter. Relieved, he shifted her weight in his arms to open the screen door and carried her inside.

Julia opened her eyes and gazed dully around the inside of the cottage. Kurt had deposited her on a couch in front of a stone fireplace and now knelt before the hearth, coaxing a small flame into a blaze. The rest of the living room was a blur, but she had the impression of an assortment of tables and chairs and late-afternoon sunlight streaming through windows.

The sunlight surprised her. It reminded her that little actual time had elapsed, even though everything before the horror of the afternoon seemed light years away. She shivered in her cocoon of blankets, trying to pull herself together.

Kurt turned. "You're awake. How are you feeling?" he asked, coming over to the couch. He picked up her blanket-covered feet and sat down, holding them matter-of-factly in his lap.

"Cold. Otherwise fine." *Not fine.* Julia looked at the fire, away from him, embarrassed at how exposed she must be. She felt raw, stripped bare.

"The doctor said to warm you up slowly with blankets and a fire. No hot baths just yet." His hands slid under the blanket to warm her feet. "You know, you scared me half out of my wits back there."

"I had to do something." Glorious warmth began to creep back into her bones, making her sleepy. She closed her eyes. "Thank you for saving my life," she said softly.

''You're welcome. Just don't do anything crazy like that ever again.''

She wanted him to keep talking. She wanted him to distract her from the nightmare that lurked close to the surface. ''How did all those people get to the beach so fast?''

''I had my cell phone in the runabout and called the sheriff's office. They contacted the park rangers and the medevac helicopter.''

His hands were working magic on her stiff calf muscles. ''You missed your true calling. You should have been a masseur.'' She had a difficult time keeping her eyes open.

''Turn over.''

That was enough to open them. ''What?''

''I'll do your back.''

She eyed his blurry form, all of a sudden not sure how far she should trust him. He had taken charge again and she had let him, too caught up in her own private hell to care.

''Relax. You're perfectly safe. I won't take advantage of your weakened condition.'' His voice held a trace of amusement. ''My hands will feel like magic.''

Tell me something I don't already know, she thought wryly.

Before she could say a word, he flipped her over onto her stomach, cocoon and all. Through the blanket he began a very slow massage of her neck. Before he reached her lower back, she fell asleep.

When Julia woke several hours later, it was early evening, judging by the low natural light casting fuzzy shadows around the room. Except for the comfortable hiss and crackle of the fire, all was quiet. She saw no sign of Kurt. She swung her legs off the couch and gingerly stood. After taking only a step in the direction she hoped led to a bathroom, her shin banged a low table.

''You really are blind.''

She jumped at the sound of Kurt's voice. ''I believe the politically correct phrase would be 'visually impaired.' I happen to be severely nearsighted.'' She squinted in the direction of his voice, still not able to make him out. ''Where are you?''

''Here.'' What she thought was a potted palm next to a table got up and came toward her.

''Would you please point me in the direction of the bathroom?''

''This way.'' He led the way down a short hallway. ''Your cosmetics case is on the counter. Mrs. Livingston didn't see your glasses anywhere in your room, so she hoped they'd be in it.''

In fact, Julia discovered a moment later, her glasses were not in the case either. No matter how many times she searched, they failed to materialize. With a sinking feeling, she closed her eyes and could almost visualize them on the bedside table at Gull Inlet. When she emerged from the bathroom, Kurt gave her the even worse news that Rob and crew would be spending the night on Fox Island because of an equipment breakdown.

''Surely they can replace it or jury-rig something.'' Julia wrapped her hands around the steaming mug of tea he put down on the kitchen table in front of her. ''Thanks.''

''They have.'' He searched through a cupboard and came up with a box of crackers. ''But by the time they got the problem straightened out, Rob decided it was too late to start back, especially with a storm in the forecast and a green crew.''

Rob was right, she knew. A Lake Michigan storm was nothing to take lightly. Thousands of wrecks littered its depths thanks to its unpredictable fury. ''They both have flights to catch tomorrow afternoon.''

''If the storm breaks by morning, they can still make it.'' She could feel him looking at her across the small galley kitchen. ''Weren't your glasses in the case?''

''No. I forgot to pack them.''

''Oh.''

Defensively she explained, ''I rarely use them, and I've never lost a contact lens before.''

He muttered something sympathetic about it working out and placed an assortment of crackers and cheese on the table. "Eat. Doctor's orders."

Hungry, Julia did. "You do this food thing quite well," she said after a minute.

"For a man, you mean."

"I didn't say that."

"But you thought it," he teased.

Neither agreeing nor disagreeing, she smiled and changed the subject. "Have you heard any more about the little girl?"

He filled her in with the good news that she was expected to make a full recovery. "Her parents would like to thank you in person for what you did. I thought maybe we could stop by the hospital this evening. They're likely heading home in the morning."

But Julia was shaking her head before he finished. "I'd like to put it behind me, and I'm sure they would, too."

Kurt leaned back in his chair, struck again by the way she wanted to distance herself from the whole thing. She certainly cared. That much was obvious from her concern about the girl. Not to mention her willingness to risk her damn-fool neck, he thought, shuddering at the memory he knew he would never forget. He relaxed as his gaze slid over her face. Her color looked better. Except that her defenses seemed less firmly in place than usual, she looked none the worse for the experience.

"I'll let them know we won't be coming. Now, what can I say to get you to go out to dinner with me tonight? Aside from the fact that Mrs. Livingston doesn't cook on Sunday night."

Julia hesitated and smiled faintly. "Tempting, but I don't think that would be a good idea."

"Coward," he mocked. "What harm could come of it? You're leaving tomorrow for London or parts unknown."

"But there's another problem," she said, not inclined to tell him that she wasn't going any farther than Cherry Beach for the rest of the summer. "I can't see and—"

"I'll drive and I won't let you walk into any walls. Promise."

"It's just that without my glasses I feel so . . ." *Dependent? Vulnerable? Out of control?*

"Defenseless?" Kurt offered.

"Yes—*no!* It's just uncomfortable, especially in unfamiliar surroundings."

"And that's your only objection?" he pressed.

She frowned, wondering what he was up to. "Yes."

"Then problem solved. When Mrs. Livingston couldn't find your glasses, I went ahead and arranged for a new pair of contact lenses. I figured you would want them in any case." Kurt glanced at his watch. "They should arrive in about an hour."

"You're joking." She was not enjoying his game. "You can't just pick up new contacts on a Sunday afternoon without a prescription, even assuming they have what you need in stock."

"Keep your pants on. Listen." He reached across the kitchen counter and pressed a button on the answering machine.

A woman's voice came through the small speaker: *"Kurt. You're all set. An optometrist in Traverse City had your friend's contacts in stock. I sent a courier to pick them up at six and he should arrive at Belle House at about seven-thirty. By the way, he's bringing along an extra pair in case you two go swimming again. Ciao."*

Julia frowned. "Who was that?"

"*That* was Chloe, my personal assistant and chief problem solver. There's not much she can't handle."

"How did you get my prescription?"

"Off the bottom of your lens case."

A small silence fell while Julia considered what he had done. Her reactions were conflicting: appreciation for his extraordinary thoughtfulness, wariness of the power he could apparently wield so effortlessly, concern over how she was ever going to pay for two pairs of expensive contact lenses plus the cost of their extravagant delivery, and not least, irritation that he'd neatly trumped her last excuse for not going out to dinner with him.

She leaned back in her chair. "Well, I guess that settles it, then. If you'll assist me up to Belle House, I'll meet you there when it's time to go."

Chapter 5

Small farms and wooded hills sped past as Kurt aimed a bottle-green Jaguar inland over narrow rural roads. The brisk winds of the early afternoon had stiffened, and an ominous wall of purple-bruised sky gathered on the western horizon, heralding the approaching storm. Eventually Kurt turned off at a quaint little inn in the middle of nowhere, the antithesis of the glitzy waterfront restaurants that abounded in the area and to one of which Julia had expected he would take her. The inside was simple yet charming. About a dozen candlelit tables filled two rooms. Most were occupied, but Kurt had called ahead, and the maître d' led them to a table for two next to a window in the back room.

Not usually a big drinker, Julia nevertheless steadily downed a glass of the excellent red wine Kurt ordered. It did its job, quickly taking the edge off. She met his quizzical look.

"That wasn't because of me, I hope." He glanced pointedly at her empty glass.

Julia's mouth widened into a rare full-strength smile. "No. *That* was because of this afternoon."

"You did well."

She tilted her head, eyeing him curiously. "I thought you didn't approve."

"I don't. What you did was incredibly dangerous." He finished refilling her glass. "And incredibly brave. That little girl owes her life to you."

"And to you," she added, meeting his gaze. "We both do."

Over dinner, they slid easily into conversation, and Julia found herself thoroughly enjoying not just the exquisitely prepared food, but—as she had earlier on the beach—Kurt's company as well. Surprisingly, he knew a fair bit about the twenties and thirties music she and Hugo favored. "I know I've heard that second number you sang last night, too."

"It's a Jerome Kern piece. Some of his pieces work well for me where a lot of others don't because of my voice."

"What's the matter with your voice?"

"It's too clear." She smiled across the table. "I should have taken up smoking."

"I like it fine just the way it is."

"Thanks, but a jazz singer is supposed to have that whiskey-roughened sound that shouts 'soul.' I can get it a little in the lower registers, but not in the upper registers." She shrugged, not particularly bothered by the problem. "We mix in a few theater songs and a smattering of vintage pop tunes and it works well enough to keep us booked."

"So who's singing the blues while you're away?"

Her laugh scattered out across the dining room, drawing the attention of the few lingering diners. "Hugo found a substitute for me," she said, still smiling.

"Hugo?"

"Sorry. My accompanist and partner. Hugo takes care of everything for me." She glanced out the window at the gathering dusk, her smile warming. "He's one of the best accompanists around. I'm very lucky to have him."

Kurt frowned. "How did you get started singing in nightclubs?"

"I fell into it after college. I had moved to London and started playing the clubs as a way to pay the rent until I figured out what I wanted to do with the rest of my life."

"And that's art."

"I hope so."

Just then, the waiter interrupted to tempt them with a trio of sinful-sounding desserts. Julia settled for a cup of tea. Kurt ordered a chocolate torte and coffee.

"More wine?" he offered, holding up the bottle.

She shook her head regretfully, already feeling its effects. "It's wonderful, but I think I've had enough. You finish it."

"Can't. I'm driving."

"Well . . ." she considered. Gray eyes met hers while he poured the last of the wine into her glass. Why had she ever thought gray eyes looked cold?

He seemed on the verge of asking another question, but Julia had reached her limit and turned the conversation in his direction. She learned to her surprise that he'd grown up on a farm northwest of Chicago.

He chuckled at her disbelief. "No, really. It's true. Have you ever heard the phrase *fin de race*?" Julia shook her head. "Shirtsleeves to shirtsleeves in three generations. It's the idea that succeeding generations in a dynasty become increasingly diminished—weaker. My father believed it and feared it."

"And you're the third generation," she guessed.

"Yes. The farm was one part of my father's antidote. It kept my sister and me away from bad influences and provided plenty of hard labor for the heir—me."

"Where did you go to school?"

"There was a prep school not far away. Dad also believed in a solid education."

"But you spent your summers up here."

"Until I was about fifteen. Then my father got really serious. Actually, some of it I enjoyed. I went on several boot-camp-style survival courses. Some summers, I worked construction or factory jobs."

"I guess it worked. You don't look at all soft."

"No, I'm not soft." He smiled. "In hindsight, I can't complain. All those summers clinging to rock faces by my fingertips or sweating in a factory were more than just a collection of adventures. They taught me independence, to take control of my own destiny, to be active rather than reactive. And for that matter, to take responsibility when things went wrong. In the end, though, all my father's efforts backfired on him. . . ."

Kurt broke off when he noticed the taut, closed look that had come over her face. "Is something wrong?"

Her hand trembled as she carefully set her glass of wine aside. "No. I just find it ironic that those who have been very fortunate in life inevitably believe they control their own destinies."

"I take it you disagree."

"What you say suggests we're responsible for all the bad or good things that happen to us. We're not. We're born. We die. For most people a lot of bad things happen in between. Some good things, too, if we're lucky. And if we're really lucky, we die before the people we love."

Julia stopped abruptly and turned her eyes away from his to stare out the window.

They sat in silence while Kurt digested that shockingly bleak bit of personal philosophy. It didn't take a shrink to see that she had personal reasons for reacting as she had—personal and obviously painful.

"You're right that many things are beyond our control," he said, feeling his way along. "And, of course, we bear no responsibility when they go wrong. I'm sorry if it sounded like I meant otherwise. We don't have absolute control. It would be arrogant to imply otherwise. However, there are many things that most people can do to affect the direction their lives take. That's all I meant."

"Sometimes there are no choices."

"Usually there are."

In the back of her mind, Julia knew she was overreacting and should stop before she made an even bigger fool of herself. But her indignation had a momentum of its own, and suddenly Kurt looked just like all the rich Northern tourists who had looked down their noses at the lazy island yokels.

She looked at him coolly. "You hold yourself up as an example, but from what you've just described, you were groomed for greatness from birth. Plus, you were born into a family that was intact, wealthy, and well educated."

"You're right. I was—*am* fortunate. Still, no matter what the circumstances of your birth, there are always choices. Do I try to accomplish something in my life, or do I use my trust fund to support a cocaine habit and a great tan? Do I ride on the coattails of my forebears, or do I use my abilities and resources to create beauty, or jobs, or places for people to live and play? I chose the latter. I think, in your own way, you have too."

"I still say that the big things in life are usually beyond our control. Disaster strikes most people sooner or later."

Kurt studied her flushed face, wishing they could talk openly about whatever was really bothering her instead of dancing around it in this frustratingly oblique manner. One of her hands rested on the table in a fist. Kurt reached over and covered it with his own. She glanced up quickly in surprise.

"Even so, there is one responsibility you do have, one thing within your control: once disaster has struck and done its damage, you have to climb back to your feet and get on with your life. You can't let tragedy control the rest of it."

As if burned, she pulled her hand out from under his. "You have no idea what you're talking about," she said flatly.

"Then tell me. You certainly seem to be in control of your life."

When had this become about her? Julia wondered. But perhaps it always had been. "Yes. I guess I am. At least I try to be." She smiled apologetically, her anger spent, but it was a sad smile. "I'm sorry I lit into you like that. It was unforgivable. And I ruined your dessert.'' She glanced pointedly at his uneaten torte.

''Forget it. You make an interesting dinner companion.''

She frowned, not sure how to take his ambiguous comment.

''I meant it as a compliment,'' he said, reading her mind, ''and the torte is still good. Try it.''

He offered her the second bite, holding up his fork. She hesitated, then reached out a hand to take the fork, but he held on so that her hand was on his when she took the bite.

He grinned wickedly at her. ''In some cultures we'd be married right now.''

''Then we'd better get a quick divorce. I'm afraid I would be poor wife material.''

He looked at her curiously. ''I've heard men say things like that, but never a woman. Usually the men are either workaholics or playboys. Which are you?''

''Well, no one has ever described me as a playboy, so I expect I fall into the first category. And you?''

Kurt shrugged nonchalantly, drawing her attention to the way his dark jacket draped perfectly across his wide shoulders and the way the white T-shirt underneath contrasted with his throat. ''I never claimed to be poor husband material.'' When he spoke, her eyes darted over the hard, masculine planes of his face to those striking gray eyes. ''So, tell me about your life in London.''

Julia leaned back in her chair, unconsciously putting distance between them. ''There's not much to tell, really. I go to work at night and to my art studio during the day, and that doesn't leave time for much else.''

''What about family?''

''I have none.'' She tensed in anticipation of the questions she expected her answer to provoke.

''Friends?''

''What?''

''Don't you have friends?''

She relaxed. ''Some. But generally I try not to let my personal life interfere with my professional goals.''

He stared at her in disbelief. "You can't possibly mean that."

She raised a quizzical brow. "But I do. Isn't that what those workaholic men you were talking about do all the time?"

"Hard work is one thing, but I know few men and fewer women who have gone so far as to sacrifice their personal lives for their careers. And none who are happy doing it. Are you happy, Julia?" He regarded her intently.

She turned uncomfortably away from a question she had been asking herself lately and without any clear answer.

Kurt downshifted onto the long driveway leading up to Belle House. The deeper drone of the engine penetrated Julia's subconscious. She blinked sleepy eyes open and gazed blankly around the car's plush interior. She couldn't have been asleep more than a minute or two, just long enough to leave her with a feeling of surprised disorientation. One minute they were chatting and the next she had zonked out again.

"You're going to destroy my ego if you keep doing that," Kurt complained.

"Doing what?" She feigned ignorance.

"I think you know. Fortunately, it doesn't happen very often. At least not this early. . . ."

"I get the picture." His potent combination of raw sex appeal and enormous wealth would be irresistible to many women. Throw in charm, keen intelligence, and power, and she suspected there must be bevies of unattached women who set out snares for Kurt Weston. Vanessa included. They would not fall asleep in the middle of a conversation with him. Julia smiled at the image of a harassed Kurt trying to stay one step ahead of a determined mob of blond socialites.

"What's so funny?" he demanded.

Smiling, she shook her head and began to hum along to an old Righteous Brothers tune drifting mournfully through the car. Kurt brought the Jaguar to a smooth stop and cut the engine, but left the music playing. A moisture-laden breeze wafted through an open window.

Julia opened sad-happy eyes when the final strains drifted away. Kurt held out a hand across the console, and she hesitated only a moment before placing hers in his. She stared at their joined hands, fascinated by the contrast. His—larger, darker, rougher, stronger—made hers look puny and unfamiliar by comparison.

"That song makes me feel like a teenager on a Saturday-night date," he murmured. "It's almost summer. The time of year when everything is new again and freedom lies just around the corner. Anything is possible."

Julia casually dislodged her hand and straightened in the seat, noticing then that Kurt had bypassed the main house and they were parked in the woods behind the guest cottage. "What—?"

"Let's go down to the beach and watch the storm roll in. It should be quite a show." He lounged carelessly against the leather upholstery. But his eyes were fixed on her, awaiting her answer, willing her to say yes and not put a premature end to one of the most interesting and enjoyable evenings he could remember.

Kurt had no doubt the attraction was mutual, if unwelcome on her part. Last night he'd discovered a fire smoldering beneath her guarded exterior. Unfortunately, something else lived there, too, some dark presence that cast a shadow over her life and apparently compelled her to keep people at a distance. Exactly as she was trying to do with him.

"I'd like that," she said, surprising him.

"Good. I'll just grab a couple foul-weather jackets."

She waited for him in front of the cottage. Then they made their way along the wooded path, following their ears toward the distant roar of surf. With the sureness of long familiarity, Kurt led her through the dark.

Trusting his sense of direction, Julia sank into the mindless beat of the elements: the musty smell of earth just before it rains, their muffled footfalls barely heard over the low moan of the wind blowing through chattering treetops, a warm hand closed tightly around hers. No matter how much she had changed in other ways, she was still a child of the earth, wind, and sea at heart. These wild, elemental forces sustained her, as necessary to her well-being as air and water. Urban life was tolerable only with periodic surfacing for breaths of fresh air, usually in a quiet seaside village she'd discovered on one of her early probes into the English countryside. It was as cheap as it was unfashionable. After each of these sojourns, she would return to London and bury herself in work until the rejuvenating effects wore off and she would escape for another fix.

When they left the protection of the trees, a gale-force wind ripped into them, snatching Julia's breath. "Better put this on!" Kurt yelled over the roar of the wind, handing her one of the yellow slickers. She couldn't catch another without turning her back to the onslaught.

Kurt caught her shoulder. "Do you want to leave?"

She shook her head, excitement shining in her eyes.

They found a dished-out nook partially protected by several scrubby bushes, from which they could view the drama unfolding around them. Crashing breakers and howling wind combined in a sustained crescendo. Swollen clouds ghosted across inky-black sky. Many miles out, bright bursts of lightning danced across the water.

"It's beautiful!" Julia cried out.

Kurt cupped her chin and turned her face to his. "Yes."

His eyes moved over her face to her mouth, and before she fully grasped his intentions, his mouth met hers in a sweet, coaxing kiss that sent tingles down her limbs. The kiss rapidly escalated in heat. Even now, having already experienced and endlessly analyzed the drugging effect of his touch, she was unprepared for the actual force of the reality.

She teetered on the brink of some wildly erotic place as elemental as the wind and waves roaring around them. She tried to hold part of herself aloof, untouched by the physical storm whirling through her, but felt herself slowly losing the battle. Within moments she *wanted* to lose the battle.

The hand that reached up to hold him at bay now clung to the neck of his slicker. A low moan tore from her throat and was lost in the roar of the storm as Kurt eased her down against the cold sand. His mouth was hot and hungry with a need that seemed to equal her own.

Moments later, lightning and its echoing blast of thunder shattered the sky, ominously announcing the storm's landfall. Nonplussed, Julia clutched at Kurt's jacket when he rose.

"It's not safe here. The storm is practically on top of us." He had to shout to be heard over the wind and surf.

Embarrassment followed confusion as she came to her senses, but went mercifully unobserved in the timely downpour that sent them scurrying up the beach. By the time they reached the protection of the cottage porch, laughing and out of breath from their mad dash through the woods, rain was slanting down in stinging sheets. Every inch of their bodies not covered by the slickers was thoroughly soaked.

Their laughing gazes met. "Here, let me help with that." Kurt carefully lifted the sodden jacket off her shoulders and then shed his own.

They stood toe to toe on the small stoop, almost but not quite touching.

"Are you going to run away this time?" His finger followed a drop of water down her chest until it met the fabric of her sundress.

"I don't know." Her legs felt weak. She thought fleetingly that she had finally met a man who passed Alex's weak-in-the-knees test.

"Why don't we go inside and find out?" He stepped away from her and held open the door to the cottage.

Julia stood in the middle of the small porch, struggling to objectively weigh the risks against aching needs that begged to be satisfied, and knowing that she was failing miserably. She sensed that the threshold on which she stood was the line drawn in the sand, easily crossed in only one direction. Kurt watched her with steady eyes, waiting for her to make up her mind. By exerting no pressure, he let her know that the decision was hers to make. She could take a chance for one night and find out what was on the other side of that door, or she could put an end to it right now and ask him to drive her up to the main house. He would, she knew.

She turned away and walked to the edge of the porch.

"Wait," Kurt ordered coolly. "It's hardly necessary to flee into the deluge. I'll see that you get back to the house unmolested."

Julia turned around. "I know." She bent down to retrieve her purse from underneath a built-in bench where she had left it earlier, and walked past him over the threshold into the dark cottage.

Chapter 6

"It's a theater renovation project we're bidding on."

Across the living room, Julia looked up from the architectural drawings she had been perusing while Kurt went off in search of something dry for her to put on. Now she watched him come toward her, noted the white terry-cloth bathrobe draped over one arm, and her heart began beating a nervous tattoo.

To cover her jitters, she turned back to the drawings littering the surface of the drafting table. "Interesting," she said quickly without really focusing on them. Her tongue felt thick and awkward in her mouth. She glanced up and saw that his gaze had drifted down her front to the edge of lace exposed under the damp top of her sundress. She shivered.

As if suddenly remembering the robe, he handed it to her. "You should get out of those wet clothes."

She gave him a crooked half-smile. "I bet you say that to all your dates."

"No. But it is a good line. I'll have to make note of it in my little black book."

Their laughing gazes held and eased Julia's tension. An

instant later they froze as hair-raising lightning and a deafening crack of thunder struck almost as one. The lights blinked.

"That and fierce thunderstorms that knock out electricity," he added.

Before Julia left the bathroom, the lights went off again, this time seemingly for good. She kept on her damp slip under the robe, not quite ready to take that final step.

In the living room, Kurt sat on the sofa nursing a drink. He'd changed into a dry shirt and chinos. Several candles cast his shadow in huge relief against a wall. A new fire was gaining momentum in the hearth.

It all looked terribly romantic, she thought, studying Kurt from the dark hallway while what little confidence she had left drained away as steadily as an ebb tide. The firelight emphasized the imposing planes and angles of his face, giving him a harsh, even ruthless look—traits she imagined most business moguls shared to some extent. Or hid.

Alex was right. In that moment, Julia understood her warning. This was not a man to trifle with.

He looked up, smiled, and rose, coming to her.

"Kurt, I . . ." She swallowed hard. "I'm not sure about this."

"I know. But there's a blasted gale out there and we're warm and safe here. Let's just enjoy the fire a while."

She nodded and let him draw her to the couch. He gathered her back against his chest. They sat in silence, listening to the crackle of thc fire while the storm raged outside. Julia felt encased in warmth, from the fire in front and Kurt's chest against her back. Candlelight and fire cast them in a warm glow. Gradually, she relaxed enough to let her head rest against his shoulder.

"It's been so long," she murmured. "I forgot how peaceful it is without electricity. No hum of a heater or refrigerator. Just the wind and fire and rain."

"Nature without all the distracting people noise. It feeds the soul."

"Yes," Julia agreed, surprised he would understand. Dear

Hugo, cosmopolitan to the soles of his Gucci loafers, never had.

When had his other arm slipped around her waist? It felt good—unfamiliar and a bit scary, but good. Warm and secure. It had been a long time since anyone held her. She closed her eyes, savoring the feeling. She wanted to feel loved tonight, even if it was only pretend. In fact, she only wanted to pretend. She wanted to slip into a dream and ease the empty ache in her heart.

Her hand moved over his to stroke and explore the long fingers. Before she lost her nerve again, she turned her head and looked at him in open invitation.

His breath released in a rush. "Yes," he answered her unspoken offer.

The first tentative meeting of mouths soon escalated into a heated clinch as banked embers flared to life—frustration and need, fear and desire, all tangled together.

Abruptly Kurt stood, pulling her up with him onto boneless legs. She swayed toward him, but he held her firmly at a distance until she looked up. "Are you protected?"

It took her a moment to understand what he meant. She nodded. "I can't get pregnant."

Still, he continued to hold her away. "I'm going to make love to you . . . *now*." He drew the words out slowly and deliberately.

This, then, was the line drawn in the sand. There would be no last-second retreat from here.

"Yes," she whispered. *Anything.*

Almost before the word left her lips, Kurt was leading her down the hall to a small bedroom. The bed was already turned down. A candle burned on each side. He was prepared.

He stopped next to the bed and pulled her into another hungry kiss that left her trembling and breathless and ready for more. Her hands became eyes of both artist and lover, carefully exploring an unfamiliar new landscape.

He moved lower. His hands parted her robe as he went until it dropped in a puddle on the floor, leaving her clad only in her slip and bikini briefs. Immediately, she crossed her arms over her chest, hands covering her shoulders. He quickly shed his own clothes until he stood naked before her. He was beautiful. Wide shoulders narrowed to a flat stomach and lean, muscled thighs. A light furring of golden-brown hair covered his chest and tapered to a line descending to his groin. Her legs wobbled when she followed the line to his jutting sex. She sank to the bed.

She had seen nude male art models before, but this was the first erect male she had ever seen. The sight was unnerving. Surely his size was unusual, wasn't it? Suddenly, she doubted her ability to bluff her way through this. She didn't want him to discover her inexperience. The whole thing was supposed to be casual.

Perfectly comfortable with his nudity, he let her look her fill, a grin starting as the silence stretched out. "Will I do?"

She jerked her eyes away from him. "Of course . . . fine," she said faintly. He raised a quizzical eyebrow.

Bloody hell.

He reached for her. She evaded, quickly crossing the room to snuff out a candle. There was another on the other side of the bed, casting a wavering light in the darkness. He intercepted her before she could reach it, and gently but firmly reeled her in.

"No," he said huskily against her mouth. "I want to see you."

She shivered.

"Cold?" He stroked her crossed arms.

"A little. Why don't we get in bed?" she whispered.

Safely hidden under the covers, she slid her arms around his neck and stopped trying to resist what they both wanted. Their mouths sought, found, and fused in a deep, urgent kiss, drenched with sex and life. The rest of the world dropped away until there were only two, a man and a woman, caught in the tight grip of Mother Nature's plan. Julia helped him remove her slip and bikini briefs and snuggled deeper into the safety of the covers. Hot palms skimmed over the curve of her shoulders, waist, hip, and thigh, leaving delicious heat in their wake. She twined her arms around him when he would have looked at her, then shuddered at the feeling of his skin making full contact with her bare chest and legs.

Kurt restrained his haste, deliberately gentling his touch, slowly building a roaring blaze from which, this time, she would not want to retreat. He gauged her moaning response when his mouth claimed her breast, triumphed when she mindlessly shuddered beneath him. Still, he held back.

He prided himself on being a generous and considerate lover, but with Julia, pleasing her became a matter of overriding importance. He wanted to give her more pleasure than she'd ever known before. With his hands and mouth, he left no part of her untouched.

Drowning in a sensual haze, Julia was hardly aware Kurt had moved between her legs until she felt him, hard and blunt, probing at her. Pressure bordering on pain intruded through the mist, and she stiffened against it.

"Relax," he choked out. "You're tight. I don't want to hurt you."

"Wait!" she gasped against the heavy shoulder pinning her down.

"Julia, don't."

Large hands captured her head and turned her face to meet his eyes in the dim light. His face was flushed with a hard, masculine passion that was at once frightening and arousing. But she saw something more there, too: tenderness and caring.

Her last bit of resistance crumbled. She drew a ragged breath and wound shaking arms around his broad shoulders. For the first time in years, she voluntarily gave herself completely over to another person's control.

Kurt held her gaze while his thrust found its way home. Soft flesh yielded to hard. She gasped. He froze, only partially inside her wet warmth. His look of confusion quickly gave way to understanding.

He knows, she thought. His searching gaze was as invasive as his body. She looked away, feeling raw and vulnerable, as if her soul were as exposed as her body. Uncertainly, she waited in their shockingly intimate embrace for what would happen next. Pain faded to wonder, fed by a growing feeling of excitement and pleasure. She thought she would go mad if he didn't do something soon.

"Are you all right?" His strained whisper brought her eyes back to his. In that instant she understood that he was holding back because of her.

"Yes, yes. Go on!"

Groaning, Kurt began to move with torturing slowness, invading by degrees. Instinctively, she matched the gradually increasing tempo. Ripples of pleasure built into waves as their bodies strained closer together. He pushed her ever higher until she rode precariously suspended on the crest of a great wave before tumbling headfirst off the edge as her release broke over her in a shimmery wave.

He groaned loudly and stiffened. After a long moment, he slumped over her, pushing her deeper into the mattress while their madly pounding hearts slowed. Then he rolled off her onto his back, carrying her along in his embrace.

Julia dreamily descended, not into reality but into a place of glowing contentment. With her head resting heavily on his shoulder, she listened to the drum of his heart, awash in a warm ocean of well-being. Surprisingly, she felt none of the awkwardness she would have expected.

Kurt lightly caressed her moist temple. "Julia?"

"Hmm?"

"Why didn't you tell—" She tensed, guessing what was coming, but unexpectedly he broke off and revised. "Do you need to take out your contact lenses?"

She relaxed. "I can leave them in overnight."

For once her inner voice of warning was silent, whether in approval or reproof she didn't know. Yet even in her blissful contentment, some sense of caution remained. When Kurt's lazily exploring hand wandered upward from her breast, she hastily snagged thc bathrobe from the floor next to the bed and pulled it on.

"Come back here," he growled, drawing her back into

their cocoon. She willingly snuggled up against him, and after she felt him fall asleep, she let herself follow.

This time gunfire shattered the lazy heat of a high southern sun. When the guns stopped, she and Jack were alone in red-stained water. Helplessly, Julia felt the small form in her arms go limp as his life seeped through her desperate embrace. He was dying and there wasn't anything she could do to stop it.

''Jack! No-o-o!'' She kicked her legs hard to keep his head above water. ''Don't go! Don't leave me. . . . Please!''

Someone was pulling her away from him. ''No! My baby! Jack!''

''Julia. Wake up. You're having a bad dream.''

Jack's lifeless little body drifted away from her straining fingertips. ''No! Stop! He'll drown.'' She struggled in vain to free herself from her captor.

''Julia, it's just a dream. Listen to me. The little girl did not drown.''

She was locked in Kurt's embrace, arms pinned to her sides. Gradually, she stopped fighting him. Cool darkness mercifully extinguished the hard Caribbean glare of her dream.

''I tried so hard, but it wasn't enough,'' she cried against his chest.

''You did fine.'' He stroked damp hair off her face. ''You okay?''

She didn't object when he peeled off her sweat-soaked robe and pulled the blankets up over them both. Thin moonlight seeping in from the now quiet sky saved the room from being totally black.

''Uh-huh.'' Her throat was raw from screaming, and her heart was racing. Nothing unusual about that. And, to her annoyance, she couldn't stop the tears. Nothing unusual about that either.

Yet everything felt different, because tonight she was not alone. For years she'd battled these terrors alone in the black silence of the night. But this time someone was with her, warm and real—a bright beacon, banishing the shadows. He was big and warm and pulsing with life. She craved it—that life, the antithesis of the dark monster that stalked her nights.

She buried her face against Kurt's chest, inhaling, tasting, wanting to merge into him. She rose up over him and found his mouth in an urgent, insistent, and very thorough kiss.

If Kurt was startled by the kiss, it was nothing to his surprise moments later when she swung a long leg over his thighs and firmly straddled him. The delicious shock of her bare skin pressed intimately against his groin erased any remnants of brotherly concern as his body sprang instantly to full attention beneath her.

At her bemused look, he shrugged. "I'm easy—especially when the reward is so delectable." His grin faded on a rising tide of need. He had never wanted a woman more. Once was not enough. Just what would be, he couldn't begin to guess. He was an addict craving the next fix. He had to have her.

Kurt wove his fingers into the hair at the back of her head and pulled her down to him, claiming everything within reach until she broke away. With reckless haste, she rose up and firmly impaled herself on him. He saw her wince. She was tight and not yet ready, the transition from nightmare to arousal too fast.

"Slow down," he groaned over his own raw pleasure. He captured her slim hips in his hands and lifted. She shook her head and pushed at his hands until he let go.

Baffled, he watched as she eased back down on him, a little more gingerly than before. He caught her face in his hands, searching for the woman behind the mask. Her eyes were shadowed with yearning and urgency and . . . sadness. That quiet sadness that lurked just under the guarded surface, just out of sight. He'd seen it on the deck at the clubhouse when she'd thought she was alone, and he'd seen it again after he pulled her out of the lake.

"We have all the time we need," he murmured.

"It's okay." It was. Her body was quickly adjusting to him. Flutters of pleasure began to shudder through her. She straightened and braced unsteady hands on his shoulders as she searched for that blissfully mind-numbing place where nothing existed except sheer physical ecstasy. A place free of despair and fear and loneliness.

But the more frantically she sought that release, the further out of reach it retreated until eventually she sank against Kurt's chest in defeat, too exhausted to move. She didn't say anything when he rolled her limply onto her back and began to massage the shaky muscles in one thigh.

"How does that feel?"

"Mmm. Don't stop."

After giving the same slow attention to her other thigh, he spread her legs and sank full length into her.

Her eyes opened. "I don't think I can do this. I'm so tired."

"Just relax," he murmured. "You don't have to do a thing."

As before, he worked his magic until soon her exhaustion slipped away with the rest of the world and she was once again swept up onto the crest of that sensual wave.

"Easy." He captured her hips to slow her pace and sat back on his heels, pulling her with him. "Do you like it there?" he asked, adjusting his position. "Or there . . . ?"

She came, shuddering and crying out.

Kurt groaned as he felt her tighten rhythmically around him. By sheer force of will, he held himself motionless above her, the need to join her barely overcome by the desire to prolong the pleasure. Some time later, after he had pushed her over the edge again, he joined her there.

Sunlight and shadows spilled over the bed through white curtains dancing in the cool morning breeze. Kurt eased out from under a slender arm, careful not to wake her. She rolled onto her back but didn't wake up. Her lashes formed dark fans on her cheeks. She smiled faintly when he traced a light finger along a gracefully arched eyebrow and down the length of her jaw. The bathrobe she'd pulled on again sometime during the night had loosened while she slept, now affording little modesty.

Kurt's gaze wandered over the flawless perfection of creamy skin and a rounded breast that rose and fell with each breath. Almost perfect, he corrected, his eyes returning to the scar above her right breast. He'd felt what he suspected was a nastier exit wound on her back. More scars criss-crossed her abdomen.

Kurt hooked a finger under the edge of the bathrobe and lifted it aside for a better look. With each discovery came more questions. A deeper mystery. This was one discovery Julia had tried hard to prevent. The slip, the bathrobe, the candles, all made sense now, even if little else did.

How had she come by those scars? And who was Jack? Because one thing he did know: she couldn't possibly have had a baby.

The cold registered first on Julia's sleep-fogged mind. Then daylight penetrated her eyelids. With morning came reality. She knew this instinctively but pushed reality away and continued to savor the dream a little longer—a precious dream that belonged in another life. Not hers. She groped for covers but her hand was caught, stilled, and kissed. Reluctantly she cracked open her eyes to find Kurt propped up on his side over her bared chest, looking at her in a thoughtful manner that struck a discordant note in her sleepy glow. Her eyes widened in alarm, and she struggled clumsily to sit up and cover up at the same time.

"Sorry. Didn't mean to wake you. I was just admiring the view. And it . . ." Kurt paused. His hand caught her chin, and his lips met hers in a gentle kiss. ". . . is magnificent."

Julia smiled and shifted uneasily. "What time is it?" She was already edging off the opposite side of the bed, straightening her robe and taking her slip from the bed as she went.

"Ten." Kurt eyed her closely.

"Oh, sod! I never sleep this late." She glanced out the window. "The storm has passed. They'll probably be back soon so Kip and Alex can make their flight. They leave from Traverse City at three." She knew she was chattering nervously, something she never did, but then she'd never played out one of these morning-after scenes before either, and it was darned awkward. "May I use your shower? Did the electricity come back on?"

"Yes and yes," Kurt answered to her back as she slipped cautiously past him.

By the time Julia left the bathroom, she was geared up for a quick, dignified exit. She flinched when strong arms unexpectedly wrapped around her from behind, trapping her against the kitchen counter.

"Why didn't you tell me you were a virgin?"

As harshly as a slammed door, the final note of the dream ended and her dignified exit went down the drain. So the fairy tale would end a drama complete with questions and lies. Because she'd rather lie than give him any kind of emotional claim on her. The whole point was to keep it casual—no strings, no involvement, no risk. She wished they could simply resume their separate lives from here, as they would ultimately in any event, and leave this magical night untarnished.

Julia steeled herself against the warm feeling of him pressed against her back. "I wasn't," she lied.

Kurt turned her around, still imprisoning her against the counter, and continued as if she hadn't spoken, merely raising an eyebrow in disbelief. "Even more puzzling, how could a woman your age who looks like you still be a virgin?"

Julia looked pointedly at his imprisoning arms, refusing to answer until he finally released her and allowed her to step away. "You know very little at all about me."

"You're right. Though not for want of trying. But your reluctance to talk about even the most ordinary subjects itself tells me something about you. Shall I continue?"

Irritation overrode caution. "Certainly! Why stop now?"

"You're obviously a very private person. You yourself said that you have few friends and live for your work. In other words, you keep people at arm's length. Which is probably why you were about to sneak out of here—"

"I wasn't!"

He went on despite her protest, "Something tragic happened to you in the past. You've closed yourself off. The scars—bullet wounds, I would guess . . ."

Julia turned pale. Black splotches filled her vision as blood rushed from her head. No one had ever seen through her so clearly, so quickly.

"Julia—"

She shook off his arm and straightened. The black splotches gradually dissolved. "So, according to you I have a meager personal life and a painful past. Sounds rather dull." She grimaced indifferently. "Now that you've analyzed my character flaws, I'd best be leaving. Alex and Kip have flights to catch."

She had the advantage of being closer to the front door of the cottage. On the way, she snatched her purse off the counter. "I'll send you a draft for the contact lenses." She was almost to the door before he caught up to her.

"Julia, wait!" He didn't touch her. Instead he braced an arm against the door so that she couldn't open it. "I'm sorry." He raked his other hand through his hair, making it stand on end.

God, he was sexy, she couldn't help noticing, even with beard stubble.

"This isn't the way it was supposed to go," he went on. "What I meant to say is, I want you to stay on here with me for a few more days. I'll have to rearrange my schedule, but I think I can manage it. If that creates a problem with your airline ticket back to London, I'll buy you another."

Julia stared at him, astonished by his arrogance. "*You* may be able to rearrange *your* schedule, but I can't mine. Last night was wonderful, but it's over." She reached for the doorknob even though he still barred the door with his hand.

His face took on a grim look, as if he were being forced to say something he'd rather not. "I'm not ready to let you just walk away. There's something between us. I don't know where it will lead, but we owe it to each other to at least take the time to find out."

Julia felt herself softening and looked away. Sometimes there were no choices, no matter how much one might wish otherwise. "I'm sorry. There really isn't anything between us. And there never can be. Please, let me go."

"I can't." Kurt looked both apologetic and perplexed by his reaction. "Look . . ." He blew out an exasperated breath and glanced at his watch. "Just don't leave Belle House before I get there. Give me half an hour to shower and change. All right?"

"Okay," she agreed reluctantly.

Kurt lifted his hand from the door but did not move aside. As she brushed past him, he stopped her. "Julia?"

She looked up and saw his intention too late. "A morning-after kiss is customary." His arms closed on her shoulders as his lips met hers in a light, nonthreatening kiss that did strike her as appropriate to the occasion. Except that the kiss was deepening by the second, and her traitorous legs were turning to spaghetti in response.

Abruptly, he released her and she staggered back a step.

"So, there isn't anything between us, huh?" he said softly.

Julia's eyes flashed her annoyance. "Just sex. A biological reaction. Nothing more."

Then she was gone. The screen door banged hollowly in her wake.

Julia fled the cottage with Kurt's words ringing in her ears. He was right. Intuitively she sensed that they had shared something rare and special. And that frightened her. It meant becoming involved. And involvements were a risky, messy business. Sooner or later it would mean pain and loss. Sooner, if she correctly understood Kurt's casual invitation. And each day, each minute, she spent with him, each confidence and each intimacy shared, would only deepen the inevitable pain in the end.

No. Her life was already strewn with broken dreams and the ghosts of those she had loved and lost. She had managed to pick up the pieces of her life once and had no intention of going through that particular hell again. Her heart, like her body, had been shattered and glued back together, but it wasn't a perfect fit. The whole was more fragile than before. A stable, predictable life was what she wanted—*needed*—and that life absolutely did not include Kurt Weston.

Chapter 7

Her promise to Kurt notwithstanding, by the time Julia reached the main house, she'd resolved to leave as quickly as possible. For once luck was on her side; Marcus greeted her with news that the boaters had returned. Alex poked her head into Julia's room while she was throwing her things into her suitcase.

"I heard you were back," Julia said, hastily tucking away her bloodstained slip. It had apparently been underneath her in Kurt's bed.

"Yeah, a little while ago. It was a wild ride." Alex came over and perched on the edge of the bed, her gaze following Julia's hurried packing. "Where have you been?"

"Walking." Julia checked her watch. "We'd better go or you'll miss your flight."

"There's time." Alex caught and stilled her hands. "Are you all right? I heard about you and Kurt."

"Heard what, exactly?" Julia asked carefully.

"You're a hero. Alfred Livingston said you nearly drowned saving a little girl."

"Oh, that."

"Yeah, that! What did you think I meant?" Alex regarded her curiously.

"Nothing. I didn't really save her life. More like we were both saved by Kurt."

"So I heard. But, according to Livingston, the consensus is the little girl survived because you got to her in time." Alex stood and gave her a squeeze. "I'm very proud of you."

Julia shrugged. "I have a feeling Kurt would have pulled it off on his own. Anyway, I'm no hero. I wasn't even thinking." She paused, her eyes going distant. "I just couldn't let it happen."

"I know. That's who you are." Alex smiled at her fondly. "Kip and I want to hear all the details on the ride back."

Abruptly Julia remembered the need for haste. "We'd better hurry if you're going to make your flight." She tucked the rest of her things into her case.

"We're ready. I just want to say good-bye to Kurt and Marcus."

"Marcus was eating breakfast on the back porch a few minutes ago when I came in." Julia picked up her luggage. "All set."

Their luggage was stowed in the boot of the sedan. Farewells were exchanged interminably. In no apparent hurry to leave, Kip and Vanessa were reliving their harrowing sea adventure. Alex was busy putting a last-minute move on Rob. Marcus showed up, and that led to another round of backslapping bonhomie. Julia glanced yet again at her watch. Anxiously she reminded her companions of their deadline. With agonizing slowness, they inched their way toward the car. Finally, Kip opened the driver's door.

Julia scrambled into the back. *They were going to make it! Oh, bugger!* She cursed silently when Kurt rounded the corner of Belle House.

Kip had spotted him, too, and naturally meant to wait.

Kurt looked momentarily startled when he took in the

little farewell scene. His eyes zeroed in on Julia. Even at a distance she could feel his reproach. Barely acknowledging the hearty greetings of the others, he descended on her.

His hand appeared on the open window frame. "You gave me your word," he said bluntly.

Julia looked up into Kurt's accusing face. A knot of dread formed in the pit of her stomach. He apparently intended to make a big deal out of it right here in front of everyone.

"Kurt!" She feigned pleasure for the benefit of their interested audience. "I'm so glad to have the chance to say good-bye in person and to thank you again for all that you did yesterday." She forced a thin smile. "We're running a bit late for the airport or I would have—"

Kurt opened the car door, cutting off her play for a smooth exit. "I'll drive you. We can talk on the way."

"No." She dropped the charade, letting the others think what they wanted. "Kip, can we spare a minute?"

"Sure. We'll wait." Kip's expression was carefully neutral.

Julia got out and crossed the driveway, leaving Kurt to follow if he wanted. She didn't stop until they reached the shade of an enormous weeping willow tree. Its streaming wands partially concealed them from the interest of those waiting by the car.

Thick silence hung in the air while Kurt simply looked at her. She could feel the tension radiating from him. He finally spoke so abruptly she flinched. "So, you're running away."

"No. I have a life, a job I'm going back to," she said evenly, determined to keep her cool. Thank heaven he hadn't learned she was spending the summer in Cherry Beach.

"Ah yes, all the work that justifies keeping everyone at a distance. You're taking the easy way out."

"My life is not easy. In any case, it's none of your business."

"It's a cop-out."

She fought to control her temper. "Look, Kurt, I'm not out shopping for a good man to pick up the pieces of my life. I don't need to be rescued from myself. It's my life and I'll live it the way I want."

"Why is your life in pieces?" Kurt pounced on her unfortunate choice of words. "What dark monster lives in your closet, Julia?"

Julia froze for an instant before turning a stony glare on Kurt. "Back off, Kurt. You're not playing fair. This was to be a limited run, a one-time engagement." She paused to breathe. Her chest felt tight. "I have a life in London. You have a life here. We both knew that. There is no room for an 'us,' however temporary."

"A limited run? You make it sound like this was some sort of part you were playing."

"Maybe it was. What does it matter? I haven't the time nor the inclination for an encore." She turned to leave but looked back briefly. "Good-bye, Kurt."

He reached out a hand to shake hers. She warily accepted what she hoped was an olive branch. But he held on when she would have released her grip.

"What I can't understand is why you did it." Kurt frowned at her. "Why wait all these years for a one-night stand?"

Julia swallowed and looked him in the eye. "It wasn't my first time." *God, she hated this.*

He shrugged. "Maybe. Maybe not."

"Not."

"Unless . . ." His mouth tightened into a hard, thin line. "Unless it was payment for saving your skin."

Julia stared at him in stunned disbelief. Heat crept up from the collar of her shirt. "Of course not!" She wrenched her hand out of his.

"Maybe you thought you owed me, so you gave me what I obviously wanted."

"No!" Julia's hands fisted in anger at her sides. Almost as quickly she reined in her emotions and her eyes iced over. "Why are you doing this?"

"Maybe I'm just used to getting to know the women I sleep with."

"Well, sorry, but I'm not available to join your stable. What is this really about, Kurt? Hasn't a woman ever turned you down before? This is probably just a matter of ego for you. You're not used to being rejected." She warmed to the idea. "With your money, women probably fall into your bed. Well, get this, I'm not looking for a sugar daddy! I've always paid my own way and I don't need you." As soon as the words left her mouth, Julia wished them unsaid.

She met his eyes and paled. He looked coldly furious. She wanted badly to flee, but pride made her hold her ground.

"Yes, I can see that you're a woman who likes to pay her own way," Kurt said icily. "Well, you paid. In spades. A real bang for the buck. And I'll throw in the contact lenses as a bonus for your outstanding—what did you call it earlier? Oh, yes—biological reaction. It was off the Richter scale."

Julia blinked in shock as the full import of the insult registered. Speechless, she could only stare as he went on.

"Maybe we could negotiate a contract for future services. It would be very lucrative."

She fell back a step and looked at him in horror.

As if realizing he'd gone too far, he reached a hand out to her. "Julia . . ."

She evaded it and, without another word, turned on her heel and left. Shell-shocked, Julia walked woodenly back to the car, too dazed to do more than go through the motions of a last, mercifully brief leave-taking. She avoided Alex's looks of concern and ignored the avid speculation on the faces of the others. They had seen enough to know that something beyond a rescue had occurred between her and Kurt. Vanessa, standing off to one side chattering at a stone-faced Kurt, looked delighted by the turn of events.

Marcus opened the car door for Julia. After she slid inside, he looked down at her sympathetically. "You're doing the right thing. Leave while you can." His voice was low, confidential. "I've known Kurt all my life. He uses people and then throws them away, especially women. They always lose. I guess that comes with having life dished up on a silver platter—'' He broke off when Alex slid into the back next to Julia. ''Take care,'' he said, closing the door.

As the sedan pulled away, Julia finally faced the questions on Alex's face. ''You don't have to worry about my baser instincts getting the better of me anymore. He now detests me.'' Her mouth twisted bitterly. ''And I detest him.''

''Is that what you were aiming for back there?'' Alex asked softly so that Kip, in the front seat, would not overhear.

''I wanted nothing more than to get on with my life. Alone.''

''Then it looks like you accomplished your goal.''

''I hope I never see the wretch again.''

Julia leaned back and closed her eyes, both against further confidences and the inexplicable tears stinging her eyelids, leaving Alex frustratingly in the dark about what exactly had happened.

The sedan turned out of sight, and still Kurt stared down the road, replaying the bitter exchange. He hadn't kept his head. He'd been brutal. She'd stood there all cool and composed after he'd caught her trying to sneak off, and he'd been incensed that she'd once more escaped behind that wall of glacial reserve. Better anger than icy indifference, he'd figured. So he'd pushed her and then hadn't been able to handle the backlash.

There had been times these past few days when he thought that maybe this one . . . Her haunted look had sucked him in, made him think he could melt the ice and bring her back to life. What a fool! The reality was that he'd barely had time to melt the surface. She was a mystery. In the hard glare of daylight, Kurt had to admit that he couldn't pinpoint with any certainty where the real Julia ended and his imagination took over. Even her virginity, which had seemed so certain in that instant of resistance, seemed improbable now. After she left the cottage, he'd searched the sheets for evidence to prove her wrong and found nothing.

But he did know she had the courage to risk her life to

save a child. And he knew she'd once suffered horrifying injuries. And he knew she had extraordinary talents.

Kurt's pager beeped. He checked the display. One of his architects.

Damn! He didn't need this. He should be glad she was gone. He had a company to run. Westco's future hung on their next bid. He'd gambled on their early success and expanded quickly. Some within the company thought, too quickly. He'd soothed their concerns; now he had to come through. Dozens of employees he valued as friends and colleagues were depending on him.

He came up here to put the finishing touches on Westco's bid. And what had he done instead? He'd spent time he didn't have chasing after a woman!

Marcus interrupted the mental thrashing Kurt was giving himself. "Don't take it too hard, Weston. She's not worth it. Vanessa says guys in college called her the queen of freeze." Marcus failed to recognize the danger in Kurt's expressionless profile. "A woman like that probably *can* freeze a man's balls off."

Kurt flicked a hard glance at Marcus. "Better watch that mouth of yours, Fuller. One of these days it's going to get you hurt."

Chapter 8

In a frenzy of industry, Julia spent the next several weeks sorting out her grandfather's finances and sprucing up the cottage to let for the off-season. In part, she owned, all this activity kept her mind off her unfortunate lapse at Breakers, as she had begun to think of it. Unfortunate but harmless in the long run, she often told herself. She dipped into estate funds to send Kurt money for the contact lenses—a bank draft in an envelope with no return address. After the first week or two she could put the entire episode out of her mind for hours at a time. In this, young Annie Cleary proved instrumental.

With school out, ten-year-old Annie became a frequent visitor at the cottage, popping in most days for a biscuit and chat, and often staying to help if Julia had something for her to do. Julia's fondness for the raven-haired sprite grew with the recognition that Annie felt a bit put off at home. Susan was busy with Annie's new baby brother and her part-time job at a medical clinic in the village. Ted's job as a school principal kept him occupied through the summer. Most of Annie's friends lived miles away in the village. The uncomplicated friendship suited Julia, and she began to save little jobs or come up with an art project to keep Annie busy.

During this time, Julia also set about finding a private investigator to look into her grandfather's death. Through Ted Cleary, she hired an ex-police officer for the job. He found nothing new and quickly weighed in on the side of the sheriff.

At the end of June, Hugo flew over for a visit. By now the season was in full swing. Throngs of summer residents and tourists jammed beaches and gift shops up and down the peninsula. Serial open-air art fairs and music festivals relined the locals' pockets and kept the visitors entertained. Hugo spent several days with her poking around the resort villages that dotted both shores of the peninsula, before flying off to visit friends on the East Coast.

In July, a blanket of sluggish heat spread over the peninsula. The regional scarcity of air conditioners forced many to the beaches, and Julia was no exception. She abandoned the cottage and sought refuge under a beach umbrella with Annie. When they could, Susan and four-month-old Dustin joined them.

In August, Julia discovered she was pregnant.

After weeks thinking she had a bug she couldn't quite shake, and then turning green and nearly fainting in front of Susan, she reluctantly drove in to the clinic for a check-up. After the exam, Susan made a few notes on her medical chart. "Do you remember when you had your last period? You left that question blank." The compact, competent-looking doctor glanced up at Julia, still perched on the edge of the table wearing a loose blue hospital gown.

"I'm not sure. I'm not very regular." She thought back. "I had one in May about the time I got here. That may be the last one."

"Let's see . . . That would be about two and a half months ago." Susan made a note on her chart. "A long time."

Something in her voice caught Julia's attention. "Not that unusual for me."

Susan looked up and smiled. "You can get dressed now. Then we'll talk."

Julia waited in the small office, ill at ease and anxious to be out in fresh air away from the medical smells. The door opened and her head snapped up. Susan smiled reassuringly as she took the seat behind her desk.

"Well? Did you find anything?"

Susan regarded Julia, her brown eyes narrowed with concern. "Yes, I did. You're pregnant."

The words hung in the air. Julia blinked in surprise. *Pregnant? Impossible!* A grudging half smile curved her mouth. "This is a joke, right? It's not very funny."

"No. It's not a joke."

Her smile collapsed. "That's impossible! There must be some mistake."

"There's no mistake. I ran the test twice. And all the physical signs are there. You're probably about two months along."

Panic tightened its grip. Julia stared at Susan, unable to accept what she was hearing. "But I'm infertile! I was told years ago that I would not be able to get pregnant. Ever."

"You mean because of your abdominal injuries?"

"Yes. My tubes were damaged, and something about scar tissue. I don't remember the particulars, but I certainly do remember the bottom line."

Susan tapped her pen thoughtfully. "I can't tell what damage was done, but it either wasn't as extensive as the doctors thought at the time or it healed better than they expected, because there is no doubt that you are pregnant." She paused, watching Julia closely. "These days most women have a pretty good idea they're pregnant when they walk in the door. Obviously, you didn't."

Julia said nothing, too stunned to form a coherent thought. Her head spun and her ears rang.

"I'm going to refer you to a specialist in Traverse City. So far, everything looks normal, but considering your history . . ." Susan rose and circled her desk to take the chair next to Julia's. "You're going to need some time to absorb all this. You don't have to make any decisions immediately. Give yourself some time. We'll talk."

Julia turned her horrified face away. This could not be happening.

In a mind-numbing state of denial, Julia stepped out of the clinic into the glare of the midday sun, clutching a pregnancy pamphlet in one hand. She paused with her other hand on the railing, waiting for a wave of dizziness to pass. Morning sickness? This could not be happening! Yet even as one part of her mind screamed that there had to be a mistake, another more realistic voice cursed the perverse twist of fate that had turned one night of insanity into *this*. Fate had dealt her another joker.

Zombielike, Julia made her way through the center of the village toward her car. Traffic was heavy. Tourists spilled from shops onto crowded brick sidewalks. The annual Cherry Beach Music Festival blared from the beach a block away, but she was oblivious to the carnival atmosphere.

She had to think. But not here. The crowd pressed suffocatingly close. She had to get back to Gull Inlet, her island of calm. She needed peace and quiet and space to sort out this disaster.

She tried to pass a slow-moving couple and didn't notice the man who cut over to block her path until she bumped up against him. The pamphlet fell from her hand. The man grasped her arm to steady her.

"Julia! Sorry. I thought it was you."

Glancing up, it took a moment before she placed the beautiful face. Marcus Fuller. "Oh, hello." She bent to pick up the pamphlet.

"Here—got it." He reached it first and glanced at the boldly printed title: "Pregnancy and Childbirth." His gaze snapped to her in surprise and something else that looked like annoyance.

Julia barely registered the odd expression before it disappeared with the rest of the world as spinning black dots merged into a black curtain in front of her eyes.

"I think you fainted," Marcus said after practically carrying her to a nearby bench. "I'd better get you back to your doctor."

"No. I'm okay. Just a dizzy spell." She frowned, forcing herself to actually focus on him. "How did you know I'd just been to the doctor?"

"I saw the paper you dropped and just assumed . . ." He looked at her sympathetically. "I'm sorry. Is there anything I can do?"

Ignoring his invitation to confide, Julia rose. "I have to go now," she said, already turning away. "Nice to see you again."

"Wait! Do you need a ride somewhere?"

"No. Thank you. My car is just over there." She waved vaguely down the block in the general direction she was headed.

"I'll walk you. In case you feel dizzy again."

It wasn't worth the effort to decline, so she let him come along.

The crowd thinned as they left the center of the village. Marcus prattled away about the coincidence of seeing her again and about his family's summer cottage on the peninsula. Julia's thoughts tumbled madly, making it impossible to focus on what he was saying for long. She gave up and tuned him out.

Good Lord, what had she done? Yesterday, that night with Kurt had seemed merely an unfortunate lapse—embarrassing, upsetting, but resulting in no permanent damage. Today, her carefully constructed world was crashing down around her ears, all because of a few hours of bliss that she could not eradicate from her head. Or her body either, apparently.

"Julia?"

"Yes?"

"Is this it?" Marcus asked.

She looked up, concentrating her thoughts. They were

standing next to her car. She wasn't sure how long they'd been there. He'd been asking about her plans to return home to London, she remembered. "Yes. Sorry. I was thinking about something else." She unlocked the door.

"Are you sure you should drive?"

"I'm fine. Thanks."

His solicitude was commendable, Julia supposed, but she couldn't handle it just then. She also didn't know what to make of it. At Breakers she'd pegged him more or less as a shallow hanger-on, a shirttail relative who grew up seductively close to all that Weston power and money and probably wanted both desperately. Perhaps she'd misjudged him, too. She'd made other, more grievous mistakes that weekend.

Belatedly it occurred to her that he'd undoubtedly concluded she was pregnant. The pamphlet, the doctor, her dizziness—it wouldn't take a mental giant to put it all together, and *stupid* was not a word she would use to describe Marcus. The possibility that he might pass the news on to Kurt loomed hideously in front of her. And while little else was clear at the moment, one thing was: if Kurt Weston was ever to learn of this, she wanted it to be when she decided and on her terms. And that was not from Marcus over a beer in the jacuzzi.

Pausing by the open car door, Julia looked back at him. "I just realized that you probably think this is for me." She smiled weakly, holding up the pamphlet. "It's not. It's for someone else." The lie sounded so lame she half expected him to laugh in her face. "I just didn't want you to think that . . ." She shrugged.

"Rest easy," he assured her, an earnest expression on his beautiful face. "I wouldn't have said anything to anyone even if I thought it was yours."

For weeks Julia fought the pull of the life inside her. But she couldn't run from it. And she was gradually losing the battle. It was mad! She had no room in her life for a child. Where she lived. Her job. Her hours.

"What are you really afraid of?" Susan asked, sensing with her uncanny radar vision that Julia's reservations went beyond the admittedly considerable logistics.

Loving and losing. Again. That was what terrified her. Her entire life structure rested on the certainty that love meant pain and loss. And anyway, what kind of mother would she be? A child deserved a loving, secure home. Could she provide one with no father? Did she even have enough love to give? Or had that part of her died with her family?

"Think about what you want deep down where you live," Susan said. "Once you figure that out, the other decisions will be easier."

Where did she live? Julia wondered. More and more it felt like a cold, bleak, empty place. And now, in the center of it was a spark of life, a glimmer of warmth. Hope. But was it too late? She'd been frozen so long.

Julia suppressed the constant questions and turned her attention to a more immediate problem. Whether she kept the baby or put it up for adoption, she had to tell Kurt. Yet she dreaded the very thought, and if it had been simply a matter of money, she wouldn't have considered it. But there were two other people in this triangle with interests different from her own. If she gave the baby up, Kurt would have to give his permission. And if she kept it, the child should have a father in its life, assuming Kurt would even consider playing that role. If not, the child could still benefit greatly by Kurt's financial support. Then, too, Kurt probably had a right to know, she admitted grudgingly, though she was at a loss as to what his reaction would be.

Probably that of a boy caught with his hand in the cookie jar, if Marcus was right. Curiously, Marcus had visited the cottage twice since their accidental meeting in Cherry Beach. During the last visit, he'd hinted that Kurt had a girlfriend—

Amanda. Julia remembered hearing the name tossed about that weekend at Belle House, the way friends do when an old familiar is absent. But Julia had never made the connection to Kurt. And she didn't entirely trust Marcus. Who knew what his agenda might be?

Chapter 9

A month later, on Saturday during Labor Day weekend, Julia pulled herself together, dressing with more care than she'd taken since learning of her pregnancy, and drove back to Belle House in a rented compact. She'd learned from Marcus that Kurt would be up for the long weekend.

The beaming caretaker, Alfred Livingston, met her at the front door. "This is a happy surprise. We heard that you'd gone back to England. I can't tell you how many times this summer I was asked about you," he said, ushering her into a sitting room off the foyer. "Between the rescue and your performance at the opening dance, you were quite a topic around here."

His smile fell. "I'm sorry, though, Rob isn't here at the moment."

"Actually, I came to see Kurt."

"Kurt isn't here either. But I expect him shortly. You're certainly welcome to wait." All the chairs in the room had been pulled away from the walls to permit cleaning behind them. "We're in the midst of getting ready for a family celebration tomorrow," Livingston explained. "In fact, Kurt hadn't planned on coming up until tomorrow, but he had a last-minute change in plans and should arrive very soon, so you're in luck."

This news took Julia aback. Marcus had assured her that Kurt would be up only *through* Saturday. Before she could ask about it, Livingston glanced over her shoulder. Julia turned, half expecting to see Kurt. Instead, Vanessa stood framed in the arched doorway.

"Julia. I thought I saw you drive up. What an interesting surprise!"

"Vanessa," Julia acknowledged coolly.

"That will be all, Livingston. I'll keep Julia company." Livingston's mouth thinned at the summary dismissal. Vanessa looked bored, as usual, and heedless of the slight.

"I'll let Kurt know you're here as soon as he arrives, Miss Griffin," he said, before making a dignified exit.

Vanessa made herself comfortable on a sofa. Seeing no other choice, Julia resigned herself to the unwelcome company and chose a seat some distance away.

"So, you've come to see Kurt. I thought I'd missed the Fourth of July."

Julia eyed her. "What do you mean?"

Vanessa smiled malevolently. "Evidently, you don't know how the game is played. One passage of arms means nothing to Kurt. You were the flavor of the week. No, in your case, the flavor du jour."

Julia gave an indifferent shrug, understanding perfectly that, with no witness who mattered around, Vanessa felt free to unsheathe her claws. "Relax, Vanessa. I'm not here seeking a rapprochement with Kurt. You have nothing to worry about." She only wished the wicked witch would take herself off so she could stew in peace while she waited for the moment of reckoning.

"Oh, it's not me." A sly smile lit Vanessa's pampered face. "Aren't you the least bit curious about the celebration Livingston mentioned?"

"Spill it. I can see you're dying to tell all." She wondered how long Vanessa had been standing in the doorway before Livingston noticed her.

Vanessa drew it out, enjoying herself. "The family is celebrating Kurt's engagement."

Julia stilled. "To Amanda?"

"The very same." Vanessa smirked.

So, Marcus was right about Kurt and Amanda. Julia steeled herself against feeling any emotion. It wasn't as if these revelations about Kurt meant anything to her personally, other than casting the entire episode in an even more sordid light—though an impending marriage was bound to color his reaction to her news.

Suddenly, the awkwardness of her presence at Belle House on the eve of his engagement party hit her. She had to get out of here. This was not the time nor the place for their meeting.

Thinking quickly, she reached into her purse for pen and paper. Ignoring Vanessa, Julia scribbled a note to Kurt, saying that it was urgent that they talk about something of great importance to both of them. She added that she was still at Gull Inlet and provided the phone number, then stared at the wording, wondering if she should be more specific. No, she decided, the tone and wording should be sufficient to give him an inkling of the nature of the problem.

Vanessa trailed Julia to the kitchen, where Mr. Livingston was putting together a tray of refreshments. Julia told him she couldn't wait after all. "Would you please give Kurt this note for me?"

"Certainly. But why don't I ring him on his cell phone?" he asked, following her back to the foyer. He produced an envelope for her note from a drawer.

"No! Thanks, I really do have to run." Julia quickly sealed the note inside and wrote Kurt's name on the front. "Please don't even mention that I stopped in." Let him think she had dropped it at the gate.

At Livingston's perplexed look, Julia smiled weakly. "The note will explain everything."

He nodded doubtfully, taking it, then excused himself to answer a phone ringing somewhere in the back of the house.

Vanessa smiled. "Well, I guess I saved you from making a spectacle of yourself."

Julia brushed past her, reaching for the door. "Good-bye, Vanessa."

Memories of the last time she had tried to escape the owner of this house gave her speed. Just outside, Julia almost bumped into a trim older woman coming in with an armful of freshly cut flowers.

"Oh, my!" The woman laughed and clutched the flowers closer.

Julia looked up and caught her breath, instantly realizing who this must be. Her hair was lighter, her face more delicately shaped, but those striking gray eyes were identical to her son's. Julia murmured a brief apology and made to move by, but Kurt's mother stopped her with a light hand on her arm.

"I don't believe we've met," she said, not waiting for an introduction from Vanessa. "I'm Pat Weston." Her fine brow creased, as if she were trying to place Julia's face. "You must be one of my daughter's friends. Are you staying over for the party?"

"No!" Julia blurted out in an appalled voice. "I mean, I don't know your daughter, and I'm not here for the party. I—"

"This is a friend of mine from college." Vanessa neatly stepped in and saved the day. "We stopped in to say hi to Rob. Unfortunately, he's out sailing and we can't wait."

For once Julia appreciated Vanessa's innate cunning.

"Oh, that's too bad," Mrs. Weston said. "He shouldn't be long, though. I know he wants to be here when Kurt and Amanda get in. Why don't you come in and wait?"

"Thank you, but I'm pressed for time." Anxiously Julia glanced up the long drive. "I'd better be going. A pleasure to meet you, Mrs. Weston. Good-bye, Vanessa."

The two women watched Julia jump into a compact and speed away.

"Interesting young woman," Pat said. "She seemed awfully nervous about something."

Vanessa gave one of her lazy shrugs. "She's probably not very comfortable here."

"Oh?"

"She doesn't fit in." At Pat's uncomprehending look, Vanessa elaborated, "She's not one of us."

Pat's eyes narrowed. "People once said that about me, too, though of course you wouldn't remember. Fortunately, a lot has changed since I first came to Breakers." She reached for the door around the armful of flowers.

"Here, let me help you with those," Vanessa said, relieving her of some of the precariously perched blooms.

"Thanks." Pat led the way to the mudroom at the back of the house. "I'm probably overdoing this party, but it's not every day my daughter gets engaged." She took the flowers from Vanessa and propped them up in the utility sink. "Your friend looks familiar for some reason. I don't think we've met. . . ." She tilted her head in thought. "I wouldn't have forgotten a lovely voice like that, or face. Interesting accent. Where is she from?"

"She's been in London for a few years."

"Oh? She isn't a model or actress or someone I should recognize, is she?"

Vanessa gave a short laugh. "Hardly."

"Well, she certainly is extraordinary-looking."

After a moment, Vanessa took her leave. But instead of retracing her steps to the front door, she followed the long hallway running along the rear of the house. When she came to the study, she checked both directions before slipping inside and securing the door behind her with a soft click of the lock. Then she made a beeline for the enormous maple desk.

Julia's note to Kurt sat on top of a pile of mail. Vanessa picked it up and pocketed it. A self-satisfied smile curved her lips as she sank down in the leather chair and reached for Kurt's private phone.

"She's gone." Vanessa propped her feet on the desk to admire her new Jimmy Choo strappy sandals. "But she left a note."

"Damn!"

"I've got it for you. Livingston is so predictable. I'm at Kurt's desk now."

"Better get out of there before someone sees you."

"Don't worry, the door is locked. I'll slip out the back in a minute. Besides, everyone is up front getting ready for Carolyn's party, which, by the way, Julia now thinks is for Kurt and Amanda."

"Perfect. Who saw her?"

"Well, Livingston. Oh, yeah, and Pat." She smiled waiting for his explosion.

"Shit! She'll tell Kurt."

"I doubt it. She doesn't even know Julia's name. And she thinks Julia and I were here together to see Rob, not Kurt. Trust me, I was flawless."

"Well, Livingston will probably flap his mouth."

"I don't think so. Julia, bless her heart, asked him not to mention she was here."

"Keep your ear to the ground. We may have to plant a substitute note."

"I doubt it. Well, I'd better run along before Kurt shows up. Remember, you owe me."

"Wait! You told me he wasn't coming until tomorrow."

"He changed his plans." She frowned at a newly discovered chip in her manicure. "There's just one thing I don't get. It's obvious why I agreed to do this for you. But what's in it for you, Marcus? She's a cold bitch—not your type at all. I should know."

"Well, babe, you haven't given me the time of day in years. Not since you started dating stock portfolios."

She shrugged. "A girl's gotta think about her future. WalMart's not my style."

"Mine either."

The trip to Belle House had been a fool's errand, Julia concluded after several weeks passed with no word from Kurt. Her gaze shifted from the blank canvas in front of her to the window. Outside, steady rain bent the dune grass. Evidently his silence was all the response she was going to get.

As the weeks of silence grew, she met his decision with a mixture of relief and disappointment. The latter, she tried to tell herself, was solely on behalf of her child. His rejection of the baby made her want to protect it all the more.

She covered the slight swell of her belly. When she felt a soft answering flutter against her hand, her eyes welled with tears. One escaped to race down her cheek before she caught it with an impatient swipe. Damn! All these unwanted emotions. Susan had warned her about raging hormones. But knowing didn't stop the flood of vulnerability. And hurt. She didn't want Kurt, but his silence stung more than she would have expected.

Through it all, the constant, nagging question loomed: to keep the baby or give it up. Her heart and her head were aligned on opposite sides of the battlefield.

One afternoon in late September, about a month after her return trip to Belle House, Julia drove down to Traverse City to visit an adoption agency. Just to see, she told herself. The woman had been kind, but perversely, the longer she talked about the wonderful couples who could provide homes for her baby, the more Julia wanted to keep it.

"What's holding you back?" Susan asked a few days later. The two women were finishing cleaning up the kitchen in the lodge after a Sunday dinner.

Julia hesitated, still not used to this level of intimacy with Susan. "I don't know if it's fair to the baby. What if I can't do it?" She shook her head and began to attack the counter with a sponge. "Blast! I'm such a mess. I want so desperately, selfishly, to keep this baby, even though the very thought terrifies me." She glanced over at Susan. "You may not believe this, but before I came here my life was as orderly and predictable as Big Ben."

Susan smothered a laugh. "Oh, I believe you. But why is it unfair to the baby?"

"Well, there's the biggie for starters—no father."

"Life doesn't always work out perfectly." Susan closed the dishwasher and turned around. "Honey, if you were a teenager, I would be begging you to put the baby up for adoption for both your sakes. But you're a grown woman. I don't know what's best for either of you. I wish I had a crystal ball. Heck, you could have your pick of men to marry and be a father for your baby. That nice deputy sheriff, Dan Farley, to name one."

Susan paused until Julia looked up. "Whatever you do decide, we'll stand by you. If you do keep the baby, you won't be alone. Ted and I will be here."

If she stayed at Gull Inlet.

The following afternoon, Julia returned home with an armload of groceries to find Alex encamped in the living room, talking on her cell phone. Papers and luggage littered the floor. Julia wasn't particularly surprised to see her, knowing it was only a matter of time before Alex came to get the answers Julia had been avoiding over the telephone.

"Hi!" Alex smiled and waved. "No," she said into the phone, "I'm talking to Julia." A moment later, she rang off and followed Julia into the kitchen.

"Alex, how nice of you to drop in," Julia said, tongue in cheek, smiling over the top of the bag of groceries. "To what do I owe this pleasure? I thought you were back east." She put down the bag and gave Alex a hug.

"I was. But I had this sudden urge to come and see why this alone thing is so appealing to you." Alex stepped back and ran assessing eyes down the front of her. "Something's different about you."

"I've gained a little weight."

Alex brushed that aside with a wave of her hand. "I can see that. It's something else." Her brow furrowed suspiciously. "What's really going on? You were supposed to go back to London weeks ago. What about Hugo and your job?''

''I quit.''

''Quit?!'' Alex looked aghast. ''Why?''

Julia drew a long breath. ''Because even on the nightclub circuit, pregnant torch singers are a bit over the top. It's rather ironic, don't you think, that the most damning evidence of engaging in the passion I sing about makes me unfit for the job.''

''In English, Julia,'' Alex said, as if she couldn't have heard correctly.

''I'm pregnant.''

Alex could not have looked more dumbstruck.

''And I'm keeping the baby.''

Alex's knees gave out and she sank abruptly down onto a red vinyl kitchen chair, her gaze glued on Julia. ''But who?'' Her eyes grew bigger as she made the logical connection. ''My, God! It's Kurt Weston's.''

Julia looked away, a telltale flush crawling up her face.

''I don't know what to say—I'm so . . .''

Smiling wanly, Julia sat down across the table. ''Well, at least I've finally seen your shock threshold. Not quite the way I'd have chosen, though.''

Alex shook her head. ''Honey-babe, you just soared over it.''

''Have you told him?'' Alex asked over dinner.

Julia shifted uncomfortably on the chair. ''Sort of. I left a note for him at Belle House six weeks ago.''

Alex eyed her incredulously. ''A note?''

Julia raised her chin defensively.

Alex waived the issue of the note aside. ''Okay. What did he say?''

''I haven't heard a word from him.''

''That makes no sense.'' Alex frowned. ''What exactly did you say in this note?''

"I told him it was urgent that I talk to him about something of great importance. What else could it be?"

"Oh, let's see: a nasty disease, a passionate desire to see him again, a lost earring." Alex ticked off the possibilities on her hand. "Still, it doesn't make sense. I would have thought he'd have been here the next day if only to—"

"Oh, it makes perfect sense, Alex," Julia interrupted, trying not to sound bitter. "He's getting married."

"Impossible! I would have heard."

"Believe it. I almost walked in on their engagement party when I went back to tell him."

"Ouch!" Alex winced. "Maybe they're keeping it quiet for some reason."

"Naturally, he wouldn't want anything as inconvenient as an illegitimate child interfering with his wedding plans."

Alex cast her a quick, surprised look. "I don't know, Julia. I saw the way he looked at you. Besides, none of this jives with what I've heard about him. Kurt Weston isn't known for walking away from problems."

"Face it, Alex, the man has hung me out to dry. Anyway, it doesn't matter. I only wanted to do the right thing for the baby. If it weren't for that, I'd feel nothing but relief. Considering his marriage, I figure I'm doing him a favor anyway."

"I wonder."

"Don't look so glum. I'm used to flying solo. I'll be fine. And I'll do everything in my power to make sure this child is, too." Her gaze narrowed on Alex. "You have to promise never to tell anyone that he's the father."

"But, Julia, maybe—"

"No, Alex. You must. He's obviously not interested. I'm doing him a favor. In return, I want to ensure that he won't come back and disrupt our lives later. I gave him a one-time chance. He rejected it. Now it's gone. I'm glad he can't know for sure what I wanted to talk to him about. That makes it easier."

"I think you should talk to a lawyer. Julia, think! He

could help with child support. And if you ever do cross paths again—''

''No.''

Alex shook her head gloomily. ''I have a bad feeling about this. Secrets have a way of turning around and biting you on the butt.''

''Hugo wants to be the father. That should quiet any speculation.''

Alex stared at her in confusion. ''So you *are* going back to London.''

''No.''

''Then I don't get it.''

''Hugo has AIDS.''

''Oh, Christ. I'm so sorry.''

''He tested positive a few years back. I only found out last year when he began to get sick. That's one reason why I could stay the whole summer. We haven't had a full schedule for over a year. I had to pick up other gigs to make ends meet.''

Julia grimly watched the rivulets running down the windowpane. ''People keep dying on me, Alex,'' she said softly.

''I'm sorry.'' Alex looked at a loss to know what to say. ''It's not fair.''

''Maybe I'm cursed. Maybe I'm dangerous.'' She turned troubled eyes to her friend. ''To you, too, Alex.''

''Nonsense,'' Alex said briskly. ''You've saved my ass too many times for me to ever believe something so ridiculous. And you're certainly not to blame for Hugo. But why does he want to be named the father?''

''It's complicated.''

''I'm all ears.''

''I think it's partly because he's estranged from his family. And partly to leave some sort of legacy—the child he could never have. And to help me out. He wants to use his estate to set up a college fund for the baby.''

''But you're not going back?''

''No. I'm going to stay right here.'' Julia stood and crossed to the window, peering out into the rain. ''I love it. And it will be good for the baby to have the Clearys nearby, a ready-made family.''

Alex sighed. ''I'm having a really hard time wrapping my mind around the whole thing. Are you sure this is what you want? Living way out here in the middle of nowhere? What about your career? And a baby! You never wanted either a husband or kids.''

''No, I didn't, did I?'' Julia turned from the window and smiled ruefully. ''It wasn't supposed to ever be an issue. I was told before I ever met you that I would never be able to have children.'' She laughed. ''What a cosmic joke—one trip to wonderland and I have morning sickness.''

''I didn't know. That explains a lot.'' Alex sighed. ''This is all my fault. If I hadn't tried to nudge up your emotional thermostat, this might never have happened.''

''No, it's not your fault. All you did was hold up a mirror to me. It reflected the sad truth about my life. Besides, you warned me about him. I'm the one who made a bad choice.''

''Maybe you're being too quick to dismiss Kurt.''

''No. He's out of the picture.''

Alex recognized from her look, her tone that the subject was closed for good.

''Okay. But are you sure you want to keep it?''

''Yes. God help me and the baby if I'm just being selfish. But this baby's mine. And I'm not giving him up.''

with the rest of the party to [illegible] the [illegible] family.

[illegible] a really great long weekend [illegible] the whole thing are you [illegible] [illegible] And a baby. [illegible] would [illegible] sort of thing.

[illegible] by the window and [illegible] I would never [illegible] That a terrific [illegible] opportunity [illegible] and I have [illegible]

[illegible] up your cardboard [illegible]

[illegible]

[illegible]

[illegible]

[illegible]

But the baby [illegible] And [illegible]

Best Laid Plans

Chapter 10

Julia lit the four red candles on top of the clown cake and carried it around the corner of the darkened kitchen. ''Happy Birthday to Nick . . .'' she began, prompting the handful of adults and children gathered in a tight knot around the table.

Her eyes scanned the faces before coming to rest on the one who gave her life meaning. Nick bounced on the edge of his chair, his face lit with joy. The four Clearys were there. Alex, too. Several boys from Nick's nursery school completed the party. One face was sorely missed: Hugo, who had visited every February before journeying on to the warmth and sunshine of Key West, had finally lost his battle with AIDS the previous summer.

Julia glanced at the Mickey Mouse wall clock above the table, mindful that the boys' parents would be coming soon to pick them up. With a flourish she deposited the cake in front of her eager son, smiling at his uncontained excitement.

''. . . Happy Birthday dear Nicky, Happy Birthday to you.''

''Wait!'' Laughing, Julia laid a hand on Nick's small shoulder, stopping him before he blew. ''Make a wish first.''

He frowned in concentration. Julia pushed the oversized

cowboy hat back from his eyes, revealing more of the springy blond mop of curls that poked out from under all sides of the hat. His hair framed his face like a cloud of sunlight. Angelic, people often said. And sometimes he was. But he also had a naughty streak a mile wide.

"Blow! Blow!" the other boys chanted.

Later, while Julia struggled good-humoredly alongside arriving parents to get the boys into the right snowsuits and boots, Alex began clearing away the birthday debris. Julia said something as she captured and stuffed a karate-kicking foot into a boot, and the answering laughter drew Alex's attention. These past years since Nick's birth had been good to Julia. She'd moved out of the shadows. She looked happy, content, impossibly younger than her thirty-one years, in blue jeans and an oversized sweater, with her hair pulled back in a ponytail. For Nick's sake, she'd finally emerged from that cocoon of privacy she'd spun around herself.

Alex had timed her visit to coincide with Nick's birthday. But she'd also come to finalize a selection of Julia's paintings for a two-artist show scheduled to begin next month at Chase Gallery in Chicago. After several years of quietly selling her paintings individually through Alex's small new seasonal gallery in Cherry Beach, Julia had agreed to the show in Chicago exhibiting a collection of her works. For Julia, it meant greater exposure and higher stakes. Alex had been after her for two years to take this step, and probably would be still if Julia didn't need the money.

Friendship aside, Alex's usually reliable instincts told her that Julia's work would be favorably received by the critics and, more important, the buyers. Otherwise, she would never have been after Julia to take this step. Because for Alex, much as she enjoyed it, art was a business. The point was to make money—for herself and the artists she represented.

Alex had a third reason for visiting at this time: something she needed to tell Julia—news already withheld too long out of concern for how she would take it.

"Motherhood agrees with you," Alex said as they finished cleaning up. For a moment, they were alone in the cottage.

Julia smiled. "He's my life, Alex." She shrugged helplessly and wandered over to the wide front windows to watch the little person who occupied the center of her universe.

Nick and Dustin Cleary were trying out Nick's new plastic sled on the low dune in front of the cottage. Although almost a year separated the boys in age, they were close pals. Almost brothers. She watched Dustin push off and jump on behind Nick. Brilliant sun and a mild February high of thirty-five degrees made for an icy, fast track. Their whoops echoed across the snow-covered inlet as they skidded down the slight incline.

Annie gamely piled more snow on top of the track to gain a precious extra vertical foot for a faster takeoff. Julia didn't have to guess whose idea that had been; Nick loved to build things. The medium didn't matter: sand, twigs, boxes, tampax, her expensive sketch paper. Anything he could lay hands on served as raw material for his projects. Just then, Bowen, a large mutt of indeterminate parentage they had adopted the year before, bounded around the side of the cottage and gave chase to the sled.

It had been harder than she'd thought. The demands of raising a child alone were exhausting, relentless, and often frightening. But she wouldn't trade it for anything in the world. The Clearys had been an integral part of the equation, exchanging child care so Julia could work part-time in Alex's Cherry Beach gallery during the times of the year it was open. But most important, they provided Nick with an extended family. She could never repay them for that precious gift.

Alex came over to peer out the window. "He's a terrific kid, Julia."

They watched the boys sneak up on Annie with snowballs stockpiled in their hats. Missiles flew, not accurately. Annie shrieked and gave chase. All three and the dog disappeared around the side of the cottage.

Julia sighed wistfully. "They grow up too fast."

"Spoken like a woman pining for another baby." Susan

came in through the back door. She wrapped an arm around Julia's shoulders and squeezed. "Great party."

"Thanks. And no, I don't want another baby." Julia's mouth quirked up. "I just want the one I've got to stay that way forever."

"Just wait, it only gets worse." Susan picked up her tote bag to leave. "When Annie turned fifteen last summer, the first thing I said to her was "Happy Birthday!" and the second was, "How dare you grow up so fast!"

Alex giggled. Julia groaned, covering her ears. "I don't want to hear this."

After dinner, a Thomas the Tank Engine video, and Nick's overdue tantrum at bedtime, Julia hugged him for the third time and tucked the blanket up under his chin. "Good night, sweetheart. I love you." And for the third time she stood to leave.

"Mama, wait! I need to ask you something."

Julia sighed but waited for him to think up something. It was his birthday.

"Thank you for the clown cake . . . and the cowboy hat."

"You're welcome, sweetheart. But you'll have to thank Marcus for the cowboy hat. That was from him."

"Oh." Nick frowned and thought some more. "Is he going to be my new daddy?"

"Goodness, no! Whatever gave you that idea?"

"Doug gotted a new daddy and his old one didn't even die. Now he has two."

Julia's smile faded. "Uncle Ted is kind of like a daddy to you," she said softly.

Nick fixed unconvinced gray eyes on her. "Yeah."

A few minutes later, Julia took her guilt downstairs and collapsed into an easy chair. Alex lounged on the sofa, an open magazine in her lap. Recently, Nick had begun to ask about his father. He'd hardly known Hugo. So far, she had simply explained that his father died, figuring, better a dead father than an absent one. As for Kurt, Julia tried not to think of him. Or second-guess decisions she had made a long time ago.

"I don't know how you do it." Alex yawned hugely.

"Who called?"

"Marcus." Alex lowered the February issue of *ArtNews*. "He wondered if you got the flowers and package he sent for you and Nick."

"Mmm. I'll have to give him a call . . ." Julia propped up tired feet and leaned her head back. ". . . tomorrow."

"Since when have you two become so chummy?"

Julia heaved a long-suffering sigh. "We're just friends. I see him maybe two or three times a year when he comes up from Chicago. Nothing's changed, Alex. We have an understanding."

Alex raised a skeptical eyebrow, glancing at the large vase of flowers on the desk. "Flowers for you. A present for Nick. And I'm supposed to believe you're just friends? No doubt *you* feel that way, but Marcus? In your dreams, babe!"

"He's helping me find refinancing, so lately I've seen him a little more." Julia shrugged. "Strictly business." But she glanced uneasily at the flowers. Last summer she would have laughed the whole thing off. Now, Alex's doubts, coming on the heels of Nick's daddy question, gave her pause.

There was a time shortly after Nick's birth when Marcus tried to push their relationship. When Julia rebuffed him, they had quickly and painlessly reached a tacit agreement to remain friends only. And they had. At least until about six months ago.

That was when she'd asked his advice about refinancing the loan on the Deer Cove property north of the cottage. The balloon payment on it would come due in about a year. Unfortunately, she didn't have anywhere near the needed money. Over the years, property taxes alone on two large tracts of prime waterfront land had severely depleted her assets to the point where, unless she could find a lender to refinance the loan, she would have to unload Deer Cove.

Marcus had met her at Sid's Diner. He barely tolerated the local hangout, but the trendier cafés down the street were crowded in the summer. He was stunned to learn that she owned the Deer Cove property. He'd immediately gone into get-rich-quick mode until she convinced him that she would give the tract to a conservation group before she would let it fall into the hands of developers. Once she knocked the dollar signs out of his eyes, he was helpful in explaining the ins and outs of mortgage refinancing. But clearly, he disapproved of her decision.

"Don't be rash," he'd argued, pointing to the sorry state of her finances. "I see the way you live. Always cutting corners. Driving one beat-up heap after another. This one transaction could set you up for life. A tract that size of prime waterfront is like gold."

But Julia felt too strongly about the matter to compromise. Seth had worked hard to preserve that land. He'd entrusted her with it. And she didn't want to see it built over with condos or "tract mansions" any more than he had.

She had met with Marcus several times since then, so far without finding a satisfactory solution to the problem. As he'd predicted, given her lack of income and dwindling liquid assets, the lenders viewed her as a poor financial risk, despite the more than adequate collateral.

Julia cast another uneasy glance at the flowers. Was Alex right about Marcus? Had their friendship begun to slide toward intimacy? Occasional wining and dining had replaced a quick lunch once or twice a year at the diner. And then there were his casual, increasingly frequent touches. . . .

"Here it is!" Alex broke into Julia's ruminations. "The announcement for your show." Alex passed the magazine across the coffee table.

Julia skipped over a blurb for a Luca Benelli show at Alex's gallery and returned to it only after eliminating the other gallery announcement on the page. There, beneath his name, was her own in bold print. Julia bolted upright in the chair, fatigue forgotten.

"Have you lost your mind! How could you pair me with Luca Benelli?"

Alex rolled her eyes. "You should be dancing a jig that I pulled it off."

Julia had never met the Italian-born sculptor, dubbed the Italian stallion by the press. But for anyone who even casually followed the fine arts scene stateside, his name instantly conjured up images of the sensual bronze nudes that had rocketed him to national prominence a few years ago. Alex had shrewdly recognized the sculptor's commercial potential early on and, despite criticism from purists that his work failed to break new ground, had given him a mutually beneficial boost up the ladder to stardom. Now, he was gaining recognition in Europe as well.

"Alex, this is crazy!"

"Why?"

"Why? Because he's Luca and I'm nobody."

"Luca was nobody when I gave him his first show in the states," Alex calmly reminded her. "Look, you want to make money fast so you can keep your land, right? Pairing you with Luca will give you exposure among big buyers. They'll come to see Luca's work and stay to see yours. It's simple."

Julia was unconvinced.

"Trust me on this one. This is my job, and I've done pretty well at it. If I thought your work couldn't hold its own next to Luca's, I would not have set up the show this way."

"What does Derrick think?" Although officially Alex's second in command functioned as Chase Gallery's appraiser and art historian, unofficially he acted as a check on Alex's occasional impetuosity.

Alex sighed. "You know what they say about a prophet in his own land."

"You're biased in my favor."

"Okay, okay. The professor gave his qualified blessing."

"Qualified how?" A worried note crept into Julia's voice.

"My, my, what a fragile ego." Alex smirked.

"Alex—"

"Take it easy. Derrick thinks we could use a few more pieces to round out the show. That's all. So far we've selected twelve from the sixteen you sent down. I'd like a few more if possible. Let's see what I find tomorrow morning."

While Julia was occupied with her job as volunteer vocal director for the high school musical, Alex was to look through Julia's stockpile for additional pieces they could use.

Mollified, Julia leaned back again and closed her eyes, only to open them a second later when another question occurred to her. "Why would a star like Luca agree to this?"

"He owes me," Alex said with an enigmatic smile. "And I showed him a picture of you. He agreed as soon as he stopped drooling."

"And I thought I was done playing run-around-the-casting-couch."

"Don't be silly. I just showed him your picture. You don't have to do anything. It should make for an interesting opening, though, the two of you together."

Julia groaned.

"Anyway, how far can he get in one night? He'll be surrounded by art groupies."

"Nowhere."

"Exactly my point."

"How far did he get with you, Alex?"

"Not nearly as far as you seem to think. I've had other fish to fry. Not that he isn't adorable with that accent and that golden mane." Alex smiled dreamily. "But I think he lightens his hair. No, not my type."

Julia laughed at that, shaking her head. "Someday you're going to have to settle down, if only from sheer exhaustion."

"I've had to kiss a lot of frogs before I found a prince."

Julia eyed her. "Ah-ha! I presume this must be the mystery man you've so carefully avoided mentioning these last few months—don't think I haven't noticed. Does this prince have a name?"

Alex squirmed uncomfortably. "Rob Weston."

"Oh, Alex! Not again." Julia made a face.

"Third time's a charm. He asked me to marry him."

Julia gave a choked laugh. "You, Alexandra Chase, marry

the bastion of industrial-strength conservatism? That's a good one."

"I said yes."

It was the rare blush working its way up from the collar of Alex's red angora sweater that gave Julia pause. "You're serious!"

Alex winced. "Hard to believe, isn't it?"

"To say the least," Julia agreed, trying to get a handle on the notion. "This is what you've been working up to telling me all weekend, isn't it? Not about Luca Benelli. I knew there was something."

"Yes—well, both, actually." She was watching Julia closely. "I didn't know how you would feel about me marrying a Weston."

It was as close as they'd come to mentioning Kurt by name since that day long ago when Julia broke the news of her pregnancy. A couple of times over the years, when Alex seemed about to broach the subject, Julia had immediately shut her down.

Julia moved to the sofa next to her. "It's a shock, I'll admit, but if Rob's the one you want, I'm glad for you. It's just hard at first to imagine the two of you as a couple. Rob is . . . Don't take this wrong; he's a wonderful man, but he leads such a buttoned-down sort of life compared to you. Are you sure?"

"Yes. I hadn't seen him for years, not since we all went up to Belle House together. Then, a few months ago, we met by chance at a fund-raiser in Boston." Alex shrugged sheepishly. "This time it clicked." After months of keeping the secret, Alex launched into an account of their courtship and didn't stop until Julia was finally convinced.

"Well, then," Julia said, standing. "This calls for a celebration. I think I have a little something tucked away in the cupboard. Be right back."

"To my best friend." Julia raised her wineglass a few minutes later, straight-faced except for her twinkling eyes. "I always knew one day you would settle down and make some wonderful man really nervous."

"I'll do my best," Alex promised with mock seriousness and took a sip. She coughed and sputtered. "Good grief! What is this stuff?"

Julia shrugged. "Not quite sure. It was on special last month at the market."

"It's swill!" Alex said, tossing back another mouthful.

"Oh, I don't know. . . ." Julia swirled the contents of her glass before taking another sip. "It has a sassy bouquet. And an unforgettably bold aftertaste."

"Unforgettable." They laughed.

"*This*"—Julia held up her glass—"is what you get when you buy champagne on a beer budget. Seriously, Alex," she said, sobering, "I wish you the best. He's a lucky man. And you're just what he needs to loosen up a bit."

But privately, underlying her happiness for Alex, the news depressed her. She didn't see how Alex's marriage into that particular family could help but affect their friendship.

Chapter 11

In April, Alex orchestrated a lavish opening-night reception for the Benelli-Griffin show. Inside Chase Gallery's handsome marble entrance, dozens of patrons, buyers, and others tightly plugged into the Chicago art scene milled about the high central atrium and two spacious adjoining rooms open for the show. For most, this opening reception for Luca Benelli's latest show was only the first stop of the evening. A contingent of men and women in glittering formal attire bound for a later charity ball rubbed elbows with the cashmere crowd on their way to a dinner or show. Black-clad waiters wove throughout the mix offering wine and hors d'oeuvres.

Alex left Julia in the atrium with two of her best clients and drifted from group to group exchanging air kisses and greetings, all the while moving toward one of the adjoining rooms. There Luca held court, every inch the urbane European in his black Brioni suit and flowing golden mane. A tight knot of well-heeled groupies hung on to his every charming word. And there were plenty of those to keep them amused.

Pleased, Alex stepped back into the atrium, surveying the

room to see that everything was in order there, too. She checked her watch. Eight o'clock: one hour down, one to go. The opening was coming off without a hitch. The tension in her back eased and her thoughts drifted happily to Rob. He'd promised to join them for dinner after the show. Absently she watched Derrick make his way toward her after seeing the Morgans on their way.

"They want *Reclining Woman II,*" he said when he reached her.

"Good," Alex nodded, pleased.

"And one of Julia's dunescapes."

Alex's smile widened. "Even better. How do you think we're doing overall?"

"Good. We probably have buyers for at least half of Luca's pieces including preshow sales. And Julia's paintings are attracting good interest, too." They both knew that Derrick's estimates were just that: estimates. Few hard sales took place in the crush of an opening.

"They're a better bargain than Luca's bronzes. I'd say we have a success." Alex glanced over at Julia, still with the Harrimans, a polite smile affixed to her composed face. They were probably putting her to sleep with details of their last cruise to Martinique, Alex guessed, feeling some pity for her.

And pride, too. Only Alex would ever know how difficult this was for her, to put her heart and soul on public display. Unlike Luca, who devoured the attention, Julia valued her privacy. At least she would be able to write her a nice fat check for her work here tonight, Alex thought with satisfaction. She watched Julia smoothly detach herself from the Harrimans and intercept a waiter carrying a tray of designer water, seemingly unaware of the attention she had been attracting all evening. The black angora dress Alex had helped select for the evening highlighted her slim figure and set off her auburn hair and creamy complexion.

"*Perfect* is the operative word here," Alex murmured.

"What?" Derrick asked.

"This evening—it's perfect."

Derrick raised an eyebrow. "Perfect is when we sell everything. But it ain't bad." He spotted the *Tribune's* acerbic art critic bearing down on Julia and hurried off to lend her a hand.

Alex turned to answer a question about one of Luca's pieces. A moment later, she nearly choked on her drink when she recognized a new arrival standing in the marble entryway. Her gaze flew across the room to Julia, who at that moment was engaged in a lively discussion with Derrick and the art critic.

Disaster! That was the operative word. Good Lord! Of all the nights for him to show up, why did it have to be this one?

Kurt Weston plucked a glass of wine from the tray of a passing waiter as he waited near the entrance for Carolyn to check her coat. Without expression, he scanned the fashionably dressed crowd of beautiful people gliding about the atrium to the light strains of Nat King Cole. Many were obviously there simply to see and be seen with the right people, and to fawn over the latest celebrity-icon. The gallery scene had never held a big attraction for him. Typically, when he wanted to acquire a piece of art, he worked quietly through his own purchaser.

"So why are we here again?" Kurt asked Carolyn when she caught up to him.

"Well, I'm here to try to wheedle Luca out of a piece for the art museum, and I thought you were here to see if one of his bronzes would suit your new building." She smiled sweetly and added, "And because you have nothing better to do on a Saturday night."

"Sadly true." One corner of his mouth kicked up while he continued scanning the crowd. He told himself that it made good business sense to meet Luca Benelli before he offered him a small fortune to create a life-size bronze sculpture for Westco's new headquarters. But he had to admit, he was curious to see Benelli's costar again, too.

The fluid crowd shifted and he spotted her.

A jolt nudged his indifference, but cynicism had it firmly

back in place an instant later. She was standing on the far side of the room, engaged in conversation with two men; the older one he recognized as a local art critic. Dispassionately he watched her smile up at the critic and say something that prompted an answering laugh.

His memory of her proved remarkably accurate given the march of time. She still had an intangible something that had once so tantalized him—the quiet reserve that hinted at hidden depths and set her apart from the hip scene. Yet he noted changes, too: a certain softness, an easiness as she gave her full attention to the two men. She was still thin, but not as rail thin as he remembered. All her curves were deliberately showcased in the soft black dress she wore.

"I'm thinking you had an ulterior motive for coming tonight." Carolyn looked at him in amused speculation. "Who is she?"

Kurt shrugged. "I guess she would be referred to as an old friend."

"Friend?" Carolyn laughed. "If that's how you look at a friend, I'd hate to see how you look at an enemy."

Across the room, the critic left, and Julia glanced absently around over the rim of her glass. Kurt knew the instant she noticed him by the way her back stiffened and her eyes widened when they locked with his. Then her startled gaze snapped down to the liquid that sloshed over the rim of her glass onto the front of her dress. He watched her mop up the damage with a napkin, then speak to the younger man. He began to lead her away through the crowd. Her eyes briefly found Kurt again. A cool mask had replaced the shock on her face. Kurt raised his glass in salute.

"My, my," Carolyn said, "you do have an impact on women. This time not good, I'd say." She looked as if she would have pursued the matter, but Luca and his entourage drifted into the atrium from an adjoining wing of the exhibit. "The reigning royalty," she said. "I'd best get on with it before you get hold of him. Remember our deal—I have first dibs."

The museum director had been smart to choose a woman

for the mission, Kurt thought, watching Carolyn wend her way through the crowd. According to the file he thumbed through on the way over, Benelli liked women. A lot of them. He ran through mistresses as casually as he changed clothes. And he appeared to be in no danger of exhausting the supply anytime soon.

When Derrick left Julia alone in Alex's office to repair her dress, she collapsed into a chair, only to pop up in agitation a second later.

Kurt Weston!

Even his name still summoned echoes of a sickening mix of guilt, shame, and anger. But that was nothing compared to the shock of suddenly seeing him in the flesh after five years. Julia did some deep breathing while she paced Alex's office, concentrating on collecting her wits. She had considered the ghastly likelihood of eventually running into him now that Alex was to marry his cousin, but had not expected it to happen here. Or so soon. Or that the moment would give her such a fright.

The door burst open and Alex flew in, a look of consternation on her face. "Brace yourself—"

"I know. I saw him."

"Oh." Alex sank back against the edge of her desk. "I tried to get over to warn you, but you were gone before I could." She peered closely at Julia. "Are you going to be okay? We're almost done. Stay here if you want and we'll collect you when the coast is clear."

Alex, Derrick, Julia, Luca, Rob Weston, and anyone else Alex happened to add along the way were to have dinner together after the reception. Alex had reserved a large table at one of the trendy restaurants near her condo on the Gold Coast.

"No." Julia straightened. "I'm not going to hide in here like a coward. What do I have to be afraid of anyway? It's been almost five years. I have to keep reminding myself that he doesn't know anything specific about Nick at all. People have affairs all the time and manage to act civilly to each other afterward. Right? Besides, he's married now.'' To the woman standing at his side?

''But, Julia, there's something you should know. . . .'' Alex shook her head. ''You never let me talk about him,'' she complained.

''Sorry,'' Derrick interrupted from the door. ''I need you both out here, pronto. Julia, remember the young couple who asked you about *After the Storm*? They seem interested. Make the rounds and talk them up.''

Julia nodded, glad to have a task even though she didn't have the foggiest idea what Derrick expected her to do.

Alex sent her a worried glance. ''We've got to talk—later.'' Then she hurried off.

Julia made a quick phone call to the baby-sitter at Alex's condo and was reassured to learn that Nick was sound asleep. Not surprising considering the hours they'd spent earlier in the day walking through the children's museum on Navy Pier.

On her way out, she paused in front of Alex's mirror and sucked in one last deep breath. She took a back hallway that opened directly into the northern wing. A quick survey of the sparse crowd in that part of the gallery assured her that Kurt was not there. Neither was the young couple she sought.

A handful of people clustered around Luca's sculptures displayed in the center of the room. Others moved around the perimeter, looking at her paintings. A hip-looking couple with matching earrings and big shoes were arguing in front of a portrait of Sid from the diner. ''No, it's definitely representational, very Andrew Wyeth.''

''But that ignores the strong underlying emotional abstraction. . . .''

Julia turned to leave, intending to slip out the way she came, then stopped short at the sight of Derrick, purposefully descending on her with Kurt and his companion in tow. ''Julia! Hold up a second.'' She stifled an urge to run and erased the tension from her face. She'd be damned if she'd let on that he affected her in any way.

Julia's gaze skipped over the woman and fell on Kurt

long enough to register an unreadable expression before she turned her attention back to Derrick and the woman he was introducing. "This is Carolyn Weston, the assistant development director at an art museum down the street."

Carolyn Weston? Julia was baffled. She'd expected to be introduced to Amanda Weston, a name she knew she would never have mistaken.

Carolyn misinterpreted Julia's confusion. "That's the latest euphemism for part-time fund-raiser, at least in my case." She held out a hand. "I've been admiring your work and insisted Derrick introduce you."

Julia looked into smoky blue eyes framed by a bright, direct, and at the moment curious face and wavy dark-blond hair. "Thank you."

Derrick turned to Kurt. "And this—"

"We've met," Kurt cut in, leveling cool gray eyes on her. "Hello, Julia."

"Kurt."

The years had been good to him. He looked the same. Except that he seemed bigger, taller, harder than she'd remembered. He wore a black suit softened slightly by the lightweight charcoal sweater he'd substituted for a dress shirt.

Carolyn wanted to hear how they knew each other, so Julia gave them a sanitized version of their meeting at Belle House. Kurt said nothing to help her out. He merely watched her performance with a cool expression. Irritated, Julia fell silent.

Carolyn filled the awkward silence. "Yes—well, I'd like to borrow Julia for a moment. Kurt," she added, over her shoulder, "why don't you talk to Derrick about that commission for Luca." With that she drew Julia over to one of her landscapes. Kurt and Derrick followed at a distance, soon engrossed in their own discussion.

"This is a dry-brush technique, isn't it?" Carolyn studied it up close. A winter moon cast still shadows over barren, windswept dunes.

Julia nodded and explained how she did it. They moved

slowly down the room until Carolyn stopped in front of a painting of Nick and Dustin peering into a bucket at the water's edge, Annie knee-deep in water a few feet behind the boys. It was not as dark as many of the others, and one of Julia's favorites. She was loath to part with it.

"I really like this one. It reminds me of my own childhood." Carolyn smiled at some distant memory. "Do you have kids?"

Startled, Julia said nothing for a moment. "Why do you ask?"

Carolyn transferred her interested gaze from the painting to Julia. "You have a way of seeing children." Her gesture included several nearby pieces depicting one or more of the kids in various settings. "A familiarity, I'd say; an empathy." She laughed. "And I have a son about that age. I confess my prejudice in thinking only another mother would see them this way."

Julia caught her breath. *A son. Nick had a brother.* She glanced at the painting, avoiding Carolyn's curious gaze. "They're neighbors of mine."

"In Cherry Beach, I assume?" At Julia's surprised look, Carolyn laughed again. "Your bio says you live near Cherry Beach, and that you studied art at the London School of Art and Design while you supported yourself by singing. Sure beats waitressing."

"You waitressed?" This woman surprised Julia. There was something fundamentally and unexpectedly decent about her.

"Surprised that a Weston would waitress? Everyone is." She shrugged a silk-draped shoulder. "It was a character-building theory my father had. I really only had to earn spending money. Dad took care of tuition, room, and board. Kurt had it worse."

"So Kurt's father had a similar philosophy?" Julia asked, confused.

Carolyn's puzzled frown slowly changed to a grin. "One and the same. Kurt's my big brother. I kept my name."

"Your brother! I thought you and he were . . ."

"Married?"

"Yes," Julia admitted. "So he married Amanda, after all."

"Amanda? Oh, you must mean Amanda Fitch. No, he didn't marry Amanda. Kurt's not married—at least he wasn't last time I checked. I guess you don't read many women's magazines. He always makes those tacky eligible-bachelor lists."

Her thoughts racing, Julia silently followed Carolyn to the next painting. A minute later, Carolyn excused herself to make a phone call. Julia was heading for the safety of the back hallway when Kurt angled over and fell into step with her.

"I like your work."

"Thank you." She saw Derrick disappear with Carolyn through the arched entryway.

"Derrick had to return to his duties," Kurt explained, following the path of her gaze.

He lingered in front of a boiling seascape. "It's a relief to be able to appreciate a painting for its beauty instead of some half-baked political statement or an ugly look inside some artist's disturbed brain."

Julia gave him a sidelong look. "I take it you're not a fan of a lot of contemporary art."

"Some, no. Some, yes. You?"

"I have my limits—like the guy who vomits paint on his canvases. So, you think my paintings are pretty? I'm more used to hearing the word 'harsh' to describe them."

"They are harsh, and they aren't pretty. They're beautiful, though."

To her acute embarrassment, he came to a full stop in front of one of her nude self-portraits. Models were scarce in Cherry Beach. Although the painting was realistic, Julia had assumed no one but Alex would recognize that she was the model, because it was mostly a back view with only a hint of one side of her face and breast. But Kurt had seen the scars.

He leaned forward to examine it closely, then turned to

her, the barest hint of humor playing around his mouth. "That must have been difficult to get right." He took a last look at the painting and moved on.

Julia felt annoying heat rise up her face.

They continued in silence. Now Kurt set the pace as he paused to give each piece its due. Julia took the opportunity to surreptitiously search the masculine planes and angles of his face for any resemblance to Nick. To her relief, except for the color of his eyes, she found none.

They were almost at the entrance to the atrium when Kurt stopped and looked at her. "You really have managed to pull it off."

Her heart jumped into double time. "Pull what off?"

"You once told me painting was going to be your second career."

She cast him a quick glance. "I'm surprised you remember."

"I remember." Their eyes held for a moment, until Julia moved on. "Do you still sing?"

She shrugged. "Mostly in the shower." For some perverse reason, she remembered he'd once said that, and his long-ago words slipped out without thought.

Kurt evidently remembered, too; she could see it on his face. "So you've turned your dream into reality. I'm impressed."

"I've been very fortunate these last few years."

"I had no idea you meant to make your move so soon."

"I didn't mean to. But I've learned since then that life can't be lived in a straight line." Reluctant to let any more slip, Julia moved on to the last painting next to the atrium entrance, passing the only other occupants left in the room, a group of three women more absorbed in their conversation than anything around them. Glancing at her watch, Julia saw it was almost nine. Relieved, she turned to find Kurt closely scrutinizing the last painting, one of Nick on the porch of their home.

"Is that your grandfather's place in Cherry Beach?"

"Yes."

"So you kept it."

"Yes." The group of women passed them by. Snatches of their conversation drifted back.

"Dreams are the door to your subconscious," one said.

"My therapist says I'm in denial . . . . I probably have trust issues," another chimed in.

"You should try crystal therapy. It releases your inner child. . . ."

Julia struggled to keep a straight face, but when she saw Kurt's mouth twitch and his eyes roll, she lost the battle and laughed. Their gazes caught and held as their smiles faded, bound by some odd connection that hummed between them. Still. She felt it. He did, too. She could see the same surprise mirrored in his eyes. And it scared her.

Noise from the atrium brought Julia back to her senses, and she hastily broke the contact. Mumbling an abrupt farewell, she turned and crossed into the atrium.

Kurt stared thoughtfully after her. From his pocket he pulled the gallery brochure he'd picked up earlier and located her biographical sketch. It didn't take long to find the information he sought: *She lives and paints in a remote part of Leelanau Peninsula.* Shaking his head, Kurt uttered a short, humorless laugh and followed Julia into the atrium.

Rob arrived at the same time and promptly invited Carolyn and Kurt to join the dinner party. Alex didn't look too happy about the development but said nothing, and Carolyn quickly accepted. Kurt glanced at Julia to gauge her reaction, but the Italian sculptor was busy moving in on her. She didn't seem to notice their addition until they all piled out of two taxis in front of the restaurant.

By mutual design but for different reasons, Julia and Luca managed to snag seats next to each other at one end of the long table. Luca had been a bit of a nuisance since he'd singled her out as his latest love interest on sight the day before, but she liked him. He was funny and talented, and so outrageous there was never any confusion about what he wanted: simple, hot sex. But using Luca as a shield had a price tag; beneath the table, Julia firmly removed his hand from her thigh.

From the opposite end of the table, sandwiched between Kurt and Rob, Alex raised her wineglass in toast, first to Julia and then to Luca. Luca followed, thanking Alex and Derrick for their excellent job and lauding Julia's outstanding effort for a first show. "She has great body of work already," he went on in his thick accent. "*Great body.*" He gave a roguish grin. Julia joined in the good-natured laughter, rolling her eyes. "I try persuade Julia to model for me. No success. But, I not give up and next year maybe we have joint show with interesting twist. Yes?"

Smiling, Julia tilted her head as if considering it. "Tempting as that is, no."

"Ah, you wound me. She crush me beneath beautiful foot." Luca's soulful brown eyes appealed to the others. "What am I to do? She refuse to believe me when I tell her of great passion I have in my heart for her." He put his hand over his heart and looked deep into her eyes. "I search for you all evening," he lied shamelessly. "You leave me to vultures."

From the other end of the table, Kurt watched Luca exude his Italian pheromones all over Julia. It made his skin crawl. It made him want to rearrange his vain face just to shut him up.

"Careful, your indifference is slipping," Carolyn murmured at his side.

"What?" Kurt glanced down at his sister.

"You look ready to skin him alive."

"What do women see in Euro-trash like that?"

Carolyn grinned. "Maybe we're witnessing the start of another great artistic union, like Stieglitz and O'Keeffe. Need I remind you that this is the guy you're ready to pay megabucks for one of his sculptures?"

"I'm seriously reconsidering that decision."

Carolyn patted his arm reassuringly. "Relax big brother, he's harmless. Trust me, the lady's completely unaffected by him."

"What, English majors study this sort of thing now?" He snorted dismissively, more interested in her impression than he wanted to admit.

"No, it's called coed extracurricular studies one-oh-one. Take heart, the only man I've seen get under her fair skin all evening is you."

Thoughtfully, Kurt looked across the table at Julia. She glanced up and their eyes locked.

Early Monday morning, Kurt buzzed his personal assistant. "Chloe, tell Frank to stop by as soon as he gets in. Have him bring everything he has on the Lost Harbor Bay proposal. And please reschedule my lunch meeting."

"What's this all about?" Frank Logan wasted no time on amenities when he burst into Kurt's office a short time later. "I pushed that project to the hilt last year and you mothballed it."

They were partners, and Frank hated being left in the dark about anything. Westco remained a private, closely held corporation, and Kurt had the controlling interest, but all long-time employees owned a piece of the pie, Frank's the largest after Kurt's.

"Because you and our other project managers had their hands full," Kurt reminded him.

"We still do. So what's changed?"

Kurt raised a hand. "We'll get to that. First give me a brief sketch of the project." Kurt was well aware that Frank had a personal interest in the project because he owned a summer cottage in the area.

"The Leelanau Grand Hotel was one of the largest of the Victorian hotels of the nineteenth century. Think Grand Hotel on Mackinac Island, only bigger. It burned down years ago. The property has been vacant ever since. We worked up plans to rebuild it in the original Victorian style, but with modern facilities, of course."

"Why wasn't waterfront property like that snapped up and developed?"

"Zoning is for minimum ten-acre lots. It's out of the way and very little of it is actually waterfront, so it just sat there."

"Are we still okay with permits and options on the property we need?"

"The options should be good. We'll need permits, but that's probably doable. The locals were generally in favor of the project. They want the jobs and they like the idea of having the old hotel rebuilt." Frank thought a minute while Kurt looked over sketches of the project. "I could put some time into it since I go up occasionally, but everyone's pretty tight right now. So who would we get to handle it?"

Kurt looked up from the sketches. "Me."

Chapter 12

May normally was a quiet time in Cherry Beach—the skiers were long gone and the summer vacationers would not arrive for a few more weeks. But this year was different. A whispering excitement hung in the air wherever locals gathered: on street corners, in offices and stores, and especially at Sid's Diner. First came rumors that the site of the old Leelanau Grand Hotel at Lost Harbor Bay had been purchased, along with several inland tracts of open land. Then came news that a big-city developer planned to begin construction of a fancy resort hotel with an adjoining marina and golf course. Julia was too preoccupied with Nick and her refinancing problems to pay much attention to the hubbub.

On a warm Saturday afternoon, she was on her knees in the garden, pulling winter mulch away from her prized pink Meidiland shrub roses when she heard a car slowly wending its way up the narrow two-track. She sank back on her heels and peered down the road. She wasn't expecting anyone. For a moment she was concerned about Annie and the boys—they had set out for the lodge a few minutes ago—but the car's cautious approach reassured her. When the low sports car appeared around the curve, Julia shook her head in disbelief. The lunatic was risking his undercarriage on this road.

She slowly stood as the bottle-green Jaguar growled to a stop a dozen feet away. *It can't be. . . .* Her stomach clenched when Kurt Weston levered his tall frame out of the car.

"So, this is where you've been living." His glance took in the cottage and shoreline before returning to her. "I think I may have passed a few of your pint-sized models on the road."

He looked at the cultivator she held in a white-knuckled grip. "I hope you're not planning to use that on me."

Julia tossed it down by the roses. "What are you doing here?" She tried to sound calm, but her voice sounded strained to her own ears.

"I was curious." He glanced around again. "I gather you never went back to London. I wish I'd known."

She bit back a reminder that he had known, and tried for a casual shrug. "I didn't realize I meant anything to you—one woman among so many."

"Yes, just another entry in my little black book." He sounded almost amused. Without waiting for a response or an invitation, he ambled around the front of the cottage, admiring the view. His expensive loafers sank deeper as he encountered loose beach sand.

Julia tagged along after him, anxiously calculating the odds of getting rid of him before the kids came to investigate.

Kurt leaned against the picnic table and picked up Nick's soccer ball, tossing it into the air. "How long has it been, Julia? Five, six years?"

"Fi—" she started to say, then caught herself. "Six, I guess." Insurance, she thought.

"All this time I pictured you on a London stage. I wouldn't have thought this was your style."

He glanced over the wild dunes.

"Peel an onion . . ."

"And just how many layers have I seen?" His flinty eyes examined her dispassionately, almost clinically.

Too many. "Not many." She had to get him out of here.

"How about letting me take you to dinner tonight?"

"Sorry. I already have plans." She glanced at her watch. "Speaking of which, I'd better get moving or I'll be late." She turned, intending to march him back to his car.

"How about some time during the week, then?"

"I can't. I'm busy." Just how long was he staying in the area?

"Nobody's that busy. Unless you're involved with someone. Are you?"

Julia hesitated, too panicky to think straight, and in that moment lost her chance to construct a convincing lie.

"You're not, are you?" Kurt pushed, giving her no leeway.

Backed into a corner, Julia lashed out. "That is none of your business. I don't owe you any answers about my personal life. I don't owe you a damned thing!"

"No, you don't," he agreed mildly.

His puzzled look doused her anger. The man could make her lose it faster than anyone she ever met, and right now she couldn't afford careless missteps. She forced an apologetic smile. "Sorry for jumping down your throat."

"Anytime." He smiled faintly.

Hearing Bowen's rumbling bark, she hustled Kurt to his car. But he stopped with his hand on the door, watching Bowen lope up the road toward them. The kids wouldn't be far behind.

"Yours?" He squinted doubtfully at the giant mutt bearing down on them.

Bowen looked even more disreputable than usual because the boys had given him a liberal trim recently when she turned her back for all of about five minutes.

"More like we're his. He adopted us. Bowen, sit!" The dog ignored her and bounded at Kurt, first giving him a suspicious sniff, then instant approval when Kurt showed he knew the magic ear-scratching trick. *Traitor,* Julia silently accused the happy dog.

"We?" Kurt asked.

"Hm?"

"You said, 'We're his.' "

"Oh." She glanced down the road. "He adopted me and the Clearys." She gestured vaguely toward the lodge. "Well, good-bye. Sorry you came so far out of your way."

"Not so far. Only about ten minutes." He climbed in and started the engine. "See you around."

With those horrifying words hanging in the air, Julia watched the Jaguar ease off over the ruts and out of sight.

"Ted," Julia began later that evening at the lodge over dinner, "do you know of any big renovation projects happening on the peninsula?"

"Renovation? No, can't think of anything."

"Except for Lost Harbor Bay," Susan said, coming in with a container of ice cream. "The biggest renovation project around here ever."

"That is a replica, not a renovation, and a loose one at that," Ted said.

Julia ignored Susan's snort and passed along bowls of ice cream to Nick and Dustin. They dove in with gusto. "That's the plan for the big resort over on the west side of the peninsula that all the buzz is about, right?"

Exasperated, Susan shook her head. "You two. One's pedantic and the other has her head in the sand."

Julia shrugged. "I've been busy. When I'm not with Nick, I'm working or talking to banks about refinancing. And the Bay Benefit Ball wants to take over my life! Whatever possessed me to say yes to that again?"

"You're a soft touch," Ted said. "And Harry Anderson's a wily old fox. He knew you wouldn't turn him down because he was a pal of your grandfather."

"Thank God it will be over in a couple weeks. At least I met my quota for the silent auction—Alex is donating a gift certificate to the gallery. She's coming up to award it personally. With your bed and breakfast weekend, my island fish boil, and Sid's free lunch for a week at the diner, I'm calling it quits."

"How's Alex doing with your paintings?" Susan passed around the last of the ice cream.

"Amazingly well. She's sold almost everything. Maybe now I'll be able to get a new loan." She frowned. "Marcus wouldn't approve if he knew, but I want you both to know that I also talked to the nature conservancy about selling Deer Cove to them for the amount of my outstanding balance."

"Frankly, I don't understand Marcus's objection to that idea," Ted said, putting down his coffee cup. "Never have. Can't see what it can hurt to at least set things in motion in case you can't get a loan. Otherwise, you could lose it to the bank, and they'd sell it to a developer."

"As a matter of fact, I had one sniffing around a couple weeks ago," Julia said.

"A developer?" Susan looked up sharply. "You didn't mention that."

"Only because until yesterday I thought he was a surveyor for the nature conservancy." Julia recounted how she'd taken a run along the Deer Cove trail one morning while Nick was in nursery school, and come across a man carrying surveying gear. "I thought it odd at the time that he parked up on the main road and hiked in without letting me know. Not only that, but when I mentioned the conservancy, he acted like he worked for them. But the conservancy director says they haven't sent anyone in there."

Dustin and Nick started poking each other and squealing.

"Boys, if you're finished with your ice cream, go play in the other room," Ted said. They waited while the boys hopped off their chairs and clattered off. "And you think this mystery surveyor may be linked to the new development at Lost Harbor Bay?"

Actually, Julia hadn't made that connection, but she would keep the possibility in mind. "Not really. I'm just curious about something I heard." More specifically, whether Kurt happened to be working in the area. What else would bring him here in the off-season? "Do you know the name of the developer on that project?"

Ted thought a moment. "Renaissance something, I think."

"Just a second." Susan dug through a stack of newspapers next to the sideboard. "Here it is . . . Renaissance Resorts." She handed the newspaper to Julia.

Julia skimmed past a sketch of a large Victorian-style inn complete with spacious balconies, gabled roofs and turrets, to the text of the article:

Groundbreaking for the $150 million, 180-unit Leelanau Grand Hotel, the cornerstone of Renaissance Resorts' major resort development, is targeted for August according to assistant project manager Frank Logan. . . .

She skipped down the text.

Renaissance Resorts is a division of Westco, a rapidly expanding Chicago firm. Originally a construction and renovation firm, Westco was founded by Kurt Weston, whose unique architectural approach . . .

The paper slipped from Julia's hand. Horrifying possibilities raced wildly through her mind before she reined in her panic. Kurt's presence here appeared to have an entirely benign explanation, she told herself, completely unrelated to Nick. She assumed Kurt knew nothing about him. But if they were to meet, wouldn't Kurt put it together? And then what would he do? She hated the uncertainty, the lack of control, and there wasn't a damn thing she could do about it. But she could and would find out more about this resort project of his.

"Mama, can we have a picnic?" Nick asked a few days later.

Halfway up a ladder, Julia glanced from the window she was washing down to Nick's hopeful face. The hot, cloudless afternoon was a sneak preview of summer. Musty smells wafted from newly thawed earth. Tender leaves seemed to chatter in their eager growth. Near the foot of the ladder, Nick played with a trickle of water she'd left coming out of the hose for him. He stopped occasionally to share a sip with Bowen.

Julia had spent the past few days combing through newspapers at the library and picking up any scuttlebutt she could on the Lost Harbor Bay project and Kurt's role in it. The news was not encouraging. He was acting manager of the project and had already taken office space in the village. Rumor had it that he'd be splitting his time between his Cherry Beach and Chicago offices for an indefinite period of time. The good news was that his presence in the area *did* seem to be entirely coincidental. He was here for business. Julia came up with a simple plan: avoid him and, above all, keep him away from Nick. Unfortunately, in a village the size of Cherry Beach, that would be a challenge. She was still working on plan B.

She glanced from her son to the stack of screens. "Well . . ." She wanted to get this done today so that she could spend tomorrow morning, while Nick was in preschool, getting started roughing in a watercolor. "We could have a picnic at the picnic table in a little while. But first I need to get a few more screens up." The upper windows would have to wait until Ted could give her a hand.

"Can I go down to the water and dig in the sand?"

"No, honey, you know you're not allowed by the water unless a grownup is with you. Why don't you dig in the sand in front of the house?"

A frown puckered his brow. " 'Cause I can't make it stay. It slides all around."

"Tell you what," she said, climbing down. "I have to do the windows on the other side of the house anyway, so I'll hook up the hose over there and we'll wet down the sand. Okay?" Unable to resist, she ran a hand through his springy blond curls, then leaned down to give him a quick hug before he wiggled away.

"Okay. I'm going to build a fort an' put cannons on it."

Julia set Nick up and then started in on the north side of the cottage.

When Kurt eased his car in beside an old Jeep next to the cottage, he saw no sign of Julia, though there were signs of activity about the place. Several damp screens and storm windows were lined up against the cottage. As he rounded the front, he was nearly bowled over by a seventy-pound streaking furball. "Down!" he ordered. The dog recognized Kurt with an outpouring of canine affection.

"Hi," a child's high voice interrupted the man-dog reunion.

Kurt looked up to find a small towhead staring at him with open interest. "Hi. What's your name?"

"Nick. But some people call me pilot." The little boy continued to watch him through wide eyes.

Kurt recognized the boy as one of the neighbor kids he'd seen walking up the road last weekend. He'd also bet the boy was the model for several of Julia's paintings in Chicago. Engaging kid, with that mop of hair and direct gaze. "Pilot, huh? How'd you come by that name?"

" 'Cause I like airplanes."

"Then we have something in common, because I do, too."

The boy considered this piece of information, then pointed a chubby finger at Kurt's Jaguar. "That your car?"

"Ah-huh." Movement visible through the front porch railing caught Kurt's attention.

Julia came around the corner dressed in sweatpants and a T-shirt, lugging a heavy old-fashioned storm window. "Nick, there you are. I just have to put the rest of these away and then we can—"

She stopped short when she caught sight of Kurt. Her startled gaze met his over the top of the boy's head. He saw a flicker of alarm before she closed up.

"Mama!" the boy exclaimed, skipping over to catch her

around her legs, heedless of her burden. ‘‘He likes airplanes, too.’’

She lowered the window to the ground and used her free arm to draw Nick against her legs. All the while her eyes were fixed warily on Kurt. ‘‘That’s nice, honey.’’

Kurt couldn’t believe his ears. He was dumbfounded. It was inconceivable! ‘‘Mama?’’ he repeated. ‘‘He’s yours?’’

‘‘Yes, this is my son, Nicholas Chadwick.’’ Her normally fluid voice sounded strained. ‘‘Nick, this is Mr. Weston.’’

The little boy was watching through big, curious gray eyes, and Kurt realized he was staring. Recovering, he stepped forward, offering his hand to the boy. The answers to the dozen questions hanging on his tongue would have to wait. ‘‘It’s a pleasure to meet you, Nick—and you may call me Kurt.’’

The boy’s chubby little hand disappeared in his much larger one. Julia ended the contact almost immediately, stepping back and pulling Nick with her, and almost dropping the window in the process. *As if I were some kind of dangerous animal,* Kurt thought. Concealing his irritation, he pulled the window from her resisting grasp. ‘‘Where does this go?’’

‘‘In the shed!’’ Nick cried happily, oblivious to the tension arcing between the two adults. The boy, at least, was bursting with excitement over his unexpected visitor. He danced ahead, eagerly showing the way. ‘‘Do you want to see my fort?’’ he called back with a look of such hope and joy that Kurt felt sorry for him. Where was his father? No husband had been mentioned in Julia’s bio for the art show. But then, neither had a child. ‘‘It’s almost as big as our house.’’

‘‘Really?’’

‘‘Seeing is believing!’’ Nick assured Kurt.

‘‘Sure, sport. I’d like to see it. Let me take care of these windows for your mother first.’’ In a glance, he took in the sorry state of the ancient storm windows stacked against the shed. They all needed to be painted—better yet, replaced.

Julia finally found her voice. ‘‘Don’t you have some wetlands to fill or something?’’

‘‘Not today.’’ Kurt smiled. ‘‘What d’ya say, sport?’’ he

called out to Nick, ''Do you want to help me finish these windows for your mom?''

''Yeah!'' Nick skipped back to circle the two adults.

''That's okay,'' Julia said quickly. ''I'm almost done anyway.''

''What about the upper ones?'' Kurt surveyed the second story, noting that the entire place needed a fresh coat of paint. The roof didn't look in great shape, either. ''You can't do those on your own.''

''I have someone who will help out with them.''

''Uncle Ted,'' Nick chimed in, dancing around them.

Geez, didn't the kid ever slow down?

''Uncle Ted?'' Kurt looked at Julia.

''Dustin's dad,'' Nick said.

''Ted and Susan and their kids live over at the lodge.'' Julia nodded in the direction of the other dwelling. ''They're distant relatives.''

Kurt carefully filed the information away. Julia had just given him the answer to one question. If *Uncle* Ted helped with the windows, that meant there was probably no significant other. The boy seemed eager for male attention. His mother, though, looked ready to pitch a fit. Where was the boy's father, this Chadwick character?

''I'll save him the trouble,'' Kurt said. ''It's going to be hot inside tonight if you don't get them in.''

Julia protested again. ''Really, Kurt. It's tricky—some of the upper ones are warped. They're hard to fit in.''

''I'm an engineer. I'll make them fit.''

Patiently working around the cavorting child and dog, within an hour he had the remaining screens washed and up and the storm windows stored in the shed for fall. Through it all, Julia hovered nearby, keeping a protective eye on Nick. She seemed nervous and transparently not pleased to have him around. They had not parted well. He had some rebuilding to do.

''Come'n see my fort.'' Nick grabbed Kurt's hand and was dragging him toward the front of the cottage. He pointed out the various features of his fort. "Here's the water where the alligators live. Mine has snakes, too."

"Good idea. I wouldn't have thought of that," Kurt said.

"An' these are pooming sticks," Nick went on.

"Pooming sticks?"

"Yeah. Poom! Poom!" Nick demonstrated, using his fingers in the universal gesture for a gun. Bowen grabbed one of the sticks. "No, Bowen!" The boy gave chase.

Kurt gave Julia a crooked smile. "Let me guess, you've never let him have a toy gun."

"No. I don't believe in them."

Kurt shrugged. "He's a boy. He'll pretend anyway, even if he has to use a stick and make up his own name for it."

"Maybe so. But I'm not going to encourage it."

Kurt nodded to the fort. "For a little guy, he makes a first-rate sand castle."

"He loves to build things."

Nick was fighting tears when he trudged back minus the stick and latched onto his mother's legs. Julia sank down onto the sand, pulled him onto her lap, and kissed his temple. Her entire being warmed and softened as she rocked the boy in her arms. Kurt couldn't take his eyes off them. He understood now the difference he'd noticed in Chicago.

"Mama, I'm hungry. Can we still eat at the picnic table?" When she hesitated, he reminded, "You promised!"

"Sure, sweetheart." Julia glanced up apologetically at Kurt, the warmth fading from her eyes. "I'm sorry, it's past Nick's dinnertime. Thanks for all your help." She stood and brushed sand off her sweatpants.

"Can't he stay?" Nick whined.

"I'm sure he has other plans for dinner, Nick." *Don't do this to me!* her eyes silently warned Kurt.

"No, I don't." He grinned shamelessly.

"Yay!" Nick hopped up and down.

"Unless you'd rather I didn't." Kurt raised an eyebrow at Julia, all innocence.

"No! No! We want you!" Nick pleaded. "Don't we, mama?"

She hesitated a long moment, but couldn't seem to resist the boy's appeal.

"Yes. We'd like you to stay." Her voice was cordial enough, but her eyes were cool. "It's not going to be much, turkey burgers and salad." She shrugged. "But if that sounds okay . . ."

"Sounds fine. I'll give you a hand."

"No, thanks!" she said with more force than necessary. "My kitchen's not big. It will only take me a few minutes." She picked up Nick's soccer ball and tossed it at Kurt. "Maybe you could kick the ball around with Nick. Soccer is his new favorite sport."

Julia escaped to the cottage and threw dinner together. She didn't want to leave them alone too long. While she worked, she dissected Kurt's reaction to Nick. He'd looked surprised—no, stunned—to learn she had a child. And it didn't seem to occur to him that he might be the father. After all her worry, after the blasted letter, he seemed not even to suspect!

Over dinner, Kurt told them about his plans for the resort at Lost Harbor Bay. He was living in one of several modular units that already had been set up at the construction site. "Contrary to what some might believe"—Kurt gave Julia a long look that left no doubt to whom he was referring—"we're not going to be filling any wetlands on the entire project."

"Oh, really—how do you propose to build a golf course without filling wetlands?"

Kurt smiled with satisfaction. "As a matter of fact, and this isn't general knowledge yet, we've just signed an agreement to purchase Little Norway, an existing golf course out that way. So you see, I'm not the rapacious pirate-developer you apparently assume."

Kurt described the indoor water park the inn would have. Nick's eyes grew big. "Tell you what, Nick, I'm going to make sure that you're one of the first kids to try it out. In fact, I think I should get your approval of the plans before we start building. You have your mom bring you into my office, and I'll show you the model."

"When? Tomorrow?" Nick's face lit with wonder.

"No, sport. We'll have to wait a couple of weeks. I've got to go to Chicago tomorrow—that's where I live when I'm not here—but I'll be back in about two weeks." Kurt winced when Nick's face fell. "Unless you can come by tomorrow morning?"

"Sorry, honey," Julia intervened. "You have preschool in the morning." She shot Kurt an accusing look when Nick's little face rose and fell again. She was quietly seething that he would issue invitations to Nick without checking with her first.

"Is that where you keep your kids?" Nick turned soulful eyes on Kurt.

"I don't think Mr. Weston is a daddy, Nick," Julia said.

Nick frowned and tilted his head the way he did when he didn't quite understand something. In his universe, all adult men were either dads or grandpas. "Why not?"

"Not all men get married and have children." Julia shifted on the picnic table bench, aware that Kurt was following this little exchange with interest. "Nick, we'll talk about this later."

Nick confided to Kurt, "My dad doesn't live with us."

"Where does he live?"

"Mama says he lives in heaven. But he didn't live with us before that."

"Nick's father is dead," Julia said evenly, not quite meeting Kurt's inquisitive gaze.

"When?"

"About a year ago." Julia stood and lifted her son off his seat. "Nick, please go up and let Bowen into the house. I think he's hungry. And put on a sweatshirt."

As soon as Nick trudged off, Julia rounded on Kurt, all the warmth and softness gone. "Just what do you think you're doing? I thought I made it clear last week that I wasn't interested."

So, the gloves were finally off. "What do *you* think I'm

doing?'' he countered, watching her closely, noticing the way she churned her bare feet into the sand.

''I think you're using a four-year-old boy to get to me. Don't ever, *ever* make promises to my son again. What do you want from me, Kurt? Another conquest?''

''You know that's not my style.''

''Do I?''

''You should.''

Julia gave him a stony glare. ''If you think you can pick up where we left off, think again. Even if I were so inclined, which I'm not, I have a responsibility to my son.''

''Ah.'' Kurt quickly reassessed the situation and made a tactical change in direction. ''I wouldn't expect you to do anything less, given your circumstances.'' He nodded after Nick.

''Good. I'm glad you understand.'' She began gathering up the remnants of their picnic.

Kurt gave her a puzzled look. ''But what makes you assume that's why I'm here?'' He read the first shadow of uncertainty in her hesitation.

''Then what do you want?''

''I came to bury the hatchet. Now that we're going to be family, I thought we should make an effort to get along. Maybe even be friends.''

Julia stopped stacking the dishes. ''Family?''

''Yes, family. Remember? Your best friend, my cousin. Wedding. August. Breakers.'' He peered at her curiously. She looked oddly panicked.

''Right.'' She seemed to relax.

''The maid of honor and best man should at least be on speaking terms.''

''I wasn't aware that was a prerequisite.''

''No, but it would make life easier for Rob and Alex if they didn't have to worry about us taking shots at each other.''

''Did Rob ask you to do this?''

Kurt sidestepped her question. ''Rob's nervous. For some

reason he's gotten it into his head that we are an incendiary combination.''

''Go figure.''

''Rob likes things to go smoothly.''

''Then he better fasten his seatbelt with Alex.'' Julia resumed stacking dishes. ''I better see what Nick is up to.''

They heard a car approaching.

''Looks like you have company.'' Kurt watched an SUV pull up.

''It's Dan Farley,'' Julia said when a rangy uniformed officer stepped out of the truck. ''He was elected sheriff last year after the old sheriff retired.'' Julia moved to pick up the tray, but Kurt blocked her path.

''Let me,'' he said, taking the tray.

Julia introduced the two men on the front porch of the cottage. The sheriff's measuring gaze moved over Kurt and narrowed on the tray in his hands. Kurt recognized immediately that he'd just been sized up by a rival. He glanced at Julia to see her reaction. She, though, seemed perfectly oblivious to the silent battle of testosterone swirling around her.

''Mama, I can't find my sweatshirt.'' Nick's high voice carried down through an upstairs window screen.

''Come on down, Nick. Dan's here.''

Seconds later, Nick cried out, ''Hi, Dan!'' The screen door banged open when he hurtled through it on a dead run.

''Howdy, pilot.'' The sheriff caught the boy up and swung him high over his head before depositing him on his feet. ''Whew! You're getting too big for that.''

''Dan, what brings you out this way on a Sunday evening?'' Julia asked as she held open the door for Kurt. ''The kitchen's in back.''

Kurt deposited the tray next to the sink and joined them in the living room. The small room was furnished with an inexpensive mix of new and old pieces, none that matched, yet somehow it all came together comfortably.

''Sid told me about the intruder you had on the Deer Cove tract. Why didn't you call?'' Dan was asking Julia.

"Have a seat, Dan." Julia pulled Nick onto her lap on the sofa and tucked her bare feet up next to her. "How did Sid know?"

"From Ted."

Julia smiled ruefully. "I'm always amazed how fast news travels around here."

"What intruder?" Kurt asked, leaning against the desk.

Dan looked up in irritation at the interruption.

"Oh, it's nothing really," she said before turning to the sheriff. "It didn't seem worth bothering you about, Dan." But at his insistence, she dutifully recited the details of the incident. "Everyone around here knows it's okay to hike through the woods or on the beach. But nobody has the right to send in a surveyor without my approval."

"We should post 'no trespassing' signs along the road."

"That seems a bit extreme."

"How far north does your property extend?" Kurt asked.

Julia looked up at him. "All the way up to the state land, just south of the old lighthouse."

Kurt raised his brow. "Quite a chunk of real estate."

"I think of it as woods and meadows and dunes, not real estate."

The sheriff's attention zeroed in on Kurt. "You've had survey crews in the area, Weston. Don't suppose this guy could be one of yours?"

Evidently the sheriff's question had already occurred to Julia. Kurt didn't like the look of suspicion on her face. "Not likely. We're on the other side of the peninsula. I don't know anything about this property other than what I just heard."

The sheriff didn't look particularly convinced, but he didn't pursue the matter. "Anything else that might identify him? Uniform, logos?"

Julia refocused her attention on the sheriff. "He was wearing a jacket that might have been company issue. Blue, I think, with a triangular logo. But I didn't notice what it said."

"All right, then." The sheriff stood. "I'll get the word

out. If we see any sign of this guy, we'll find out what he's up to.'' He flipped his notepad closed and slipped it into the front pocket of his shirt. ''Just one more thing. There's a rumor that you're thinking about selling off some of that acreage. Any truth to that?''

Julia glanced at Kurt, looking none too happy about discussing it in front of him. ''I've talked to a land preservation group about turning over some property to them. But''—she sent Kurt another quick glance—''I haven't put the property up for sale. Nor do I plan to in the future.''

''Probably someone heard the rumor and sent the guy in for a look-see. Well, I guess I'd better be going.'' The sheriff edged reluctantly toward the door.

''Thanks for coming out, Dan.'' Julia followed. The boy was draped around her neck. Kurt saw the sheriff's eyes rest on her for one last, hungry moment. ''Mr. Weston was just leaving, too, I believe,'' Julia added.

''See you at the Bay Ball, Julia,'' the sheriff called from the porch.

''Bye, Dan.''

Kurt stopped on the threshold and looked down at her. ''Think about what I said, Julia. It would be real nice for Alex and Rob if we could bury the hatchet.'' He reached over and ruffled Nick's curls. ''See you in two weeks, sport.''

Chapter 13

The sight of Kurt ensconced in the second booth at Sid's the following day at noon unsettled Julia more than she wanted to admit. It brought home that he was here to stay, and that she was going to have to deal with running into him like this. His suggestion that they become friends was absurd. She'd aim for civil.

The Bay Ball committee members were gathered in their usual booth near the rear, all except their chairman, Harry Anderson. The trio in Kurt's booth were huddled over papers, and Kurt hadn't noticed her and Nick come in. Julia took Nick's hand and tried to pull him past without stopping. That proved about as successful as trying to sneak dawn past a rooster. Nick's sneakers squeaked as he dug in his heels at the edge of the booth.

"Hi, Kurt!"

Kurt and his colleagues looked up in unison. "Hello, Nick," he said. "How was school?"

"Okay. We learned about glass eyes. You get 'em when you look in the sun too long. An' you can do lots of tricks with 'em. Mrs. Twitt puts hers in Mr. Twitt's soup. An'—"

"Nick." Julia tugged on his hand. "Mr. Weston is in the

middle of a meeting. Maybe you can tell him about the Twitts another time.'' By this time, Kurt and the man and woman with him all wore broad smiles. The woman had on a beautifully tailored canary yellow suit perfectly suited to Madison Avenue but guaranteed to stand out in Cherry Beach. She had quick almond-shaped eyes that darted from Kurt to Nick to Julia and back to Kurt. In contrast, everything about the man looked rumpled, from his unruly brown hair to the baggy sport coat.

''You learned that in school?'' Kurt asked Nick.

''Yeah, in a book.''

''Nick, we'd better be going. Sorry.'' Julia began to pull Nick away.

''Wait.'' Kurt glanced up at her. ''I'd like to introduce you to my associates.'' He introduced his assistant, Chloe Fronzak, and assistant project manager, Frank Logan. ''Nick here will be consulting with us on the design for the water park. Right, sport?''

''But I thought you were going someplace this day,'' Nick said, suddenly remembering the invitation to Kurt's office.

''I am. As soon as I'm done talking to Frank and Chloe. But I'll be back in two weeks. Don't forget.''

''Okay,'' Nick said. His face lit up again.

''Julia Griffin . . .'' Chloe mused, studying her. ''Why does your name sound familiar?''

''Chloe has a Rolodex memory when it comes to names,'' Frank said.

''The lost contact lenses! That was you, wasn't it?'' She looked Julia over with even more interest.

''Yes. Thanks for all your help on that,'' Julia said, and then to them all, ''I have a meeting, too. It was nice to meet you.''

Kurt watched her drag Nick to a table in back, where they joined several others. Harry Anderson, president of the local bank, came in a moment later and stopped at Kurt's booth.

''Mr. Weston.'' The courtly old gentleman's magnanimous smile added more wrinkles to his creased face. ''It didn't take you long to discover the natives' favorite hangout.

This is fortunate. As chairman of the Bay Benefit Ball, I would like to enlist your support and attendance at our upcoming event. But I won't keep you now. I see that you're busy, and my committee awaits as well.'' He nodded toward the booth where Julia and the others waited. ''Let me know if you would like to buy some tickets. We have a silent auction as well, if you have anything you would like to donate.''

After Harry left, Kurt turned to Chloe. ''Figure out something for the auction—season passes for the golf course or something. And buy a block of tickets. Save one for me, and give the others away as you see fit.''

''The ball is on June fourteenth, and you don't return until the sixteenth,'' she reminded him.

''I've had a change in plans.''

''Anything else we need to talk about?'' Frank asked.

''Yes, one last thing: can either of you tell me why one of our people would be checking out property over on the east side of the peninsula?'' Kurt stabbed a long finger on a map. ''Here.''

''She's doing it again.'' Susan voiced her disgust to Alex as they watched couples on the dance floor at the fifth annual Bay Benefit Ball.

The two women stood near the entrance of the musty second-floor ballroom above the village hardware store. Built by lumber barons before the turn of the century, the ornate ballroom with its molded plaster ceilings and huge chandeliers was one of the few remnants of that gilded era. Out on the dance floor, Julia smiled up at Sheriff Dan Farley, shook her head, and gestured apologetically toward the tables where the silent auction was set up.

''They don't come any nicer than Dan Farley, and he's been smitten for years.'' Susan sighed. ''I've figured out her unwritten code of conduct. She'll dance, but never more than one dance. She rarely accepts a date, and then only if others are present. And she never, under any circumstances, socializes with the summer inhabitants. Except for Marcus."

"Hmm." Alex was mildly bored. She glanced away from Julia and the sheriff to survey the milling crowd. New York Spring Fashion Week this was not. No diamond-encrusted socialites here. No fashion police. Everyone wore the best they could dig out from the back of the closet. This was strictly a local affair, the last before the more affluent vacationers began trickling in over the next few days—and filling up her gallery, she hoped.

"I'm beginning to think Nick was an immaculate conception," Susan said.

"Well, there was Hugo."

"Oh, please! I'm not going to dignify that with an argument."

Alex smiled at Susan's outburst but offered nothing more.

Obviously frustrated, Susan complained, "I'm tired of seeing her keep every man she meets at arm's length. And believe me, I've thrown some very nice men in her path."

"Yes, I know. She's mentioned that."

"Oh, quit looking like that, Alex. I know perfectly well my efforts are not appreciated." Her gaze returned to Julia, who was now inspecting the auction tables. "Just once I'd like to see a man strike a few sparks," Susan said wistfully.

"Well, who knows? Maybe tonight's the night." Alex watched Kurt Weston's slow progress through the bottleneck under the arched entrance to the ballroom.

Susan snorted. "That would be worth the price of admission."

"Hello, Kurt," Alex greeted him coolly when he approached the two women a few minutes later.

"Alex." Kurt lightly kissed her cheek. "Rob misses you. For a minute I thought he might ditch his work to fly up with me tonight." His eyes came to rest expectantly on Susan. Alex made the introduction. "You must be Julia's neighbor—distant cousins, I think she said." He took Susan's offered hand, regarding her with frank interest.

"Yes." Susan looked him over with equal interest. "But I confess I'm surprised—I didn't realize Julia knew you."

"We met several years ago, and again in Chicago at her show."

"That's odd. We were reading the newspaper about your project and she never said anything—" Susan broke off with a puzzled frown.

"Julia said you stopped by to see her a couple of times," Alex said. "Funny you never mentioned your work here when we saw you in Chicago."

Kurt shrugged. "It was still under wraps."

"I always thought these things took a lot of time to get off the ground," Alex persisted.

"They do. This particular project has been in the works for a couple years."

"What a coincidence that your project *happens* to be here, in Julia's backyard."

"Mmm." Kurt leisurely scanned the crowd.

"I didn't think you spent much time in the field these days."

"We're shorthanded at the moment."

Impatient with his calm refusal to be drawn out, Alex resorted to her usual bluntness. "I have to hand it to you, Kurt. Somehow, you've managed to convince Julia that you just want to be friends." That got his attention.

Kurt's eyebrows snapped together in a scowl. "And you don't believe it?"

Alex eyed him uncertainly. "I haven't figured out yet exactly what you want," she admitted. "Maybe you're trying to outflank her. Let's just say I find it hard to believe your presence here is mere coincidence."

"Well, Alex, when you have it all figured out, you be sure and let me know. While you're at it, perhaps you might rethink your assumption that I'm some kind of predatory despoiler of innocent women, because I think you'll discover that it has absolutely no basis in fact." Kurt then excused himself and strode off, leaving the two women with very different expressions on their faces. Alex looked thoughtful, and Susan looked incredulous.

"You can close your mouth now," Alex said to Susan.

Across the room, Julia patrolled the auction tables, making sure everything was in order. The band launched into a Righteous Brothers tune, and she glanced up at the sudden shift in style.

"I believe this is our song."

Julia stilled, forgetting everything at the sound of the voice behind her, low and soft in her ear. She turned slowly to face Kurt. "You're supposed to be in Chicago."

"I came back early."

Over the years, Julia had observed that men in tuxedos usually fell into either of two groups: the great majority, who looked like they were playing dress-up; and the lucky minority, who looked like they'd been born to wear them. It figured that Kurt would fall into the latter group. And that made her suddenly self-conscious to be wearing the same midnight blue gown she'd worn five years ago when she danced with him at Breakers. Never mind that she wore it every year to the Bay Ball and that it never bothered her before.

"So, may I have this dance, Miss Griffin?" He gave her an engagingly crooked smile. "Just a dance between friends." When still she hesitated, he added, "It's not a life-altering event."

She nodded. "I can't leave the tables for long." She didn't need to ask what he meant by "our song." She hadn't forgotten anything about that long-ago night, and intended to prove to both of them that it meant nothing. "Did you request it?" she asked, looking for something to say when his arms went around her on the dance floor.

"I thought it suited the occasion."

Julia wondered why but decided not to ask. Just being in his arms again unsettled her enough. She felt as though she'd been thrown back five years to the ballroom at Breakers. "We should be able to find something to talk about," she said, trying to maintain a distance.

Kurt pulled away a few inches to look down at her. "Do you always talk when you dance?"

"Don't you?"

He smiled. "Usually I don't find it necessary when I have a woman in my arms."

"Now, why doesn't that surprise me?"

Kurt chuckled and they lapsed into another silence until the number ended. Julia left his arms stiffly and would have retreated to the auction tables then, but Kurt caught her hand.

"How about one more for old times' sake?" He nodded to the table. "Looks like you've been replaced."

Julia glanced at the tables and saw that he was right. She also saw that they were the center of considerable attention. Well, not so much she as Kurt. The natives were eager to get a look at the big-city developer.

"Just between friends, Julia. Nothing more. Unless . . . ?" He looked at her closely. "Correct me if I'm wrong, but that night we spent together was nothing but a harmless fling to you, was it?"

She tried to keep her voice light, casual. "Of course."

"I'm not missing anything, am I?"

"No."

"Good. Then there's no reason why we shouldn't at least attempt to be cordial—for Alex and Rob." He patiently waited for her answer, seemingly unperturbed by the couples swinging wide around their little tête-à-tête.

"You win—the dance part, not the friend part. I'm still not sure about that."

In answer, his right arm slid around her waist, pulling her close. She looked up into his hard, handsome face to see whether he gloated, but was surprised to see only warmth there and quickly looked away. *Don't.* She told herself firmly. She didn't want to remember how it once was between them when nothing could come of it.

"You can relax this time around," he teased. "You're perfectly safe."

Mortified that he'd noticed she'd been straining to hold

herself away from him, she forced her taut muscles to relax, but that brought them disturbingly closer. His chin rested on top of her head and his arms tightened, pulling her into an intimate embrace. Insidious heat crept through her from every point of contact with him. The room felt suddenly stifling. She couldn't get enough air. All at once she was frightened.

When the final note sounded, she pulled free and was halfway across the dance floor before Kurt realized what had happened. His thoughtful gaze followed her hasty retreat.

He had his answer. She was not as indifferent to him as she pretended.

Six years ago, when she'd walked out of his life without a backward glance, he'd tried to forget her. He thought he had. And if she occasionally infected his dreams, clearly his memory of her had been exaggerated by nocturnal fantasy. Then he'd seen her again at the art show.

Yes, he had his answer, he thought, watching her run away from him just as she had before. But this time around, he did not intend to let her off so easily. This time he'd drawn a better hand. Patience and time were on his side.

Julia darted through the couples on the dance floor, determined to put as much distance as possible between them. She ignored the utterly astonished expression on Susan's face and didn't stop until she reached the safety of the women's lounge. That's where Alex found her several minutes later, sitting in a quiet corner of the room.

"You okay?" Alex sank down onto a faded silk settee and kicked off her heels.

"I feel like such a fool. The man makes me crazy!"

Alex decided it was long past time to risk venturing into forbidden territory. "So the chemistry's still there, huh?"

"Oh, I don't know!" Julia shook her head in disgust. "If that's what it is, then it's chemistry run amuck. Badly." She looked as if it pained her to make the admission.

"Maybe you ought to go out with him. Get him out of your system."

"Now, there's an idea," Julia said sarcastically. "Let's

complicate everything even more. Besides, he claims he just wants to be friends.''

Alex almost laughed. ''Oh, I'll bet you could get him to change his mind on that one.''

''I would never do anything that would risk messing up Nick's life.''

''I don't get the feeling he even suspects he's Nick's—''

''I don't either.'' Julia waited while an elderly woman tottered out of a stall. ''Not unless he's a bloody good actor,'' she went on in a lower voice. ''Or a monster. But that's exactly the point: whatever he suspects, or doesn't suspect, he's a wild card, and that makes him dangerous and unpredictable.''

Two qualities Julia had zero tolerance for, Alex mused gloomily.

''Come on.'' Julia stood. ''Harry will be announcing the auction winners in a few minutes. Then we can leave.''

''FYI,'' Alex whispered as they slipped back into the ballroom. ''Kurt was headed for the bidding tables after you raced off. I'd bet my new Benz he goes for your fish boil.''

But he didn't. Fifteen minutes later, Kurt walked off with Alex's gallery credit and tickets to the local summer stock theater.

''I'll be darned,'' Alex said to no one in particular. ''He's smarter than I thought.''

The Monday after the Bay Ball, Kurt asked Chloe to call and set up a time for Nick to come in and see the water park models.

''Any particular time?'' Chloe asked.

''No. This afternoon when he gets out of school is fine, or anytime later in the week that I'm free.'' He paused at the door to his office. ''Oh, and if Julia wants to talk to me, tell her I'm not available.''

Kurt ignored Chloe's questioning look and crossed his office to the windows behind his desk. From his second-story vantage, he had a panoramic view of the unfolding lake scene. Already, a few walkers strolled along the boardwalk. Beyond lay the beach and, to one side, a large grassy field with a playground that doubled as the site of various summer events, starting with the Cherry Beach Music Festival. Tucked off on the other side, behind a narrow spit of sand, nestled the harbor and a picturesque little village of fish and smokehouse shanties. Beyond that stretched the brilliant blue bay. Kurt watched one of the tall ships being readied for its morning excursion on the lake. A handful of tourists waited on the dock to board. In a matter of days, lakeside activity would explode.

Kurt heard Chloe's muffled tread over the plush new carpet, but he didn't turn from his perusal of the shoreline.

"They're going to stop in just before noon, when Nick gets out of school."

"Did she say anything else?"

"No, except she did ask to speak with you. I told her you were unavailable."

"Okay. Thanks."

Chloe paused on the threshold. "It's a beautiful day. Would you like me to order a picnic lunch for the three of you?"

Kurt turned from the window and sat down behind his desk. "No, thanks. Not today."

After Chloe pulled the door shut behind her, Kurt leaned his chin on steepled hands. Just in case Julia was tempted to tell him to get lost after the Bay Ball, he wasn't going to give her the opportunity. Patience, he reminded himself—and patience happened to be a trait he'd developed in spades over the past ten years.

Julia looked at the phone after Kurt's assistant rang off. She'd been about to call him and put an end to his impromptu visits when his assistant called to schedule Nick's visit to Westco's offices. She accepted because Nick was counting on it, but she still intended to curtail future meetings with Kurt.

No good could come of any association with him, she told herself for about the hundredth time since the Bay Ball. The risks were too great. But even as she justified her decision, she remembered the way Nick's puppy eyes had followed Kurt, all eager and hopeful and adoring.

It was just plain bad luck that Kurt had appeared when Nick was beginning to realize what his life was missing: a living, breathing father of his own. But he had a father of sorts in Ted, she thought defensively. And they had a good life here. They had family, friends, a safe home and community. Everything they needed. They were safe. *Safe.*

Chapter 14

Two weeks later, Julia met Marcus at the diner to hear about a possible loan for Deer Cove. As she slipped into the booth, she took in Marcus's bronzed beauty and conspicuously *GQ* look, totally out of place at Sid's. It was July fifth, and Cherry Beach was bursting with visitors. She'd left Nick and Dustin in Annie's care at the village beach so she and Marcus could talk without interruption.

"I've found a lender to refinance Deer Cove," Marcus announced.

"Outstanding! Who? When can I talk to them?"

He smiled. "Hold on. It's somewhat unconventional."

They waited while Sid brought coffee for him, tea for Julia, and took their lunch order.

"What do you mean by unconventional?" Julia asked as soon as Sid left.

"The lender is a private individual that I do some work for. I approached him about making you a loan, and he's willing. It's yours, Julia."

Some of her excitement dimmed as questions arose. "Why is he interested when all the mortgage companies consider me a bad risk?"

"Because the property itself is worth far in excess of the loan amount."

"But that was true with the banks, too," she pointed out.

"Right. Except that an individual doesn't have to follow all of the internal rules for approving loans that an institution does. He has a lot more flexibility. The only downside is that certain terms might be a little stiffer than what an institution would require."

Marcus looked edgy as he slipped in that little detail.

"Such as?"

"Slightly higher interest. Not bad, though," he added quickly. "And a shorter loan period—five years max. It will be like a bridge loan until you find another."

Julia mulled it over. That would mean that in a few years she'd be right back at square one, caught in the same financial bind. On the other hand, her options were not plentiful. The land conservancy wasn't ready to commit yet. She'd been unsuccessful in finding a lender on her own. Her choices boiled down to selling now or grabbing Marcus's five-year reprieve.

He leaned forward. "Take it, Julia. It's a good deal. The best you're going to find."

"I hadn't thought about going to an individual. It feels riskier than dealing with a bank."

"Don't kid yourself. An individual is more likely to cut you slack than a faceless institution."

"Five years. Not what I'd hoped for. But, as you say, it would buy me time."

Marcus looked reproachful. "It's a good deal. I put my reputation on the line to get it."

"Forgive me, Marcus." Julia sent him a look of apology. "Here you've gone to all this trouble and I . . ." She gave a helpless shrug. "I'm nervous. I really do appreciate all your efforts. So, when do I get to meet this man and his buckets of money?"

"You don't. I'll set it up with his lawyers and bring you the papers to sign."

Julia blew out a breath. "All right then—let's do it."

He smiled. ''Good.''

By the time they finished lunch, people crowded the entrance waiting for tables. While Marcus was over at the cash register paying, Kurt came in with an attractive woman in an expensive linen 'resort' ensemble. She looked as out of place in Sid's as Marcus. Kurt, with his dress-down Friday look, blended in superficially, although he was too big and imposing to blend in completely anywhere.

Ironically considering all her angst, in the two weeks since the ball, Kurt had kept his distance. Not once had she found herself alone with him. Even when she took Nick to Westco's offices to see models for the new resort, others had been around. They'd run into him several times at the village park after nursery school, but when the boys switched to their summer playschool schedule, they hadn't seen him again. The ever-active village rumor mill had it that he was spending time with a comely summer resident. Perhaps this was her in the flesh. In hindsight, Julia was glad she hadn't found an opportunity to have that little talk with Kurt.

She drew Kurt's notice when she slid out of the booth to leave. His gaze veered sharply to Marcus when he joined her in the narrow aisle. She thought it odd that Marcus hustled her out the door with barely a nod to Kurt.

''So, he really is here,'' Marcus said as they made their way through heavy pedestrian traffic toward the harbor, where he'd parked.

''Kurt?'' Julia looked puzzled. ''I thought you would know that since you represent him.''

His head snapped up. ''I don't do much work for him anymore.'' He didn't elaborate, but after a moment added, ''I heard about the hotel project. I was surprised to find out that he actually moved up here.''

''He comes and goes.''

''I hope he's not giving you any trouble.'' Marcus watched her intently.

''No,'' Julia could answer honestly.

He took her hand as they dodged tourist traffic in the street. On the other side, a tennis-racket display in a shop window caught his eye and he stopped to take a closer look. "I heard that his lunch date is here cooling her heels until her divorce is finalized. Then she'll probably be off to Europe on her settlement, where she can console herself with a new honey."

Julia studied him curiously. "You sound bitter."

He shrugged, his attention still on a racket. "Women have it easy. An attractive woman can marry a sugar daddy and no one bats an eye. Married or divorced, she's set for life."

"Only if she's willing to be a trophy wife married to a man she doesn't love," Julia protested.

Marcus snorted. "Sounds like a good exchange to me. I never heard any complaints from my mother until the well ran dry."

Julia stared at him, her disgust tempered by sympathy, but he was still peering in the display window and didn't notice. "Are you saying the best way for a woman to find security or happiness or whatever is to marry money?"

"No, the best way is to inherit it," he said with a grin.

"Really, Marcus!"

He finally turned to her and saw that she was not amused. "Come on, I'm joking." He gave her his most innocent wounded-puppy look. "I personally find the whole business obnoxious."

Julia was quiet the rest of the way to the waterfront. This was the dark side that Marcus usually kept well hidden. She'd caught glimpses of it over the years. The flashes of greed. The sense of entitlement. Yet, for years now, he'd been a loyal and generous friend to her and Nick. He touched base with them two or three times a year, always concerned about their welfare, ready to help if he could, even remembering Nick at Christmas and on his birthday. And he never asked anything of them in return. Over time, Julia's early suspicion of him had softened until gradually she'd come to trust him.

"How long are you in town?" Julia asked when they reached his car.

Marcus ran his hand along the roof of the exotic black

sports car—he always drove something new and racy. "Just long enough to attend Mother's party tonight." His beautiful mouth twisted in distaste. "Sure you won't change your mind and come with me? You would save me from an evening of excruciating boredom."

Julia smiled faintly. "Sorry. Can't. I have to rehearse for the music festival." Several times a year, she played in a local band. They called it School's Out because, except for her, they were all teachers. Across the street in a grassy park, a large white awning was being erected over the festival stage.

"I wish I could stay to see you," he said wistfully. "I wish I could stay to protect you—" His eyes locked on her in sudden, earnest intensity. "Julia, stay away from him."

"Who? Kurt?" The warning in his voice alarmed her.

"Don't make the mistake of thinking he's changed, because he hasn't. He uses people, especially women. Then spits them out and walks away without a backward glance." Marcus gripped Julia's forearm hard enough to hurt. "I don't want anything bad to happen to you or Nick."

Julia extracted her arm from his grip. "There's no need for you to worry. His attention appears to be elsewhere. And even if it wasn't, I'm certainly not interested." Julia smiled fondly at Marcus, touched that he cared. Impulsively and to his obvious surprise, she leaned over and kissed him lightly on the cheek. "But thanks for your concern. And for finding me a loan."

Across the street, returning to his office with lunch in hand, Kurt witnessed the disturbing sight of Julia bestowing a kiss on Marcus Fuller. Equally disturbing was the distinct impression they gave that their acquaintance was of some duration and closeness. The sight was so unexpected that, had Kurt not just seen them leave the diner together, he might not have trusted his own eyes. What on earth was she doing with that little weasel?

Kurt watched Julia smile and wave at Marcus as she headed for the beach. Marcus climbed into his drug-dealer car and thundered off down the narrow waterside street.

Where had Marcus found money for wheels like that? Word was, the Fuller family law firm was floundering under Marcus's mismanagement, and Charles Fuller was threatening to take over again. Kurt had pulled what little business he'd been sending their way after Westco's chief accountant hesitantly confided his suspicions that Marcus was padding his bills.

Kurt debated a moment, decided work could wait, and followed Julia across the street to the park. By the time he caught up, she was pulling sandwiches out of a cooler at a picnic table already occupied by Nick, Dustin, and a teenage girl Kurt figured must be the Cleary daughter he hadn't yet met. The boys interrupted their lunch long enough to greet him with loud enthusiasm. The girl eyed him with interest.

Julia glanced up at him in surprise. "That was a quick lunch date."

Kurt held up a white bag, taking care not to let his eyes stray down the long, bare legs exposed below her short skirt. "Take-out. I couldn't wait for a table. It's too nice to be indoors, anyway. Mind if I join you?"

"Sit by me, Kurt!" An eager smile lit Nick's face as he scooted over closer to Dustin.

Julia introduced Annie to Kurt while she passed out drinks. Kurt spent a few minutes quizzing Annie about her year in school and her interests before turning to the squirming boys. "So, how come I haven't seen you two pirates tearing around here lately?"

They both guffawed loudly. Dustin explained, " 'Cause it's summer. Now we get here before we used to."

Kurt looked at Julia for clarification. "Summer playschool gets out half an hour earlier than nursery school did," she explained.

While Kurt munched on his sandwich, the boys plied him with endless questions about the water park, questions they'd asked and he'd answered on other occasions, but they loved hearing about it and had many grand ideas of their own. As soon as Kurt finished eating, they dragged him off to play soccer.

"He's gorgeous, Aunt Julia," Annie said dreamily, her gaze glued on Kurt as he dribbled the ball down the field.

"I thought your taste ran more to boys who were a little less intimidating." Julia marked Kurt's thoroughly masculine face and build.

"He's not intimidating. He's nice." At that moment, Kurt was being dragged to the ground laughing while Nick and Dustin struggled to pin his arms to the turf.

"You used to like skinny boys with sweet smiles," Julia said almost wistfully.

"Yeah, and I used to read the Babysitters' Club books, too."

Julia sighed, half wishing she could keep her not-so-little buddy from growing up. Growing up and leaving. "Don't you have to get back to the ice-cream parlor?" Annie had a summer job there.

"Yeah." She began gathering up her things. "The worst thing about this job is that I used to really like ice cream."

Julia laughed. "Thanks for watching the munchkins for me, honey."

"No problema." Annie gave Kurt a last look. "You know, Aunt Julia, you could do a lot worse," she said before setting off across the park.

If you only knew, Julia thought, wandering over to the boys and Kurt. Evidently, Kurt had given in, because now all three lay sprawled together catching their breath. Annie was right. He was a gorgeous-looking man. She winced when she saw vivid grass stains on his white shirt and khaki trousers.

"Those stains are going to raise a few eyebrows at your office."

He grinned, climbing to his feet. "And disappointment, I imagine, when I dash their lurid fantasies."

"Probably," she agreed with a grudging smile, "although that wasn't what I meant." Then she directed her attention to Nick and Dustin. "Boys, we have to leave in a few minutes. If you want to swim, this is your last chance."

"Yeah!" they chorused, leaping to their feet and running

for the beach. Julia thought Kurt would go back to work then, but instead he walked with her to the beach.

"I see that you're performing in the festival this weekend," he said.

Julia nodded. "Should be fun. The theme this year is sixties music. Are you coming?"

"Wouldn't miss it."

They reached the edge of the water. Julia kicked off her sandals, letting the cool water lap over the tops of her feet. Kurt sat down on dry sand a few feet from the water's edge.

"I thought you gave all that up."

"I have, for the most part. This is just for fun, very low-key." Julia stepped back from the water and sat down a few feet away from Kurt, stretching her legs out on the sun-baked sand. "We play mostly jazz classics, some folk and rock. Anything we feel like."

They lapsed into companionable silence, watching the boys splash around until Nick ventured too far out. Julia got up and called him back. He wheedled, but she held firm.

"Must be tough raising Nick on your own," Kurt said when she sat down again.

She was silent a moment. "Sometimes, but I've never regretted having him. He's my heart and soul," she added quietly, gazing out at Nick.

Julia's simple declaration of love, the uncompromising exclusivity Kurt sensed, dealt a blow to his carefully planned siege. Nick held exclusive rights to her heart. Everything Kurt had seen and heard about her since coming to Cherry Beach indicated that she had no intention of letting anyone else gain a foothold there. Not Marcus. Not Luca Benelli. Not the good sheriff. And not him.

"Whatever you're doing must be working, because he's a great kid," Kurt said after a time.

"Thanks."

"Was Nick's father lucky enough to know what a fine son he had—before he died?"

Her gaze snapped to his, searching for something. "Yes, I think he did."

"I gather you never married him."

Her eyes cooled. "No."

Kurt saw the curtain come down. She seemed to draw away without moving an inch. "And you don't want to talk about it anymore."

"Right." She turned her gaze to the water. "Tell me about your project here. I'd like to hear more about it."

Kurt saw the tension ease from Julia's face as she watched the boys, saw how her eyes gradually softened again. Had she loved Nick's father? He felt a stab of envy whenever he thought of the faceless man who had somehow managed to breach her defenses. He never should have let her go so easily six years ago. He should have put his instincts above his pride and business interests.

"I understand if you don't want to talk about it," she said, misunderstanding his silence. "You must get enough of it at work."

"No, it's not that. I was thinking about something else. What would you like to hear about—the water park?" he joked.

She groaned. "Anything but. Nick will be talking nonstop until bedtime about shipwrecks and cannons that shoot water. Tell me about the first Leelanau Inn. What was so interesting about it that you would want to build another?"

Kurt told her about its architecture and history, surprised at how easy it was to talk to her about his work. When he would have stopped, she prodded him with more questions until finally he had to leave for a meeting.

"Wait!" Julia stood, too. "You never said how it burned down."

"That's another mystery." Kurt watched her brush sand off her legs. "Some say the flamboyant owner, one Charles Berkley, a railroad mogul, was carrying on an affair with a married guest. Her husband, a rough chap by the name of Black Jack Skinner, showed up and caught them in flagrante delicto. He retaliated by setting fire to Berkley's inn. Investigators never had enough evidence to officially pin the fire on Skinner. There were other more mundane possibilities, but I think the fire was an act of passion by Black Jack." Kurt's gaze skimmed lightly up Julia's long legs, and then further, to her beautiful, fascinated eyes. "Passion, love, jealousy, betrayal are emotions of fire. A man can act irrationally when engulfed in flames."

"Great job, everyone," Stuart, the group's de facto leader declared. A broad smile split his ruddy face as the band coasted in the afterglow of their success. His approving eyes included Julia and the three other members of School's Out, who were packing up their instruments in a small tent set up behind the festival stage. Onstage, the headline act was loudly tuning up.

Julia blotted her heated face with a white towel, grinning as she listened to Stuart chatter on. He was always charged after a performance. They all were.

"Marsha," he singled out the keyboardist, "you were seamless; all you guys were. Julia, honey, you need to quit your day job. Such a waste. I was worried for a minute there that we were going to have some of those college boys up on stage with us. You blew them away."

"I'm rusty," she said.

"I don't think anyone noticed," the drummer said, eyeing her black leather miniskirt, spike heels, and tank top. "They were too busy checking out your leather. You know, you look more like a biker chick than a flower child."

"Yeah," Stuart grinned. "You think you know someone and she turns out to be a sexy biker babe."

Julia laughed, used to their teasing, but tugged at the hem of the leather skirt as she sat to change out of the heels. It was the closest thing to sixties rock garb that she and Annie had managed to scrounge up in the drama department's costume bin. They'd used it in *Grease* last year.

"So, who wants to stick around and check out the competition?" Stuart asked as they finished gathering up the last of their equipment, which was minimal because they hadn't needed their own sound system.

The others were willing, but Julia passed. "Sorry. I have to run by the market and then pick up Nick." Susan and Ted had brought the boys in to see the group's afternoon performance and had Nick with them now at the lodge.

"Where're you parked?" Stuart asked.

"In the medical clinic parking lot on Elm."

"Let me drop this stuff off at my car and I'll walk you over."

"Thanks, Stuart, but I'll be fine." She stuffed the heels into a large purse. "Nothing ever happens in Cherry Beach." She called out a last "bye" and raced off, in a hurry to get to the market before it closed.

Away from the lights and activity of the festival grounds, the village was dark, deserted, and silent. Only the light from the small corner grocery repelled the rapidly closing night. Julia dashed through the nearly empty store, throwing into the cart as much as she could carry the two blocks to her car. Back outside, with her vision obscured by the full bag of groceries, she failed to notice a man who moved to block her path until she stumbled into him. Murmuring an apology, she tried to step around him, but the man moved with her, bringing her up short again.

Startled, Julia looked up into pale blue eyes starkly lit by the store lights behind her, and felt real fear. She'd never seen eyes like these before. Cold. Dead. They were set in a scruffy, foxlike face topped by a thatch of grimy ginger hair.

"See, I told you it was her," he said in a rusty voice, glancing briefly over his shoulder. Julia made out the shape of a second man in the shadows. "Where ya going so soon?" the dead-eyed one asked, wrapping Julia in the stench of stale beer. "Party's just getting started."

They must have followed her up from the festival. Julia didn't allow her fear to show. When she'd played the clubs, she quickly learned that cool detachment was the most effective deterrent to unwanted attention. But those clubs had not catered to lowlifes like this. And she hadn't been alone.

"Excuse me," she said coldly, trying again to pass.

"What's your hurry?" He caught her arm. "What say you, me, and my friend here—"

"Take your hand off me!" Despite her best effort, she couldn't keep a quaver of fear from her voice. She tried to pull away, but the bag of groceries hampered her, and his grip only tightened. Although he was slightly built and had no advantage in height, he was wiry and strong.

"Maybe we shouldn't," the other man said, emerging from the shadows. He was bigger and, to Julia's relief, didn't appear to be as drunk as the wretch who had her arm.

"Shut up," the little one hissed. She heard someone come out of the store behind her. The man quickly dropped her arm. "Okay. Sorry," he whined, holding up his hands in surrender. "I just thought you—"

Julia didn't wait. She brushed past him with a quick look that caught the sidelong glitter of feral eyes before she fled into the darkness. Clutching the bag of groceries close, she hurried along to her car. The darkness swallowed her up, and at first made her feel safe. Then she heard a noise. Belatedly, she regretted not having gone back into the store when she had the chance. But she was already late to pick up Nick, and really, nothing ever did happen in Cherry Beach.

Another voice buried deep in her psyche whispered, *Bad things can happen anywhere.*

No! She pushed that other paranoid voice away. Nevertheless, she cast an anxious glance over her shoulder into the darkness.

When she turned, movement melted into shadow. She briefly considered and rejected ditching the bulky groceries; they couldn't afford it. Probably her imagination, she tried to reassure herself, not very successfully.

Heart pounding, she quickened her pace. She heard sounds of whispery movement behind her. Or was it her own ragged breathing and pounding heart? Seconds later, the distinct crunch of stones on a gravel drive behind her gave the answer she dreaded.

One or both were following her. As unobtrusively as she

could, she dropped the groceries into some bushes she passed and picked up her pace.

Please let it start on the first try, she prayed as she fumbled with her free hand in her purse for the keys to the Jeep.

"Wait, Julia!"

In her panic, she didn't recognize the voice and ran. A hand grabbed her just short of the Jeep. Julia struggled to get free. A fraction of a moment later, recognition dawned, and she stilled, sagging in his grip. Relief and then fury rapidly replaced her fear.

"Jesus, Kurt! What do you think you're doing sneaking up on me like that?" She shoved furiously at his broad chest, but it was like trying to move a brick wall. "Do you get your kicks out of making women think you're Jack the Ripper?" He was backing her toward the car as she ranted. She finally noticed, and angrily tried to push him away. "I though some creeps were—" Her diatribe ended in a startled gasp when he roughly jerked her up against his chest.

"Shut up!" he hissed in her ear. "They still are, and I'd like to get us out of here without a knife in my back, if you don't mind!"

Abruptly Julia stopped resisting the backward momentum and cast a fearful glance around the solid wall of his chest. There, at the edge of the parking lot, in the dim yellow glow cast by a single light at the rear of the medical clinic, skulked the vile creature with the soulless eyes and his large companion. They were slowly closing in. Kurt turned and faced them, shielding Julia from their view.

The little one edged forward. "Hey, man, she don't want you. Just go away and you won't get hurt."

"Sorry, guys, my wife is undoubtedly flattered by your attention, but we have a son at home who needs to be put to bed and a baby-sitter who needs to go home." Kurt spoke easily, as if they were all reasonable people. "Get in!" he muttered under his breath to Julia.

Julia unlocked the driver's door, trying to be unobtrusive about it, but she was scared. Her hands shook so badly it took her a while just to get the key in.

"That true, girl? What he said about you'n him being married and having a kid?"

Could this get any weirder, Julia thought, stifling a hysterical urge to laugh. "Yes, it's true," she played along. The door gave a rusty squeak as she eased it open.

The big one edged into position to the rear. It looked like the little one was directing him. Now the little one eased closer, toward the front of the car, all the while watching them through cold, flat eyes. His mouth stretched back in a parody of a smile. "You know, I think I believe you. But guess what—I don't give a flyin' fuck!"

"Get in!" Kurt shoved her from behind. The two thugs lunged forward.

Julia scrambled in. She heard the sickening sound of the car door connecting with flesh and bone, and immediately another thud and a moan. In the next instant, just as she managed to jam the key into the ignition, Kurt jumped in behind the wheel.

"They're going to be madder than wet cats in about five seconds."

It took Kurt two tries to get the cantankerous Jeep started. By that time, the small one had stumbled to his feet. He cradled an injured arm against his midsection. In the glare of the headlights, Julia saw a steel blade dangling uselessly from his limp hand. He glared at them malevolently as Kurt shoved the Jeep into gear and sped out of the parking lot in a hail of gravel.

Kurt drove back to the festival grounds in silence. He was so exasperated with Julia for wandering around alone, after dark, in a get-up that made her look like page one of a *Playboy* spread, that he didn't trust himself to speak. If he hadn't left the festival shortly after her set . . . If that bigger thug had been more determined . . . Damn! He couldn't even think about it without breaking into a sick sweat. From a block away, he'd seen her talking to someone in front of the grocery store, her outfit a dead giveaway.

When a second man stepped into the light, Kurt knew she was in trouble. Like a torturous replay of the scene on the beach all those years ago, she'd run unerringly into danger. Why hadn't she run for the safety of the store?

Kurt glanced across the Jeep at Julia. She stared unseeingly out the windshield, a shell-shocked expression on her face. Her usual cool reserve was MIA. Kurt put aside for the moment his urge to blister her ears.

"Friends of yours?" he asked.

She drew in a ragged breath and managed a pained half smile. "Right. I would have introduced you, but you seemed in such a hurry." Her smile collapsed. She reached over and touched him, letting her fingers rest lightly on his bare forearm. "I don't know how I can ever thank you. I would have been in big trouble if you hadn't come along."

He looked at her hand on his arm, enjoying the look and feel of it more than he should under the circumstances. "Know who they are?"

She shook her head. To his disappointment, she removed her hand and wrapped her arms around herself. "No. They must have come from the festival. They seemed to recognize me." She looked up when he stopped behind his car, parked in his private space across the street from the festival grounds. "It was probably my outfit that attracted their attention."

Kurt raised an eyebrow. "Undoubtedly." *And every other man with a pulse.*

"Well, thanks again." She evidently assumed they were finished and that he was going to get out there.

"Come on." He got out. "We need to find your friend, the good sheriff, and let him know what happened. He was here before I left. Maybe they can still catch them."

She peered out at him, a harried, apologetic look on her face. "I can't. I'm already late to pick up Nick. He'll be exhausted. I'll call Dan as soon as I get home."

"Okay," Kurt agreed, "but I don't think you're in any kind of shape to be driving home alone." *And certainly in no shape to meet up with those two pieces of shit again,* he thought. "Let me grab the phone from my car. We can call in a report on the way."

He was back shortly and punched in the number on his phone while he drove. "If they're not complete idiots, they've probably gone to ground by now, but—"

"You're hurt!" She was staring at the blood-stained handkerchief on his lap.

"Take it easy. I'm fine." He checked the small cut on his left forearm—a parting gift from the little asshole with the big blade. He fervently regretted not being able to stick around to make sure the son of a bitch went to jail. Preferably with his ass in a sling. But it seemed more prudent to get out of there while they could.

Kurt twisted his arm around so Julia could see for herself that the cut was minor. But instead of reassuring her, she looked as though she was about to be sick.

"My God, Kurt, you could have been killed by those two!" Her horrified gaze was frozen on the blood. "How could I have told Nick? It was all my fault—if I hadn't . . . I'm so sorry."

Kurt pulled off to the side of the county road and stopped the Jeep.

"What have I done?" she whispered.

"Julia, listen to me!" He tilted her chin up even with his face and waited until her eyes cleared.

Julia focused on Kurt's face. The concern she saw there made her cringe with guilt and regret.

"You are not to blame for the actions of those animals. You did nothing to deserve what they did to you. And you're certainly not to blame for my involvement." He peered at her closely. "You okay?"

No, she wasn't. How could she tell him that the violence and blood brought back the evil monster? And how could she possibly tell *him,* the man who just risked his life to protect her, that she wasn't sure but she may have made a terrible mistake five years ago and in the process done him a horrible injustice? And, by the way, did he or didn't he suspect that Nick was his son?

She could hear noise from the phone. The 911 operator. She drew a head-clearing breath. She had to do what was best for Nick. As things stood *now,* not five years ago. But just what was best had begun to blur.

"I'm fine," she said. "I want Susan to look at your arm when we pick up Nick."

He put the phone to his ear. "Yes, can you patch me through to the sheriff?"

"No, a butterfly bandage will not 'do the trick,' " Susan insisted again. "Every time you bend your wrist or twist your arm it's going to want to open up again."

Kurt scowled across the lodge kitchen at Julia's back, which was shaking suspiciously. "What are you laughing at?" he groused. But really, he was glad she could see some humor in it. She'd still looked rough around the edges when they arrived at the lodge.

Julia turned from the sink. "You're not going to win this one. *Doctor* Cleary doesn't lose arguments with patients, even you." Kurt noticed that she was careful not to let her gaze drop to his arm. "You're not afraid of getting a few stitches, are you?"

"*No.* It's just a damn nuisance—waiting around in the ER half the night until they can drag some poor slob out of bed to do it. I know the drill at these small-town hospitals." He glanced at Susan with a coaxing grin. "I bet you could do it here."

Susan looked from Julia to Kurt. "I only have a topical anesthetic. It would sting."

"I've done it that way before."

"Then let's get to it." Without further ado, Susan dug into her kit and lined up the supplies she would need on the island counter. "Julia, why don't you go and check on the boys? And tell Ted we have company." To Kurt she added after Julia left, "She doesn't deal well with blood."

"I noticed." He watched Susan's face while she cleaned the cut. "Does it have something to do with those scars of hers?"

Susan's hand stilled. Finally, she shrugged. "Could be. She's never said. Anyway, it's her story to tell if she wants. Now, tell me what happened tonight—the whole story, not that fairy tale you gave before."

Later, Kurt drove Julia and a sleeping Nick the short hop down the road to the cottage. "Let me take him," Kurt said when she struggled with Nick out of the Jeep. He caught the boy up, not giving her time to consider whether or not she ought to protest.

She led him upstairs to Nick's room and turned down the covers. Kurt watched as she tucked him in, then lovingly smoothed the blond curls away from his forehead and dropped a kiss there before straightening. Without meeting his eyes, she led the way outside. They stood on the dark porch looking out over the shadowy dunes.

"Let me know where my car is tomorrow and I'll come and pick it up," she said.

"Fine." He'd hoped she would invite him in for a nightcap, but sensed from the way she'd hustled him outside that she was on guard again. She'd been uncomfortable having him watch her put Nick to bed.

"So, are you all right? Really?" she asked, glancing at the bandage on his arm.

"I'm fine. Really." He smiled.

"Well, then, thank you again. Somehow, that seems inadequate under the circumstances. If there's anything I can—"

"There is one thing," he said. She waited. "I'd like to think that we can be friends—that we can finally put aside the past. You know, we actually get on quite well when you forget that you don't like me."

"Is this where I'm supposed to fold?"

"It would sure make things easier. Is it so difficult?"

She tilted her head in thought, but the smile was in her voice. "Yes."

He laughed. "You know, your problem is as plain as the nose on that beautiful face of yours."

"What problem?" she asked indignantly.

"You're chicken."

"I am not!"

"Well, as Nick says, seeing is believing."

Julia smiled. "Okay, okay, I give up. Friends."

Chapter 15

As the summer unfolded, so too did Kurt's plans for Julia. He took full advantage of their truce, aware that the mind and body cannot long sustain a state of constant alert, that over time one becomes first inured to a threat and eventually lax in its face. Inch by inch, he outflanked her defenses. He took to stopping by occasionally on his way back and forth to the work site where he was still quartered. Sometimes he brought a pizza or a picnic lunch. Once, he took Julia and Nick out to eat. As Julia became accustomed to his presence, she began to relax. It wasn't a total capitulation. She still watched him, weighing. And sometimes, when she didn't know he watched her, he saw a shadow cross her face—fear, regret, indecision—he wasn't sure what.

One morning, Chloe announced, "I have an update on that surveyor out on Julia's property."

Kurt glanced up from his desk. "Good."

"What I have doesn't lead far. One of the local surveyors we used finally admitted he was hired to do a little moonlighting, no questions asked. That much we suspected. He claims he never saw who hired him. He says it was done by phone and he was paid in cash by mail."

"He must have sent his report somewhere."

"To a post office box in Chicago in the name of MAF Enterprises." Chloe frowned. "The problem is, I can't find anything on this outfit. No telephone number. No address. No reference to it anywhere. Nothing."

Kurt deliberated a moment. Something about it teased him, just out of reach. He sighed and gave up. If Chloe couldn't crack the puzzle, it probably couldn't be done.

"Find out exactly what he was asked to do—and what area he was hired to map. At least that might give us a clue about why this MAF is interested in the property. Get Sam Livingston on board if you need an investigator." Kurt flipped through his Rolodex and handed over Sam's card. "He's located in Traverse City."

"Do you want me to pass this information along to the sheriff?"

"Not much point."

Chloe left his office to pick up a call at her desk. Kurt slanted his chair sideways to look out the large window behind him. The only sound in the room was the cool hum of the air conditioner. Not surprisingly, the good sheriff and his minions had found no trace of the thugs who accosted Julia. And now another dead end. All these loose ends bothered him.

Outside, Cherry Beach sizzled in an August heat wave. Pedestrian traffic was light, but the beach was crammed. Old-timers claimed that a hot summer meant a cold winter. Kurt hoped not; a cold winter might slow construction, although by December they should have the exterior of the inn substantially roughed in.

Kurt checked his watch. Maybe he should knock off early and see if Julia would let him take Nick for a swim. The boy was probably napping on the cot set up for him in the studio while she worked nearby. If he waited an hour, she might be persuaded to stop and join them. As an added inducement, Kurt decided he would pick up some fish and chips at the fish shack down on the dock. He had to leave for Chicago soon to take care of Westco business he'd neglected too long, and might not see them again before Alex and Rob's wedding next weekend.

"I did find out something about that other matter you wanted me to look into," Chloe said when she returned. "There is a mortgage recorded on that same piece of property. It's held by a local savings and loan in Traverse City."

"Anything on the southern parcel?"

"Nothing recorded. It apparently came to her free and clear on her grandfather's death. But she is delinquent on property taxes for both parcels. She's paying it off a little each month."

Kurt quickly came to a decision. "See if you can find out anything about the terms of that loan on the northern parcel—Deer Cove."

Chloe gave him a sharp look. "Look boss, I know you haven't asked for my opinion, but Julia is not going to like you prying—"

"Just do it," Kurt ordered brusquely.

She drew herself up to her full height. "Yes, Mr. Weston. But how do you suggest I do it? They're not going to hand over the information because I smile pretty and say please."

Kurt sighed. "Chloe, calm down. I'm only trying to strengthen her position. Someone has an eye on that property. I suspect Julia doesn't want to sell but can't really afford to keep it. The property is so valuable that she may be playing way out of her league."

"Oh." Chloe gave him a knowing smile. "So, you're going to play the hero."

Kurt rolled his eyes. "Hell!"

"That still doesn't solve my problem."

"Tell them we're interested in buying the loan. Make it worth their while."

Julia caught the phone before the second ring. Alex's husky voice came over the line. "So how did the fish boil go?"

"Alex! Hi." Julia glanced at Nick across the boat shed

she had converted into her art studio. He stirred briefly on the narrow cot but didn't wake up. "It was fine." Dan Farley had won her fish boil and invited his two deputies and their significant others to share the evening.

"How are the wedding plans going?" Julia stared indecisively at the canvas she'd been practically falling asleep over. A lazy heat weighted the air, making every movement an effort. She decided to pack it in for the day. It was so blasted hot! She'd take Nick down to the water when he woke up.

"That's the other reason I called—you are to bring Nick along and stop all this worrying. There will be a bunch of kids and two nannies. He'll have a great time. Everyone in the family says to bring him." Alex and Julia had both assumed Nick would stay with the Clearys when she went to Belle House for Alex's wedding, but the wedding coincided with their vacation plans.

"Yes, that's what Kurt says, too. So it looks like I will." The decision to bring Nick into the middle of the Weston stronghold had not been a comfortable one. But in the end, she couldn't see what harm it could do. And the alternatives—letting him go away with the Clearys for two weeks, or worse, leaving him with a baby-sitter—were even less acceptable.

"Good! I'm glad you came to your senses. What are your travel plans?"

Julia smiled at Alex's brisk tone. "We'll probably ride up with Marcus on Friday and then come back on Sunday with Kurt aboard the Westco jet." Nick was going to be in ecstasy when he found out. She and Kurt had decided to keep it a secret and surprise him.

"I'm glad you're getting to know Kurt. Maybe he's not the villain you thought."

"Maybe not," Julia agreed.

"Don't you think it's time you talked to him about Nick? I've thought about this, and the more I get to know Kurt, the more convinced I am that he's clueless about Nick."

Julia tended to think so, too. But that didn't fully exonerate him; he was still the man who had ignored her letter all those years ago. How could he explain that? Although remote, one possibility had gradually gained ground: perhaps he'd never read the letter. Perhaps, in anger, he'd thrown it out. Or never gotten it. However specious, the more time she spent with Kurt, the more attractive this possibility became. And that frightened her.

"Hello?" Alex said into the silence. "Did you faint? Forget I mentioned it."

"Sorry. I was just thinking. Actually, I have been considering talking to him about it." Julia almost feared that voicing the idea aloud would set it irrevocably in motion.

"Has something happened?"

"No." Only that when she watched Nick and Kurt together, the not knowing was tearing her apart. "It's just that all of those grand reasons I had for keeping them apart seem feeble when I see them together. I just don't know anymore."

"Oh, honey, I think you're headed in the right direction. Talk to him and get to the bottom of all this. But *puh-lease,* do me a favor and wait until after my wedding."

"Whoa! Slow down, Alex. I said I was considering talking to Kurt about it. But first I want to find out a little more from Marcus. And there's someone else I should talk to at Belle House." Livingston might remember whether Kurt got her note. "But don't worry, I wouldn't dream of dropping that bomb in the middle of your wedding."

"Nick, honey, wake up. We're here." Julia leaned down to nuzzle Nick's temple, inhaling his salty little-boy smell while she unfastened the seat belt. He blinked open sleepy eyes and stretched out pudgy hands. Julia scooped him up and headed for the front door of Belle House. Marcus followed with their luggage. She and Nick were to share a room here because this was where Alex was staying. Marcus would be staying next door at Vanessa's.

"Where's Kurt?" Nick mumbled, yawning and peering around at the big house curiously.

"I don't know, sweetheart. He may not be here yet."

"He said he would take me swimming in a pool."

"I know. He will. Let's get settled first and then find Alex."

One of the temporary staff hired to help with the wedding showed them to a bedroom on the second floor. This room, like the one she had stayed in five years ago, opened onto the rear gallery and connected through the bathroom with the room next door where Alex was staying. A sea green gown, covered in protective plastic, hung from a hook on the closet door. The maid of honor gown, Julia assumed. Through the open window she could hear the buzz of conversation punctuated by occasional high-pitched squeals of children.

"There's a lunch buffet on the patio," the young man told them. "Come down after you're settled in."

When he left, Marcus turned to follow. "I'll see you downstairs. Remember what I said. Don't make the biggest mistake of your life. Kurt can be one ruthless son of a bitch."

Brows knit with worry, Julia stared uncertainly at the door, replaying the disturbing conversation they'd had on the ride up. After Nick fell asleep in the back seat, Julia had come out and simply asked Marcus if he'd ever talked to Kurt about Nick. She'd found it hard even to broach the subject of Nick's paternity because they'd never openly acknowledged or discussed it. To her relief, Marcus said that he had not told Kurt—at her own request, he'd reminded her.

She would have dropped the subject then, but Marcus hadn't. "Please tell me this doesn't mean you're considering telling Kurt."

"What would you say if I were?"

"I'd say you were flirting with disaster. Julia, do not tell Kurt. As sure as I'm sitting here, if you tell him that Nick is his son, you will lose Nick. The Westons would never allow one of their own to be raised by an outsider. At best, you might get some visitation."

"But before, you accused Kurt of using people and abandoning them."

"Women—*you,*" Marcus said harshly. "Not his family, especially not his own son. He'll take him from you, Julia. It won't matter to him who he hurts in the process—you or Nick."

"No." She shook her head in denial. "He wouldn't do that."

"Wouldn't he? Are you willing to take that chance?"

"Even if he wanted to, he couldn't take Nick away from me. No court would allow it—I'm his mother. I've raised him."

"You're assuming a level playing field. It isn't. Open your eyes. All the players are on his side of the field. He has all the money, all the power, all the influence. And if you think that doesn't matter, you're not living in the real world. Hired guns win in court. Judges know who funds their war chests. And baby, it ain't you!"

Nick's squeal as he leaped high above the bed yanked Julia back to the present. "Nick! Stop jumping on the bed!" she snapped. He cast her a quick, hurt look before scrambling down. Julia pressed a hand to her forehead. "Listen, honey," she said with a reassuring smile, "this isn't our house. We have to be careful of other people's things. Come on." She took his hand. "Let's get you cleaned up for lunch."

Alex burst in a minute later with a glad cry and open arms. By the time she brought Julia up to date on the wedding preparations and then herded them down to the patio, the crowd there had largely dispersed. The children and some of the adults had gone to the pool. Nothing was scheduled for them until the rehearsal dinner later that evening at the clubhouse. A few adults lingered around a half-dozen umbrella tables. Alex's brother, Kip, sat at the nearest table talking to Marcus. Julia spotted Kurt's mother and sister a few tables away.

After they settled Nick next to Marcus with a plate of

food, Alex took Julia over to introduce her to Rob's parents and Kurt's mother and sister. Rob's mother had a last-minute question about the guest list, leaving Julia alone with Kurt's mother and sister. Carolyn Weston recognized Julia from the art show in Chicago, but her surprise at seeing her here was evident.

"I didn't realize you were Alex's maid of honor," Carolyn said. "Rob said something about a woman and her son coming." She turned to her mother. "Mom, this is the artist who did that painting I gave you for your birthday."

"Really! Wonderful!" Gray eyes studied her so intently that Julia wondered if the other woman remembered her. "I dearly love that painting. In fact, it's hanging prominently in the family room. I'll have to show you later."

"Thank you," Julia said. To Carolyn she asked, "Which one did you get?"

"The one with the two boys on the beach bent over looking at something and the girl farther out in the water."

Julia nodded. It was one of several she'd half hoped wouldn't sell.

"I assume your son was one of the boys?" Pat Weston's gaze fell on Nick. "He's adorable. All that blond, curly hair . . . It looks just like your hair did, Carolyn, when you were little. Kurt's, too, only his was a little darker." A smile broke across her face. "Speaking of *my* baby boy," she said, lightly touching Julia's sleeve, "here he is now, late as usual."

Across the patio, Nick spotted Kurt at exactly the same time.

"Kurt!" He scrambled from his chair and hurtled along an intersecting path.

Kurt swung Nick up in a high arc and caught him close against his chest. "Hi, champ! I missed you."

A dimpled grin split Nick's face. "Mama's here, too."

Both pairs of smoky gray eyes turned in unison. Julia felt Mrs. Weston's hand tighten on her arm as she got her first close look at Nick.

"I see that." Kurt laughed. "And do you know that the

lady your mom is talking to is *my* mom? And the other one, with the mop of hair, is my little sister."

Nick gave Carolyn a dubious look. "She doesn't look so little."

"No," Kurt agreed with a teasing grin at his sister, "she doesn't, but we men are not supposed to say such things to the ladies." He ignored his sister's indignant snort and turned to Julia. "Hi," he said with casual familiarity. Suddenly, Julia found herself the uncomfortable center of interest as Kurt unexpectedly leaned down and gave her a light peck on the cheek. "How was the trip up?"

"Fine. Yours?" she asked, automatically taking Nick from Kurt when he stretched out his pudgy arms, then letting him wiggle down to the ground.

Nick pulled on Kurt's pant leg. "Will you take me swimming?"

"Sure," he agreed, "if your mom says it's okay."

"She said I could. I'm gonna get my suit."

"Wait!" Julia snagged Nick as he began to dash away. "Eat first. Then we'll go over."

"Go eat, Nick." Kurt nudged him along. "I'll wait."

"I'm sorry," Pat Weston said, suddenly coming to life when Nick ran off. "I'm forgetting my job as hostess. You must be famished," she said to Julia. "Go, fill up a plate before they take the buffet down. You, too, Kurt."

"Well, well," Carolyn murmured as Kurt and Julia walked away. "How interesting."

"What's interesting?" Pat asked, watching them, too.

"When they met—or I should say, became reacquainted—at the opening reception for Julia's show in Chicago last April, ice flew in both directions. From the looks of things now, I'd say there's been a thaw. She lives down in Cherry Beach, you know."

"No, I didn't know." Pat's troubled gaze rested on Julia and Kurt as they joined Nick and the others at the far table.

"It's odd." Carolyn hesitated. "I only met her that one time, but I could swear she said she had no children."

She shrugged, glancing back to her mother. "Mom, what's wrong?"

Pat shook head to clear it. "Nothing, honey." She patted her daughter's hand reassuringly. "Just an old woman's imagination running away with her."

Chapter 16

Julia would rather have avoided the gathering poolside and taken Nick far away from Weston turf. She was probably overreacting. Still, she couldn't shake the feeling that Pat Weston might already suspect more about Nick than she logically should, based on one minor physical similarity to Kurt. Julia shuddered at the idea. Not for a second had she expected trouble from that quarter. She would have to be especially careful around Pat.

Alex walked over to the pool with Julia, Nick, and Kurt, but didn't stay because she had a list of last-minute wedding matters to attend to. The crowd ebbed and flowed as wedding guests migrated between the tennis court, pool, beach, and house.

"Mama! Watch!" Nick demanded from the top of a water slide.

Julia stood in waist-deep water, wearing a high necked tankini that covered her where she needed it most, waiting to catch him. He slid down headfirst. Laughing, she caught him up, letting his momentum toss them backward underwater. Kurt followed Nick down the slide and dove underneath, grabbing them and bringing them up together. As they surfaced, Nick squirmed away, leaving Julia pressed smack up against Kurt's wet chest. She easily freed herself, but the contact left her flustered and breathless. She shivered when a breeze feathered her heated skin.

Kurt touched her goose-bump-covered arm. "You're cold."

"Yes, I think I'll sit out a bit." She looked around for Nick and located him splashing back and forth through a miniature waterfall.

"I'll keep my eye on him," Kurt said.

As Julia climbed out of the pool, Marcus lifted his drink and called to her from where he lounged with Vanessa at a table conveniently near the cabana's wet bar. Julia waved but opted for a deck chair under an umbrella nearer the pool. After a while, the warm sun and fresh air made her drowsy. She lazily watched Kurt from behind the safety of dark glasses.

Why did everything have to be complicated with him? Why did she have these messy emotions where he was concerned—and this annoying physical reaction? She reluctantly admired the way his muscles flexed and glistened as he moved through the water chasing after his nephew, Andrew. She was fully aware of the slow heat building between them since their truce. Kurt might think he was pulling a fast one on her, but she wasn't stupid. She knew he was moving in on her. What he didn't know was that she had deliberately let him, so that she could have a chance to look him over while she worked though her decision about Nick. It was a dangerous game. She had to keep a clear head because the stakes were dear. And that had become increasingly difficult.

Kurt looked over at her—seeming to know that she watched him behind her dark glasses—and held her eyes until, finally, she glanced away. Oh, yes, he knew she watched.

* * *

"Julia? I'm sorry. Did I wake you?" Her eyelids felt like sandpaper over her contact lenses as she cracked them open to find Pat Weston standing over her.

"No. That's okay." Blinking, Julia automatically glanced around for Nick and found him sitting with Kurt and Andrew at a table piled high with Legos. They each had a tall soda in front of them and were intent on their building project. "I must have dozed off. I didn't intend to." *Especially not in the opposition's camp.*

"Alex asked me to remind you to try on your gown right away. She said to insist because otherwise you would manage to forget again." Mrs. Weston smiled at Julia's groan.

"Too bad she has only one bridesmaid to worry about."

"Why don't you walk back with me? The seamstress is working up at the house now, so if you need any alterations, this would be the time. Kurt will watch your son," she added, following Julia's gaze.

"Okay. I'll just be a minute, Mrs. Weston."

"Please, call me Pat."

She waited while Julia checked with Kurt to make sure it was okay to leave Nick with him. As they started across the wide expanse of lawn toward Belle House, Pat asked whether Nick would be okay with the other kids that evening while the adults were at the rehearsal dinner.

Julia nodded. "Nick is usually more okay about being away from me than vice-versa," she admitted. "And he's having a lovely time playing with your grandson."

"Some kids are more independent than you'd like. Kurt was like that, too." After a moment, Pat broke the short silence that had fallen. "I have to ask you a question that's been bothering me—have we met before? You look familiar for some reason, and I've been racking my brain trying to place your face. Could it have been with Kurt? You two seem to know each other quite well."

Julia was momentarily taken aback by the question, but answered levelly. "I think we might have met briefly years ago when Vanessa and I dropped by to see Rob."

"Oh, I didn't realize you knew Vanessa."

"We were in college together. Alex, too."

"I see." Pat paused to speak to a gardener. When they resumed walking, Julia expected Pat to pick up the thread of their conversation. She was relieved when instead, Pat asked about her work, skillfully drawing her out until the direction of the questions began to lead back to Kurt and his residency in Cherry Beach. "So you live only a few miles from Kurt's new project?"

"Yes, I guess it would be about that—as the crow flies. I live on the opposite side of the peninsula."

Pat smiled and patted Julia's arm. "I'm glad Kurt has a friend nearby. That always makes it more pleasant when one is new to an area. I believe Carolyn mentioned that you and Kurt go way back."

"Did she?" Julia tried to sound casual. "Actually, no. Before this summer we had met only once before."

"Oh? When was that?"

Near the house, the path ran along a perennial border that had caught Julia's attention on the way down. "I'm not sure. It must be six years ago, at least." She leaned over an airy profusion of tall, salmon-colored blooms. "How beautiful! Is this Clara Curtis?" she asked, neatly derailing Pat's interrogation.

Pat gave a grudging smile, evidently recognizing the move. "So you're a gardener, too."

"I dabble. Nothing like this. I'm envious." She skimmed her hand across the tops of the daisylike blooms. "I saw a picture of these in a catalogue but thought the climate would be too cold."

"These have come back year after year. You shouldn't have a problem in Cherry Beach." Julia straightened and they continued toward the patio. "I'll dig some up for you to take back. I understand you and your son will be flying home with Kurt?"

Before Julia could react to Pat's latest step in the dance, she was distracted by the sight of Mr. Livingston fussing with a cart on the patio. Julia's step faltered; he was another wild card. She was about to turn away when he looked up and saw her. *Blast!* She had hoped for a chance to talk to him about the letter, but the timing couldn't have been worse with Sherlock at her side.

He clambered to his feet, a smile of recognition lighting his weathered face. "Miss Griffin! What a delight it is to have you here with us again."

"My goodness, Alfred," Pat said to Livingston when Julia left to try on the dress. "I haven't seen you so lit up since you bought that old Thunderbird. She certainly seems to have won you over."

"That she did," he agreed.

"Let me see if I have this right: Julia came up for a weekend with Alex and Kip to visit Rob." Livingston nodded. "Just when was that?"

"Can't say for sure. It was a few years back. I can check the log."

"Yes. Please do. And check to see if Kurt was here then, too."

"That I do know. Kurt was here."

"You're sure?"

"Absolutely. It was Kurt who pulled Miss Griffin and that little girl out of the riptide up in the park that spring. It happened before you arrived."

"I remember. The little girl nearly drowned. You're saying that *Julia* is the woman who dove into the riptide after the girl?" Pat asked in astonishment.

"Yes."

"So Julia Griffin is the singer?"

Julia's sense that events were quickly spinning out of control only heightened when she stood before the mirror staring in dismay at the bridesmaid's gown. The gown itself was exquisite, a silky, sea green column. No ugly bridesmaid's dress this. The problem was that it rose over only the left shoulder, leaving her entire right shoulder bare. Most likely Alex had instructed the maker to flip the design, and it hadn't been done. One of the female staff knocked on her door and Julia sent her off in search of Alex.

Downstairs in the kitchen, unable to locate Alex, the maid handed the problem over to Pat. "What exactly is wrong with the dress?" Pat asked.

"I think she said the wrong shoulder is bare," the maid replied.

Vanessa, in tennis whites, eavesdropped with avid interest, momentarily forgetting the drink in her hand and her doubles partner waiting on the court. "Maybe she has a wart." She smirked. "Does she have a wart, Kurt?" Vanessa asked as he came into the kitchen with Carolyn and the two boys.

"Who?" Kurt asked from the refrigerator.

"Julia."

Kurt shot Vanessa a warning glare and looked pointedly in Nick's direction. "What's going on?" Kurt asked his mother after he handed out glasses of lemonade to the boys and sent them outside. His mother had the maid repeat what Julia said.

"That doesn't sound like her." Kurt frowned. "Did you say one of the shoulders is bare?"

"What doesn't sound like Julia?" Alex asked, breezing into the kitchen.

"Julia apparently refuses to wear the gown," Pat explained to Alex.

"You must be joking. She would wear a brown bag if I gave it to her."

"I don't know," Vanessa said, clearly enjoying herself. "She always was vain."

"Oh, please." Alex rolled her eyes.

"Most women are," Vanessa insisted. "Julia is a prima donna. She barely talks to anyone."

"Careful, dear, your claws are showing," Pat warned Vanessa quietly.

Kurt gave Vanessa an annoyed look as she took a pull from a bottle of Evian, preferred drink of the rich and self-absorbed. She seemed willing to say or do anything these days to keep the wolf of boredom at bay.

When Alex got the story straight, she rushed off in search of the seamstress.

The excitement over, Vanessa sauntered back to the tennis courts and Carolyn went after the boys, leaving Kurt alone in the kitchen with his mother.

"So, I take it there really is something wrong with the dress?" she asked.

"I think so."

"And you know what it is?" she persisted.

"I have a good idea."

"And you're not going to tell me?"

"What do you think?" he asked.

"I used to be pretty good with a sewing machine. Maybe I should go up and—"

"No, mom," Kurt firmly cut her off. "Let them handle it."

The seamstress miraculously salvaged the dress, but the day headed south again during the rehearsal dinner when Julia observed signs that Alex was unraveling. The dinner itself was as large and protracted as the preceding rehearsal in Breakers's chapel had been simple and brief. Although the wedding party was small, the number of extended family members present for the dinner made up for the dearth. The two families appeared well pleased with each other. They had every reason to be; they were cut from the same expensive cloth. But as the evening wore on, Alex began to look brittle and overbright. Julia watched Alex take a quick gulp from a drink someone shoved into her shaking hand.

At that point, Julia began searching the crowd for Kurt, looking for an ally to help get Alex out of there. He'd taken his job as her escort seriously, smoothing the way for her most of the evening. But he'd been pulled away a while ago by Alex's father, ostensibly to look at Kurt's sailboat. Julia suspected that was merely a pretext to curry Westco business. The Chases never minded mixing business with business.

An hour later, after relieving Nick's baby-sitter, Julia went through the connecting bath to Alex's room. Stripped to her slip, Alex stood in the cool breeze coming through the screen door. The tip of a cigarette glowed in the dark.

The cigarette was a dead giveaway. Alex only smoked in rare moments of extreme stress.

"How's Nick?" she asked, turning from the door.

"Fine. Sleeping." Julia switched on a light and searched her friend's face. "Okay, Alex, what's wrong?"

"Nothing's wrong." She blew out a stream of smoke.

Julia gave her a pained look. "You may be able to fool a lot of people, but right now my baloney meter is in the red."

"I think I may be making a mistake."

"What kind of mistake?"

"Marrying Rob."

Julia sat down in a chair. "What happened between this afternoon and tonight?"

"The firm descended."

Which, Julia knew, meant her family. "So? They seem pleased with Rob."

"That is the problem." Alex laughed, but it had a hysterical edge to it. "They never approve of anything I do. It's like a barometer—if they push in one direction, I'm usually better off going in the other. And now, when I'm about to take the most important step of my life, I discover they're ecstatic about it because it's such a good alliance for the firm. My parents, who make marriage look like a blood sport, highly approve of 'the match,' as they so quaintly call it."

Julia knew she had to calm Alex down before she did something she would regret forever. "I can see how that would give you pause. But Alex—"

"Rob and I are so different."

"Alex . . ."

"You yourself once called him a bastion of industrial-strength conservatism. Maybe I'm deluding myself thinking it could ever work between us. There are a lot of other fish in the sea—''

''Alex! Slow down.'' Julia pointed to the other chair. ''Sit.'' She waited until Alex did. ''First, when I said those things, I spoke in surprise and ignorance. I have long since come to view you and Rob as perfectly suited for each other.''

''Really?'' Alex looked at Julia uncertainly.

''Yes, really. Second, you and your family may have reached the same end, but you got there by entirely different paths. It's mere coincidence that you happened to arrive at the same place. And third, there may *not* be a lot of fish out there for you. There may be just one.''

''Oh, Julia . . .'' Alex's eyes sparkled with barely suppressed tears. ''It's just that I'm so scared I'll end up like them. It's hard to break free of the past.''

Julia smiled wanly. ''I know.''

They were interrupted by a soft knock on the door. ''That will be Rob,'' Alex said.

Julia rose. ''I'll see you in the morning. If you need me, I'm right next door.''

''Thanks.'' Alex gave her a tight hug. ''I don't know what I'd have done without you all these years.''

The next morning, Julia wished that her own problem could be solved as easily. She and Nick ate an early breakfast in the kitchen under the watchful eye of Pat Weston while most of the other inhabitants were still in bed. In Pat, Nick found an attentive audience. She was affectionate and interested. The combination drew him like a magnet. Julia watched uneasily. She had to have it out with Kurt before long—as soon as they got back to Cherry Beach.

''Come on, pilot. Let's go see if Aunt Alex is up yet.'' Julia held out her hand and Nick hopped down from the chair and took it. She leaned down to whisper a reminder in his ear.

"Thank you for the breakfast, Mrs. Weston," he dutifully piped out, then grinned.

"You're welcome, you rascal." Pat smiled and opened her arms to him. "Come here and give this old lady a hug." Nick scampered across the kitchen into her arms. "He's a delightful child," Pat said to Julia over Nick's head.

"Thank you." Julia held out her hand again for Nick and led him out.

His high voice echoed down the hallway. "Then can we go see if Andrew and—I forget their names—those other kids are up? Can I stay up there tonight with them? *Please?*"

Julia looked down into Nick's pleading face. Carolyn's son, Andrew, and several other children were sleeping in a third-floor dorm room with one of the nannies. Nick badly wanted to join them. "We'll go see if they're awake. But I'll have to think about tonight."

Alex was still sleeping and Nick wanted to play with the kids, so Julia left him in the nanny's care and seized the opportunity to take a head-clearing run. Clad in blue running shorts and a white T-shirt, Julia jogged up the winding road.

Kurt laid his tennis racket down on the patio table, where his mother was sitting over her coffee, and mopped his brow with the white towel slung over his shoulder.

"How was your match?" she asked.

"These kids are getting quicker every year. I barely eked out a win in a third-set tiebreaker." Kurt poured a tall glass of orange juice and downed it in one long swallow.

"That *kid* was league champion this year. They all gun for you." Kurt had gone through college on a tennis scholarship. "Someday soon, they'll overtake you."

Puzzled by the uncharacteristic jab, Kurt cocked a quizzical eyebrow at his mother. She'd been testy since he'd arrived yesterday, and he couldn't fathom the reason. Maybe the pressure of the wedding and a houseful of people were getting to her. He noticed Nick, sitting with the other kids eating breakfast. "Where's Julia?"

"She went out for a jog a few minutes ago. I'm surprised you didn't see her."

"She must have gone south."

As if reading his thoughts, his mother said, "You can probably catch her if you want. Maybe you simply need to try harder and get your priorities straight."

Kurt gave his mother a baffled look. He'd have to make time to have it out with her later today. In the meantime . . . Kurt rose and picked up his racket. "You can tell me what that's supposed to mean later."

He caught Julia a mile up the road and fell into step with her. "Thought I'd join you."

Julia skeptically eyed his prissy white tennis shorts and shirt. A slow, smug smile curved her lips. "Okay, if you think you can keep up."

Twenty minutes later, Julia wished she hadn't goaded him with that smart-ass remark. As a seasoned runner, she'd snobbishly assumed he wouldn't be able to keep up with her. Belatedly, she remembered a vague reference he'd made about doing "a little light jogging." He was intent on making her pay, and she was equally determined that this contest of wills would end in no worse than a draw. Talking was out of the question. Her only consolation was that he wasn't talking either. By sheer grit, she was still with him when they reached the channel on their way back.

Julia paced along the bank, cooling down, hands resting on hips, chest heaving. She looked over at Kurt, who was doing much the same, except that he'd removed his shirt on the run and now mopped his face with it. They exchanged grudging smiles, acknowledging a draw.

Kurt ambled over to her. "How long have you been running?"

"Since I was a teenager." Julia's eyes followed the slow descent of a rivulet of sweat through the golden-brown hair on Kurt's chest. It made her insides do a little flip. He reached over and tucked back a stray lock of hair that had escaped her ponytail. Her insides flopped.

"Why do you do it?"

"Why do I do what?" Her voice sounded distracted and husky to her own ears.

"Run. Were you in track at school? Do you run distance races? Do you run to stay in shape?"

"Oh, let's see. . . . No, no, and that's a side benefit, but not my main motivation. Why do you always ask so many questions?"

"I'm interested in the answers. So why do you do it, then?"

Julia sent him an exasperated look, but he just grinned lazily back. "It helps me sleep." She checked her watch. "I've got to get back."

"The wedding isn't until six."

"I know, but Alex has a hair stylist and manicurist coming to the house."

"How is Alex?"

Julia knew he was referring to the night before. "I hope okay. I haven't seen her yet this morning. She has a case of prewedding jitters brought on by close proximity to her family. Thanks for your help, by the way."

"Speaking of close proximity, I was wondering if you'd like to get away from the hubbub for a couple of hours. Nick, too. There's a beautiful place near here I'd like to show you."

Julia thought a minute. It sounded wonderful to get away from the bustle at Belle House. Safer, too, she mentally added, thinking of Pat. "I'd like that. Let me check with Alex. I'll let you know."

By tacit agreement, they kept an easy pace the last half mile to Belle House.

Chapter 17

They met at noon in front of Belle House. Julia found Kurt waiting for them beside a Land Rover, and he buckled Nick into the back seat next to a backpack and a cooler. "How's everything in the bride's camp?" he asked when they were under way.

"Actually, fine."

"You sound surprised."

"I am, a little. For a while last night, Alex sounded ready to call the whole thing off. But this morning, she's done a total turnabout. It's like she's on a Valium drip—everything is wonderful." Kurt chuckled and Julia added, "Rob did *something* last night to calm her down."

At that, Kurt laughed harder. Nick joined in for the sheer fun of it. Julia couldn't help a grudging smile in response. "Not everything can be fixed by *that*."

"No," he agreed, grinning, "not everything. But in this instance . . ."

She rolled her eyes. "How is everything in the groom's camp?"

"Calm. You know Rob. We spent the morning sneaking my things out of the guest house and their things in." Alex and Rob secretly planned to spend tonight in the cottage and leave on their honeymoon early next morning.

After a few miles, Kurt turned off the rural blacktop onto a dirt track that wound up a long incline. Thick woods and brush closed in, scraping the sides of the truck. When they could go no farther, he squeezed the SUV into a small opening in the brush. "Now we walk," he announced.

The trail narrowed and steepened until it turned into a nearly vertical, two-foot-wide ribbon of sand. "This is a sand dune!" Julia exclaimed, at first not recognizing it for what it was because of its camouflaging cloak of woods. Ahead of her, Kurt hauled Nick up the steep path.

"Just wait until we get to the top." Kurt glanced back at her with a look that held the promise of something grand ahead.

"It's a sand slide," Nick called out. "Like a water slide, only it's sand."

A minute later, Kurt and Nick disappeared over the lip at the top. Shortly, Kurt reappeared, offering his hand, and pulled her up and over. Julia stopped, catching her breath. Before them lay a vast, untracked bowl of sand perhaps a half mile across. Beyond the bowl, crests of successive hills marched into the distance to Lake Michigan. Silence expanded to the far horizon. While Nick tore around, they stood side by side and drank in the landscape.

"I used to come here when I was a kid." Kurt's rich voice blended with the hollow hum of air moving across the great expanse.

"It's beautiful," Julia whispered, flashing him a rare, full-wattage smile of appreciation.

They ate there so they could leave the backpack. After lunch, they set off across the sand. Nick soon tired and Kurt swung him up onto his shoulders.

When they crested the rim of the next bowl, Kurt did a slow turn, taking in the great, open expanse. "I've always loved this place. Sometimes, here, the summer light glitters on the sand with such intensity that it almost hurts to look at it, it's so beautiful."

Julia glanced at him, surprised that a builder would see it that way. Marcus looked at wide-open spaces and saw development potential. And here Kurt, the builder, saw it as she did—a place already perfect.

Nick wiggled down from Kurt's shoulders and raced off toward a high cornice. Kurt followed, and soon the rush of unbroken air circulating inland from the distant lake swallowed up their voices. Many miles away, in that great stretch of breathing blue, Julia could make out an island. She felt dwarfed by the immensity of the landscape. She was an ant, a speck of creation, lost in the middle of the great expanse. Nick and Kurt had disappeared from view. It felt as though she were alone on the earth.

But then she caught sight of them, small figures at the peak of the dune. She reminded herself that she wasn't alone anymore. She watched Kurt take Nick's wrists and whirl him around and around in a circle until his tiny body was horizontal to the ground, his feet swinging out over the edge of the drop-off. It struck her that she wasn't afraid for her son. Just a few short months ago, she wouldn't have trusted this man with the family goldfish. Marcus had to be wrong about him. She watched Kurt and Nick leap off hand in hand, sinking into the slope below.

It looked . . . right.

Julia tasted tears on her lips before she realized she was crying. By then it was too late to stop them. They welled up from some huge reservoir and streamed down her face unabated. She turned away from the blurry figure closing in on her across the sand.

Kurt caught her shoulders and turned her around. "Julia, what's wrong?"

She shook her head. "Nothing."

"You're crying." He drew her into the warm circle of his arms, holding her, lightly stroking the back of her head.

"I'm fine—really." But she made no move to pull away. She took the comfort he offered, letting her forehead rest against his shoulder. The tears stopped. "Is Nick okay?"

"He's busy digging a giant hole." She felt his warm breath against the top of her head.

"Kurt—" she began, then stopped before she blurted it all out. This wasn't the time, with Alex's wedding only hours away. She took a deep breath and straightened.

"What is it?"

Julia shook her head, stepping away from him. "There's something I need to tell you, but this isn't the time. We'll talk when we get back to Cherry Beach."

Kurt watched her, curious, but he didn't push for answers. Julia gazed out across the vast expanse. "It's easy to imagine that we're the last people at the end of the world," she said.

Their eyes caught and held. "Or the first—Adam and Eve." Kurt gave her a light, quick kiss before Nick caught up to them.

The wedding proceeded on schedule at six that evening in the Breakers chapel. An abundance of candlelight and flowers turned the chapel into a fairy-tale setting. As Julia preceded Alex down the aisle, the hum of anticipation hushed. Here and there Julia recognized faces among those gathered: Derrick, from the gallery; Vanessa, Marcus, and various Chases and Westons; and Kurt, standing next to Rob at the end of the aisle, his gaze on her as she walked toward him. Less than an hour later, it was over. The crowd began a slow migration across the road to the clubhouse for the reception.

Champagne flowed like tap water from a crystal fountain in the middle of the room. Tables overflowed with appetizers: smoked salmon pâté, beluga caviar on toast points, miniature goat-cheese tarts, and more. Alex had arranged with the band to have Julia sing for the bride and groom's first dance, so after dinner Julia made her way through the crowd to the bandstand.

Watching from the bar, Marcus drew deeply on a cigarette. He didn't think much of the sappy song she sang, but she looked hot and she could sing, he'd give her that. Even though he knew from personal experience that it was all a tease, her beauty stirred him. He liked to imagine her silky voice in his ear as he rode her. It might almost be good enough to make him forget how annoying he usually found her. He tossed back the last of his drink.

"*. . . I will feel a glow just thinking of you . . . and the way you look tonight . . .*"

"Marcus!" Vanessa interrupted his fantasy. "We're waiting downstairs. Do you want to do a line with us or not?"

"Yeah, coming. It'll have to be a quick one. Bartender!" he snapped, "do you think you could manage to get me that refill in this lifetime?" In answer, the expressionless bartender seemed to shift into even slower gear. Marcus scowled. The working stiffs knew who they had to suck up to and who they could blow off. They hustled for the great Kurt Weston.

Nervously, Marcus wondered if Julia had said anything to Kurt about Nick. Probably not, he reassured himself again. He hadn't noticed any difference in how Kurt treated Julia or the kid after they came back from wherever they sneaked off to this afternoon. How they'd managed that, Marcus still couldn't figure. He'd had one or the other almost constantly under his eye since their arrival. For a while this afternoon, it had felt as though his future was about to be blown to hell. He had to keep better tabs on her until he could come up with a new plan. He had to keep that bastard out of her life and get her to sign the damn loan agreement. Otherwise, all his plans were shit.

After her stint onstage, Julia borrowed Alex's phone to check up on Nick. She'd relented and agreed to let him spend the night upstairs in the dorm room with Andrew. Reassured that all was well, she returned to the reception, but the close press of people eventually wore thin, and she slipped outside to the quiet deck.

Kurt joined her a little while later. "Thought I'd find you here." He leaned against the railing next to her.

"You must be psychic."

"I just know you."

"Oh, really?" Julia turned sideways against the railing to face him, a small smile of disbelief curving her mouth.

He eyed her. "You have a low tolerance for crowds. And you've been avoiding me ever since we got back from our little outing this afternoon, although I'm not certain whether it's the kiss or that I saw you cry that bothers you the most."

"Not bad," she said lightly and waited for him to make his next move. It didn't take long.

"So which is it, the kiss or that I saw you cry?"

"Both," she admitted with uncharacteristic candor.

Unlike this afternoon when he caught her by surprise, this time she knew he was going to kiss her.

"I've been wanting to do this all evening," he murmured, cupping her face in his hands. "You are rare . . . beautiful . . ."

From the first gentle contact and the accompanying zing through her bloodstream, the kiss went beyond the mere epidermal. This was not the brief, friendly peck of this afternoon. Julia's shocked gasp of recognition was smothered under the increasing demand of Kurt's mouth as he gathered her more tightly in his arms. It all came back to her—passion so intense it swept away caution, hunger so urgent it was both pleasure and pain. She wound her arms around his neck and hung on as the storm whirled through her.

She had tried to forget. But she hadn't. Not really. He'd been there in her dreams all these years. And despite everything, she wanted him. It was familiar, the same as before, only more vivid than her faded memory. Then she remembered Nick.

Julia turned her head away, gulping air. "Kurt, this isn't a good idea. I don't want to get involved."

"Too late." He pulled her closer.

"Kurt! Wait!" she said more firmly, pushing away. "This isn't right."

"It feels perfect to me."

"There are things you don't know," she said in desperation.

He finally released her, looking none too happy about it. "Then tell me," he demanded.

"Not here. Not now." She turned and walked away.

He caught up to her just inside the ballroom and took her hand, firmly propelling her around clusters of chattering guests, making a beeline for the nearest exit. He leaned over and said in her ear, "We'll leave, then, together, and go someplace quiet where we won't be disturbed. You can talk all you want."

"No! When we get back to Cherry Beach we'll talk." He continued walking. She dug in her heels.

"You're making a scene," Kurt warned calmly.

They were attracting attention, Marcus's in particular. He was bearing down on them with a strangely frantic look on his face.

"*I'm* making a scene!" she hissed. "This is not just about you and me. I have Nick to think about. And I shouldn't need to remind *you,* Mr. Let's-be-friends-for-Alex-and-Rob, that this is their wedding reception!"

Kurt muttered a curse and let her go. "Okay, I'll give you some time, but don't ask me to pretend this didn't happen. And know this: I'm not a threat to either you or Nick."

She met his unwavering gaze. "Yes. You are."

Much later, Kurt walked along the gallery, his formal white shirt untucked and open to the cool night breeze. Soon after the episode with Julia at the reception, he'd helped sneak Rob and Alex to the guest cottage, moved his own things into Alex's room, and then joined a late-night poker game downstairs. He'd last seen Julia shortly after Marcus had spirited her off to the dance floor. On reflection, Kurt found Marcus's pronounced agitation perplexing. He'd looked wild, panicked, desperate, and more dissolute than usual from liquor or whatever poison he was into these days. Incredibly, Julia hadn't seemed to notice any of it.

Kurt had puzzled over the peculiar friendship between Julia and Marcus ever since seeing them leave the diner together. How had they hooked up? What did she see in him? More troubling, what did he want with her? Because Julia wasn't his usual type. Marcus's taste in women ran to blond, built, and ready to rock. Or wealthy. Could that be it? The land? But the land could have no value to him unless she was willing to sell it or develop it, which she'd made clear she wasn't. So how could he benefit? Kurt shook his head—no way that he could see. Still, he didn't trust Marcus's earnest charm around Julia. He'd learned long ago that leeches only smile when they're sucking blood. Perhaps he'd have Sam Livingston do some digging there, too.

A high cry interrupted his ruminations. He glanced down the dark balcony, but saw no one. Then it came again, this time an indistinct muttering that he traced back to the open window to Julia's room. When her cries grew louder, he tried the door. Locked. He circled around through his new digs and entered Julia's room through the shared bath.

Twisting and turning, relentlessly pursued by her demons, Julia fought through the mental maze of her nightmare. It came as a one-two punch. It always did. First, the paralyzing horror, the racing heart and popping sweat. Then the gut-wrenching nausea as reality slipped in, a reality worse in some ways than the nightmare. The open door to the past allowed all-too-real monsters out. And pain. So much pain.

She came out of the nightmare crying, anguish dulling the shock she would otherwise have felt at finding herself cradled on Kurt's lap as if she were a child. "I promised my mother I would take care of him and I didn't," she choked out, hovering between two worlds.

"Who did you promise to take care of, Julia?" Kurt rocked her.

"My brother." Someone rapped lightly on her door. Kurt hugged her tighter.

"What happened to him?"

She shook her head, pressing a hand over her mouth to stifle her cries.

The knock came again, more insistent this time. Kurt shifted her off his lap. Thinking he was leaving, she held on. "Don't go."

"I'm not." He rose, then lifted her in his arms and gently propped her up against the headboard of the bed. "Someone's at the door. I'll be right back."

"Only Carolyn," he said when he returned a moment later. "She heard noise and wondered if everything was all right."

Julia said nothing. Kurt sat on the bed beside her, drawing her over so that her back rested against his chest. She exhaled slowly.

It's over; they're together; there's nothing you can do . . . she silently chanted a litany she had repeated countless nights in countless variations over the years. Deliberately she relaxed tense muscles, concentrating on how good it felt to be held. *I am not alone.*

Kurt felt a tremor go through her as she exhaled. Her head fell back against his shoulder and she closed her eyes. Her arms and legs were crossed in pathetic defense against whatever horrific memory tortured her. His heart ached for her.

Kurt's eyes roamed over the distinct line of cheekbone and jaw, down the slim column of her neck to the deep vee of a maddeningly revealing T-shirt and beyond, over lean thighs and long bare legs. An oversized armhole exposed the creamy outer curve of one breast. Without thinking, he reached up and caressed its cool softness with his hot palm. She didn't move, didn't say anything, but her nipples puckered into hard points against damp cotton. Kurt's heart hammered.

He had to stop this now before it got completely out of hand. He wanted her, but not like this. He wanted to help her, not take advantage of her. He wanted her to trust him. On the other hand, a contrary little voice said, this might be the only opening she would ever give him.

"I should leave," he said abruptly.

Julia clutched at his retreating hand. "No. Don't go yet."

"I can't stay without making love to you," he said in a strangled voice.

"I know." It didn't matter anymore. Need overrode caution. She needed him to stand between her and the cold emptiness that threatened to consume her. She needed him to affirm life in that ultimate and most basic human way, to fan the spark already tingling along her bloodstream. In the end, one night couldn't matter so very much—whatever his reaction when she dropped her bomb—as long as she made sure of one thing. "I don't—I'm not protected. You would have to . . ."

He took pity on her awkward attempt to discuss birth control. "I can wear a condom. But are you sure you want to do this?" He peered at her intently.

"Yes, I want to have sex with you," she said evenly.

"Sex," he repeated, as if weighing her deliberate choice of that emotionally bankrupt word for it. "Julia—"

"I'm a big girl," she said, cutting off his attempt to save her from herself.

"So you are."

He turned her chin toward him and covered her mouth, kissing her gently. Slowly, he shifted around until she was in his arms and they were lying together on the bed. Julia raised her hands to his face, exploring like a sculptor, running her fingers over his features and through his hair until the monster vanished and there was only Kurt with her. He rose up over her and stroked her gently, running his hands down her sides, over her thighs, caressing her breasts until she was mindless with pleasure.

In one slow, smooth motion he peeled off her nightshirt. Automatically, she crossed her arms, her left hand covering the scar below her right shoulder, her right going to the scars on her abdomen.

"Turn off the light," she whispered.

"I want to see you." His hands circled her wrists, warm

and gentle. "Trust me, Julia. Don't hide from me anymore. I would never hurt you."

Uncertainly she let him remove her hands and pin them loosely against the bed on each side of her head. He stared down at her exposed body for a long moment and finally back up to her eyes.

"You are mythically beautiful."

Tears filled her eyes.

"Don't cry." He caught a tear with his tongue, then moved to her lips.

She trembled when his cotton undershirt brushed against her nipples. His open dress shirt fell along both of her sides to the bed, enclosing them together behind a curtain of white. She protested when his mouth moved away, and an instant later gasped when he tenderly kissed the scar below her right shoulder. Giving her no time to marshal any resistance, he moved on to her breasts, palming one, while he drew the nipple of the other into his mouth and slowly ran his tongue over it. She shuddered and her fingers dug into his shoulders.

This was what she wanted: the feeling of life beating through her veins, obliterating everything else. Sharing it with Kurt. For a time, not having to resist the connection that stretched between them, to simply give in to gravity.

Kurt straightened on his knees above her, his hot gaze devouring her as his hand moved to his zipper. Then he froze. "I'll be right back."

Dazed, Julia watched him disappear into the bathroom. She drew a ragged breath in a vague attempt to restore some order to senses careening madly out of control, then stopped herself. This was exactly what she wanted: this pulsing, insistent, driving force of life at its most basic.

He returned seconds later and held up several small squares for her to see, then quickly stripped off his shirt and undershirt.

Julia stared at his broad, well-muscled chest. His hands dropped to the front of his slacks and her eyes dropped with them, watching as he hooked his thumbs under both slacks and shorts and pushed them down in one smooth motion.

Then he was next to her, pulling her into his arms, shuddering at the full-length, skin-to-skin contact. His hands moved over her body, caressing her, loving her. Julia exulted in the solid, warm feel of him under her hands, the weight of him on top of her.

"Julia . . . sweetheart, I can't wait any longer," he said between kisses.

"Yes." She wanted him inside her, filling the empty ache, with a single-minded purpose she dimly knew would shock her to her toes were she able to feel shock, which at the moment, thankfully, she was not.

She heard him fumbling with a foil wrapper. Then he was over her, between her legs, spreading them wider, penetrating by slow degrees. She trembled from pleasure so intense it bordered on pain.

Another kind of delicious agony began, catching her up and hurtling her helplessly toward a cliff. She tried to back away from it, to at least slow it down, but it was no use in the face of the primal need drawing her on. All she could do was wrap her legs around his waist and hang on as she went over the edge in a free fall.

She wasn't sure how much time elapsed—seconds or minutes—before she heard him murmur something she couldn't quite catch. All she knew was that she wanted to drift forever in this warm current of serenity. She didn't want to move. She didn't want to return to reality. Gradually she realized that although he had ceased moving, he was still hot and hard and pulsing inside her. And it began all over again.

He captured her head in his hands and their mouths fused as he began to take long, lazy strokes that rendered her senseless to all but the rekindled need building inside her. They moved together until rippling waves of pleasure built into a single long crest. She hung suspended, beyond reason or restraint. "Kurt!" she whispered hoarsely, and this time they tumbled into the abyss together. His harsh groan summed up all the frustrating months of waiting.

After a while, he rolled onto his back, bringing her with

him so that her head rested against his shoulder and her legs tangled with his. Julia lay hushed in the circle of his arms, floating in a sleepy sea of contentment until she fell asleep.

Sleep was more elusive for Kurt because he had to come to terms finally with the indisputable conclusion that she was imprinted on his soul. When he'd come to Cherry Beach he'd meant either to exorcise the myth that had nagged him all these years or possess the reality. Now it seemed only the latter would be possible.

"Okay, honey, you go in and pick out a pair of shorts and a shirt and clean underpants. I'll wait right here for you. Be real quiet so you don't wake your mom. Can you do that?" Nick's solemn nod made Pat Weston smile. She gave him a quick hug. "That's my boy." She cracked open the door to the room and sent him in. Seconds later he reappeared with only a shirt and a scared look on his face.

"Something's wrong with Mama. Her arm isn't . . ."

Pat couldn't understand what he said next because he started to cry. She tucked him behind her and stuck her head into the room. In an instant, she took in the scene on a sharp intake of breath. A familiar tousled head shared the pillow with Nick's mom. They lay spoon-fashion, Kurt's large arm contrasting with the fair skin underneath. Pat guessed that from his shorter viewpoint, Nick hadn't seen Kurt behind his mother, only the masculine arm wrapped around her. It must have looked like Kurt's arm belonged to Julia. The sheet had slipped off their shoulders, and it was apparent that both were naked underneath. Pat shushed Nick, who had seen enough to let out a relieved cry of recognition, and quickly backed them both out of the room.

Pat was helping Nick fasten a pair of Andrew's shorts a few minutes later when Carolyn shuffled into the kitchen in pajamas and bathrobe. "I hope it's okay that I borrowed Andrew's shorts for Nick—his mom is still sleeping."

"Kurt's sleeping in her bed, too," Nick piped up.

"He is?"

Pat scrutinized her daughter. ''You don't sound very surprised.''

Carolyn shuffled over to the coffeepot. ''She had a nasty nightmare last night, or rather about two this morning. Kurt got there before I did. He probably didn't want to leave her alone.''

That appeared to make sense to Nick. ''Mama has bad dreams sometimes. Sometimes she frows up in the toilet. But it's okay, 'cause dreams aren't real so they can't hurt you—that's what Mama says.''

''That's right, honey.'' Pat steered him to the patio door. ''You go on out now and Mrs. Livingston will help you get some breakfast on the patio.''

Carolyn frowned over her coffee. ''I wonder what her nightmares are about.'' Then she glanced up. ''Mom, you look like a disapproving nun. Kurt probably stayed to offer a little comfort and fell asleep.''

''Rather an extreme sort of comfort, from what I saw.''

Chapter 18

Julia woke by slow degrees, gradually becoming aware of a large, warm body curled around her naked backside. It took a few more seconds for her brain to fill in the blanks. Her heart thumped in panic.

She heard children's voices coming from the patio below the window.

Nick! How late was it? At least eight, she guessed, unable to read the bedside clock without her contact lenses. He could walk in on them.

How on earth had she gotten into this? She knew, of course. Her reasoning skills were never great after one of her nightmares. But this time they'd reached a new low. What had seemed like a good idea last night when she was weak and needy looked like insanity in the light of day.

Gingerly she eased out from under Kurt's arm, trying not to wake him, and reached for her glasses. She preferred to be up and dressed before he woke.

"Looking for this?" Kurt asked as her feet touched the floor. Julia shoved on her glasses and whirled around. With a wicked, come-and-get-it twinkle in his eye, he dangled her nightshirt from one finger.

"You're awake!"

"And *you* are sneaking away."

"Kurt, we don't have time for this right now. Nick could walk through that door any second. You've got to get out of here."

"He's having breakfast on the patio. I just heard him."

Julia was aware of the warm perusal Kurt had been giving her naked self while she perched on the edge of the bed. She refused to let her discomfiture show.

He dangled the shirt closer, inviting her to make a grab for it. Instead, with as much dignity as she could muster considering she wasn't wearing a stitch of clothing, she rose, walked across the room to the closet, and wrapped herself in a white terry-cloth robe.

"Well done."

She ignored the amused gleam in his eyes. "We have to talk, but first we have to get dressed before someone happens in on us."

"We'll talk now. You have a way of bolting, given half a chance." He got up and unhurriedly picked up his boxer shorts from the floor. As he stepped into them, he caught the direction of her gaze and followed it to his arousal.

"Want to go back to bed and make me a happy man? No? Pity."

He walked over to the hallway door, locked it, and turned back to her. "Why do I have the feeling that you already regret what happened between us last night?"

"Because I do. It was wrong. I'm ashamed of what happened. I apologize for throwing myself at you. Sometimes when I have bad dreams I'm not . . ." She couldn't find the words to explain and finished lamely, "I'm not quite all there." She straightened. "Regardless, what I did was not fair to you, and it was horribly disrespectful to your family to do it here. I'm sorry. I hope that we can remain friends, because I have come to value our friendship." Julia thought that about summed it up.

Kurt listened calmly to her speech. "So that's it, then.

You intend to turn this into another one-night stand. We go back to being . . . ?"

"Friends," Julia said firmly. "Kurt, I have a son to think of."

"Is this really about him?"

Julia's eyes narrowed. "What's that supposed to mean?"

"Are you sure you're not using Nick as a shield against me?"

"That's not fair! Just because I'm not willing to be your sex partner—"

"Oh, I want more from you than just sex. Wait!" He caught her arm as she stalked past toward the bathroom. "We're not finished."

"Yes, we are!"

"Indulge me a moment. Play a little game with me."

"We don't have time for games," she hissed impatiently.

"It won't take long. You owe me," he added, shamelessly playing on her guilt. "I need some answers. I'll ask a few questions, and all you have to do is answer true or false, but you have to be honest." He nudged her into a chair and took the other one. "True or false: you're afraid of me."

She shot him a disparaging look. "That's ridiculous. We just had sex."

"True. You've been running away from me ever since we met. True or false: you hide things about yourself."

"I like my privacy."

"True. You're desperate that people not find out things about your past." Julia jerked up out of the chair as if he'd poked her, but his arm shot out and pressed her back as he tossed out his next question. "True or false: you're as wildly attracted to me as I am to you, and it scares the hell out of you."

"False! On both counts."

"True, on both counts. You're attracted to me. You hate it that you are, but there it is. And it scares you because you can't control it."

Julia sprang out of the chair, this time avoiding the reach

of his arm. "Your presumptuousness is surpassed only by the enormous size of your ego!"

"And what really scares you is that this might be more than just sex." Kurt stood and started toward her. "Why? What monsters haunt your dreams? Why does the thought of something more than a quick fuck send you diving for cover?"

Kurt stalked her across the room. The blood pounded in her head as each accusation hit home with devastating accuracy. How had she gotten into this? *Damn! Damn! Damn!* "Must you always psychoanalyze people?" She edged closer to the bathroom.

"Only when someone I care about seems bent on messing up her life, and mine."

"Well, you might care less about me soon."

Kurt cocked a dubious brow at her. "You mean when you tell me your deep, dark secret?"

"Yes." She slipped into the bathroom and locked the door behind her.

"Don't count on it," she heard him mutter through the closed door.

Julia covered her temples with her hands and saw the man's shaving kit on the counter. Of course—Kurt had moved in next door when he gave up his place in the cottage to the newlyweds. That's why he'd been close enough to hear her last night.

In the shower, she hashed out her options. Foremost, she wanted to end this latest muddle with Kurt on a better note than the last time. All three of their futures depended on an amicable resolution.

When she turned off the shower, Julia could tell from the sound of water running in the sink that she was not alone. She anchored a large bath towel firmly under her arms before she emerged from the shower stall. Without her glasses, Kurt was just a blurry lump over by the sink, but she could smell toothpaste and soap, and knew that he'd stopped what he was doing to watch her. "What are you doing in here?"

"Keeping an eye on you."

"Why?" He came toward her and didn't stop until he was so close that his features were fairly distinct and she could smell his shaving cream. He still wore only boxer shorts.

"I want proof." At her look of incomprehension, he went on. "If screwing me meant nothing, prove it. Show me. You shouldn't mind indulging me again. After all, you did it just a few hours ago, so what difference could it make?" As he talked, he traced a finger down her chest to her cleavage. Goosebumps rose on her arms. He hooked the towel and gently tugged just hard enough to bring her even closer or risk losing it altogether.

She tried to read him. "And if I do, you'll leave me alone?" she asked, calculating the odds that he was on the level. But her mind was already clouding. Her traitorous body *liked* his outrageous proposal.

"If you prove it."

She nodded and tried to sound indifferent. "Okay, but we'd better get on with it because—"

He released the towel with one quick tug. His hands roved over her in a tactile inspection, generating fire at points of interest until Julia felt breathless and dizzy. As inevitable and unstoppable as the rising sun, heat built to a feverish ache. She was ready even before he pulled her hard against him.

If their coupling during the night could be likened to the ebb and flow of a long summer storm, sometimes frenzied, sometimes soft and gentle, this time was as cataclysmic as a Caribbean hurricane. Reason drowned in a tidal surge of desire. Even when he lifted her onto the counter between the two sinks and knelt between her legs, doing things to her she had never imagined wanting to have done, she could summon no resistance, only small moans as her body sang to this new pleasure. And when he stood and pushed his way inside her, she clung to him in need, ignoring the lingering soreness for the pleasure.

Afterward, Julia leaned her forehead weakly against Kurt's damp shoulder, her arms loosely circling his neck as returning awareness of their stark surroundings dispelled the afterglow. Her rapid breathing mirrored his, hollow-sounding echoes of each other in the quiet bathroom. She grimaced in sudden embarrassment at the feel of cold, hard ceramic under her bare buttocks and Kurt still lodged inside her.

When she nudged him in the shoulder, he took his time easing away from her. Ignoring first his outstretched hand and then his narrowed eyes, she hopped off the counter unassisted. She winced when her feet hit the floor, and gingerly stepped over to pick up her bathrobe.

"Now we're even." She pulled on the robe, cinching it tightly in front, and fished her glasses out of the pocket.

Kurt leaned against the counter, watching her. "Lady, if that's what you think of as recreational sex, you ought to turn pro, because you'd be a gold mine with a little training."

Julia swung around, eyes flashing, but her retort died on her lips as her gaze riveted in horror on his limp penis. "You wretch! How could you?"

"How could I what?" He scowled, looking down at himself.

Incoherent, she slashed her hand at him and finally sputtered, "You didn't wear a condom, did you?" She didn't wait for an answer.

He followed her into her room. "Julia, I'm sorry—it was a mistake." He caught her arm as she furiously searched her luggage for something to wear.

She wrenched away and rounded on him. "A mistake? God, I must be suffering from terminal stupidity."

He watched her yank on underwear, slacks, and a shirt. "I forgot. We both got carried away." He realized then that he'd never seen her really angry before. Not like this. She was livid, practically in tears. She was also scared, he saw suddenly. "Calm down."

"Don't patronize me. Do you think it's easy to raise a child by yourself?"

Kurt gripped her by her shoulders to stop her frantic

packing. "Listen to me. If anything should happen, I will take care of you."

Beyond reason, Julia jerked free of his hands and lashed out with scathing sarcasm, "Oh, that is rich, under the circumstances!" Abruptly, she turned on her heel and marched into the bathroom.

"What circumstances?" He stood in the doorway as she prepared to insert her contact lenses. Already she was closing up, drawing that opaque curtain between herself and everyone else. "I think I finally get it. This Chadwick jerk knocked you up and then split, leaving you to raise Nick on your own. That's it, isn't it?" She said nothing, but her hand, poised to insert a lens, so trembled that she had difficulty performing the task. "Understand this: if you had my child, I would never desert you or the child. I would make sure that you were both well provided for."

Finished with her contacts, she fixed him with a cool look, her anger now firmly in check. "Don't treat me like some bimbo you can buy off and sweep under the rug." She made a quick swipe with her lipstick, then tossed it and the rest of her things into her purse.

Kurt scowled. "Damn it, Julia. I wouldn't buy you off. I wouldn't have to. Let me clarify: if Nick were my son, he would be with me." *And you would be, too,* he added silently. "No kid of mine is going to have an absentee father."

"With you?" A flicker of panic rippled across her cool facade.

"Why does that surprise you? Do you think I would walk away from my own child?"

"Nick has a family."

Kurt puzzled over her odd response. Her face had lost so much color she looked ready to topple over. "Nick needs a father," he countered gently.

"Well, fortunately for you, it's not your concern."

He reached for her hand and drew her into a loose embrace. She offered no resistance, but her spine was ramrod-straight. "I'd like it to be. Don't run away this time."

Julia barely heard him. Cold fear squeezed her chest. *If*

Nick were my son, he would be with me. She pushed out of his arms. ''It's over—I proved it in there.''

''Oh, no, sweetheart. You didn't come close. All you proved was that you want me as much as I want you.''

Julia shook her head. ''It was over five years ago.''

''Six.''

''What?''

''Six years ago.''

''Yes,'' she agreed.

''No. It was never over between us and I doubt it ever will be.''

''So all your grand talk about just wanting to be friends was nonsense.'' She glared at him.

''No—''

''You've been trying to get my back to the floor ever since we met. It's about sex. Another conquest.''

''That would make this a whole lot easier for you, wouldn't it? Do you really think I'm that hard up for a warm place to put it?'' Kurt shook his head in exasperation. ''I think we both know that what's between us goes beyond sex. No matter how great that is, it's just a symptom. The real question is, why are you so unwilling to acknowledge it?''

''Maybe because if I can't see this thing you're talking about, it doesn't exist.''

''If it didn't exist, you would never have gotten into bed with me the first time, let alone the second. And you would not be running so fast and scared now.'' An insistent knock sounded on Kurt's bedroom door. ''This isn't over, Julia,'' he warned. ''If you think you can just waltz in and out of my life again, you're wrong. I'm not going to go gently into the night this time.''

If Nick were my son, he would be with me. Reeling from what Kurt had said, Julia searched for Nick among the early risers breakfasting on the patio. She would gather him up and find Marcus. Flying home with Kurt was out of the question.

But the children had gone on a walk, she learned. And Marcus had yet to put in an appearance. With Alex already gone on her honeymoon, he was the only one left she could turn to for help. She declined Mrs. Livingston's offer of breakfast but begged for a cup of tea.

"In the kitchen," she directed her. "Not much call for more than coffee out here. And Mrs. Weston might be able to tell you where the children were headed."

"They went for a walk up the beach," Pat told her a moment later, setting a cup of tea on the island counter for Julia. Although on the surface Kurt's mother seemed cordial, there was a noticeable chill in her eyes that made Julia uneasy.

"Have a seat," Carolyn invited over her breakfast when Julia was about to leave. "Cassie won't keep them out long, because it's supposed to rain. I thought it would be all right since you and Kurt aren't leaving until this afternoon."

Julia carefully set her cup down. "There's been a change of plans. I need to get home earlier, so Nick and I will try to catch a ride with Marcus this morning."

Carolyn sent her mother a quick look. "I'm sorry to hear that," Pat said. "But before you leave, I'd still like to show you where I've hung your painting, if you have a minute."

"We could do it now," Julia suggested.

Pat led the way down a short hallway to a spacious sunroom. Julia could tell this was where the family spent much of their time. Family photographs hung in clusters on several walls. She spotted her painting prominently displayed above a white marble fireplace and wandered over to it.

"It's a lovely setting," she said, meaning it. The bright, open space complemented the summer theme and colors of the painting. "I confess I had half hoped this piece wouldn't sell, but it looks perfect here." She glanced at an adjacent cluster of photographs of children playing on a beach, her attention caught by the eerily familiar face of a young boy with curly blond hair, gray eyes, and an impish smile. Pat came up next to her.

"That's Kurt when he was about six," she said. "His hair is a little darker, but it's amazing, isn't it? The resemblance between my son and yours."

Julia struggled to cover her shock. Her safe little world was crashing down around her ears. "Yes, it is. It's remarkable how similar children can look in photos as long as their coloring is the same." She tried for casual, but her voice wavered. Desperation created inspiration, and she continued, "It must be something about cameras. Nick looks just like childhood pictures of my father."

As if on cue to rescue her, a hung-over looking Marcus poked his head into the room and, seeing them, came in. After a minute, Pat remembered she had muffins in the oven and left.

"I heard you were looking for me. Everything okay?" he asked as soon as they were alone.

"Oh, God, Marcus! You were right about Kurt. If he finds out about Nick he might try to take him." She quickly gave him an abbreviated version of her conversation with Kurt this morning, carefully omitting that she'd slept with him. Marcus immediately offered to give them a lift back to Cherry Beach, and they agreed to meet in forty-five minutes.

"Thank you, Marcus. I've got to rethink this whole plan. Promise that whatever happens, you won't tell him." She touched his sleeve urgently.

Marcus covered her hand. "Of course. When are you going to realize I'm on your side? I'm glad you've come to your senses."

"No one can know now, at least not until I have a chance to think this through—especially not Kurt!"

"Exactly what am I not supposed to know?" Kurt asked, coming into the room. Vanessa trailed along in his wake.

Julia snatched her hand from Marcus's sleeve. Panic rendered her speechless.

Marcus stepped into the void. "You'll have to excuse us, Weston. We were discussing a personal matter."

"Which evidently concerns me. So why don't you run along and let us discuss this in private." Kurt's glance included Vanessa in his dismissal, but she ignored him.

"Oh, but it does concern me," Marcus said, draping a familiar arm around Julia's shoulder. His voice was rushed, almost eager. "I think we can tell him, don't you, darling?" He smiled at Julia. At her look of alarm, he reassured her, "It's okay. Everyone will know sooner or later. You can be the first to congratulate us, Weston." Julia watched in wretched suspense as Marcus smiled triumphantly at Kurt. "Julia and I are engaged to be married."

The strangled gasp she heard was her own. She wondered fleetingly if she looked as stunned by Marcus's announcement as Kurt did. Her own astonishment left her beyond expression.

Finally, Kurt uttered a short laugh of incredulity. "You've got to be joking."

Marcus's arm tightened around Julia's waist, stopping her instinctive move toward Kurt. She felt as if she were trapped in a hideously surreal dream.

"It's no joke," Marcus said.

"This is ridiculous!" Kurt exclaimed.

"Believe it." Marcus made no effort to hide his satisfaction.

For a moment, Kurt looked ready to cram his gloating smile down his throat. Instead he turned cold, measuring eyes on Julia. "I want to hear it from you. Is this what you've been hinting at that you had to tell me?"

Marcus's fingers bit a painful warning into Julia's arm. She tried to think past the ghastly moment, racking her brain unsuccessfully for a way out short of the truth. She refused to risk losing Nick. She needed time to consult with a lawyer and think all this through rationally. Damn Marcus for doing this to her.

"Yes," she heard herself say. She flinched under Kurt's look of contempt.

"How long have you been engaged?"

"Since last week," Marcus said. She couldn't bear the look of betrayal that twisted Kurt's face before it hardened.

"You've been a busy girl. Why was it so hard to mention?"

Julia flushed. "Alex—we thought we should wait until after the wedding."

"I see." As he turned to leave, he seemed to remember something and stopped in midstride. "Your son is back."

As soon as Kurt and a pleased-looking Vanessa left, Julia angrily shook off Marcus's arm. "Damn it, Marcus! Have you lost your mind?"

"It was the best I could do in a pinch. You looked ready to faint. And actually, in hindsight, I think it may be the perfect solution—it will keep him away from you. Did you want to tell him the truth?" Julia grimly shook her head. "I didn't think so. Go collect Nick. I'll be back as fast as I can."

"They've been seeing each other for years, so it really isn't all that sudden."

Julia heard the tail end of what Vanessa was saying to Carolyn and Pat when she entered the kitchen a minute later. In addition to Kurt and the three women, several other wedding guests were present, but no Nick. On Julia's entrance everyone fell silent—confirmation, if she needed it, that they'd been discussing her supposed engagement to Marcus. Vanessa acted as though the whole debacle were a parlor game for her entertainment, while Kurt stood expressionless on the far side of the large kitchen.

Vanessa broke the awkward silence. "Congratulations on your engagement." She smirked. There were several murmurs of assent, but conspicuous silence from the Weston contingent.

"Thank you." Julia glanced around uncomfortably. "I was just looking for Nick."

Carolyn started to say something but broke off when the

two boys, each clutching a muffin, clattered into the kitchen from the patio with the nanny, Cassie, close on their heels.

"Mama!" Nick ran across the room into her arms. "You're awake."

"Yes, I am." Julia forced a smile and hugged him tight. "And we've got to get ready to go because we'll be leaving very soon."

"But I want to play soccer with Andrew," he whined loudly. "Cassie said we could."

"Sorry, pilot. We have to go home." Julia noticed his shorts. "Where did you get these?"

"Nana got—"

"Nana?" Julia interrupted.

"That's what Andrew calls her." Nick pointed a short finger at Pat, who smiled fondly at him. "an' she said I could, too." Julia looked over at Pat and was taken aback by the censorious look the older woman returned.

". . . an' then Nana took me up to get my clothes," Nick was saying, "but I got scared 'cause I thought your arm looked funny, but it was Kurt's arm, an' then Nana said we should go an' get Andrew's shorts." Too late Julia realized what Nick had seen, and froze in horror as he innocently delivered the final stroke. "Mama, why was Kurt sleeping in your bed? I asked Nana but she said I had to ask you."

Julia's mortification was beyond anything she could ever have imagined. Her face flamed and a dull roar sounded in her ears. The sudden hush in the room was tangible. Everyone seemed to have heard Nick's question. As if in slow motion, she saw shock register on their faces as they gaped first at her and then Kurt. All except Pat Weston.

Pat must have seen them together! That's why she'd received a chilly reception this morning and an even icier one a minute ago after the announcement of her engagement. What must they think of her? She felt filthy—ostensibly engaged to one man while another man's semen dripped into her underwear.

Julia finally managed to break the dense silence that had descended. "We'll talk about it later, Nick," she whispered.

At a loss for what to do next, she raised her gaze in agony, desperately trying to summon a way out.

Rescue came from the quarter she least expected. "Cassie," Kurt spoke up, "take the boys outside for their snack. Then, if there's time before Miss Griffin leaves, they can play soccer in the front yard."

"Yes, Mr. Weston." The nanny quickly crossed the room and took Nick's hand. Julia mumbled something about having to finish packing and beat a hasty retreat from the kitchen. A moment later, Kurt cut Vanessa off in midsentence and strode toward the doorway through which Julia had disappeared.

His mother caught his arm as he passed. "I'd like to have a word with you, Kurt."

"Later, Mother."

Kurt heard water running in the bathroom when he let himself into Julia's room. He figured he was a fool for coming within a mile of her when he was this angry, but damn it, she owed him some answers. The longer he thought about it, the more her engagement to Marcus had *bogus* written all over it. She'd looked as astonished as he'd been when that little shit had made his gleeful announcement. But then, why hadn't she denied it? And if their engagement wasn't what she'd been hiding from him, what was? What secret could be so important to her that she would suffer through the kind of public shame she just experienced in order to protect it? She'd just stood there, looking as though she thought she deserved to be stoned in the village square, until he hadn't been able to stand it anymore.

Julia emerged from the bathroom a minute later with a towel cinched around her hips. She still had on her shirt.

"Were you able to scrub away all that sin?"

She spun around to find him lounging in one of the easy chairs. "What are you doing here?" She'd thought they were finished. Yet here he was, apparently ready for the next skirmish. She began to doubt her chances of escaping Belle House with any skin intact. Her messes were feeding off each other, compounding at every turn until finally they'd outstripped her ability to keep up.

"We could just sew a scarlet *A* on your shirt."

She flushed. "You shouldn't be here. It will only make matters worse."

"Too late. When eight people know something—not to mention two little boys prone to chatter—you can assume that everyone will know, including your fiancé."

She glanced nervously toward the door and then back to his cold, measured stare. "Look, if it's an apology you want, I'm truly sorry I got you into this. I know it must have been dreadful for you to have this all come out in front of—"

"Save the mea culpa. I'm not interested."

"Then what?"

Evidently reading the direction of her thoughts, his dark gaze slid down her body to rest on the towel she clutched, and he laughed at her. "Don't worry, sweetheart. I'm not into sharing. I came for some answers. The more I think about this engagement of yours, the more the pieces don't fit. Come on, you and Marcus? It doesn't add up."

"You said yourself that Nick needs a father."

"Not Fuller."

"Why not?"

"What do you know about him? What makes you want to marry him of all men?" Kurt looked baffled.

"He's a good man. He's good with Nick."

Kurt snorted derisively. "Lady, you've been had—in more ways than one."

Julia's back stiffened. "I don't owe you any explanation. I'll marry whomever I please." She snatched a skirt out of her duffel and started toward the bathroom, only to have her path blocked by Kurt, who had the advantage in distance.

"Oh, yes, you do owe me. Remember? I'm the guy you invited into your bed last night without bothering to mention that you were engaged. And I'm going to tell you a little about the man you're planning to marry whether you want to hear it or not, because somehow, for some reason I haven't quite figured out, he's managed to bury you under a pile of bullshit!''

Julia shrugged. ''Go for it, if it will make you feel better.''

Kurt scowled at her. ''This is a guy to whom the concept of a hard day's work is a curiosity. He's a parasite. He lives off people. For him it's become something of a cottage industry because most of his get-rich-quick schemes blow up in his face. He's always one scandal away from a prison sentence, and probably would be there already if it weren't for his family.

''You say he's 'nice'? Smooth, yes, charming, maybe, but not 'nice.' Con men are never nice. I'd bet my last dollar that he wants something from you. And tempting as you are, it's not you. I doubt he's capable of loving anyone but himself. I don't know what it is. Maybe your land.'' She shifted uneasily at the mention of her land, and his eyes narrowed. ''Watch your back. Greedy men can be dangerous.''

''Thanks for your concern,'' Julia said as coolly as she could with a towel wrapped around her naked bum and her heart in her throat. ''But the man you describe bears no resemblance to the man who's been my friend for many years.''

''Suit yourself.'' Kurt gave an indifferent shrug and leaned against the doorjamb, continuing to block her escape. ''But if he's so great, why was I the one in your bed last night?''

She looked away but answered evenly. ''I told you before—it was the nightmare.''

''So if Marcus had been here instead of me, you would have slept with him?''

She met his eyes, dying a little inside. ''Exactly.'' When had his good opinion come to matter so much? she wondered, watching his gray eyes take on an even more wintry hue.

A light tap at the door preceded Marcus's lowered voice from the hallway. ''Julia? Let me in.'' The doorknob jiggled. Fortunately, Kurt must have thought to lock it.

''Speak of the devil . . .'' Kurt muttered.

''Please leave!'' Julia hissed at him.

"Why?" he asked with a humorless smile. "All the action is right here."

"I'll be down in a minute, Marcus," she called out.

"Let me in!" he demanded in a more insistent whisper. "We need to talk."

"I'm changing my clothes. I'll see you downstairs." She turned to Kurt, "Go!"

"Now that we're engaged, I think it would be all right if you let me into your room. I'll turn my back." Marcus's voice was muffled, but clear enough to convey his growing irritation.

"This is getting more interesting by the second." Kurt crossed his arms, showing no inclination to leave.

Julia glared at Kurt, then called out, "Please, Marcus, I said I'd be down in a minute."

"Maybe you don't know him so well after all." Kurt's eyes were gleaming as he took a catlike step closer to her.

She stiffened when he reached out a hand and traced a warm path down her cheek. "Kurt!"

"Don't blame me; you made up the rules. Now you have both a fiancé"—his arm wrapped around her shoulders, cutting short her flight as his mouth lowered to tease the back of her neck—"and a lover."

Julia broke free of his light hold and hurriedly pulled on underwear and skirt beneath the towel before discarding it. Dressed, she met the amused gaze that mocked her attempt at modesty.

"What happened to your aversion to sharing?" she asked over her shoulder as she hefted her luggage and headed for the door.

"It doesn't appear that I am."

Outside, the marble gray sky looked ready to drop its load as Marcus stowed the luggage in his car and Julia collected Nick. Already the first few drops splattered dry earth, creating a musty smell that had Marcus hurrying awkward farewells to the gathered Westons. As they pulled away, Julia looked back at the man who had been sometime friend, twice lover, and now, more than ever, adversary. That thought saddened her even as it sent a chill down her arms. Once again he'd managed to threaten her carefully constructed life. Not since Nick's birth had she felt such fear and uncertainty about the future.

After Marcus's car turned out of sight, Pat looked at her son. "Would you please explain to me just what is going on between the two of you?"

Kurt sighed. "We'd better discuss this inside," he said as the rain came.

Pat chose the same place as for her earlier, disappointing conversation with Julia. Kurt wandered over to Julia's painting and glanced at it. "I know it must have been unpleasant for you to walk in on us this morning."

Pat interrupted him with an impatient wave of her hand. "Is that what you think this is all about?"

"Isn't it?" he asked cautiously.

She planted her hands on her waist. "Well, walking in on my son in bed with one of our guests was hardly the high point of my day, but it pales next to the fact that I have a grandson I didn't know existed until two days ago!"

"What on earth are you talking about?"

"Don't you know? I'm talking about Nick. Your son."

A rueful smile smoothed out his irritation. "So that's what this is all about. I don't know if it will come as a relief or a disappointment, but Nick is not my son. To be quite frank, before last spring, it had been six years since I'd seen Julia. Nick is four."

She picked up a large glossy photograph that Alfred Livingston had found for her and handed it to Kurt. "Then how do you explain this picture of the two of you taken here at Breakers *five* years ago. The staff photographer took it at the season-opening dance. Look at the date, Kurt! Eight months before Nick was born. Open your eyes," she added, pointing to the same photograph that had caught Julia's attention earlier. "The boy looks exactly like you at his age."

Chapter 19

It was a symptom of her apprehensive mental state that Julia couldn't settle down the next day. Endless tossing during the night left her feeling tired and edgy. In the morning she took Nick and Dustin into the village to run errands, then dropped them at the lodge with Susan. She yearned to take the afternoon off and sleep, but the pressure to produce and sell overrode that luxury. So she rolled open the studio doors and went through the motions of working. In fact, she spent considerable time watching marshmallow clouds slide across the cobalt blue sky.

She wouldn't be able to work with the studio doors open much longer. The day had a restless feel that mirrored her mood, a hint of chill that presaged the imminent change in seasons. In another week, Nick would be starting school in the village kindergarten. Julia sighed at the thought as she slid a Rachmaninoff CD into the boom box. She leaned down to scratch Bowen's ears until he grew bored and loped off.

As she worked, the weekend debacle at Belle House was never far from her mind. It was the not knowing that made her edgy. There were too many wild cards in the deck—

Pat Weston, for one. How strong were her suspicions, and would she voice them to Kurt? Julia fervently prayed that with Marcus in the picture, Kurt would realize it was over between them and keep his distance. Yet, unexpectedly, she also found herself mourning the inevitable loss of his friendship. Somehow, without fully realizing it was happening, they really had grown close. She would miss that. And she was not the only one who would miss him; already Nick was talking about building a tree fort with Kurt's help. But at least until she could consult with a lawyer and decide the best course of action, Kurt would be off limits for Nick, too.

Frequently as the afternoon wore on, she found herself nervously looking over her shoulder to the open wall, half expecting to see Kurt standing there. So, for an instant, she doubted her eyes when she glanced up and did see him framed in the wide opening, silent and unmoving. For a time, he continued to regard her with an unreadable expression. Heart pounding, she waited for him to say something.

"It was five years ago," he finally said. His eyes did not leave her face as he came into the studio toward her.

She smothered a rush of panic. "I'm sorry? What was five . . . ?" Her voice trailed off when he tossed two large photographs down on the worktable in front of her. Warily she picked up the one on top. It showed them dancing together in the ballroom at Breakers five years ago. The date was neatly noted in the border. She dropped the photo and didn't bother to pick up the other one, which she could see was of her onstage that same night.

He eyed her coldly. "I think you know perfectly well what I mean—it was five years ago, not six, when we met."

"So?" She hid her shaking hands under the worktable.

"Nick was born eight months later."

"Oh." She feigned a look of dawning understanding. "So you think—"

"Nick is my son."

She gave a short laugh of disbelief. "This is unbelievable! One time five years ago and you think you're a father. Do you do this to all your old flames who have kids, or am I just lucky?''

''I've been very careful to prevent this from happening. You've been my only slip.''

''I find that hard to believe.''

''Frankly, I don't care what you believe.'' Julia met his eyes briefly. He looked cold, remote, dangerous—a stranger. ''We can do this the hard way or the easy way,'' he went on. ''Is Nick my son?''

Her mind raced, considering options and consequences, risks and benefits, and settled on the prudent course. She wasn't going to admit anything without consulting an attorney. ''As I already told you,'' she said, working to keep her voice steady, ''Nick's father died a year ago. But I can see the only thing that will satisfy you is proof.'' She slid off her stool. ''It's in the house.''

In silence, Kurt followed her across the yard. She left him in the living room while she went upstairs to find the papers she hoped would allay his suspicions. When she returned, he dropped a thick document onto her desk. He'd been looking at the loan agreement Marcus had arranged for her, she realized, irritated at his intrusion. She handed him two documents: the first, Nick's birth certificate, identifying Hugo as his father; the second, Hugo's will, leaving the bulk of his modest estate in trust for the education of his son, Nicholas Jason Chadwick. She watched Kurt carefully inspect each document. At length, he pulled a small notepad out of the pocket of his sport coat, briefly wrote something in it, then handed the papers back without comment.

''Where's Nick?'' he asked, turning toward the door.

She eyed him in confusion, uncertain whether her ploy had worked. ''He's playing with Dustin. Why?''

''Tell him I'll be by this weekend to get started on that tree house.''

''I don't think that's a good idea.'' She expected an argument, but he merely nodded his acquiescence and left.

She scurried after him across the porch and yard to his car, desperate to know if he believed her, but not wanting to give him any reason not to. When it looked as though he was going to get in his car and drive off without another word, she could stand it no longer. She had to know.

"Well, I'm glad I was able to put all this to rest so easily. It must be a great weight off your shoulders." Her words rang hollow and over-bright in the silence.

He stopped with his hand on the open car door and looked at her. "If you're asking whether I bought that dog-and-pony show in there, the answer is no. I know desperation when I see it. And lady, right now you're so desperate you'd do just about anything to keep me from the truth. You see, the disguise you normally wear so well slips when it comes to Nick."

Julia suddenly became aware of the barely leashed fury behind his icy exterior. He hated her. The force of it hit her like a physical blow. "What will it take to convince you?"

"A blood test."

Panic tightened its grip. "That's ridiculous! I won't agree to it!"

"Oh, but you will. From now on we play by my rules. And believe me, you're not going to like them at all. In fact, you will regret this day for the rest of your life because this is one battle I intend to win."

Looking at the ruthless set of his mouth, she believed every word he said. Feeling sick and sweaty, she stared at him as he climbed into his car and started the engine. In the next instant, fierce anger caught up to her fear as the threat to the very heart of her life hit home. She would win because she had no other choice.

She straightened. "Are you threatening me, Mr. Weston?"

He sneered at her through the open car window. "Call it a warning shot across your bow, *Miss* Griffin. I don't need to resort to threats. My next shot will hit you broadside." He began to back out, then shifted into neutral. "By the way, you'll be making another big mistake if you sign that loan agreement in there." As if to justify his interest in the matter, he added, "Just looking out for my son's future."

Shaking uncontrollably, Julia stood until his car rounded the curve of the inlet road. Then she sank down onto her knees in the dirt.

"He's not your son! He's mine!" she screamed at his departing car. Her wail lifted in the wind to join the lonely chorus of gulls and waves and rustling dune grass.

Chloe had to run to keep up with Kurt as he strode across the outer office toward his inner sanctum. "I cleared your schedule for today. Is there something I should know?"

He ignored the question. "Good. Did you talk to the bank about Julia Griffin's outstanding loan?" Chloe trailed him into his office. He stared out the window at the few visitors enjoying the waterfront this late in the season.

"Yes. They're happy to sell her loan for the price you authorized, but—"

"Buy it. Have them continue to administer it."

"But, Kurt, the loan is nearly at the end of its life and there's a rather large balloon payment due soon."

"When?"

"Three months. The bank turned down her request for an extension."

Kurt's mouth twisted into a grim half smile. "All the better. See to it immediately. And get Sam Livingston on the phone. He's the private investigator I had you contact about our mystery surveyor. After I finish with him, put me through to my lawyer."

"I'll get right on it." But still she lingered in the doorway until he looked up, surprised that she was still there. "How was the wedding?"

"Enlightening."

"What's with him?" Frank asked Chloe as she softly closed the door to Kurt's office.

"I don't know, but I don't like it." She sat down at her desk and reached for her Rolodex.

A minute later, Kurt was on the phone with Sam Livingston. "I've got another job for you."

"Some people can't stay out of trouble," Livingston said with the easy familiarity of a childhood friend. "What's up?"

Kurt heard Livingston's chair squeak as he got down to business. "I need you to dig into the backgrounds of two people."

"Got my shovel right here. Who?"

"Hugo Chadwick. He died about a year ago in London." Kurt rattled off the address he'd copied from the will. "I want to know who he was, what he did. And Julia Griffin." Kurt heard Livingston's chair squeak again in the momentary silence.

"The babe you've been chasing."

"*Was.* And I wasn't chasing her."

"Whatever you say. How deep do I dig?"

"I want to know everything. Especially anything having to do with the birth of her son, Nick. It was here in Cherry Beach, five years ago this February. Her doctor, any medical records you can get your hands on, the men in her life—especially men, even casual." Kurt heard Livingston's boots hit the floor with a muted thunk.

"Not looking at a paternity rap, are you?"

"No. I'm bringing one."

Ted found Julia a lawyer the next day, one who specialized in family law, and she was able to get an appointment to see him a few days later. In the meantime, a process server delivered Kurt's opening salvo. Susan was shocked when Julia showed her the complaint. "You're being sued by Kurt Weston! Whatever for?"

"Read on," Julia said grimly.

Susan skimmed the allegations, reading key parts aloud as she went:

"On . . . defendant delivered a child, Nicholas Jason Chadwick . . . Defendant was unmarried from the date of conception until the birth of the child. Plaintiff

wishes to institute a paternity! *proceeding against defendant, Julia Griffin . . . Defendant became pregnant with the child in Harbor Springs . . . on June . . .*"

Susan's voice trailed off, her eyes wide with shock. "So he is Nick's father."

Julia subdued a hysterical urge to scream. "Wonderful. If even you believe it, what chance do I have?"

"Well, is he Nick's father?"

Julia was silent as she considered how much she should tell her. What if Susan had to testify at some future time? Then she realized that if things went that far, it wouldn't matter anyway. And suddenly, she wanted to tell her the truth. Maybe that would erase the bad taste left in her mouth ever since she'd lied to Kurt.

She met Susan's puzzled gaze with an apologetic look. "Yes, he is. I'm sorry, I should have told you before this."

"It's okay. You didn't owe me an explanation." But she still looked confused. "Why is this coming up now? I thought you told him before Nick was born?"

"I left Kurt a note. Apparently he never got it."

"Oh, Julia."

She looked away from Susan's sympathy. "I was going to tell him after Alex's wedding. Then it was too late. Kurt's mother seemed to suspect from the first. It turns out Nick bears a striking resemblance to Kurt as a boy."

Susan squeezed her hand. "Hey, this will all work out."

"He hates me. He'll do everything he can to get Nick away from me."

"You don't know that. Kurt is a reasonable man. He's angry now, but that's natural. Give him time. I think he cares too much about both you and Nick to hurt you."

Julia felt a twinge of hope until she remembered the look on Kurt's face and his chilling prophecy. He intended to exact his revenge in blood—*hers.*

* * *

By Ted's account, Henry McGinn had left a big-city law practice at his wife's urging, to retire to the resort life up north. But McGinn found the endless rounds of golf and beach-walking dull, so he'd compromised and set up a part-time practice on the other side of the peninsula in the county seat.

Julia studied him while he reviewed Kurt's complaint, and was satisfied with what she saw: a certifiable triple-A personality from the top of his neat comb-over to the toes of his shiny Allen-Edmonds. He was coolly professional rather than friendly, and not physically imposing, yet there was something scrappy about him that she found reassuring. She didn't need a friend. She needed a fighter, someone who could go toe to toe with Kurt's lawyers.

McGinn looked up from the complaint. "If I am going to represent you, I need to have answers to certain questions that you may find uncomfortable. I assure you that nothing you say will leave this room without your approval. Obviously, the first question is whether Mr. Weston is in fact your son's biological father." When Julia hesitated, he gave her a stern look. "The truth, mind you."

"Yes."

"Are you sure? Were you sexually intimate with any other man within a month of the estimated date of conception?"

"I'm sure." His silence prodded her to add, "There was no one else."

He nodded, satisfied, and then questioned her briefly about the nature of her relationship with Kurt and the reason for his delay in bringing the suit. Finally, he leaned back in his chair. "The first thing we need to do is file an answer acknowledging Mr. Weston's paternity."

"No!"

He held up a hand to forestall further protest. "Please, hear me out." He waited until she nodded. "It would be useless to continue to deny the truth. Useless and possibly harmful to your case when your deception is exposed. Ultimately, it can only weaken our position and credibility, and for no good reason, because the fact of Mr. Weston's paternity eventually will be proved no matter what we do.''

''There must be something you can do to stop it!''

''No,'' McGinn said firmly. ''His attorney will request a blood test—may have already—and the court will grant it automatically. If there is a match, and there will be from what you've told me, paternity will be presumed by the court.''

Kurt's cold vow echoed sickeningly in her head: *''From now on we play by my rules.''*

''Your case is quite simple,'' McGinn was saying. ''It all boils down to setting child support for you and establishing visitation for the father, if he so desires.''

''What about custody?'' She crossed her arms, holding herself together.

''Do you have reason to think Mr. Weston will seek legal or physical custody?''

''I think he'll try for both. It's what I fear most. Can he succeed?''

''That would be extremely unlikely. On this, at least, I can offer you some peace of mind. When parents disagree over custody, a judge must determine what's in the best interests of the child. It would be highly unlikely to award physical custody to the father in a case such as yours where there is a long-established custodial arrangement with the mother.''

Julia felt weight lifting from her shoulders as hope cautiously resurfaced. Maybe they would be all right after all.

''What makes you think Mr. Weston will seek custody?''

''He once told me that if Nick were his son, he would be with him. That, and I've crossed him in an unpardonable way. I doubt he'll be happy until he brings me to my knees. Taking Nick would accomplish both objectives.''

McGinn gave her a skeptical look that said he thought she was being overly dramatic. ''What he might want in the heat of the moment and what he'll be able to get are two very different things. His lawyers will give him a reality check if necessary. Are we agreed, then, that I'll go ahead and file an answer admitting paternity?''

''Do I have a choice?''

He smiled at her grim attempt at humor. ''In theory, yes. In practice, no.''

''All right then, I agree.''

''I'll move this along as quickly as possible. We'll meet again before the hearing.''

Before she left, Julia asked him to take a look at the loan agreement Marcus had left for her to sign. ''I'm not a business lawyer, but I'll take a look. We'll go from there.''

Julia left McGinn's office a little calmed and drove to the gallery. She'd cut back on her hours there after the success of her show—financially she now did better with her artwork than she could at the gallery—but this week she was filling in for a student who had to return to college before Alex closed up for the season. That reminded her that Alex should have returned from her honeymoon yesterday. She needed to call her before she heard any gossip about the lawsuit.

Cautiously upbeat for the first time in days, Julia was humming when Marcus's father came into the shop. She recognized him from Alex's wedding, although somehow they had never been introduced.

''Mr. Fuller.'' She smiled as she crossed the gallery to him. He was a flushed, dissipated version of Marcus. The resemblance was unsettling.

''Oh, good! You know who I am.'' He smiled and took her hand. ''When I heard that you work here, I had to come by and welcome you to the family.''

Taken aback, Julia gaped at him. With all her other worries, she hadn't given Marcus or their sham engagement much thought after they'd returned to Cherry Beach. He'd called once to ask whether she'd signed the contract for the loan, but she and Nick had been on their way out and they hadn't talked long.

''I know, I know; I'm not supposed to talk about it. Marcus said the two of you still had things to work out.'' He shrugged affably and admitted, ''Actually he told me to stay away from you, but I was having lunch next door and couldn't resist."

A boozy lunch, Julia guessed. He smelled as if he'd been pickled in gin.

"I can't tell you how happy I am that my son is finally thinking of settling down. He's had a lot of wild oats to sow, and frankly, I wasn't sure he ever would. But enough of that. *You* must be a very special lady."

"You're very kind, but—" Julia shook her head.

"Say no more. I understand." He winked and diplomatically changed the subject. "I suppose Marcus told you that I was a friend of your grandparents."

"Seth?" Julia asked, surprised again.

"No, the Marches. I represented your grandmother on a few matters at the end."

"I had no idea." She frowned. Brittle shards of childhood memories hovered just out of sight. She struggled to pull them into view, but she had blocked them too successfully for too many years to do so easily now.

"I can't imagine why Marcus never mentioned the connection," he went on.

"Maybe he doesn't remember," Julia said, distracted. What was she missing? Whatever it was dangled tantalizingly out of reach.

"Of course he does, especially considering . . . Well, maybe you're right. It was years ago."

"Considering what?" Her attention sharpened.

Charles Fuller shifted and glanced away. "I'm sorry, my dear, I was thinking of another old family friend. I'm not very good at remembering things anymore."

And not very good at lying, either. Julia was as baffled by why he would be lying as she was sure that he was doing so. What could he be hiding?

Marcus stopped by later that night to see if she'd signed the loan agreement. He wasn't happy to learn that his father had visited the gallery. His handsome face twisted into an angry grimace. Nonplussed, Julia glanced uneasily at Nick, who was staring wide-eyed at Marcus.

Marcus seemed to recollect himself the next instant. "I didn't want him bothering you." He blew out a breath and fell silent. Finally he looked up. "Dad is in the early stages of some kind of dementia, and mother is hell-bent on keeping it quiet. His drinking makes it worse. Half of what he says is off the wall." He frowned. "So what did he say?"

Julia cast a sidelong glance at Nick to see if he was still listening, but he was again hunched over the Legos Marcus had brought him. "Mainly, he welcomed me to the family. You'd better tell him the engagement is off. There's no need to go on with the charade."

"Why? I'm willing."

She sent a meaningful glance at Nick. "I'll tell you after I put him to bed."

Nick chose that moment to dart over with a handful of Legos and shove them under Marcus's nose. "Can you help me put it together?" he asked with a hopeful smile.

"Sorry, Nick, maybe another time." Marcus smiled and patted Nick's head in careless dismissal. "I need to talk to your mom now."

Julia saw the hurt in Nick's eyes and scooped him up on her lap. "I'm going to take you up to bed in a second, honey."

"Did he talk about anything else?" Marcus persisted.

"Do you have something particular in mind?" Julia asked, watching him closely.

"No. It's just that he often gets people and events mixed up."

"Well, he did mention that he used to represent my grandmother."

"Really. That's interesting. I wonder if it's true."

Marcus was edgier than usual. His nervously bouncing foot gave him away. Was it from embarrassment over a mentally deficient parent or from fear that his father had revealed something Marcus didn't want revealed? "He knew my grandparents' name—March. He wondered why you hadn't mentioned the connection to me.''

Marcus shrugged. ''I honestly had no idea. If he did represent her, it must have been before I joined the practice. Did he say anything else?''

''No. That was about it.'' He relaxed slightly, as if he'd narrowly avoided a pitfall. Or did she just see what she was looking for?

Immediately she felt ashamed. Marcus had been a true friend for years. She must not let Kurt's condemnation of him infect her own perception. On that guilty thought, Julia headed for the stairs with Nick. ''I'll just be a minute,'' she said over her shoulder.

She hurried Nick along with brushing his teeth and pulled the covers up over his Elmo pajamas. ''Good night, sweetheart, I love you.'' She gave him a tight squeeze.

When she turned to leave, Nick stopped her. ''Mama, does Marcus like me?''

Julia sat down next to him and peered into his serious face. ''Of course he does.''

''He never wants to play with me,'' he said glumly.

She stroked through his blond curls. It was true. Although Marcus always brought a gift for Nick, he seldom paid much attention to him. Unbidden, the way Kurt treated Nick came to mind.

''Kurt plays with me.'' Nick echoed her thoughts. ''But he never comes anymore.''

She looked at his dejected face and her heart twisted. ''He will, sweetheart. Kurt likes you very much. And I know Marcus likes you, too. It's just that he doesn't know how to play with kids. Some adults are like that.''

When she went downstairs, Marcus was seated at her desk. He stood and tossed aside a magazine. ''Julia,'' he began firmly, ''I don't want to put pressure on you, but you have to sign those papers or the offer will be withdrawn. It may not be quite what you'd hoped for, but as your lawyer, I don't think you have much choice here.''

Julia knew what she had to say would displease him. ''I

have made a decision, just this afternoon. I appreciate so much all you've done for me on this, but I can't take the loan."

"Why not?" he asked incredulously. "If there's something in particular that's bothering you, let's look at it."

"I don't have it. I gave it to a lawyer today to answer a couple of questions." She could tell he was offended by that and rushed on. "It doesn't matter anymore. Everything has changed. I have to get out from under that debt. The land conservation group has finally agreed to buy Deer Creek for the amount of my outstanding debt, plus a little extra." She paused. "Kurt has filed a paternity suit. I need the money to pay my lawyer."

"That son of a bitch!" Marcus exploded, surging to his feet.

She filled him in on Kurt's lawsuit, her meeting that morning with McGinn, and her negotiations with the conservancy.

"You know I can get you more money than that," he said when she finished.

"I know. Thank you. But this way accomplishes Seth's objective. I owe him that."

"Do what you have to. But about McGinn's analysis of your case—I think he's overly optimistic that you'll retain custody." Concern wrinkled his brow. "He doesn't know Kurt. My advice to you—and it's extreme—is to leave the country. Don't admit anything. Take Nick and go back to England before he can get a blood test. You'll be safe there and I can handle your affairs here."

Running had been her first instinct when the process server had delivered Kurt's complaint. She'd run before. She could do it again, even if it meant leaving this place she had come to love so well. But she didn't want that for Nick, to start over away from friends and family. If McGinn proved right, Nick would have the father he needed, she would still have her son, and they could stay right here.

She shook her head firmly. "I can't do that."

"Then marry me!" he blurted out. "I'm serious. You

must know how much I care about you. The only reason I haven't asked before is that I didn't think you would accept. Think about it. A mother, a father, a child, a complete family—that's what the judge would see. It would be difficult even for Weston to overcome."

Julia felt a tug of regret looking at his earnest face. "I'm touched, Marcus. More than I can say. But it wouldn't work—I'm not wife material." She made an apologetic face. "At this moment, I very much wish I were."

"At least let things stand as they are. Let everyone think we're engaged. An engaged couple will look better to a judge than a single mother."

She nodded slowly. That made some sense. "All right. As long as we agree that the arrangement is temporary and either of us can break it off at any time."

"Agreed. And Julia, just to be on the safe side, make sure your passports are in order."

When she walked him out, he stopped on the threshold and drew her into a light embrace. Then he leaned down and brushed her lips in a gentle, brotherly kiss. At first she found the kiss pleasant enough, until Marcus, encouraged by her acquiescence, began to kiss her in earnest. Instantly revolted, she jerked away from him.

Surprise quickly changed to irritation on his face, and then both disappeared behind a smooth mask. Julia broke the awkward silence. "I'm sorry. It's not you. I'm not interested in that kind of relationship. With anyone."

"It's okay," he reassured her with a thin smile. "I'm sorry, too."

But behind their polite expressions lay the unspoken fact that on at least two occasions she had not been averse to Kurt's attentions.

After Marcus left, Julia changed into her nightgown and settled down to ring Alex. She yawned as she dialed, utterly exhausted after days of worry on top of many fitful nights. Her wandering gaze caught on the lower file drawer of her desk. It was ajar. But she hadn't been in there in days, and she had a child lock on it to keep Nick out of her files.

Marcus. He'd been sitting at her desk when she came downstairs. What possible interest could he have in a bunch of old bills? Perhaps he'd been looking for note paper or something.

Alex answered after several rings, and Julia dismissed her suspicions as silly.

"Julia! Thank God. I tried to get through to you all afternoon."

"I was at the gallery most of the day. How was the honeymoon?"

"In a word, wonderful. I'll tell you about it later. There's something important I need to warn you about. Take a deep breath and sit if you're not already." Alex paused as if she was gearing up for something big. "A rumor is raging through the Weston clan that Kurt is about to sue you to prove that he's Nick's father."

"He already has," Julia said matter-of-factly. "Several days ago."

There was a short, stunned silence before Alex's voice rushed over the line. "Does this mean you told him? You sound so calm. What on earth is going on?"

"No, I didn't tell him. I think his mother figured it out. And I'm much calmer now than I was before I met with my lawyer this morning. He says Kurt won't be able to get custody of Nick. It will all boil down to visitation and child support."

"Thank God," Alex said again. "I've been worried sick. Rob said he's never seen Kurt like this before."

"Like what?"

"Rob called it 'battle mode.' After we heard the rumor, he stopped by Westco. Kurt would barely talk to him and refused to talk about you at all. Rob said the whole office seemed tense. Everyone was giving Kurt a wide berth."

Julia shivered and held tight to McGinn's assurance that she wasn't going to lose Nick.

"There's more." Alex hesitated. "There's another rumor, although I can scarcely credit it, that you're engaged to Marcus."

"We do have an arrangement of sorts." After gaining

Alex's promise not to tell anyone, even Rob, Julia began to untangle fact from fiction.

Alex groaned when she finished. "What surprises me most is that you slept with Kurt again. It's been years—I didn't think you even remembered how," she added dryly.

"I wish I hadn't."

"You do have a knack for choosing inopportune moments."

"To say the least," Julia agreed ruefully.

"When is the hearing?"

"McGinn thought it would be soon, maybe a couple weeks."

They talked for a few more minutes about Alex's plans to come up over the weekend to supervise the gallery's closing. Then Julia dragged herself upstairs to bed and instantly fell into the first good night's sleep she'd had since Alex's wedding.

Chapter 20

Several weeks later, in a cold October rain, Julia and Susan pulled up in front of the county courthouse. They waited in the hallway outside the courtroom until McGinn arrived. After a quick inspection, he nodded his approval of the taupe-colored suit and silk blouse Julia had carefully selected for the occasion. Pulling her into a quiet corner, he reminded her that, because she had formally acknowledged paternity, the sole purpose of the hearing was to establish temporary support and visitation. ''We're last on the docket, so the courtroom will be pretty much emptied out,'' he added.

Inside the courtroom, when their case was called, Julia took a seat at the defense table next to McGinn. The judge, a large, florid-faced man who appeared to have little humor left after years on the bench, flipped through the last file on his desk. Kurt's lawyer stood and identified himself for the record as Ben Rosen. He looked expensive and not from the area. Julia glanced over at the plaintiff's table and met Kurt's gaze. His gray eyes were as cold and hard as granite.

In short order, Rosen waived a blood test and offered temporary support in the amount of $4,000 per month, which

McGinn promptly accepted on her behalf. Julia had little time to be stunned by that staggering sum before the judge briskly moved on to the key issue of temporary visitation.

Rosen stood. ''Mr. Weston requests weekend visitation and Thursday evenings while the parties attempt to work out custody.''

''Will you be seeking some sort of joint custody arrangement then?''

''Yes, Your Honor.''

''Then I'll give you two months to try to work something out with the defendant. In the meantime, custody to remain with the mother. Every other weekend with plaintiff, plus one evening per week. Thanksgiving to plaintiff. Christmas to defendant.''

The judge rattled off visitation times so quickly that it took Julia a moment to grasp it.

''Thirty-six-hour weekend?'' Rosen asked without pause.

''No!'' Julia came to her feet, tensed for battle. McGinn was tugging her back into her seat. She hissed urgently to him, ''Nick's never been farther away from me overnight than the lodge.''

''Counselor, please remind your client that she is to remain silent.'' The judge sent her a black look.

McGinn gave her shoulder a warning squeeze as he stood. ''Yes, Your Honor. We request that you reconsider your decision as far as overnight visitation. We do not feel it is in the child's best interest to be separated from his mother overnight at this time. The child is very young, is not used to being away from his mother at night, and does not even know the plaintiff well.''

''Plaintiff?'' The judge looked at Rosen.

''Your Honor, the boy did spend considerable time with plaintiff over the summer. They are not strangers. Furthermore, defendant has only herself to blame that the relationship between father and son is not stronger, given that she withheld the critical information of plaintiff's paternity—even lied about it—right up until my client filed this suit. Defendant cannot now use the fact that Mr. Weston does not know his own son as well as a father should, to bar him from having the opportunity to get to know his son better.''

Sighing, McGinn shook his head. ''Your Honor, we need to focus on the best interest of the child here, which is his mother's primary concern. We merely request that visitation be set during this adjustment period so as to exclude overnight visitation, which the child might find traumatic. When and how plaintiff learned that he is the father of a child born out of wedlock is irrelevant to these proceedings. But, for the record, Miss Griffin did try to communicate the fact of her pregnancy to plaintiff by a written note that apparently did not reach him.''

The judge raised a hand to forestall Rosen's response. ''Given that defendant does not argue that Mr. Weston is unfit to care for the child, defendant's request is denied. Every other weekend overnight visitation to plaintiff.''

McGinn kept his hand on Julia's arm to warn her against further protest.

''Thirty-six-hour weekend visitation, Your Honor?'' Rosen asked.

McGinn interjected, ''We would of course prefer a shorter period, say, twenty-four hours.''

''We'll begin with twenty-four and reevaluate when we meet in a couple of months.'' The judge closed the file and stood.

And that, Julia realized in dismay, was that.

Outside, the rain had stopped for the moment, leaving behind a dense, penetrating fog. Julia and Susan stood talking to McGinn on the sidewalk in front of the courthouse. From above came the mournful honking of an invisible formation of geese. Suddenly, their ghostly shadows coasted by overhead. Julia shivered and drew her coat up around her neck. McGinn thought that their only chance to avoid the overnight visitation was to work out a deal privately with Kurt. He and his lawyer and sister had just come out, and they formed their own huddle some distance away.

"I'll be in touch with Rosen to hammer out a permanent visitation agreement," McGinn said. "I'll see if there's any wiggle room on the overnight, too. But better get used to the idea. Even if I can work something out for now, overnight visitation will be part of the final order."

On the courthouse steps, Kurt questioned his own lawyer. "What do you know about her lawyer, Ben?" His hard gaze slid over to where Julia stood talking with her lawyer and Susan Cleary. She looked composed now after her brief outburst in court. He watched her pull her coat together over the sleekly feminine suit underneath, obviously chosen to evoke an image of the boardroom rather than the art room. It worked. She looked beautiful, businesslike, and remote.

"McGinn's good. Used to have a top-drawer practice downstate before he came up here to retire. The retirement didn't take, so here he is. He's no pushover, if that's what you're asking."

"Do we have a chance?"

Rosen shrugged. "Hard to say. It might help if we could make Miss Griffin look a little less perfect. So far, my investigator has gotten squat to help us from the locals. My own mother would love her. As far as I can see, her only step off the straight and narrow was you."

"Maybe we're going about this the wrong way," Kurt mused. "Try looking at the people around her—Marcus Fuller, for one. On second thought, don't bother; my own investigator is already doing that. We can regroup when I hear from him." Carolyn tugged on his arm, but he ignored her. "When can I see my son?"

"Kurt!" There was a warning note in Carolyn's voice that made both men glance up just as a photographer began snapping their pictures. With him was a young man who'd been sitting at the back of the courtroom.

"Damn!" Rosen muttered under his breath. "I had a bad feeling about him. No comment!" he snapped in answer to the reporter's rapidly fired questions.

"How bad do you think it will get?" Kurt asked grimly as the pair made a beeline across the steps for Julia's camp.

The two women looked at the photographer with varying degrees of surprise and confusion. McGinn, though, veteran that he was, instantly sized up the situation and hustled the women off.

Rosen shrugged. "You're too well known and the story is too juicy not to attract some attention. Depends on how slow the news is. I warned you that it would become part of the public record as soon as we filed suit."

"She didn't leave me with much choice."

Rosen parted with them at Kurt's car. Carolyn was going with Kurt to Cherry Beach to pick up her own car. Kurt felt her watching him as he drove. Finally, he said, "Okay, what is it?"

"You could have given her more time before you filed a lawsuit. At least tried to work it out."

Kurt's face hardened. "Your sympathy for her is difficult to stomach, Carolyn."

"It's going to be tough for her when she finds out what your plan is."

"I have a right to my son, too, and if she gets hurt along the way, she has only herself to blame. For almost five years I've had a son and didn't even know it. For five years she's kept him away from me, time I can never get back. She didn't say one word, even this summer when I thought we had become friends. Even when she saw how quickly Nick and I took to each other. Christ, the kid is starved for a father's attention. No! Her betrayal of both Nick and me has spared me any concern I might otherwise have felt for her."

When he fell silent, Carolyn ventured softly, "You must really love her to want to hurt her so badly."

Kurt snorted. "I feel nothing for her except contempt and a scary desire to strangle her."

"Her lawyer said she sent you a letter," Carolyn pointed out.

"Another lie."

"Okay, then why do you suppose she didn't tell you about Nick?"

He shrugged, impatient with her. "You're the psychologist."

"It would have been advantageous to her—especially financially. My impression is they could have used the money. I keep wondering what she thought she had to lose. Ask her."

"There is no explanation that would excuse what she's done."

"That may be, but I know if circumstances had been different and I thought Andrew's father might take him away from me, I would have gone to the end of the earth to stop that from happening."

"Thanks for the tip," he said coolly and picked up his cell phone. "Have you got someone in place yet?" Kurt asked when Sam Livingston answered.

"Yeah, my brother Dennis."

"He's a photographer!"

"It's a perfect cover."

"Make sure he keeps his mind on the job. I'm not paying him to take pictures of birds."

On the way home, Julia dropped Susan off in front of the clinic and continued through town to the county road running north to Gull Inlet. She'd arranged to have Nick go home from school with one of his pals and had a couple of hours before she picked him up.

Distracted, she didn't at first notice the unfamiliar pickup following at a discreet distance. At times it was completely hidden in the gray mist. In the off-season, she usually recognized the few cars of her neighbors. She would have pulled off onto the grassy shoulder to let it pass, except the driver seemed content with her slow pace through the thick fog. Dismissing it, she was alternately worrying about whether Kurt's suit against her would make the newspaper and thanking God for finally sending clear proof this morning that she wasn't pregnant. The pickup's horn jerked her back to the present.

Alarmed, she saw that it was riding her bumper. Her speed had crept up too high to safely ease off onto the grass. The driver leaned on the horn again, inching menacingly closer until no more than dust could be separating them. *Jesus!*

Heart racing, adrenaline pumping, she pressed hard on the accelerator, negotiating through the fog more by memory and instinct than vision. Shuddering, the old Jeep opened some distance with the truck. But the pickup soon gobbled it up. It was on her and then beside her in an instant.

She caught a quick glimpse of the driver, recognizing him before he veered threateningly into her lane. Then, playing cat and mouse, he eased off, blocking any escape to the rear. They were flying through a gently sloping meadow, but woods crowded close to the road just ahead.

She made a split-second decision to take her chances in the field and sent the Jeep careening over the edge. Instinctively, she turned the wheel in the direction of the fall line. The soft, wet earth and tall grass grabbed at the Jeep's bouncing wheels, slowing it down until it rolled to a stop some distance from the road. After a moment, she heard the pickup roar away.

Her teeth chattered, and her hands shook so badly she couldn't get her seat belt off. She gave up and cradled her head in her arms against the steering wheel. Thank God Nick hadn't been in the car, was all she could think.

She heard another car creep past in the fog. The high pitch of the engine identified it as a small car, not the truck returning. She heard it pull over.

"Ma'am, are you all right?" Julia looked up into the anxious eyes of an unkempt young man who looked no more than twenty, and exhaled in relief. His blue jeans had holes in the knees and his chin sported a spotty blond stubble.

She assured him that she was fine. He'd been too far behind to see the accident.

They examined the Jeep. It looked all right and the engine still ran, but it was evident it would have to be towed out of the field. "Let me give you a ride home, or wherever you need to go," he offered. Julia accepted gratefully and they slogged back across the muddy field to his ancient Volvo. When she began to tell him how to get to the cottage, he exclaimed, "Why, I've just rented a little place in Gull Inlet!"

Julia sent him a quick, interested look as he pulled onto the road. Ted had mentioned that he'd rented the beach shack to a nature photographer. She'd been so preoccupied by the approaching hearing that she'd nearly forgotten. Unheated and perched on the windswept rim of the inlet about halfway between her place and the lodge, it was more suited as a summer camp than for this time of year. "I was surprised to hear that anyone would want to rent the place in the fall. It's not much."

"It's perfect for me. I'm a photographer," he explained. "I shoot mainly birds, wildlife, that sort of thing." He pointed a thumb over his shoulder toward the backseat, which was indeed strewn with loose photos and camera equipment. "Lot of species stop off here for a rest."

"You do realize it's unheated and has no running water."

"There's a wood stove." He grinned and shrugged. "It's a five-star resort compared to some of the winter camping I've done to get shots. You must be my other neighbor." He introduced himself. While she pulled herself together, he spent the rest of the ride trying to impress her with the hardships he'd faced on some of his shoots.

"Thanks for the lift, Dennis." She slid out of his car and waved as he turned around and bumped off toward the shack. Then she went inside and rang up Dan Farley. She was almost positive the man in the truck was one of the thugs who had accosted her after the music festival last summer—the little one with the scary eyes. Dan and his deputies had never found either one.

Julia and Nick spent a quiet weekend at the inlet. The Jeep was in the shop being checked over, and Julia didn't want to go anywhere anyway. Time with Nick suddenly seemed more precious than ever. The thought was never far from her mind that there would soon be times when he was away from her. On Sunday morning, she knew she could no longer put off telling him that Kurt was his father. The story had made the local papers Saturday, and on Sunday it leaped to national news. Alex called to commiserate. A Chicago paper had gotten hold of the pictures in front of the courthouse and a picture of Julia and Kurt at Alex's wedding. "Why is this even news?" Julia stared at a Tribune blurb: *Weston scion sues former London singer*. The story wasn't front-page news, but it was prominently featured in the Metro section.

"Sex, secrets, money, power, glamor—the usual reasons," Alex said.

Telling Nick about Kurt proved difficult. To Nick, Hugo was his father, even though he couldn't really remember him. At first he thought she meant she was going to marry Kurt, and he was overjoyed that Kurt would be living with them.

"No, sweetheart. I'm not marrying Kurt." His face fell. "Wait, Nick." She pulled him close. "You're going to get to see him a lot. He'll still be your daddy even if he doesn't live with us. He's not your stepfather—Hugo was like that to you. Kurt is your real father, like Uncle Ted is Dustin's father."

"Like Doug's daddy?" Nick frowned.

"Right. Doug's daddy doesn't live with them anymore, but he still sees Doug a lot." Julia closed her eyes and prayed for Nick's sake that Kurt lived up to the role he'd wrested from her.

"But Kurt doesn't come here anymore. Maybe he doesn't want to be my dad." Nick's worried eyes sought her reassurance.

"Oh, no, sweetheart. He very much wants to be your dad. The only reason he didn't spend time with you before is that he didn't know you were his son. He just found out."

"Why didn't he know?" His face looked curious and hopeful.

"It was a terrible mistake, Nick. I thought he knew, when

he really didn't. But now that he does know, he can't wait to be your dad.'' Julia knew she was putting a shiny gloss on a flawed picture, a picture that she'd created but that Nick would have to live with.

Chapter 21

"Miss Griffin . . ." a reporter shouted at her.

Julia fended off a microphone and tightened her grip on Nick's hand as she pushed through the melee outside Nick's school the next day.

A half-dozen reporters trying to get pictures and statements jostled aside twice that many parents waiting to pick up their children after the morning kindergarten session. The reporters pressed in on Julia and Nick, blocking their way. Anxious that she would lose him, she picked him up and held him tight against her chest. "Please let us through. I have nothing to say."

"You heard her," a voice called out over the din. "Let them through or I'll throw the lot of you in jail." Relief flooded through Julia at the sight of Dan Farley's fair head bobbing up behind the line of reporters. "Come on." He steered them through the throng to his police cruiser.

"My car . . ." she said as he bundled them inside.

He held out his hand. "Give me the keys. I'll have my deputy bring it out."

Nick chattered excitedly as they left the reporters behind. But between Julia and Dan there was a new distance that hadn't been there three days ago when he'd come out to take her statement about the car accident. Now he and the rest of Cherry Beach knew the truth about Nick's parentage and her own history with Kurt Weston—or at least the sensationalized stories the newspapers were passing off as the truth.

Dan cleared his throat. "Have these guys been bothering you at your house?"

Julia shook her head. "No. I'm getting calls on my answering machine, but no one has come to the house." She took a deep, calming breath and forced tense shoulders back against the vinyl seat. The sight of all those reporters, their callous aggression, unnerved her. "There were only a couple at school this morning."

"They followed you in from the inlet. I've had a deputy posted at your turnoff since Saturday afternoon. He radioed in that there were several guys parked there, waiting for you. We can't do much when you're out in public, but we should be able to keep them away from your house. As long as they don't come in by foot through the woods, which wouldn't surprise me." He glanced over at her. "The good news is, I expect the frenzy will die down in a few days."

"Thanks, Dan. I appreciate your thoughtfulness in putting one of your men out here."

He kept his eyes on the road. "Weston is picking up the tab. It was his idea."

"Oh." They lapsed into silence. When Dan slowed for the turn into Gull Inlet, Julia noticed the police car tucked in between some trees near Mrs. Hornig's house. She'd been oblivious to it when she passed by earlier.

As they neared the cottage, Dan said, "I've been rethinking our assumption that the guy who ran you off the road is the same thug as the one last summer. After what I've seen today, I'm looking at these reporters. One of them might have been trying to stop you and went overboard—these guys will do anything to get a picture. When you went off the road, he panicked and split."

Dan cut the engine and silence engulfed them. A cool

breeze stirred autumn leaves set ablaze by the midday sun. But for once, Julia was oblivious to the inlet's staggering beauty.

"That would make sense except they weren't around three days ago," she pointed out.

"There was at least one: the guy who took your picture at the courthouse. It doesn't take these guys long to pick up the scent."

Julia hoped Dan was right. Admittedly, she hadn't gotten a good look at the driver. But she worried that in his rush to find an easy answer, he was too willing to ignore other possibilities.

"I hope you're right about them being gone soon. . . ." Her voice trailed off. She glanced around uneasily.

"Something wrong?"

"No—well, I don't know." She got out of the car, scanning the yard. "Nick, stay in the car a minute." He was busy in the backseat using an action figure as a police radio.

Dan met her in front of the car. "What's up?"

"Probably nothing, but the dog usually comes running when a car pulls in. Bowen!" she called out. They heard a muffled answering bark from her studio. "He's inside."

She ran over and pushed open the door. Bowen launched himself out, practically knocking her down in his eagerness. "You scared me, you mangy mutt! How did you get in there?" she asked with mock severity. "You better not have gotten into any of my stuff."

Julia heard the sound of a small motor start up in the distance—a motor boat or a dirt bike, she couldn't tell which. She hoped dirt bikers weren't using the dunes again.

Dan came out of her studio holding up an uneaten half of a rawhide chew. "You give him this?"

"No." She looked at it, baffled.

"I'd better take a look inside." He loped toward the house. "Stay with Nick," he ordered over his shoulder. Julia saw him draw his gun before he disappeared around the corner and up the front porch. She understood then: he suspected someone had lured Bowen into the shed. A minute later, he came back to the edge of the porch and motioned for her to come.

"I assume you didn't leave things this way?" he asked when she stepped inside.

Julia stared at the mess. "No," she whispered. The contents of her files were scattered everywhere around the desk. Across the room, the closet door stood open and several boxes had been taken out and upended on the floor.

"This looks like more work of those paparazzi," Dan said tersely. "I'll bet he was here when we drove up. Probably went up the back trail on that dirt bike we heard."

Dazed, Julia walked slowly toward a pile of photos spilled on the floor. "It could have been a thief. Maybe someone thought I have money because of the Westons."

Dan shook his head. "Whoever did this was looking for information, not things."

He appeared to have thought of something else. She could almost see the wheels turning in his head. "Henry McGinn is your lawyer, isn't he?" She nodded, puzzled. "Funny, a few weeks ago someone broke into his office and really messed up *his* files. Looked a lot like this. We had no leads. Now I'm thinking there may be a connection with this." Dan glanced at her. "You don't seem surprised about McGinn's break-in."

"No. I knew about it. I asked him to look at a loan document for me and it ended up lost in the mess. It didn't matter. I decided not to go through with it anyway."

"What about your file in the paternity case? Anything missing there?"

"Not that I know of." She made another slow turn around the room, taking in the destruction. Outrage began to push aside shock as her mind started functioning again. A stranger had invaded her personal sanctuary, violated it, and for what? To ferret out purely private matters and splash them across the media.

Dan turned to the door. "I'm going to check in with my deputy and have him look along the road. Maybe we can get this creep."

* * *

Julia arranged to meet with Kurt at Sid's diner a few days later. His first visitation with Nick was scheduled for that evening. As a precautionary measure, she parked a short distance away. Although Dan's prediction had proved accurate—the reporters' presence had indeed dwindled during the week as they chased off after new stories, unfortunately leaving Dan and his deputies no closer to solving the break-in—she didn't want to push her luck. Kurt apparently had no such qualms, she saw as she turned the corner. His Jaguar sat right out front, announcing to anyone who cared that he was inside.

Kurt watched her cross the diner and slide into the booth opposite him. She was dressed in fawn-colored slacks and jacket rather than her usual jeans. He'd expected her to look anxious by now, even panicked, ready to throw herself on his mercy. Instead she looked annoyingly confident and composed, as if she fully expected him to agree to whatever it was she wanted from him.

She smiled her thanks when Sid set a cup of tea on the table in front of her an instant after she sat down. Then she looked up at him, her face serious, restrained. "Thank you for agreeing to meet with me. I didn't want to discuss this in front of Nick tonight."

"You told Chloe you would make it worth my while if I met with you. I'm waiting." He already had a good notion of what she wanted. Her attorney had been trying, unsuccessfully, to negotiate a visitation schedule that did not include overnight visitation. He'd come anyway, just for the pleasure of turning her down.

She nodded and got down to business. "Nick is not ready yet to leave home overnight. He needs time to get to know you better. He—"

"Is it Nick who's not ready, or you?"

"Both," she admitted. "But I'm here on Nick's behalf, not my own. What I—"

"Let me be perfectly clear: I won't give up one minute of time with my son."

"I'm not asking you to." She leaned toward him intently. He noted the determined set of her jaw. "I *want* you to spend as much time as you can with Nick, for his sake. Right now with the alternate weekend visitation and Thursday evening, you'll average fourteen hours a week, and for at least a third of that, Nick will be sleeping." From her bag she pulled a pen and pad with days of the week marked off. "What I propose is sixteen hours, spread out more evenly during the week and weekend, at your convenience, more like this. . . ." She drew in one long block of time and two shorter blocks. "You could have two to four times every week—whatever works for you—rather than the way it is now. And none of it at night when he's sleeping."

She looked up from the notepad. "But I have several conditions. First, no overnight visitations during this interim time. Second, you spend the first couple of times with him at Gull Inlet to give you both a chance to become reacquainted. Third, I don't want him anywhere near the construction area unless it's a very brief visit and you're right next to him every minute. I would prefer that you get another place away from there altogether." She took a breath. "And last, you let me know your schedule ahead of time and stick to it. I won't have Nick jerked around to accommodate last-minute changes in your business schedule."

She sat back in the booth and waited. Expectant silence hung between them.

It pissed Kurt off that she'd made him an offer he couldn't refuse. He wanted to send her away empty-handed. But more, he wanted that extra time with his son. As it now stood, on the odd weeks he would have Nick for a total of just two hours. What was in it for her? Why was she willing to give up time to him when previously she'd been determined to keep him out of Nick's life altogether? "Frankly, I'm surprised that you could bring yourself to make such an offer."

"Why? Because you think this is some sort of tug-of-war over Nick? Despite what you think of me, I've always tried to do what I thought best for him."

"And you thought not telling me about him was best?"

"I did try to tell you about him—"

"You expect me to believe that after everything that's happened?" he asked incredulously.

"It's the truth." Their eyes met and he almost did believe her. Almost. "And later, yes, based on the facts as I knew them, I thought it would be best not to tell you."

"You had no right," Kurt said harshly.

"I had every right!" She quickly caught herself and gritted her teeth. He saw her glance across the half-full diner. Several patrons hastily averted their eyes. "This isn't going to get us anywhere, and it's only going to hurt Nick if he sees us at odds." She sighed wearily. "So what's your answer? Do you agree?"

"I have one condition of my own." He eyed her without expression. "I keep the entire Thanksgiving holiday, four days and nights, just as the judge ordered."

Julia looked at him a long moment, evidently saw that he wasn't going to budge. "Okay." She began sliding out of the booth, but paused at the edge and looked at him steadily. "Don't hurt him, Kurt. I know how you feel about me, but don't take it out on him."

"He was *what?*" Kurt's astonished gaze snapped back across his desk to Sam Livingston's amused face.

"Gay. Hugo Chadwick was gay."

"So they were not . . . ?"

"By all accounts, they were friends and business partners. Nothing more."

Kurt examined the photos Sam brought back on the morning red-eye from London. Julia in a glamour shot. Hugo Chadwick, handsome in that narrow-faced English-upper-crust way. "But she lived with this guy."

"If you count having a separate flat in his town house, yeah. Her life in London was most remarkable by what it didn't include. For a woman who looks like she does, with a job like she had, there were no men in her life. I don't just mean that she didn't have a steady boyfriend—or girlfriend, for that matter—she apparently didn't date at all. She took art classes, worked in her art studio, sang—mostly in nightclubs, but sometimes in larger cabaret productions—and once or twice a year she took vacations to the seashore, by herself."

Kurt drummed his fingers. "What do you know about her life before London?"

"Just the bare bones, so far. Sad story. She was born in the British Virgin Islands. Mother died a few months after giving birth to a brother, Jack. Julia was twelve. Father and brother died four years later in the Bahamas under unclear circumstances. Found out that much from sketchy records at Briarwood Academy, where she enrolled after their deaths at age sixteen."

Where she met Alex, Kurt recalled. "Silk-stocking school. Who footed the bill?"

"Maternal grandmother, Mary March. She set up a trust for Julia before her death." Sam leaned forward in his chair. "Now here's the odd thing: Charles Fuller was the trustee who paid all Julia's bills at Briarwood. Turns out the Marches lived in Chicago, too. They evidently knew Charles well enough for Mary to designate him trustee of her granddaughter's trust."

"I'll be damned," Kurt muttered. Was this the source of the inexplicable connection between Julia and Marcus? Why had neither ever mentioned it?

"Other than that . . ." Sam shrugged. "If it's dirt you're looking for, I didn't find any."

"What about Marcus?"

Sam snorted. "Well, you know I could never stomach the guy, even when we were kids. He grows shady schemes faster than a chia pet. Unfortunately, he also covers his tracks pretty well—it's going to take a while. In the meantime, I got a copy of his rap sheet.'' He handed it over. ''He's the original Teflon kid—nothing sticks. This is interesting, too.'' He pushed another sheet of paper across the desk. ''Twice in the last five years he's been investigated by the attorney grievance commission. He seems to have a nasty habit of misusing client funds. Both matters were later dropped by the clients.''

''Probably paid them off, or Mommy and Daddy did.'' Kurt wearily rubbed the back of his neck. ''Keep on him. Her, too. Find out what you can about this trust. She doesn't live like a trust-funder.'' He frowned. ''She might be able to buy a better defense than I thought.''

Sam eyed Kurt. ''I'm going to presume on our friendship and give you some advice. Don't turn this into a personal vendetta. It could destroy everything in its path: you, her, and your boy. I've seen stuff like that happen, an' it ain't pretty. Maybe you ought to kiss and make up. It'd be a hell of a lot more fun.''

Kurt smiled thinly. ''Thank you, Ann, for your advice, but I have no interest in kissing her or doing anything else with her.''

''Pity.'' Sam gave an offhand shrug. ''So you're bent on revenge.''

''No,'' Kurt snapped, giving an impatient tug at the neck of his tie. ''This isn't about revenge. I'm indifferent to her. It's about my son.''

''Ah-huh, whatever.'' Sam got to his feet. ''I gotta find a shower.''

A few days after meeting Kurt at the diner, Julia was to meet with McGinn to discuss the status of the ongoing negotiations, but her Jeep wouldn't start. Dennis happened by and fiddled with something under the hood until the heap sputtered to life. By then, though, it was too late, which was tremendously frustrating because Julia was frantic to know what Kurt was up to. So far, the visitations were going well.

She barely saw Kurt when they handed Nick off. For his part, Nick was thrilled to be seeing Kurt again.

"Use the child support and get your car fixed," McGinn advised over the phone when she called. "That's what it's for. Or get something new. You'll be able to afford the payments."

"I'll think about it," Julia said noncommittally. The money offended her sense of self-reliance. And it felt too much as if Kurt was buying her off. She'd opened a bank account in Nick's name with the first support check.

"So what's their position?" Julia asked, changing the subject. "What does Kurt want?"

At McGinn's hesitation, Julia braced, sensing that she wasn't going to like what he would say. "He's willing to let you keep physical custody until Nick is a teenager. Then he wants Nick to live with him." She heard McGinn sigh. "So far, I haven't been able to budge them on that."

Julia took a calming breath. It could be worse. "What are Kurt's chances of winning if I refuse and this goes to court?"

"I wish I could say that he has no chance. Unfortunately, this case is not turning out to be the legal slam-dunk I had expected, for a couple of reasons. First, Mr. Weston appears to be dead set on steering Nick through his teenage years. Of course, this could change—he could get married, have new priorities. Second, unlike the vast majority of litigants, Mr. Weston has the financial resources to mount a campaign to reshape the boundaries of current law. His attorney has already contacted expert witnesses who are willing to testify that a teenage boy is better off with his father than his mother."

Julia's stomach churned as Kurt's promise ran through her head: *You will regret this day for the rest of your life because this is one battle I intend to win.* "Are you saying you think Kurt would win?"

"No, no. I doubt the judge would want to order a change in custody to take place so far in the future. Mr. Weston would likely have to raise the issue again when the time comes.''

''But you're not sure.''

''I can't guarantee anything.''

''So, if I don't agree to this arrangement, they'll try to get it in court?''

''Unfortunately, maybe not. Rosen says Kurt will try for full custody immediately if you don't agree and the matter goes before the court.'' McGinn quickly added, ''I think he's bluffing. His case for that isn't strong, in any event. He's probably hoping to force a quick settlement to keep it out of court. They hired a private investigator by the name of Sam Livingston to dig up dirt on you—play up your nightclub-singer past. Most of it sounds like nonsense, except one matter could present trouble—Marcus Fuller. I was unaware that you are engaged.''

Julia struggled to regain a measure of control. ''And if we are?''

''That could be a problem. According to Rosen, Fuller has been arrested for drug possession and possession with intent to deliver. In more recent years, he's been investigated by the state attorney grievance commission for misusing client funds.''

Julia closed her eyes, stunned by these new revelations about Marcus. But hadn't Kurt warned her? She felt shaky and cold. ''Kurt's going to win this, isn't he? They're going to make me look like a loose floozy with bad taste in men.''

''They may try, but they're not the only ones who can play that game. Remember, it's not about winning the moment, it's about winning the case. Now, about Marcus Fuller. Did you know about his record?''

''No. Could it be true?''

''Most likely—arrests, I expect, not convictions. So he never said anything?''

''No.'' Julia hesitated. ''We're really only what you'd call, I guess, distant friends. I see him when he's up here, maybe twice a year or so, a little more often the last six months because he's been helping me with that land problem I asked you about."

"Then this engagement of yours is for show?"

"Yes. At first it was to throw Kurt off track with Nick. Later, we thought it would look good to the judge."

"Then dump him," McGinn said bluntly. "He just became your biggest liability."

"I already have—about ten seconds ago."

Chapter 22

Winter closed in early over the peninsula. On a brilliant Saturday morning in late November, when Kurt drove out to Gull Inlet to collect Nick, the ground was covered by several inches of heavy new snow. Bent branches dripped their melting load in audible plops. The wet snow wouldn't last the morning, he predicted.

He hadn't been out to the inlet since those first few visits with Nick. Since then, Julia had dropped Nick off at the house Kurt had rented in Cherry Beach and promptly picked him up at the appointed time. Kurt guessed the arrangement gave her a sense of control over the visits, in part because it ensured that he wouldn't stretch the agreed-upon times. But yesterday, she called his office to ask that he pick up Nick at the cottage instead.

Three weeks had passed since their lawyers' last round of settlement talks. Three weeks of silence without a hint of the anticipated counteroffer from McGinn. Julia had been similarly close-mouthed. In front of Nick, she continued to maintain an upbeat, surface friendliness toward Kurt, doing everything she could to facilitate the transitions for Nick. But outside Nick's presence, she was chilly and formal.

What were they up to? Kurt mused. He'd alerted Sam and Dennis Livingston to keep a close watch on her. If she was getting ready to run, he wanted some warning.

Two other cars, in addition to Julia's battered Jeep, were parked in the side yard next to the cottage when he pulled up. One had an official logo of the state Department of Environmental Quality on the driver's door, and Kurt wondered what the DEQ was doing out here.

Kurt found Julia on the front porch talking to an outdoorsy type who looked like an Eddie Bauer spin-off: fortyish, brown hair, neatly trimmed beard, wire-rimmed glasses. They were turned slightly away from him, looking to the north, and neither noticed when he came around the corner.

"It can't be that bad," Julia was insisting, "even if they are toxics. I run along that back trail all the time. I would have noticed if those barrels had been there before."

"I hope you're right," the man said. "It's very disappointing. We want the parcel, but I can't take the chance without knowing more. The conservancy's funds are limited." He scratched his forehead under the brim of his cap. "I know you're in a bind, but if we could delay the closing a month or two . . ."

"I don't have a month or two. I need to sell *now*."

"I'm sorry. I can't—" Eddie Bauer noticed Kurt and broke off.

Julia glanced around at Kurt with a vague, startled look, then recollected herself and introduced them. "Excuse me," she then said to the man. "I have to get my son. I'll just be a minute."

Kurt followed her inside. "What's going on here, Julia?"

"It's none of your concern," she said, continuing toward the stairs.

"It is if it affects Nick. What are you doing?"

She stopped and planted hands on hips, glaring at him. "And just what do you think I'm doing? Evidently you suspect me of something."

"I think you're getting ready to cut and run."

She looked surprised, her arms falling unnoticed to her

sides. Then her mouth twisted into a wry smile. "You do assume the worst of me."

Kurt shrugged, unmoved. "With good reason."

"Daddy!" Nick tore down the stairs past Julia and flung himself against Kurt's legs.

Kurt swung him up in his arms and searched his face in wonder. Nick had never called him "Daddy" before. Kurt had been hesitant to suggest it, not wanting to push him.

"Mama, I'm hungry," Nick complained, wiggling out of his arms. "You forgot breakfast."

"You're right, honey, I did." Her harried gaze shifted back to Kurt. "They showed up early. Would you mind stopping somewhere and getting Nick breakfast?"

"How about I get him something here?" He wanted answers before he went anywhere.

Julia hesitated, then nodded. "All right. I was going to scramble an egg. Everything is on the counter."

In the kitchen, Kurt broke an egg into the skillet. Nick stood on a stool next to him, watching him push the egg around the bottom of the pan.

"You don't do it like my mama," Nick observed.

"Oh? How does she do it?"

The small shoulders lifted in a shrug. "It doesn't stick like that when she does it."

Kurt's mouth twitched. He found it difficult to keep his eyes off the boy. His son. The words prompted a tug of wonder, love, protectiveness, and pride all rolled up together.

"Nick?"

"Huh?"

"I liked it when you called me Daddy."

Nick looked up at him seriously. "Mama said you would."

"She did, did she?"

"Yeah. She said if I wanted to, I should."

"What else did she say?"

Nick's brow crinkled in thought. "She said, if you love somebody, you should show it . . . and not be afraid," he recited, then grinned in evident satisfaction that he'd gotten it right.

"Your mother is a smart lady," Kurt said after a moment. He scraped the egg onto a plate, added toast and orange juice, and set the lot down on the table in front of Nick. While he watched Nick scarf down his breakfast, Kurt tried to piece together what was going on. "Nick? Were you there when the man outside came this morning?"

"Yeah," Nick said around a mouthful of egg. "Two mans came in two cars."

He knew Julia would not approve of him pumping Nick for information, but he didn't care. The boy was a sponge. And right now Kurt needed information.

"What was your mom talking to them about?"

"Well, the one man said he wanted to buy the land, 'cept someone named Anonymous said it had toxic dumps on it, so he couldn't . . ."

At length, Kurt thought he had a pretty good idea what was happening. Julia had arranged to sell the Deer Cove property, on which he now owned the mortgage, to a nature conservancy, represented by the Eddie Bauer on the porch. But the deal was threatened because the DEQ inspector and the conservancy representative, tipped off by an anonymous informant, had discovered drums of presumably toxic waste dumped on the property. Apparently, the DEQ inspector was presently out looking for more toxic sites.

"Mama needs the money to pay for the balloons."

The balloon payment due on the mortgage, Kurt translated.

"Maybe we should get Uncle Ted to help." Nick looked up at him worriedly.

"I've got another idea. How about you and me sticking around today and helping your mom ourselves?"

"Yeah!"

"Good. Finish your breakfast. I'm going to make a phone call."

Julia straightened from the porch railing when he and

Nick came out. Kurt looked around. "Did Eddie Bauer bail on you?"

"Who? Oh, yes. He's gone." She sounded as if the air had been let out of her tires.

"What about the DEQ guy?"

"He's still out there somewhere." She waved vaguely to the north.

"Show me where these supposed toxics are."

"Daddy said he's going to help you," Nick chimed in.

"He did, did he?" She lost the distracted look. Although her voice was neutral, the look she sent Kurt was anything but. "Nick, run upstairs and brush your teeth."

As soon as Nick gave up trying to weasel out of it and went inside, she turned on him. "Butt out, Kurt. This is none of your business. I'm not cutting and running—"

"I know. I jumped to the wrong conclusion."

"Fine. Now go."

"Look," he muttered, "you're a little out of your element here. I may be able to help."

She eyed him warily. "Why would you want to help me?"

"I owe you."

"Why? Because you misjudged me?"

"In part."

"What's the other part?"

"Daddy," he said simply. She looked confused. "You helped my son say 'Daddy.' "

She nodded and looked away.

"I know something about real estate. Your choice." He shrugged indifferently.

"Okay," she agreed after a moment, but she didn't look happy about it.

When Nick returned, they walked north along a track through the woods that started at the back of the cottage. The trail cut through Deer Cove up to the county road. The dump site sat about a hundred yards in from the county road. When they got there, the DEQ inspector was examining a half-dozen fifty-five-gallon drums littering a clearing next to the trail. Kurt could see at a glance that the drums had not been there long. For one thing, ruts from the delivery truck were still visible under the melting snow. Unfortunately, several lids had popped off, spilling the contents. Probably when they were pushed off the truck, he figured.

"Now what?" Julia muttered. Kurt looked up to see Sam walking down the trail from the direction of the road.

"He's with me. Sam Livingston."

"I don't want your spy on my property," she said tightly.

"He might be able to track down who did this."

"Only if he works for free, because I won't pay him a dime for his time."

"I will," Kurt said, then left to meet him.

Julia held Nick back while the two men joined the DEQ inspector among the drums. Kurt and the inspector rejoined her after a few minutes. The inspector hadn't found any other sites.

"Good. Maybe the conservancy will still go through with the deal," Julia said to him.

"I doubt they'll want to assume the risk without more testing. If they buy knowing the spill is here, they assume liability for the cleanup. The good news is, it looks like the spill hasn't permeated the ground, because it's frozen. We can't know for sure without more testing. If it is contained on the surface, this might be inexpensive to clean up."

"What would be considered inexpensive?" she asked.

"Oh, under fifty thousand."

She sucked in a breath. "And if it's not contained?"

"Depends on how far it's traveled in the soil and groundwater. We could be looking at six figures, easy. But I don't think that's the case," the inspector added quickly.

"Think this is the work of some rogue hauler?" Kurt asked him.

The inspector nodded. "Could be. They charge a low price to haul the waste away and then dump it instead of paying for interment in a licensed landfill. Or it could be a small industrial user who decided to get rid of a batch of solvent for the same reason. Whoever did it was sloppy;

they missed part of a label on one of the drums. We'll try to trace it."

Sam and the inspector left to search for evidence along the county road. Kurt walked back to the cottage with Julia and Nick.

Kurt broke into Julia's grim reverie. "Why don't you ask the bank for an extension on your balloon payment?"

She eyed him suspiciously. "How did you know about that?"

"Just put two and two together. I heard you tell Eddie Bauer you needed the money in two weeks." He nodded up the trail at Nick. "And Nick said you needed money to buy balloons."

"I tried that already. It didn't work."

"Tell them about the spill. They shouldn't be too eager to jump into the middle of a possibly expensive cleanup."

That hadn't occurred to her. It was worth a try. Of course, it wouldn't replace the forty thousand extra she'd negotiated above the amount of the mortgage. She'd counted on that to pay her legal fees. And there was always Marcus. As he reminded her weekly over the phone, he still had a buyer willing to pay a whole lot more than the conservancy. Or she could use Kurt's child support. There was a certain perverse appeal to that idea.

At Kurt's new winter car, a Lincoln, she gave Nick a kiss. "I'll pick you up in a couple hours." She looked across the hood at Kurt. "I'll come to your place. And thanks for the other."

He nodded. "Remember, I'm picking up Nick on Wednesday for Thanksgiving."

Later that evening, long after Julia had collected Nick, Kurt handed Livingston a bottle of beer from his refrigerator and took a long pull on his own. "Curious that the conservancy got this anonymous tip right before the deal was to close."

"And too close to her loan deadline to do much testing,"

Livingston added. "I discovered something else. All three drums that spilled had marks showing they'd been pried open. None of the others had the same kinds of marks."

Kurt sat down at the table, his face set, his eyes narrowed as he drew the logical conclusion: the lids hadn't popped off when the drums were shoved off the truck; someone had deliberately opened them afterward. "If it looks like a setup and smells like a setup . . ."

"Yeah. I've been thinking the same thing. But who?"

"Whoever didn't want her to sell Deer Cove to the conservancy."

When Kurt arrived at the cottage on Wednesday, Nick was beside himself with excitement to be returning to Belle House. He couldn't wait to see Andrew and Nana. Silently Julia handed Kurt Nick's suitcase and watched him stow it in the trunk of the Lincoln.

"I forgot Sylvester!" Nick yelped and raced back inside.

"His teddy," she explained, glancing at Kurt. And then, "He's not ready for this."

"No?" He raised a mocking brow, looking pointedly after Nick.

"He hasn't left yet."

He leaned against the car, looking fresh and relaxed in jeans and a sweater. "Did the bank agree to extend your loan?"

"Yes. You were right about the spill. Their attitude took a remarkable turn when they heard about it—one hundred and eighty degrees, in fact."

"Good. Sam thinks he's found the source of the solvent. He traced it to an auto parts contractor in Traverse City, but the owner's not admitting anything. Sam notified the authorities. Maybe they can get him to talk." Kurt's expression darkened. "There's more. Marks indicate the lids were pried off *after* they were pushed off the truck."

"But why?"

"Was anyone else interested in that property? Someone

who might have wanted to stop your sale to the conservancy?''

Aghast, Julia suddenly understood. ''You think someone did this deliberately. Here! On my property. Not just to get rid of the stuff.''

''It's possible.''

Marcus? Surely not. She pushed aside such thoughts, shaking her head. ''That can't be. Maybe it was just senseless vandalism.''

''Maybe,'' he agreed, but he sounded unconvinced.

She was still trying to make sense of it when she saw Nick returning with Sylvester clutched securely under one arm. Her focus shifted abruptly. ''Promise me you'll take good care of him. He's just a little boy. Don't let anything happen to him.'' Her voice sounded strained and pleading to her own ears, but she didn't care. She would get down on her knees and beg if it would ensure that her baby came back to her safely. ''And promise that if he gets homesick you'll bring him back,'' she added quickly, before Nick could hear.

She hugged Nick again, then matter-of-factly, without any outward show of her distress, buckled him into the booster seat. At the last minute, Nick suddenly seemed to grasp that he was leaving his mother behind. ''Mama, can't you come with us?''

Julia sat down on the edge of the seat next to him. ''Oh, sweetheart, I can't. One of us has to stay and keep Bowen company.''

''Uncle Ted can.''

''They're all going away for Thanksgiving. You know that.''

''But I'll miss you.'' Nick's brow furrowed anxiously.

''And I'll miss you. But you're going to have so much fun. Remember, you get to see Andrew and Nana again, and I'll be right here waiting for you to come back.''

Nick smiled tentatively and nodded. Julia shut the door, smiled, and waved at him through the window, then quickly turned away.

Kurt could see this was hard for her. But she maintained her composure for Nick's sake, easing his way as she had all along. And for that, at least, she had earned Kurt's reluctant respect and gratitude.

"Julia . . ." He stood in the open driver's door.

She turned and met his eyes. He noticed the shininess of hers and how it lightened them to sea green.

"I promise," he said.

Julia nodded, not trusting herself to speak. She watched the sandy road until long after the dust settled, and then slowly wandered back inside. The cottage felt cold and empty. The next four days stretched out forever in front of her.

She had barely hung up the phone after talking with Alex on Thursday evening when Marcus called and wanted to go out for a drink.

"I can't. I can barely keep my eyes open." *And I need to be here in case Nick calls.*

"This doesn't have anything to do with what Weston's lawyer said about me, does it? I can't believe even Kurt could stoop that low. Those arrests were bogus— they were dropped, for God's sake."

"I know. But my lawyer said it would be best if I kept my distance until Nick's custody is set. I don't want to take any chances." Julia closed her eyes. She wished he would stop calling. She didn't want to listen to more dire warnings about Kurt. They only added fuel to her anxiety. "What are you doing up here this time of year?"

"Mother decided to have a quaint Thanksgiving in the north woods before they head down to Palm Beach. I'm bored stiff. So, did you close the deal with the conservancy?"

"No. It didn't go through. Last Saturday they discovered a toxic spill on the property."

"No kidding. Where? How bad is it?"

"Probably not too. The stuff has already been traced to a local manufacturer," she added to gauge his reaction. "The police are looking into it."

A short silence followed. "This is unbelievable. How did they trace it?"

"A label on one of the drums."

"You should have called me right away! You're going to need another buyer."

And you just happen to have one. "Actually, I'm okay. The bank extended my loan."

"They did? Great. For how long?"

"Long enough for everything to settle down. It was Kurt's idea to ask for an extension."

"Christ, Julia, did it ever occur to you that he could be behind the spill?"

"Why would he be? The property is too far from Lost Harbor Bay to do him any good. Besides, he's the one who suggested I ask the bank for an extension."

"I can think of a couple of reasons," Marcus said shortly. "For starters, keeping you up to your neck in debt so you can't afford to put up a good fight for Nick."

Julia didn't sleep well for a second night in a row. On top of missing and worrying about Nick, she couldn't stop thinking about what Marcus had said. She still favored the theory that her property had not been specifically targeted at all, that it had just been a remote place to unload the stuff. But if her property had been targeted as Kurt and Marcus had both suggested, she could come up with only three people with even the slimmest of motives.

Marcus was one. He'd opposed her deal with the conservancy from day one. Not so long ago she would not have even entertained the possibility that he could be part of such a duplicitous scheme, but after McGinn's disturbing revelations, she was no longer sure. As distasteful as it was, she could not ignore the possibility that he had an agenda at odds with hers.

That led to the second suspect: Marcus's mystery buyer, about whom she knew nothing except that he wanted the property and would pay far more for it than the conservancy. Who was he? Could he want it badly enough to resort to such drastic measures to kill her deal with the conservancy?

Finally, there was Kurt. But upon reflection, he seemed the least likely of the three. It wasn't that she trusted him, exactly. But clandestine dumping of toxic chemicals didn't seem his style. He operated in the open, his threats and tactics unmistakable. Deliberately so, to force her surrender, she imagined. She doubted he would resort to this sort of back-alley crime. His hiring Sam Livingston to dig up dirt from her past was of a different stripe altogether. And if he was the villain, would he be so eager to turn the matter over to the authorities? She would check to see if he really had.

The next morning, the inlet had a deserted feel under a threatening gray sky. The Clearys had gone to relatives downstate for the holiday. Mrs. Hornig up on the county road was with her son. Even Dennis, the bird photographer, who always seemed to be around lately, had gone away for a few days. She and Bowen jogged the half mile to Mrs. Hornig's house to feed her cat. On the way back, Dan Farley overtook them in his police cruiser.

"Everything quiet here?" He produced a biscuit for Bowen.

"Too quiet. What are you doing on paparazzi patrol?" Media attention had largely disappeared, and Dan had recently cut back his watch.

"I've got a couple guys off for the holiday. Sorry to hear about the spill on your property." He shook his head in disgust. "Bad business."

"How did you hear?" She leaned down by the open window to get out of the brisk onshore breeze.

"State police. Sounds like they expect to nail whoever did it. Hope so."

So Kurt *had* turned the matter over to the police, Julia concluded, relieved.

"Gloomy day," Dan remarked. "Forecast is for snow tomorrow."

"It's early for a big blow." Julia straightened and cast a worried glance at the leaden sky. She didn't like to think of Kurt driving Nick back through a bad storm. Or worse, not being able to get through at all.

"We usually get at least one dump before Christmas. Wouldn't surprise me if this is it."

Julia was working in her studio later in the afternoon when Bowen started barking outside. She assumed Dan was making the rounds again, and considered going out to invite him in for a cup of tea. She would have welcomed the company. But things had changed between them. There was a new distance on Dan's part. He'd relegated her back to outsider status, an attitude mirrored by some others in the village. She stood, stretching the kinks out. She used to crave this sort of isolation. Now it just felt lonely. She jumped when the studio door slammed opened.

"Mama!" Nick catapulted across the room into her arms. Kurt stepped inside behind him.

Julia knelt and hugged Nick tightly, fighting tears of relief and joy at having him back. For two days she'd tried to close her mind to how much she missed him. Now her emotions threatened to swamp her. "I've missed you so much," she warbled unsteadily.

She forced herself to relax her grip on him. "What are you doing back so soon?" she managed in a more normal voice, glancing from Nick to Kurt. "I didn't expect you until Sunday. Are you okay?" Automatically she stroked his forehead, examining him closely.

"I'm not sick," Nick said, burrowing back into her arms.

Julia raised questioning eyes to Kurt.

"We thought we'd spend the rest of the weekend in Cherry Beach," he said matter-of-factly. Evidently, he didn't want to say more in front of Nick. He didn't need to.

"Thank you," she said gratefully.

He nodded. ‘‘I’ll be by tomorrow morning to pick him up for the day.’’

‘‘Why don’t you spend it here?’’ Julia suggested on impulse. ‘‘I can throw something together for lunch.’’ She hated the idea of Nick leaving again so soon.

‘‘Let’s play it by ear,’’ Kurt said on his way out.

Chapter 23

During the night it started snowing. In the morning, Nick crawled into her bed and they snuggled together under the down comforter, listening to the icy bite of snow against the windows while he told her about the turkey dinner and Nana and Andrew. By midmorning, eight inches had fallen, and Julia expected that Kurt would call and cancel. She was surprised when he showed up an hour later, and aghast when she realized he still intended to take Nick.

"You must be joking!"

"About what?" Kurt's eyes narrowed on her.

"About taking Nick out in this blizzard. I won't allow it!"

"Won't allow it?" There was a hard edge to his quiet voice. "You don't have a choice."

Julia tried to be more diplomatic. "The forecast is for as much as a foot more snow. Spend the day here if you want, but please don't take Nick out in this."

He considered and finally shrugged, relenting more easily than she expected. "Okay. As long as I can borrow your Jeep if this keeps up."

She opened her mouth to warn him about the Jeep, then

shut it, and nodded. "Make yourself at home. Nick is upstairs. I'll just make up some sandwiches for lunch and then go work in my studio." She glanced around the living room, looking for things he and Nick could do inside. "There are toys and games in the closet over there." She gestured to a door across the room. "Books are up in Nick's room. We only get two TV stations."

"We'll manage," Kurt said on his way up the stairs to Nick's room.

Outside, the inlet had disappeared in a whiteout. Even in the lee of the cottage, icy needles stung her face as she waded through deep snow to her studio. Anxiously Julia willed the storm to stop soon. If it didn't, Kurt would be stuck with them until the county got around to digging them out.

Around four, Kurt ducked into the studio, slamming the door against the howling wind. "I'd better take off. Nick's asleep."

"How did you manage that?" Nick rarely napped during the day anymore.

"I think he's a mite tuckered out from our Eskimo raiding party across the dunes."

Julia stilled. "You took him out in this?"

If Kurt noticed warning signs of an impending explosion on her face, he blithely ignored them. "He had a blast."

"You must be out of your mind!"

"We had fun." He scowled back at her. "I seem to recall that you once liked a good storm."

"It's a full-scale blizzard out there and he's a four-year-old child!"

"Nearly five. And he was perfectly safe with me."

Infuriated, Julia glared at him, but he refused to acknowledge his stupidity.

"If you coddle him so much, you'll smother him. He'll grow up weak."

Her spine stiffened. "So now you're an expert on child rearing, and after only two short months. Imagine that."

His gaze hardened. "It doesn't take an expert to see that you're an overprotective mother."

A charged silence followed. "Your arrogance is frightening. He's a four-year-old child. His life is fragile. Ask any parent who's ever lost a child. It can be snuffed out . . ." She shuddered and didn't finish the thought. "Awful things happen. You have to be cautious."

"Are you speaking from personal experience?"

His softly spoken question caught her off guard. She thought about Sam Livingston's investigation into her life, wondering how thorough it had been. "I expect you know all about me by now," she answered coldly.

"On the contrary, I suspect I've seen only the tip of the iceberg." He studied her without apparent emotion, as if she were a foreign creature he was examining. "It's going to be damn hard for us to work together as a team when you see the world through these phobias of yours."

"Reasonable concerns," she insisted.

"This is obviously a subject we're going to have to discuss at length. Unfortunately, I don't have time right now if I'm going to make it home."

Holding on to her temper, Julia dug into her coat pocket for the keys to the Jeep and dropped them into his outstretched hand. "Yes. You'd better go."

After he left in a swirl of snow, Julia instantly regretted giving in to her spite and letting him go out in the storm. She should have told him about the Jeep. McGinn had cautioned her against stirring up any more hostility. While she waited for him to return, she cleaned her brushes. After a few minutes, when he still hadn't, she began to worry. What if he actually managed to get some distance away and got stuck? He could get lost in the whiteout.

When she went outside after him, the Jeep was nowhere in sight. She pulled her hat down to her eyes and followed the tire trail through the snow. Away from the protection of the buildings, the world dissolved into a spinning white emptiness. It was impossible to tell where land and sky met. The thin light was already beginning to fade into darkness.

With her head down, she didn't see Kurt until she plowed into him with a teeth-rattling jolt.

"What are you doing out here?" he shouted over the roar of the storm.

"I was worried that you would get stuck," she shouted back.

"I did."

When they reached the lee of the cottage, he explained, "Your four-wheel drive isn't working. I was only getting power to two wheels."

"That's odd," Julia said, glancing away.

"You knew," he accused, squinting at her through the stinging snow. She turned away toward the cottage. "You knew it wasn't working and let me come out here and risk my neck."

"I didn't think you would get out of the yard," she said defensively. "I came out looking for you when you didn't come back right away."

"I could have gotten out there too far to get back and had to spend the night in this!"

Julia forced an apology through gritted teeth. "I'm sorry. I was angry with you. But even with four-wheel drive you wouldn't have gotten through this."

"I'd have made it. Why didn't you tell me it wasn't working this morning?"

"I didn't want you taking Nick out in this. It wasn't safe even then."

"So you lied."

"I didn't lie . . ." Her eyes shifted away from his. ". . . exactly."

"No," he agreed, "you merely withheld critical information. It seems to be a habit with you," he added contemptuously. Without waiting for a reply, he stomped up the steps of the back stoop and opened the door to the mudroom.

Julia hurried inside after him and blocked the door to the kitchen. "Please. We're obviously stuck with each other for a while. Let's not take our disagreement inside in front of Nick. I am sorry. It was petty of me not to have told you."

Kurt didn't look any happier about the situation than she felt, but he nodded. "Don't worry, *Mom,*" he said dryly. "I have no intention of arguing in front of Nick. This may be the poor little guy's only chance to have both of his parents under the same roof."

Inside, Nick was still napping. Julia put on a Mary Chapin Carpenter tape in the kitchen and got started on dinner. While she worked, Kurt sat at the kitchen table and made a few business calls on the phone. At first she was uncomfortably aware of his presence in the small space, but eventually the low drone of his voice faded into the background as she peeled potatoes for soup. Dinner was civil. For Nick, they managed to mask their differences.

Not wanting to risk their fragile truce, after putting Nick to bed she went downstairs only long enough to bring Kurt bedding for the sofa before retreating to the safety of her room. She'd offered to have Nick sleep with her so Kurt could have Nick's room, but he'd declined.

They lost power sometime during the night. Even after five years of living through numerous power outages, despite their inconvenience, the profound silence still moved her. But she had hoped it wouldn't happen with Kurt there. With no electricity, there could be no refuge in the studio today. And they would be even more confined in the cottage because the wood stove didn't provide much heat upstairs. Usually during winter outages, out of necessity, she and Nick turned the living room into a camp and slept there.

Reluctantly she left her bed to go down and light the stove.

When Julia padded downstairs with pajamas showing under an oversized Norwegian sweater, Kurt was just putting a match to wood in the stove. He thought her sleep-smoothed face and tousled hair made her look young and cuddly and ravishing all at once. According to Sam's report, she was thirty-one, but at that moment she looked like a teenager.

The fire caught, sending flames licking and crackling over the kindling. Hearing the noise, Julia stopped on the stairs and fumbled in her pocket for her glasses. "I thought you'd still be asleep," she said in evident surprise.

"Go back to bed. I've got it." Kurt stood.

She continued down the stairs. "I might as well stay up now. Nick will be up any minute." She covered a yawn. "If you want a shower, better do it now before the water cools off completely."

Julia made pancakes on the wood stove. While Nick and Kurt ate, she went back upstairs and got dressed for outdoors. They were going to need a supply of wood, and right now it was buried under a mountain of snow. Looking out her bedroom window, she was relieved to see the snow had nearly stopped. But deep drifts covered the entire inlet, including the road out. Everything was white except the starkly contrasting skeletal shapes of trees off to one side and the sullen bay to the other. Between woods and sea, the dunes formed smooth white waves. In the distance, smoke rose from the lodge's smokestack. That meant the Clearys had gotten back yesterday after all, she thought, her spirits rising. Their furnace could only be running on the generator, and that had to be turned on manually.

By midmorning the clouds moved off, and the sun took the bitter edge off the cold. They were clearing snow from the front porch, which had borne the brunt of the wind, when Nick gave a squeal and pointed toward the water. Annie, in snowshoes, pulled Dustin on a sled.

"Aunt Julia!" Annie called out, puffing up the incline.

Julia met them at the edge of the porch and reached for Dustin, but with his longer reach, Kurt snagged the giggling boy and swung him up onto the porch to her. Then he did the same with Annie, snowshoes and all. "Am I ever glad to see you!" Julia gave Annie a hug. "I wasn't sure until this morning that you got through."

"We got back yesterday afternoon," Annie said, still puffing. "It was really bad. Dad had to plow us through at the end. Mom called but your phone is dead." Annie glanced uncomfortably in Kurt's direction, evidently unsure how she should treat him. "She wants to invite all of you over this afternoon. I brought an extra pair of snowshoes for Mr. Weston to use. Mom thought Mr. Weston would have a cell phone and wanted me to ask you to call her."

"The phone is in my car," Kurt said. "But how did your mother know I was here?"

Annie and Julia exchange knowing looks. "Binoculars," Annie said.

"Dad called for the plow," Annie told Julia before leaving to go back to the lodge, "but they're real busy in town. They won't come until the county gets the main road plowed anyway."

Julia explained to Kurt, "Ted usually plows the inlet road. Except when we get this much snow, his truck can't handle it." She hesitated and looked away before admitting quietly, "It might be another couple days before they get to us."

"Thanks for coming to my rescue," Julia said to Susan later at the lodge. Kurt, Ted, and the kids had gone outside to sled on the hill next to the lodge. Worn out from shoveling, Julia opted to watch from inside with Susan. Outside, Kurt was pulling Nick up the hill. She watched them together, laughing at something. Kurt reached over and gave him a hug, and Nick hugged him back tightly. She stared at their faces.

They loved each other.

Susan shot her a worried look. "You all right? He's not badgering you about the lawsuit?"

"The lawsuit? No. We agreed to a truce for Nick's sake. Kurt is being perfectly amiable, the perfect guest. He shoveled a ton of snow, split kindling, he's nice to Nick. If he weren't threatening to take my son away from me . . ." Julia fell silent, her gaze distant.

The words hung in the air. Susan prodded impatiently, "Then what?"

Julia blinked. "What?" she asked with a blank look on her face.

Susan heaved a sigh. "Then what is the problem?"

''It's just that . . .'' Her brow furrowed. ''I don't know . . . He's big.''

''Big.'' Susan looked baffled.

''He's hard to ignore.'' Julia shook her head in disgust. ''And we got into an argument over him taking Nick out into the middle of the blizzard yesterday. I was upset that he'd done it, and he accused me of being an overprotective mother. I got mad and did something really stupid.'' After Julia finished telling Susan about the Jeep fiasco, she looked over at her. ''I suppose you think he's right about me being an overprotective mother. You've implied as much before.''

''No,'' Susan said after a second. ''I don't think you're overprotective. You're cautious. Most mothers are. Fathers tend to push children to take risks and mothers try to protect them. Somehow it all balances out.''

Julia raised a doubtful eyebrow. ''Sounds like a recipe for war.''

''It works,'' Susan insisted. ''If the parents are committed to making it work.''

Hoping Susan or Ted would invite Kurt to spend the night, Julia delayed their departure as long as she could. It didn't happen despite her blatant hints. They walked single file, following close to the water, where much of the snow had been scoured away and what remained was packed by their earlier passage. Julia led, holding Nick's hand, and Kurt brought up the rear, pulling the sled. Bowen bounded back and forth between them. They stopped before crossing the dunes to put on snowshoes and settle Nick on the sled. Then they threaded their way through drifted valleys. All around them, wind-sculpted cornices rose dramatically, wave after wave of silent, untouched white.

As they neared the cottage, Julia felt the first snowball land weakly on the back of her leg. She turned in time to see Nick launch a second round, a joyful grin on his face. She ducked to avoid an incoming missile from Kurt and ended up taking it on the chest. He called out an apology. But at the sight of his unrepentant grin, she let him have it.

She had a good arm and didn't spare it, lobbing them in faster than a pitching machine. It was no coincidence that they all seemed aimed at his head. What did it matter that she felt a perverse satisfaction when she clipped him on the chin? That his yelp was music to her ears? Only she would ever know how much she enjoyed it. Even McGinn couldn't begrudge her a little innocent revenge.

"Sorry," she echoed his earlier apology. But as Kurt wiped melting snow from his face, he must have glimpsed the triumph on hers, because instead of resuming the fight, he began lumbering purposefully toward her. From the gleam in his eye and the hard set of his jaw, she knew the game had moved to a new level. Pretending not to recognize the threat, she tossed a snowball at Nick, then turned toward the cottage as casually as she could in snowshoes. "Come on, Nick. Time to go inside."

Out of the corner of her eye, she could see Kurt stalking her, undeterred, gaining on her with every waddle and cutting off her path to the cottage. *To hell with dignity!* A hysterical giggle bubbled up as she made an awkward dash for the cottage and nearly tripped in her haste. Similarly hindered by his own gear, Kurt took off in slow-motion pursuit. Julia realized at the last moment that she wouldn't make it, and cut away from the cottage. He changed course to match, lumbering along hard on her heels, steadily gaining on her. She hazarded a glance over her shoulder and couldn't help laughing at the sight.

"No, Kurt!" She held out a hand to ward him off and was still laughing when he launched himself at her. They landed in deep snow, a tangle of arms, legs, and snowshoes. Though she could hardly move as it was, he took the added precaution of pinning her arms down into the snow on either side of her head.

"It'll take more than a few snowballs to get rid of me, Julia," he warned, not bothering to hide his amusement, "even though you could probably start for the Cubs. And forget about trying to pawn me off on the Clearys again. Oh, yes," he added sarcastically, seeing the startled look on her face, "did you think I missed your little manipulations?" His gray eyes gleamed inches from her face. "You're going to have to deal with me, so you better get used to it."

Chapter 24

Kurt peered across the living room at Julia from under half-closed lids, watching her stroke a light hand across Nick's temple as he slept on the couch. "Tell me about my son."

Julia's hand stilled. "What do you want to know?"

"Everything. Your pregnancy, his birth, when he talked, walked, smiled, his school, friends—everything I've missed."

At first he thought she wasn't going to answer. After a minute, she carefully extracted herself from under Nick's head and disappeared into the closet. She came out with several picture albums and handed them to him. "Tea?" she offered on her way to the wood stove to refill her mug from a pot warming on top. She had to edge around the mattress they'd brought down from Nick's bed, and Kurt wondered which of them she intended it for. She came back and settled into the chair next to his, tucking her long legs up underneath her.

The single oil lamp bathed the immediate vicinity in a warm glow but left the rest of the room in shadows. A gust of wind rattled its way through a leaky storm window, setting the lamp's flame dancing. It flickered over her face. Even in old jeans and a baggy sweater that nearly swallowed her up, with her hair pulled back in a ponytail and her face free of makeup, he found her incredibly alluring and had to mentally distance himself from the effect she had on him. A difficult feat given their close confinement. The chemistry between them had always run hot. At least on his side, though he had every reason to believe it ran both ways. It must, in order to overcome the preternatural self-control that would otherwise have kept her out of his bed in the first place and that, according to Sam's reports, had kept her out of other beds.

Kurt stifled a sigh of frustration. He couldn't afford to do something foolish, such as mistaking a normal physical reaction to their extended proximity for something more.

"Nick was born here on a February night." Her beautifully modulated voice interrupted his brooding. "It had snowed off and on all day."

"You mean he was born at the hospital in Cherry Beach," he clarified.

"No, I mean right here, in this chair." She patted the upholstered arm.

"Isn't that taking your aversion to hospitals a little far?"

"Believe me, a home birth was never part of my plan, but my options were not real plentiful. He came faster than usual for a first baby. I was scared to death—" She stopped, then started again in a more composed voice. "The important thing is, Susan got here in time for his birth and there were no complications." Julia's face softened into a smile. "He was perfect."

"Are you saying you were all by yourself out here through your entire labor?"

"Yes. Except the most important part, his birth."

"How long?"

She shifted uncomfortably, evidently embarrassed by his questions. "A few hours, I guess. At first I thought it was just discomfort because I'd been shoveling snow."

The image of her all alone, in pain, while she gave birth

to his son, made his blood run cold. *By her choice,* he reminded himself, hardening his heart.

"Anyway," she went on, "we drove to the hospital the next morning, stayed one night, then I brought Nick back here, and this is where we've been ever since."

She picked up one of the albums and opened it. "This was taken the day I brought him home from the hospital." Her voice warmed as it always did when she talked about Nick. Kurt moved to the ottoman in front of her chair, and she passed the album to him, leaning forward so she could see over his shoulder. "He didn't have much hair at first." Kurt heard the smile, felt her breath on his ear. He inhaled a scent he remembered well—light, airy, floral. "And these were taken a few days later. . . ."

They spent nearly an hour going through all three albums. She'd meticulously chronicled every event in Nick's young life. Most of the photographs were of him at progressive ages, although he recognized a few other faces: the various Clearys, Alex, even Marcus in a couple. Julia appeared rarely, and Kurt could imagine her artistic eye behind the camera in most of the shots. She was there in a few though, one holding an infant Nick beside a beat-up car that must have preceded the beat-up Jeep she drove now. That was another thing that struck him, the evident thrift of their lives. He could see no signs pointing to a cushy trust fund—no fancy vacations, or cars, or other luxuries people tended to memorialize in snapshots.

"Must have been hard, way out here alone with a baby," Kurt remarked when Julia returned from the cellar with a dusty bottle of Scotch from her grandfather's stash. He moved back to the other chair, taking the albums.

Julia tried to read his face to determine whether there was a hidden dig in his comment, but could see none. "It was, at times," she answered honestly. "But I wouldn't trade it for anything. He has brought meaning to my life."

He didn't say anything to that. She contemplated him as he took a sip of the Scotch. A look of pleasure smoothed the hard planes of his face.

Maybe this was her moment—maybe the only one she would ever have. He looked more relaxed and approachable than she'd seen him since this whole nightmare began.

"I can't lose him, Kurt," she said quietly. "He's my life. He's all I have. Someday you'll have other children. Nick would always have one foot on the outside of your new family. With me, he'll always be at the center." She looked at him imploringly. "*Please,* I'm begging you, be reasonable. Give up your demand for custody—"

"Be reasonable?" His face had hardened in an instant, and Julia recognized her mistake. "You think *I'm* being unreasonable to want to be a father to my son? It's the only reasonable response to this entire mess, which you created by neglecting to let me in on the minor detail that I had a son in the first place. I've always wondered—was it too much bother to tell me? Or could you just not stomach having to share him?"

"I did try to tell you. I thought I *had.* I left a note—"

"I can't believe you're still spinning that fairy tale. I got your note. It contained a bank draft for the contact lenses, but nothing about a baby."

Julia flinched at the contempt in his eyes. "I left a second note. *Please!* Listen."

He shrugged. "I'm not going anywhere." But his face assumed a bored expression.

She marshaled her thoughts. This was it. She doubted she would get another chance. "When I learned I was pregnant, I considered giving the baby up for adoption," she began. "Susan said that I would have to get your consent as well."

"So you decided to keep the baby to avoid telling me," he said flatly.

"No! I decided to tell you either way. It just got me thinking about it. Marcus offered to handle it for me, but I declined."

The mention of Marcus's name caught his attention, so she elaborated. "I wasn't sure if he was passing information on to you about my condition. You see, early on I was under the impression that he was some sort of personal troubleshooter for the Westons—that it was his job.''

''He did some work for me, but that was never part of the job description.''

''Well, anyway, he called up to Belle House for me—this was close to Labor Day—and found out from someone that you were going to be there over the long weekend. So I decided to drive up and talk to you. I didn't think it was something I should tell you over the phone.

''When I got there, the entire household was in the middle of preparing for a party the next day—your engagement party, it turned out. You weren't there yet, but they expected you shortly with your fiancée. I realized then that I'd made a dreadful mistake by not calling you ahead of time. So, I left a note for you and got out quickly, saving us all from an embarrassing scene. Then I waited to hear from you. And when I didn't, I assumed I had your answer—that you were not interested in being a father to my child—which, considering the nature of our brief relationship and your engagement, I didn't question.''

At length, Kurt raised his glass to her in a mocking salute. ''You know, I have to hand it to you, you almost had me for a minute.''

''But it's the truth! How else would I know about the party and your engagement?''

''You didn't know.''

''Yes—''

''No, because there never was an engagement or an engagement party at Belle House, or anywhere else. Your research is faulty.''

Julia shook her head in disbelief. ''But everyone was talking about it.''

''Who?''

''Well . . .'' She thought back. ''Vanessa, Mr. Livingston. Even your mother,'' she added as the memory surfaced. ''She had cut some flowers, and I practically knocked her down when she came in through the front door. She thought I was one of your sister's friends. I remember she asked if

I'd come for the party. And Mr. Livingston might remember. I gave him the note."

Kurt raised a cynical brow. "My mother asked if you were one of Carolyn's friends?"

"Yes. I think so," she hedged. "It's hard to remember the details after all these years, but I think your mother must have been expecting some of Carolyn's friends and assumed I was one."

Carolyn. Suddenly, it occurred to Kurt that *she'd* had an engagement party at Belle House a few years ago. What year had that been? He couldn't pin it down.

At length, he shook his head, voicing the critical fact she couldn't explain away: "If you'd come and left a note with Livingston, I'd have gotten it. Not to mention, if you'd been there just before I arrived, Livingston would surely have told me. And he didn't."

"It could have been misplaced."

"Forget the damned letter!" he bit out impatiently. "Why didn't you tell me last spring when you saw I didn't know?"

She looked away from the cold accusation on his face. "Nick and I had made a good life together. I needed time to think." She hesitated, then decided to lay it all out. "And I needed time to see what kind of father you would make before I risked telling you."

"And you decided *not* to tell me."

"No! I decided I would tell you. I could see how good you were with him and how attached to you he became."

"Lady, I sure don't remember you telling me. But I sure as hell do remember you denying it to my face when I came here and asked you point-blank."

Julia felt as though she were drowning, fighting for her life—or at least the best part of it, which had long ago taken up residence in Nick. "Alex asked me to wait until after the wedding. I agreed. I almost told you anyway, at the dunes the morning of the wedding. Remember?" She looked at him beseechingly.

He nodded reluctantly. "You kept hinting that you had something to tell me when we got back to Cherry Beach."

"Yes. Then, after we . . ." Julia swallowed her embarrassment. "The next morning when I was upset because you hadn't used a condom, you jumped to the conclusion that I was worried about being abandoned like Nick's father had done. And you told me not to worry, because if Nick were your son he would be with you. Kurt, try to understand!" she pleaded. "I couldn't tell you then. I thought if I did, you might try to take Nick away from me."

Kurt tried to ignore the anguished appeal in her eyes, even as he cursed silently for not making himself more clear at the time.

"And your engagement to Marcus? Was that another lie?"

"Yes. Marcus made it up on the spot when you overheard me saying that we couldn't tell you about Nick. I went along with it because I had no choice."

"Except the truth."

"That was no longer an option."

This much of her story, at least, he believed. All the pieces fit. "Let me guess: Marcus opposed telling me all along."

"He predicted you would react by taking Nick away from me," she admitted. "And it turns out he wasn't far off the mark," she added bitterly.

"So he knew about Nick from the beginning."

Julia nodded. "I never told him exactly, but he discovered it when we literally bumped into each other on the street the day I'd learned I was pregnant. He saw the pregnancy pamphlet I was carrying and put the pieces together."

And if Marcus knew, Kurt thought, *Vanessa might have known.* The two had been thick for years. "You said Vanessa was at Belle House when you came to talk to me."

"Yes." Julia smiled humorlessly. "She enjoyed rubbing my nose in your engagement to Amanda . . . your *supposed* engagement to Amanda."

Kurt didn't say anything. First Marcus and now Vanessa. He didn't trust either one. Yet both figured in Julia's account of the day she claimed to have left the note for him. Maybe, as improbable as it seemed, Julia wasn't lying. Because if she was, she had just stupidly crawled way out on a limb by involving in her story any number of people who could send her falling with a word. By her own account, there were at least three people who had seen her at Belle House the afternoon she claimed to have left her note.

But if her story was true . . . God, he could barely stand the thought of what might have been, the wasted years. If her story was true, Vanessa had lied to her about his supposed engagement. To what end? And what had become of the note?

"You'll get married, have other kids . . ." she was saying. "Think how stressful it would be for your wife and children to suddenly have to share their home with a teenager, almost a stranger to them. And how awful that would be for Nick. Teenagers have enough to deal with already."

"Gee, I had no idea I had a fiancée waiting in the wings. You know something I don't?"

"I know you're the type of man who sooner or later will marry and have kids."

He shrugged. "Maybe. But you could, too."

"Me?" She looked faintly appalled. "No. I will never marry and I will never have more children. Nick is all the family I'll ever have. Or want. On that score you can rest assured. I *promise* you will always be his only father. And I promise you will be able to see him as much as you want. I won't try to keep him away from you."

She leaned forward intently. "Consider the reality: I'm here when he gets home from school. I've arranged my life so I can be here with him. With your schedule, he would come home to an empty house, or a housekeeper, or someone other than you or me. Please, I'll do anything you want to accommodate you. Just don't take him away from me. Or at least let him make the choice when the time comes."

"Would you move?" he asked abruptly.

"Move?" She looked momentarily dumbfounded by the question. She glanced around the cottage. "I never thought . . . This has been our home."

Kurt watched her steadily. "You could keep the cottage and come back summers."

She shook her head slowly. "I couldn't afford two places."

"I could."

It felt as though sand were shifting beneath her feet. She was suddenly not sure what, exactly, they were talking about, and suddenly utterly sure that McGinn would heartily disapprove of this conversation. Something important had just taken place; Kurt's expression was unreadable, yet different than before. She didn't know what it was, or what had brought it on, but she sensed the change might be in her favor, and the last thing she needed to do was muck it up.

"Maybe this is something we should work out through our lawyers."

"Perhaps," he agreed with that same unreadable expression.

She pondered Kurt's question when she went upstairs to get ready for bed. Would she agree to move—she assumed he meant closer to him—if in exchange he would drop his custody petition? The answer was a no-brainer.

When she came down, she brought extra blankets and a book. She was wearing flannel pajamas and a wonderfully hideous velour bathrobe she'd been meaning to give to Goodwill.

"Nice," Kurt said. But his teasing smile said he'd guessed she'd deliberately dressed down because of him. She had. Only it wasn't supposed to *look* deliberate. It was supposed to demonstrate her indifference to him and discourage some of the looks he'd been giving her.

She dropped a pillow and two quilts on the mattress. "You take the mattress." The glance she sent him was brief, impersonal.

"Then where are you going to sleep?"

"I'll sleep in a chair. I'm going to stay up and read a while anyway."

"Forget it. I'm not taking your bed. You and Nick can take the bed. I'll take the couch."

She shook her head. It was the obvious solution, but she didn't want to be that close to him. Not while she slept. She needed a zone of privacy. "The couch is too short for you. Use the mattress. When I'm ready to sleep, I'll move Nick down with you and take the couch."

She had no intention of doing anything of the sort, but he didn't have to know that.

Kurt shrugged and picked up one of Seth's boat-building books.

"Tired?" His question startled her awake a while later. The words on the page swam in front of her face. "Why don't you go to bed?"

She blinked. "Not yet," she mumbled. "I'm at an interesting part right now."

Kurt laughed at her. "Then the rest must be riveting." He turned over on the mattress and within minutes appeared to be asleep.

Julia shivered in the cold draft of the rattling window behind her and pulled the blanket higher around her shoulders. Even Bowen had sense enough to move closer to the warmth of the stove. She should go upstairs for another blanket, but she was too tired. With relief, she let her heavy eyelids fall, not bothering to remove her glasses or turn off the lamp.

In her dreams, strong arms picked her up and laid her down in a soft bed. She snuggled close to the delicious warmth, drifting down into deeper sleep.

Kurt woke a few hours later, surprised that he'd managed to fall asleep at all. Surprised, too, that some time during the night he'd turned toward her and now held her close, her back and legs molded to his entire length. The scent of her hair and skin, the feel of a soft breast against his arm, teased him to instant, hard arousal. Without thinking, he nuzzled the soft skin along the nape of her neck, that slender, feminine arch that so tantalized him whenever she wore her hair up or pulled back in a ponytail. She sighed in her sleep and snuggled back against him, seating her bottom more firmly against his groin.

Kurt stifled a groan and eased away, careful not to wake her.

She turned over and stretched an arm across the empty side of the bed. On impulse, he leaned down and kissed her lightly on the mouth. "There is still that between us, too," he whispered in agreement. A corner of his mouth turned up in a wry half smile.

Unbelievable, he thought as he edged along the length of the mattress, careful not to disturb Nick on the couch. Her betrayal, the lawsuit: either one should have killed any desire he felt for her. Neither had. Even more confounding, despite the rocky start, he'd thoroughly enjoyed being snowbound with her, and regretted having to leave. He admired the life she'd made here. And, to his surprise and against his better judgment, he found himself helplessly drawn both to the woman she was and the woman he sensed she could be if she ever shucked that emotional straitjacket she had herself strapped into. He was, quite simply, in grave danger of falling under her spell again.

After stopping to build up the fire, he took his cell phone to the kitchen.

By slow degrees, Julia became aware that someone was shaking her shoulder. "*Julia . . . Wake up a minute. I have to go. . . .*"

She cracked open an eye to see Kurt's fuzzy outline leaning over her. She was on the mattress. Vaguely she remembered being enveloped by a warm body. It hadn't been a dream, then.

"Go?" she mumbled, fumbling with the glasses he handed her.

"I have to go to the office. There are things I have to make sure get taken care of at the work site because of all this snow."

Julia peered up at him, failing to understand how he expected to get there. Her eyes drifted down his wide shoulders and long legs. He looked freshly groomed, energized, and impatient to be about his business. She felt at a severe disadvantage. "But you can't . . ." She propped up against the couch, gathering her robe together in one hand and pushing her hair out of her face with the other. "Not unless you plan to snowshoe out."

She heard the *thwap, thwap, thwap* of a helicopter approaching. The suspicion grew that it might not be the Coast Guard helicopter passing by, but Kurt's mode of transportation.

"My ride," he confirmed.

Julia's eyes narrowed on his back as he left the cottage in a blast of cold air. If he had the means to leave, why had he waited until today?

"So, you want to tell me what's really going on here?" Sam peered across the polished expanse of Kurt's desk in Cherry Beach. "It might help me do my job if you level with me."

Kurt turned from the snowy scene outside his window. In the two days since he'd flown out of Gull Inlet, the village roads had been cleared and his staff had trickled back to work. Preliminary reports from the job site indicated no significant damage from the early blizzard. "Other than adding another man to protect Julia, you are to proceed as planned."

"To protect Julia," Sam repeated slowly. "Let me get this straight: now I'm to *protect* the woman you're squared off against?"

Kurt ignored his jibe. "And Nick. Look, we suspect that whoever dumped those toxics deliberately targeted Deer Cove—we assume, to thwart the sale to the conservancy."

"Right."

"Except it didn't work because I let Julia have an extension on her loan. Whoever it is likely still wants the land. I doubt they're going to give up now. My guess is Marcus Fuller fits in here somewhere, although he can't be the big money."

Before Sam could respond, the door to the office opened, and Kurt's mother bustled in with the air of a woman on a mission. "Darling, I'm glad you're here." Halfway across the room, she noticed they were not alone. "Oh, Sam! How are you, dear?"

"Mother, what are you doing here?" Kurt's question brought her attention back to him.

"I was just on my way to Chicago and decided to stop and see you."

Kurt struggled not to show his exasperation. "You shouldn't be out driving in this."

She sent a brief, pointed glance toward Sam. "I have something to show you that relates to our phone conversation yesterday."

Kurt's interest sharpened. He'd called to see if she could verify Julia's story about going to Belle House when she was pregnant. When she hadn't remembered any such visit, he'd been more disappointed than he wanted to admit. Now, at the leap of hope he felt, he reminded himself that it no longer mattered. It would be nice to confirm her story, but either way, he'd made his decision. Still, he was impatient to know. "It's okay. You can speak freely in front of Sam."

"Well, I know you said it wasn't important, but I thought it might be." She perched on the edge of a chair. "I don't think I would have remembered at all if Alfred hadn't nudged my memory. There was so much commotion at the time, and we had such a brief exchange. Anyway, it was over the Labor Day weekend five years ago, just as you said on the phone. You remember, that was the weekend of Carolyn's engagement party."

She dug a red leather notebook from her shoulder bag.

He nodded at the vaguely familiar book. "What's that?"

"Why, it's one of Alfred's visitor logs, darling." She came around the desk to him. He heard the undercurrent of excitement in her voice. "See? Right here, in the Saturday entry: *Miss J. Griffin stopped to see Kurt but could not wait. Left note.*" Pat's finger slid down the page. "Then here's an entry noting your arrival from Chicago with Amanda Fitch half an hour later.''

A muscle flexed in Kurt's jaw. ''I had no idea Alfred's logs were so detailed.'' He'd known of their existence, of course—they were humorously known as the ''family archives.'' Alfred Livingston considered it part of his job to chronicle the comings and goings at Belle House. Kurt used to find it amusing. Not anymore.

Sam chuckled. ''Dad has that sense of history, you know.''

Kurt saw the distracted frown on his mother's face. ''What is it, Mom?''

''Well, now that I've had a chance to think about it, I do remember bumping into her at the front door that day. She was with Vanessa. The odd thing is, I was under the impression they had stopped by to see Rob, not you. And Julia seemed nervous, in a big hurry to leave. I found it odd, even then. But things were so hectic, I didn't give it much thought.''

Kurt said nothing. He simply turned and walked over to the far window to stare sightlessly out over the roiling gray water beyond the breakwater. She'd been telling him the truth all along.

Pat sent a questioning glance at Sam, and he shrugged. ''Darling?'' she ventured.

Chloe's voice came over the intercom. ''Kurt, your lawyer is on line one.'' Even as he crossed the room to turn off the speaker he'd inadvertently left on, she added, ''Oh, and you wanted to know as soon as the car dealership delivered the new car to Julia—''

Kurt picked up the phone, cutting off the intercom.

''Very generous.'' Sam grinned when Kurt hung up.

''They've been riding around in an unreliable piece of junk.''

From where I sit,'' Sam said, ''it looks like your plan has made a little detour. First, you gave up a golden opportunity to foreclose on her mortgage—''

''What mortgage?'' his mother interrupted.

"Julia's," Sam answered, his shrewd gaze on Kurt. "And now you give her a car."

"My objective remains the same." Kurt paused thoughtfully before saying, almost more to himself than to them, "There is often more than one way to win. And sometimes, it's staring you right in the face."

Phone service and electricity weren't restored to Gull Inlet until Tuesday, but to Julia's amazement, they were plowed out on Monday within hours of Kurt's departure. A full-size highway plow, sent over from the work site at Lost Harbor Bay, muscled its way through the drifts. On Tuesday morning, an even bigger surprise landed at her door.

As soon as the phone was working, she called McGinn and told him what had happened over the weekend, ending with her cautiously optimistic impression that Kurt might be willing to drop the lawsuit if she and Nick would move closer to him when his project here was done.

"Well," he said when she finished, "would you be willing to move?"

"In an instant. If it guarantees I won't lose custody of Nick."

"Think carefully; you'll have to live with your decision. Are you sure?"

"Yes," she answered firmly. "It's a small price to pay for peace of mind. And it would be good for Nick to be near his father."

After a moment of silence, when Julia thought they might have been disconnected, she heard McGinn clear his throat. "My dear," he said solemnly, "you are a remarkable woman." He sighed. "So be it, then. Much as I would like to fight this on principle, sometimes compromise is the smart way to go. And my gut is telling me this is one of those times."

"What do you mean? You said Kurt didn't have a strong case."

"It shouldn't be. But he appears ready and able to go to

the mat. Not to mention that we have a judge who's up for reelection next year and a plaintiff who will soon be the biggest taxpayer in the county."

And I'm a nobody, Julia filled in. She'd already made her decision. Nothing McGinn said changed anything, but it made her nervous to hear him voice fears she'd had all along.

Please don't let Kurt change his mind, she prayed.

She lifted the curtain over the kitchen table and eyed the shiny new Volvo all-wheel-drive station wagon parked next to her old Jeep. She loved it. It was a beautiful champagne beige with butter-soft heated leather seats, sunroof, and every bell and whistle she'd ever imagined and a good many she hadn't. She hated it. It was a slap in the face. She'd always been proud of the life she provided for Nick. But she couldn't compete with Kurt. She couldn't even afford reliable transportation.

"What should I do about the car?" The practical part of her wanted to keep it, gratefully. Her pride wanted to send it back.

"Keep it," McGinn said decisively. "Your Jeep's in lousy shape. Consider it child support."

Three to one, she tallied, with McGinn firmly in the same camp as Susan and Ted. Only Marcus urged her to give it back. He'd arrived on her doorstep late in the morning on his way downstate after the snowstorm and had been bluntly curious about the new car sitting in her yard.

"Well, then," McGinn said, "I'll get in touch with Mr. Weston's lawyers and try to settle the matter."

Chapter 25

When Julia and McGinn arrived at Kurt's office the following Monday, they knew little more about Kurt's intentions than they had the week before, for Ben Rosen would only confirm that Kurt would drop his bid for custody if she would agree to certain conditions to be laid out at the meeting. Julia wore an attractive cream cashmere suit—one of Alex's altered castoffs—which she thought, gave her a businesslike look rather than the bimbo image the media had tried to create for her. She was glad she'd worn it when Kurt's perky assistant, Chloe, ushered them through the lobby past a half-dozen openly curious employees, who quite obviously recognized her from all the media hype. Chloe led them to a conference room overlooking the harbor. Kurt and Ben Rosen entered almost on their heels, and Chloe left, leaving the four of them alone.

When they were seated, Kurt steered the conversation into friendly, impersonal talk about the recent storm, seemingly in no hurry to get to the main event. Instead of putting Julia at ease, the delay had the opposite effect. In response to her questioning look, McGinn reassuringly patted her sleeve. "Relax," he whispered. "This feels like détente."

Nonetheless, he turned to Rosen. "We'd best get on with it. I have a court date this afternoon and Julia has to pick up Nick."

At Kurt's nod, Rosen began. "Then I'll try to make this as brief as possible." He flipped open his notes. "As I indicated on the phone, Mr. Weston will forgo all attempts to gain custody of the parties' minor son now and in the future if Miss Griffin agrees to meet certain conditions, which I will enumerate."

He paused to clear his throat. Julia perched tensely on the edge of her seat, her gaze riveted on him, aware that she herself was the object of Kurt's scrutiny.

"First," Rosen said, "the terms of this agreement are to remain confidential between the parties, whether or not Miss Griffin chooses to accept it."

Julia nodded, and McGinn agreed, "We have no problem with that."

"Second, the child's surname will be legally changed from Chadwick to Weston."

"Agreed," McGinn intoned at Julia's nod.

"Third, Miss Griffin agrees to consult with Mr. Weston regarding major decisions affecting their child."

Again Julia nodded her acquiescence and McGinn agreed.

"Fourth." Rosen paused, glancing at his client. Kurt signaled for him to continue. "Except for the summer months, which Miss Griffin is free to spend with her son at Gull Inlet, she and her son are to reside with Mr. Weston. At present that means sharing Mr. Weston's residence in Cherry Beach, but at some point in the future it will mean moving with him to his home in Illinois."

Julia's confused gaze veered from Rosen to Kurt. "I assume you mean we will be living near you, but in separate residences."

Kurt watched her steadily, but it was Rosen he addressed. "Explain, Ben."

"The last condition, Miss Griffin," Rosen said, his expression when he faced her curiously sympathetic, "is that you marry Mr. Weston."

Dead silence met Rosen's astonishing statement. Rosen looked stoically resigned to an impending storm, McGinn stared at Kurt as if seeing him for the first time, and Julia's spine stiffened as if she'd been shot. Her face drained of color. Only Kurt, staring back at Julia through slightly narrowed eyes, showed no expression.

"Marry you?" Julia choked through stiff lips. An unpleasant thought occurred to her and fed a mounting sense of betrayal. "You can't seriously think I'd fall for such a transparent scheme." Anger hardened her voice and brought color back to her face.

When she began to push away from the table, McGinn laid a cautionary hand on her arm to forestall a hasty departure. "My client is right. This whole thing is a sham. *Drop* his bid for custody? He couldn't even *bring* a custody petition if they were married—"

"What scheme, Julia?" Kurt interrupted McGinn, holding up a hand to secure his silence.

Julia gave a bitter laugh. "It's simple. You marry me, establish a home for Nick, divorce me, keep Nick."

"No." Kurt shook his head.

"What protection does my client have you wouldn't try exactly that?" McGinn asked. He gave an indignant snort. "In all my years in this business, I've never heard *anything* quite like this."

Rosen cleared his throat. "Your client would be well protected. Let me explain the details of the agreement."

"Please, do," McGinn muttered.

"If Miss Griffin satisfies the conditions I've already spelled out, at the end of one year she may, if she so desires, divorce Mr. Weston, and he will agree not to seek physical custody then or in the future. He would, of course, still expect reasonable visitation. In addition, Mr. Weston will transfer into her name the sum of one million dollars to serve in lieu of alimony and child support. So as not to create an incentive to divorce him, Mr. Weston will transfer the same amount of money to Miss Griffin if she *does* stay married to him. Either way, as long as she sticks out the year, she ends up with her son, and becomes a very wealthy woman.''

''What if he divorces her before the year is up?'' McGinn asked.

Julia pushed her chair back from the table and walked woodenly away from them until she came to a stop in front of the wall of windows overlooking the harbor.

''She gets custody automatically,'' Rosen replied. ''And the money.''

The ground was sliding out from under her. She leaned against the reassuringly solid windowsill and stared out at the bright, cold blue beyond the deserted harbor. Vaguely she noted the lonely silhouette of one of Seth's beauties still bobbing at its mooring despite the lateness of the season.

Behind her at the table, the two lawyers huddled together, poring over the details of the settlement papers Rosen had prepared. She listened with half an ear as she tried to review her options. But the specter of losing Nick clouded her ability to reason. She was tired. Months of uncertainty had already taken their toll. And now, when she'd thought it was finally over, she simply could not bear the thought of enduring even worse and, in the end, maybe losing.

A year.

She was going to have to do this. Her fingers tightened on the edge of the sill. Her stomach churned. Her head felt as if it would burst.

Marriage meant intimacy, involvement, loss. All that she'd spent most of a lifetime trying to avoid, pouring her hopes and dreams first into her music and art, because it was safer, and then into Nick, because it had been impossible to do otherwise. She didn't want it. She was afraid of marriage—especially to Kurt, who put her in danger of experiencing the very emotions she wanted to avoid. Kurt could break her heart if she let him.

She sensed rather than heard his approach. He would never give up his fight for Nick. Even if she went to court and won now, he would try again later.

He came up behind her and said softly, "What do you have to lose, Julia?"

My heart, my soul. The life I've meticulously constructed, piece by precious piece, out of ashes. "And if I refuse, what then?" she asked without turning.

"Then I'll do whatever it takes to get custody," he confirmed in a matter-of-fact voice that left her in no doubt that he would do exactly that.

"Why are you doing this?" She turned and looked at him.

"Because it's the only way we can both have what we want."

"One year, no money, no marriage unless we decide we want to at the end of the year."

"No more compromises. This is an all-or-nothing deal." When she didn't say anything, he went on. "Look, I wouldn't be doing this if I didn't think we could make a go of it."

"By forcing me to marry you?" she said incredulously.

"Not forcing—asking." His jaw tightened. "We get along well, or did until all this came up. We enjoy each other's company. There's no other man in your life, or we wouldn't be having this conversation. We both want Nick. And this is what he wants most." His voice held the same quiet assurance Julia had found soothing in other circumstances. "You know it."

It was a low blow. She did know it. "Just what kind of marriage are you proposing?" She hated the tremor in her voice. "Is this some kind of business arrangement, in name only, or . . . ?"

"No, I want a real marriage. This is a real proposal." At her look of contemptuous disbelief, he grew defensive. "Do you think I'd be doing it this way if I thought for one minute that hearts and flowers would work? I thought this way would be easier for you—to lay it all out, to eliminate as much risk for you as possible." He searched her face. "Do you want to hear me profess my love for you, Julia? Do you want to hear me say that I've never met anyone before you that I've wanted to share my life with? Do you want me to beg you most humbly to be allowed into your life?"

She sucked in a sharp breath and warbled an appalled "No!"

In an instant, his eyes cooled. "Good. Just so you understand that I don't want a sham marriage and a mistress on the side. We'll share a bed."

Julia stiffened. "I see. So is that all spelled out in there, too?" She waved at the table and the papers McGinn was studying. "The number of times per week I have to perform to earn the jackpot and keep my son?"

He gave her a look of disappointment. "We can work that out on our own."

"You ask a steep price."

"The alternative could be steeper for you."

"Or you." Julia pushed away from the window and started back toward McGinn, saying over her shoulder, "I'll think about it and let you know."

Overhearing her, Rosen glanced up from his papers. "The offer is good until noon tomorrow. Then it's off the table. Stay here as long as you like, or you may take it elsewhere."

McGinn glared at Kurt. "Now, look here. There's no call for these strong-arm tactics. At least have the decency to allow Miss Griffin a reasonable amount of time to consider your proposal"—his mouth twisted around the word—"if that's what you call it."

"Take it," Kurt said with an indifferent shrug, "or leave it." He turned and walked out, followed by his lawyer.

Clamping down her outrage, Julia joined McGinn at the table. "Is there any hidden danger in there I need to worry about?" She glanced briefly at the offending document.

"No. It's all very simple and straightforward, basically what you heard. Marry him, stick out the year, and he gives up any later claim to custody and the money. You'd be set."

She closed her eyes, feeling panicky and numb at the same time.

"You don't have to do this," McGinn added. "The odds are still with us."

"But you can't guarantee I will keep my son, now *and* in the future."

"No. I can't." He hesitated, then said, "I don't think a man makes an offer like this unless he's more than a little in love with the woman. It's a huge gamble for him. He's got to make you want to stay, or he loses everything."

Julia closed her eyes. *No.*

"That could work to your advantage. Even if you turn him down, he might not want to hurt you by taking Nick away from you—at least for now."

"I think you're wrong."

"Maybe." He sighed. "Why not sleep on it? We can discuss it again in the morning."

"That won't change anything. I'd rather get it over with." Julia stared at the papers. Abruptly she picked up a pen. "Where do I sign?"

McGinn flipped to the back page and she hastily scribbled her signature on the designated line. She stood, fighting a sudden bout of light-headedness, and shrugged on her coat. Behind her, McGinn hurriedly shoved papers into his brief-case and scrambled to join her, leaving only a signed copy of the agreement on the gleaming cherry table.

Kurt's office adjoined the conference room. He was there, talking to Rosen, when Julia and McGinn strode past the open door without a word. Rosen opened the connecting door and spotted the document on the conference table. "Well, well, that was fast," he said on his way across the room to retrieve it. Only the hard set of Kurt's face hinted at the tension he felt.

"You won," Rosen announced as he came back in, "if that's what you call it."

Kurt exhaled slowly as tension eased out of his shoulders. He'd won the first inning. But there was a long way to go before he knew whether he'd win the game.

Suddenly energized, he jumped up from his chair. "Let McGinn know I'm reserving Julia's church for the first Saturday in January. If she wants to plan it, fine. Otherwise I'll turn it over to Chloe. And remind him that the terms of our agreement are confidential.'' Kurt frowned at the ceiling. ''She can say we're getting married for Nick's sake, if she wants, but nothing more.''

''I sure hope you know what you're doing,'' Rosen said doubtfully.

Me, too, Kurt agreed silently. Because he'd just bet all three of their futures on it.

''I hope you know what you're doing, Julia.''

Julia pressed her free hand against her temple. Alex wasn't taking the news of her impending marriage at all well. This was their third telephone conversation in four days. Each was proving more difficult than the last. It didn't help that she couldn't disclose the terms of the agreement.

''Look,'' Julia said with a touch of impatience, ''couples get married because of pregnancies all the time. It's called, 'doing the right thing.' This isn't much different.'' She glanced from her watch to Bowen, waiting patiently at the front door. It was late Saturday afternoon and she had only an hour until she was due to pick up Nick at Kurt's house. The thought of Kurt tied her stomach up in knots. If she could get off the phone, she could still get in a short, calming run before she had to leave. An early December thaw had cleared most of her route.

''Have you seen the divorce statistics lately?'' Alex asked sarcastically.

''Well, at least we'll have tried. And if it doesn't work out, what would be so bad about a divorce?'' Alex seemed momentarily speechless, and Julia quickly changed the subject before she revealed too much. ''You're the one who always told me not to rule out marriage.''

''But not to someone you've been giving a damned good show of hating! Listen, Julia, it's obvious that there was always something between you and Kurt. I've even hoped that maybe it would eventually develop into more. But there's something wrong about this whole thing. Maybe you need to slow down.''

Julia sighed. History was working against her. And how could she convince Alex when she was having a hard time convincing herself? Meanwhile, the specter of the wedding loomed ever closer, only three weeks and counting. Chloe called almost daily to consult about it.

Julia waited for Alex to wind down, then asked, "Was it in the *Tribune* today?"

"Yeah, a splash about your upcoming wedding, and a regurgitation of the paternity mess."

"I guess I'm not surprised," Julia said grimly. "My phone's been ringing off the hook. Dan had to put an officer up at the county road again. I can't figure out how they know so fast." At least, thank God, they hadn't gotten wind of the mad bargain she'd made with Kurt.

"I think they can smell scandal in the air. Like dogs."

After a minute, Julia begged off. "I want to take a run before I pick up Nick."

"A run, huh? I'd lay odds you've been doing a lot of that lately. I don't know what it is you're not telling me that just might make some sense of all this, but one thing I do know: whatever it is, you're not going escape it by running. Not this time."

"Alex . . ." Julia's voice held a note of warning.

"Oh, all right. But you'd better think about this. *Hard.* Bye."

She'd barely hung up when the phone rang again. Thinking it was Alex calling back, Julia automatically reached for it instead of letting the machine get it. "Alex?" She heard only a wheezing breath. By now inured to reporters, she waited only an instant before muttering an annoyed "No comment" and starting to hang up.

"I'm no reporter." The cold, expressionless rasp on the other end stilled her hand.

"Who are you, then?"

"A friend." She dismissed him as a kook and was about to hang up. "You're in deep shit. I have information that can save your skin."

Curiosity won out over better judgment. ''What do you mean?''

''That rich guy, Weston, hired a guy I know to do a hit on you. He wants you gone so he can have the kid.''

''Who is this?'' Julia demanded.

''That don't matter,'' the voice rasped. ''Main thing is you got to get away.''

Shuddering, she cut off the creepy voice, then chided herself for letting him spook her. This wasn't the first weird call she had received—only the most deviant.

She pulled on sweats and a pair of running shoes. Outside, she followed Bowen along their usual route down the inlet road toward the lodge. From the lodge, they would turn north along the beach, past the cottage to a path that eventually wound through dunes and woods until it connected with the old back road where the toxic chemicals had been dumped.

She'd barely started when Dennis came out of the dunes onto the inlet road just ahead. He waved and patted Bowen while he waited for her. When she jogged up, he grinned and pointed at his watch. ''You're late.'' Vapor condensed in the cold air as he spoke.

Julia laughed. ''Am I that predictable?''

He tilted his shaggy blond head and grinned. ''You're definitely into routine.''

She glanced at the two cameras slung around his neck. ''Finding any interesting subjects?''

The expression on his face turned sublime. ''I shot some trumpeter swans up past your cottage yesterday. It was awesome. They're endangered, you know,'' he added with hushed reverence. ''I'm heading up that way now. Hope the light holds.'' He doubtfully assessed the overcast sky and fading light.

Julia shivered in the chill wind coming in off the lake and began to run in place to keep warm. ''Might see you up there, then,'' she said as they parted in opposite directions.

They often met like this. She rather liked it. He was a nice kid, full of passion about his subjects. He'd presented her with some terrific photos of Nick and Dustin that she intended to mount and frame. A wedding present, he'd said with that Peter Pan grin of his.

When she passed the lodge, she waved at Susan, working in the kitchen. Fifteen minutes later, she turned inland, away from the raw wind and sullen-looking water into Deer Cove. Bowen led the way, sticking close to her except when making an occasional diversion to check out an interesting smell. She remembered Kurt telling Nick that for Bowen, sniffing was like reading the newspaper: his nose told him who had been by lately. Nick had found the notion funny and she'd heard him repeat it countless times, beginning proudly with, "My dad says . . ."

As they neared the old back road, Bowen bounded off into a stand of trees to their right. Julia heard him barking ferociously at something. Please, not a skunk! she wished fervently, having already suffered one such encounter. "Bowen! Come!" she yelled impatiently.

He reappeared, hackles raised but smelling like his usual doggy self. "Good boy. Come on, we have to get back." He growled at the trees. "What did you find in there?" She peered into the dark shadows but couldn't see anything.

"Come on," she urged, suddenly uneasy. It was nearly dusk, and they still had to go through the dense woods bordering the old road.

She picked up the pace as the path dropped into an open valley. On the far side, the old two-track lay hidden beyond the edge of the woods. Bowen stayed with her, but his nose and eyes were alert and searching. Once more as they neared the road, he wanted to veer off into scrubby growth. Julia nervously called him back. "You're making me spooked," she muttered.

They were a dozen yards short of the trees when a loud explosion shattered the stillness of the valley. Julia stumbled and nearly fell before catching herself and instinctively sprinting for the line of trees. *A hunter,* she thought, legs pumping and heart pounding. The property was posted against hunting, but that didn't always keep them out.

"Bowen, come!" she shrieked when he faltered uncertainly behind her.

Just as they reached the first trees, another shot boomed out, splintering a chunk of bark off a trunk in front of her.

Oh, God, No! They were shooting *at* them. There must be at least two—the shots seemed to have come from different places. Hunters, or . . . ? *He's going to kill you so he can get the kid.* She nearly doubled over in agony. *No! Please, not that.*

Panicked, she failed to sidestep an icy spot she'd been avoiding all week. In sickening slow motion, her foot slipped sideways, snagged on a downed branch, and then she was hurtling forward. The frozen ground rushed up to meet her in a breath-stealing crash. For an endless moment, she couldn't move, couldn't breathe. Finally, she managed to suck in great gulps of air.

She made it as far as a sitting position. Bowen padded back to where she sat. He whined and poked his nose into her face. Hideous pain radiated up from her arm across her shoulder. She fought the urge to vomit and forced herself to look, imagining blood streaming from her shoulder. There was none, and for a moment that confused her.

Bowen whined anxiously.

The monster was back. She could feel it coming.

They had to get away from here. Cradling her injured arm, she struggled to her feet and stumbled off the path into the woods after the dog and away from whatever was back there.

She couldn't make it far, but the woods were dark, providing cover. When they came to some thick brush, she called to Bowen, and they hunkered down behind a fallen tree. Shaking with pain and fear and cold, she waited. Soon a shadow moved down the trail, then another not far behind. The first stopped just beyond her at a curve in the trail. She held Bowen's muzzle with her good hand to keep him silent.

"See her?" the second one called out.

"No," answered a familiar rasping voice, "too dark." He peered into the woods.

"Thought for sure I saw her go down," the second one said.

"No blood," the first replied.

Chapter 26

Kurt frowned at his watch. Julia was twenty minutes late to pick up Nick. ''Did your mom tell you what her plans were for this afternoon?'' Nick glanced up from a mountain of Legos on the floor of Kurt's living room long enough to shake his head.

Kurt paced over to the windows facing the street. Until today, she'd always been punctual enough to set his watch by. He wondered if this was her small way of getting back at him. She was angry, he knew. She felt manipulated, forced into signing the agreement. But he dismissed the idea almost as quickly as it occurred to him; Julia would never use Nick to punish him.

Something was wrong. Probably that damn Jeep of hers. She hadn't returned the Volvo as he'd half expected, but she wasn't driving it, either.

He tried calling her at the cottage. When he got her machine, he called Dennis.

''Where's Julia?'' he demanded without preamble when Dennis answered.

''Don't know. I saw her out running an hour ago, but she should be back by now. Something wrong?''

"She's late to pick up Nick. Look to see if either car is gone."

"Hang on."

Kurt's fingers beat a worried staccato on his desk.

A few seconds later, Dennis was back. "They're both there, but I can't see any lights on inside the cottage." Kurt could hear the new worry in Dennis's voice.

"Go over. If she's there, call me on my cell phone. Do you have the number?"

"Yeah."

"If she is there, tell her I'm bringing Nick home. If she's not . . ." Kurt didn't need to finish.

"I'll start searching the route she runs."

"I'll be there in a few minutes." Kurt thought quickly. "What way does she usually go?"

"South to the lodge, north along the shore to the state forest border, then inland through Deer Cove to that overgrown two-track where the spill is, then back to the cottage."

"If she's not home, go backward around her route."

"Right."

When he arrived at the inlet, Kurt stopped at the lodge first. He hadn't heard from Dennis and hoped maybe Julia was talking to Susan and had simply lost track of time. No such luck. Susan said she'd passed by over an hour ago on her run. Ted got up from the dinner table and grabbed his jacket and a couple of flashlights. Susan kept Nick with her.

"It'll be all right," Ted assured Susan at the door, outside of the children's hearing. "I'll let you know as soon as we know anything." Unspoken by all three was the fear that it would take something truly serious for Julia to fail to come for Nick.

They took Ted's Bronco. The cottage was open. A quick search confirmed she wasn't there. Nor was the dog. For Kurt, actually seeing the deserted cottage and both vehicles parked outside drove home the gravity of the situation. It was dark, the temperature had fallen below freezing and was still dropping, and she had probably been out now about two hours. She could be anywhere on the remote, largely inaccessible terrain.

"We'll find her," Ted said, nudging him in the direction of the Bronco. They drove around the cottage and picked up the dirt trail Julia and Kurt had followed to the dump site several weeks ago. The track was nearly impassable in places. They crawled along in four-wheel drive. Neither man said much. Kurt scanned the woods while Ted concentrated on the road.

"There!" Ted exclaimed as they rounded a bend. The headlights outlined two people and a dog in stark relief against the black woods.

Relief washed through Kurt when he recognized Julia being propped up by Dennis's arm around her waist. He sprang from the Bronco. "What happened?" he asked, moving to her other side to help. He took in the scratches and bruises on her face, the arm clutched protectively across her midsection, the hollow look in her eyes. But she was alive and in one piece.

"Careful!" Dennis warned. "She's in a lot of pain over there. I think she may have broken something."

Kurt thought she looked half frozen. And nearly in shock.

Dennis echoed his thoughts. "She's really out of it. I found her walking about a quarter mile up the trail, her and the dog. She wasn't moving very fast."

"What happened, Julia?" Ted asked, peering into her face.

"I fell," she said through bloodless lips.

"Let's get her into the truck. Ted, turn up the heat." Kurt took Dennis's place on her good side and carefully lifted her in his arms. "Put Bowen in the back, Dennis."

On the ride back to the lodge, they decided that Ted would stay with the kids while Susan came with Kurt and Julia to the hospital emergency room. When Kurt got out to take Ted's place at the wheel, Dennis pulled Kurt aside, his face troubled.

"I didn't want to say anything in front of the others, but

I think this is more than a slip and fall. She said monsters were shooting at her.''

Kurt looked doubtful. ''Dennis, she looks like she's practically in shock.''

''I heard the shots.''

X-rays confirmed a clean break in Julia's left arm just below the shoulder. Susan gave her a strong sedative to relieve the pain while they waited for the specialist to arrive and set it. ''Good,'' she said when Julia fell asleep. She spent a few minutes cleaning the scratches on Julia's face, then tucked another blanket around her. ''Come on,'' she said to Kurt. ''We may as well grab a cup of coffee. It'll be a while.''

Kurt glanced worriedly down at Julia. Even in sleep, her face looked strained.

Susan gave him a sympathetic smile. ''She's going to be fine.'' She stepped out into the corridor ahead of Kurt. ''I doubt if she'll have to stay overnight.''

''She can't go home,'' he said sharply.

''No,'' Susan agreed. ''She'll come back to the lodge for a couple of nights.''

''There's something you should know. . . .'' Over coffee, Kurt told her what Dennis had said. ''So if you still want to put her up, I insist on being there, too. And I'm going to have someone watching outside. It would be better if I took her to my house.''

''Not for Julia,'' Susan said. ''She won't be able to tell us what really happened until tomorrow, anyway. In the meantime, take whatever precautions you feel are necessary.''

Kurt nodded.

''Who would want to hurt her?'' Susan asked.

''I don't know.''

''It just isn't fair! All these bad things have been happening lately, and I'm not even including your lawsuit.''

''Yes, let's not go there,'' Kurt agreed dryly.

"The lunatic that ran her off the road, the toxic spill, the break-in at her house, the weird threats on her answering machine, and now this," she ticked off.

"Tell me about them—not the toxics, the others." He knew generally of the break-in and her car accident from Sam, but suddenly the sheer number of these incidents made a suspicious-looking pattern.

Susan was surprisingly forthcoming, giving him details he had not been aware of, details that intensified his suspicion that Julia was in danger.

"She's had a string of bad luck going all the way back to that incident with those men after the festival last summer, when you came to her rescue."

"Or perhaps good luck that she's come through it all in one piece," Kurt said slowly. "And if that's the case, she must be running on fumes by now."

"I hadn't thought of it that way. You don't think there's some connection?"

"I don't know." His mouth drew into a taut line. "But I intend to find out."

The next morning, Ted came down from Julia's room, drew Kurt aside, and reported that her fall had indeed been precipitated by someone shooting at her. Kurt's first reaction was pure, blinding rage. His second was to summon the sheriff.

When Julia came downstairs later with Susan, it seemed as if a sea of faces watched her careful progress. Dan Farley was there with one of his deputies. Sam Livingston and Dennis stood nearby, each with a coffee mug in hand. And of course, Kurt was there. "Well, well, the gang's all here," Julia muttered to Susan, trying to cover her jitters. Kurt met her at the bottom of the stairs.

"How are you feeling?" he asked, taking her good arm and guiding her to a nearby chair as if she were an invalid. Or maybe he thought she was still drugged up.

"Fine, I'm not even drooling anymore." She forced a

wan smile. "Hello, Dan," she said as the sheriff came over and took the chair next to hers.

"I'm sorry about your accident. Weston filled me in some, but I need to ask you a few questions." The room quieted expectantly. Susan came in from the kitchen, passed out more coffee, and sat down next to Ted. "So far, it sounds like you had a close encounter with someone hunting on your property. Maybe mistook you for a deer?"

"It wasn't an accident," Julia said firmly. "It was still light; they had to have seen us. Bowen and I do not look like deer."

Dan shrugged. "Bowen might. Were you dressed in bright colors?"

"No, but—" She grew indignant when she saw Dan and his deputy begin to relax, ready to write it off as a mere hunting mishap. Kurt scowled at Dan and looked about to say something, but she beat him to it. "There were *two* shots and they came from different locations. The second one hit a tree barely a foot above my head. We were out in the open, perfectly visible. It was not an accident." She finally had Dan's full attention.

"Well, I guess that puts it in a different light," Dan conceded reluctantly, looking glumly resigned to the reality that he wasn't going to get off easily this time.

Kurt sent Dan another disgusted glance. "About time."

Dan's face colored, but otherwise he ignored Kurt. "Did you actually see anyone?"

"Yes." She described the incident clinically, without expression. "There were two men. They followed me onto the back road after I fell. Bowen and I hid in the woods. It was getting dark. I could hear them talking, but I couldn't see them very well. They searched around a while and then they left."

"Oh, my God . . ." Susan murmured.

"Did you hear what they said?" Dan asked.

"It wasn't a lot. Something like, 'I thought I saw her go down,' and the other one said, 'No blood.' I remember that."

Dan was writing it all down.

Abruptly Kurt stood. ''We can't ignore the possibility that some—or all—of the mishaps Julia has suffered over the last few months are related and not accidents.''

Dan bristled. ''I don't plan to ignore anything. Or anyone,'' he added, looking pointedly at Kurt. Turning to Julia, he asked, ''Anything else you noticed about them.''

''The voice of one of them. Someone called just before I left to run. I dismissed him as another kook. I think he was one of the men. It was his voice. . . .''

The whine of the kids' video in the distance drifted through the quiet. ''What about it?'' Dan prompted.

''It was raspy, rough, sort of like metal grating. I'm almost positive it was one of them.''

''What did he say?'' Dan asked.

Julia hesitated, glancing at Kurt, who was leaning against the mantel, intently following Dan's questioning. She'd been doing a lot of thinking about that call. ''He said I was in danger, that someone was going to try to kill me.''

''Who?'' Kurt asked softly. She met his eyes and could tell he knew what she was going to say.

''You.'' Her voice was barely a whisper. ''He claimed you hired someone to kill me so you could have Nick.''

Kurt made no move to defend himself, and her words were still hanging in the air when Dan said, with what Julia thought was an unseemly amount of satisfaction, ''Well, Weston, looks like you have some explaining to do.''

Sam Livingston had been silently watching the interview from the sidelines, but he now spoke up in Kurt's defense. ''The call was obviously an attempt to set Kurt up. The guy knows her routine—when and where she usually runs. He calls, supposedly to warn her, and then takes a shot at her minutes later. The fact is, Kurt has been spending thousands to protect Julia. We've even had my brother living here to keep an eye out for any problems.''

Julia was flabbergasted when Sam nodded to Dennis, standing next to him. She remembered all those chance meetings with him, how he always seemed to be nearby. He'd been spying on her for Kurt.

"After the chemical spill," Sam continued, "I hired an additional man to patrol the area. Unfortunately, my man was called away by a family emergency and has been gone for the last couple days. Otherwise we might have caught these guys."

Dan looked unimpressed. "How do I know you three weren't the ones?" His gesture included Kurt with the Livingston brothers. He pointed at Dennis. "You knew all her movements, I'll bet." Then he turned to Kurt. "Motive. Opportunity."

Julia saw that nothing would please Dan more than to nail Kurt. They'd rubbed each other wrong from the start. Dan had resented Kurt from their very first meeting on her front porch. And Kurt, in his turn, had questioned Dan's competence beginning with the incident last summer after the music festival. This was Dan's chance to take Kurt down a peg.

Around Julia, accusations flew. Everyone had something to say except Kurt, at the center of the storm, who seemed inscrutably above it all as he watched her steadily, waiting. For what? And then she knew, as if he'd said it aloud. Before her an escape hatch appeared—her way out of the wedding. All she had to do was support Dan in casting this cloud over Kurt. Even if nothing stuck, his reputation would suffer and, along with it, any attempt to gain custody of Nick.

"You're wasting your time, Dan," she said over the hubbub. "It's not Kurt."

She knew it with a bone-deep faith that defied easy explanation. She didn't know how or why she knew it. She just did. This man who loved her son so well, who had held her protectively on the way back from the hospital, who had gently kissed her forehead last night when he thought she was too whacked out on drugs to know—this man was not a murderer.

"You know of someone with a better motive?" Dan shot back crossly.

"No, I don't," she admitted. "But that's the problem, isn't it? It would be stupid for him to murder me when we've been in the public spotlight, and I don't think anyone would call Kurt stupid. I trust him with my life,'' she said softly. ''In fact, he's probably already saved it twice.''

''Before or after he knew about Nick?'' Dan muttered.

''Dan, I'd have recognized any one of their voices.'' Her glance included Kurt and the Livingston brothers. ''It wasn't them.''

''He could have hired—'' Dan persisted, but Julia interrupted him.

''Kurt is not a murderer.'' Her eyes connected with Kurt's and she couldn't help being warmed by the approval she saw there. For a moment, she wished she could trust him with her heart as easily as with her life.

''If we assume for the moment that you're right,'' Dan said, pulling at his collar in frustration, ''then we have zip to go on.''

Kurt broke his silence. ''What about those two thugs that accosted her last summer? I heard that Julia thought one of them might be the guy who forced her off the road.''

They all turned expectantly to her. ''I don't know. The shorter one did have a gravelly voice.'' She shook her head. ''I'm not sure.''

Dan promised to look into it and pass along their earlier descriptions of the two men to other area law enforcement units. After a few more questions, he and his deputy left with Dennis to search the crime scene for evidence.

Kurt immediately turned to those remaining, his gaze lingering longest on Julia. ''Thank you. If all of you hadn't vouched for me, the good sheriff would probably have me cooling my heels behind bars right now.''

Ted rejected that with a wave of his hand. ''And if you hadn't raised the alarm as soon as you did, Julia might not have made it back at all. A fact Dan did his best to ignore.'' Ted heaved a sigh. ''He's a good man for the usual problems we have here—the occasional domestic dispute, juvenile pranks, that sort of thing—but I'm afraid he's in over his head on this one. If he doesn't bring in the state police, I think we should.''

"The problem now," Susan said with a worried look, "is how to protect Julia and Nick."

Sam nodded. "That's what I've been wondering. They can't stay here."

"We get them out of here as soon as she can travel comfortably," Kurt said decisively.

"That should be tomorrow," Susan put in.

"We could take her up to my parents at Belle House," Sam suggested.

"No." Kurt shook his head slowly. "Someplace farther away."

Julia listened with growing annoyance to them deciding her future. "So Nick and I are supposed to go off and hide indefinitely?"

"Nothing so drastic." Kurt drew her down next to him on the sofa. "Here's my plan. We move the wedding forward to next Saturday. Until then, you'll stay somewhere safely away from here. We should probably move the ceremony, too—the chapel at Breakers will do for that. After we're married we'll remain in Chicago until Sam and the authorities get to the bottom of this."

At the mention of moving the wedding to mere days away, Julia tensed.

"Sounds like a good plan to me," Sam approved. "I doubt you'll have to be away long," he consoled Julia, misunderstanding the cause of her distress. "This whole thing feels about to break wide open. My police source says the owner of the machine shop is close to giving up the name of the hauler. Once that happens—assuming at least some of these incidents are connected, and my gut says they are—it's all going to go down."

"If Sam is right, you could be in even more danger until everything is wrapped up," Kurt pointed out.

Susan and Ted murmured their approval, making the verdict all but unanimous.

Four pairs of eyes watched and waited for her response. Julia racked her brain for a logical alternative. "All right," she finally conceded.

* * *

Early the next morning, Sam accompanied Julia and Nick to Chicago aboard the Westco jet. There they settled into Kurt's penthouse apartment overlooking the Lincoln Park Zoo and Lake Michigan, not far up the Gold Coast from Alex's flat. The Radenbacher was an architectural gem. It had been one of Kurt's early restoration projects. From the manager, Julia learned that Kurt still owned the building. And from Sam she learned that the apartment was not his main abode. That was the family farm some distance outside the metro area.

Julia and Nick made a startling discovery upon entering the apartment. "Mama, look!" Nick said, pointing across the living room to a spot on the wall that had already captured Julia's openmouthed attention. Her paintings—she eventually counted three—adorned walls throughout the rooms, in breath-stopping company: here near a Matisse, there behind a Remington bronze. Kurt had purchased them immediately after the spring show, Alex told her later that evening. But because the transaction had been made through an intermediary, she, like Julia, had only discovered the true identity of the buyer when she visited Kurt's apartment for the first time.

Alex returned the following evening leading a confusing array of people and covered clothing racks that quickly sorted themselves out into the proprietor of a bridal salon, her assistant, and a dozen wedding gowns. "Alex, what is all this?" she protested.

"You need a gown."

"Maybe I do, but I'm sure I can't afford even the cheapest thing here." She should have seen this coming. Alex had been aghast the day before when Julia had admitted that she hadn't given much thought to the matter of a wedding dress, what with nearly getting killed and all, but supposed she could wear the cream cashmere suit Alex had passed on to her.

The eavesdropping proprietor was quick to correct Julia

and protect her sale. ''Mr. Weston instructed me to send the bill to him for whatever you want. And he set no limit,'' she hastened to add, evidently concluding the situation called for bluntness.

Julia leveled a cool gaze on Alex. ''You called him about it.''

''Come on,'' Alex cajoled, ''you need a real gown, not one of my old things. That suit wouldn't fit over your cast, anyway,'' she pointed out pragmatically. ''If you won't take it from him, I'm going to buy one for you. So take your pick.''

Julia sighed. What difference did it make at this point, anyway? To some extent she would be financially dependent on Kurt as long as she and Nick lived away from the inlet. And to protest overmuch would simply invite questions she was not free to answer.

Julia addressed the hovering woman, ''Do you have something that doesn't look so much like, well, a wedding dress? I think something other than white would be preferable.'' She looked pointedly down at the top of Nick's head. ''And obviously something that will fit over this.'' She indicated the cast and sling.

The woman relaxed and gave an understanding nod. ''I think I have just the thing.''

From several gowns, Julia selected an ivory sheath with a matching jacket and no train or veil. She could fasten the jacket at the top and let it drape over her broken arm. It was simple, flattering—or would have been without the ridiculous-looking cast—and even though it didn't provide as much armor as the cashmere suit, at least it didn't look hopelessly like a wedding gown, either. The proprietor took it with her to make a few adjustments.

''Don't let the money bother you, Julia,'' Alex said on her way out. ''To someone like Kurt, a dress like that is pocket change. It means nothing.''

''Then why do I feel like he just stuck a few more bills in my garter?'' Julia muttered to herself after closing the door behind Alex.

* * *

On Friday, they boarded the Westco jet for the return flight north. On this trip Alex and Rob swelled the passenger list to five.

"Mama, will Andrew be there when we get to Nana's?" Nick asked her.

"I don't know, honey," Julia answered. "We'll find out very soon, though." Gazing out one of the jet's small windows at the wintry-white scene below, she wondered whether Kurt would be there waiting for them. She had spoken to him several times since leaving Cherry Beach and knew that he had his hands full clearing his schedule in order to take a few days off after the wedding.

Alfred Livingston met them at the small airstrip and answered both questions. Andrew and his parents had flown up yesterday, he informed Nick as he, Sam, and Rob quickly transferred luggage several feet from the jet to the van parked next to it on the snow-covered tarmac. "The jet is going to fly down and get Kurt now."

But before that could happen, an accident at the work site interceded. A carpenter was injured, and Kurt appropriated the Westco jet to fly the man to a specialist in Chicago. "I'm sorry to leave you on your own with my family tonight," Kurt apologized to Julia over his cell phone as he began the drive north. "I'll see you in a few hours." Julia looked out the window at the swirling snow. He would be lucky if he made it before midnight.

Dinner was a low-key affair, much to Julia's relief, with none of the usual prewedding fanfare she had been dreading. The children ate early in the kitchen, which left only Carolyn and her husband, Alex and Rob, Pat Weston, and Julia to dine together later at the long dining room table. Considering the dreadful circumstances surrounding her last departure from Belle House, Julia was pleasantly surprised at the warmth with which Pat welcomed her to the family.

Predictably, her encounter with the "hunters" and her broken arm were keen topics of conversation, although she couldn't add much to what the others had already heard; Sam's predicted breakthrough had yet to happen. Oddly, though, the reason they had come together—the wedding itself—was barely mentioned. It was an awkward subject that everyone at the table, following Pat Weston's lead, gamely tried to dodge. Yet their private speculation was almost a tangible thing lurking beneath the surface of the conversation. Julia sensed that each was undoubtedly questioning the circumstances of her sudden marriage to Kurt.

At eight, Julia said good night and took Nick along to their room. Her early departure before Kurt arrived was cowardly and bound to fuel further speculation, but in truth, she did want to avoid seeing him. His absence made it easier to face tomorrow.

The rest of the group began breaking up at ten, and by the time Kurt let himself in at eleven, he saw only Rob and Sam lingering over drinks.

"Pour me one of those," he called out from the foyer.

Chapter 27

Kurt didn't notice Marcus sitting in the shadows until he stepped into the living room. He paused an instant before continuing across the room. "Fuller." He nodded coolly. "Didn't expect to see you here."

"Just got in myself," Marcus replied. "Couldn't miss the big event. Congratulations, by the way."

"Wasn't sure you were going to show up," Rob groused at Kurt, eyeing him as he handed over the drink. "It was damned awkward at dinner with the groom AWOL."

Kurt sank into a chair. "We had an accident at the work site." He spent a few minutes filling them in, then excused himself and went up to his rooms on the third floor.

Shortly, Sam joined him there. "It's going down," he said as soon as the door closed. "The owner of the machine shop gave up the name of the hauler. He admitted it was a cash deal, a very good deal. Unfortunately, the name turned out to be phony—"

Kurt muttered an oath.

"Wait! The guy was suspicious enough that he got the plate number off the truck. The state police are checking it out. All I know now is the truck was registered to a Chicago address.''

''Chicago again.''

''Yeah, our boy Marcus's home town,'' Sam said. ''Speaking of which, my guy down there did a little digging through the probate court records and came up with some interesting news about the March trust. We still don't know how much money was originally put in, but it's a matter of public record that more was added at the time of the grandmother's death.''

''So what happened to it? Julia has hardly lived like a trust-funder.''

''No,'' Sam agreed. ''I think it's time we ask her about it.''

''After the wedding,'' Kurt said firmly.

''We should talk to Marcus, too.''

''Not yet. We need more evidence. At this point we don't know for sure that he ever had anything to do with the trust.'' Kurt thought a moment. ''Start with Charles Fuller. Better yet, any March relative that might know something. But be discreet. We don't want to tip Marcus off.''

''Right.'' Sam nodded his agreement. ''What do you make of him showing up here now?''

''Julia must have told him. She's very loyal to him.'' Kurt's mouth thinned in frustration. ''I have no idea what he's up to. Make sure he doesn't get her off alone. I want him watched.''

The next morning, Alex delivered breakfast to Julia's room. The ceremony was scheduled for noon, with a luncheon afterward at Belle House for the few dozen family and friends who would attend. By ten, the Clearys had arrived and Susan joined Alex in helping ready Julia for the event. ''We brought Bowen up,'' Susan told her. ''After the reception, we're going up to Mackinac Island to see the Christmas lights and we won't be home until tomorrow night.''

They worked around her broken arm, careful not to snag the gown on the cast as they dropped it over her head. Numbly Julia let them decorate her.

After anchoring Julia's hair on top of her head, Alex stepped back to evaluate the result. She smiled. "I always said you could turn burlap into haute couture, but what you do for that gown ought to be a sin." Suddenly remembering something, she dove for her tote bag. "I almost forgot." She came up with a piece of ivory satin that matched the gown. "A sling!"

After Susan finished adjusting the new sling, Julia fixed a hollow gaze on her image in the mirror. A response was expected, and she made one. Alex and Susan exchanged worried looks.

"You know," Susan said gently, "you don't have to go through with this."

Julia noticed their concerned looks and straightened. "I'm just nervous." She summoned a reassuring smile for her two dearest friends. "Thank you both. I don't know what I would do without the two of you."

"Well, we're not going to give you the chance to find out," Alex said briskly.

Kurt's gaze was riveted on Julia as she came down the aisle of the small chapel to him. He had never seen her look more beautiful or more remote. She had on her composed stage persona, and he couldn't see beyond it. Her hand, when he took it, felt cold. Midway through the brief ceremony, he felt her tremble. He searched her face and realized she was barely holding on. For the first time since setting his plan in motion, he questioned the wisdom of muscling her into a marriage she quite obviously did not want.

It was time. Julia tried to pull herself together. The minister waited expectantly for her to say the words that would bind her to Kurt. But now that the big moment was here, she couldn't seem to force the words out. She felt dizzy and couldn't get enough air. Alex made a strangled sound from the first pew where she sat with Nick and Rob. Behind them, others began to stir uncomfortably. At first, Kurt's hand tightened almost painfully on hers, but then he eased his grip, allowing her to easily disengage hers if she so desired. She looked at him and saw compassion and disappointment on his face, which was worse than anger would have been. He gave her hand a reassuring squeeze. God, she was going to have to marry this man who saw too much.

Her whole body stiffened. Unsteadily she pushed out the words, "I do."

The gathering heaved a collective sigh of relief. All that was left was for Kurt to agree, which he promptly did. Seconds later it was over, their bargain sealed for better or worse. He leaned down and kissed her lightly on the lips before they turned to greet their well-wishers.

For the first time, Julia noticed Marcus next to Vanessa and glanced at Kurt in surprise. He must have invited him. But why? Considering their mutual antipathy, it seemed odd. And then they were engulfed, and the thought drifted away. "Aunt Julia," Annie called out as she squeezed through. "You look really rad. And your ring . . . Wow!" They both stared at the wide, jewel-encrusted band Kurt had slipped onto her finger moments ago. It had a substantial, old-world flavor that reminded Julia of his buildings.

"Thank you, honey." She gathered her little buddy close. "You look beautiful, too."

A luncheon buffet was laid out back at Belle House. Julia negotiated the afternoon on automatic, making the correct remarks, smiling on cue, but always aware of Kurt, dramatically handsome in black at her side, and of the hand that often rested lightly at her waist.

She was returning from the powder room when she encountered Marcus in a back hallway and saw that he meant to talk to her. He'd given his congratulations with the others, but without any great enthusiasm. She expected from the look on his face that she would soon be privy to his true feelings whether she wanted to be or not.

"Julia, I have to talk to you—"

''Please, not now, Marcus. I know you mean well, but this is hardly the time.''

His handsome face flushed in offense. Still he persisted. ''There may not be another . . .'' His voice trailed off when someone stepped around the corner.

Julia spun around. ''Sam!'' How long had he been standing there?

''Kurt wanted me to check on you, *Mrs.* Weston.'' She wasn't sure for whose benefit he emphasized her new marital status. Although he spoke to her, his hard gaze was fixed on Marcus. ''He thought you might want to escape the crush, and rest.''

''Yes, I would,'' she agreed readily. It was dark, she was exhausted, and most of the guests not spending the night had left. She, Kurt, and Nick were to spend two more nights at Belle House before flying down to Chicago on Monday. It was an odd arrangement for a wedding night, but she hadn't wanted to go on a honeymoon or to leave Nick. The only hitch was that her things had been moved to Kurt's room, and she had no idea where that was. ''If you could tell me the way. I'm just going to look in on Nick first.''

''I'll show you,'' Sam said. ''Kurt's quarters are up on the third floor, too.'' He swept her away, giving her no time to say more than good night to Marcus and leaving him glowering after them. At the end of a corridor, Sam opened a door that looked like any other, and guided her into a small mahogany-paneled lift.

''I assumed the only rooms up here were the kids' dorm rooms,'' Julia said while the cab hummed up to the third floor.

''Kurt likes his privacy, so he usually stays down in the guest cottage or up here.''

They looked in on the children. Satisfied that all was well with Nick, Julia left him in the nanny's capable hands. Sam showed her down the hall to Kurt's room. It turned out to be an entire suite, with a bedroom, bath, and sitting room with a kitchenette tucked into one corner. The furnishings were rich, with an emphasis on comfort: colorful Kasak tribal carpets covered the floors; built-in bookcases lined the walls; and there were large easy chairs and a sofa that was as soft as a feather bed.

Mentally drained, she hadn't budged after Sam left, and was nearly asleep on the sofa when a soft knock sounded at the door a few minutes later. Carolyn poked her head in. "I thought, with your arm, you might need help getting out of your dress." She smiled and ventured farther into the room. "Alex is occupied in a game of poker."

"And winning, I'll bet. She usually does." Julia stood. "Yes, thanks. I could use some help. If you would just unzip it, I can do the rest." Julia eased the jacket off first.

"Actually," Carolyn said as she crossed the soft carpet, "I've wanted a chance to tell you how glad I am that this has worked out for the three of you." Julia presented her back, and Carolyn unzipped the gown. "I was hoping it would from the start, when I saw that Kurt was in love with you. But then he was so angry. I've never seen him like that."

Julia stilled. "Kurt never loved me. He loves Nick, and I'm . . . well, in the way. As Vanessa once so charmingly put it, I was merely the flavor of the day." She immediately regretted having spoken so frankly, but what Carolyn said alarmed her.

"Vanessa!" Carolyn snorted in disgust. "She's been after him for years. If she said that to you, it just means she saw it, too." She began to untie the silk sling at the back of Julia's neck. "You'd better hold your arm."

Distracted, Julia automatically followed Carolyn's direction. "He certainly has an interesting way of showing it."

She slipped the gown off Julia's good side first. "It makes perfect sense in a warped way. He was being such a jerk because he loves you. Ordinarily, Kurt's not unreasonable or mean. He's as fundamentally decent a man as I know. . . ." Carolyn's voice died. Julia felt a draft on her bare right shoulder. She didn't need to see Carolyn's face to know what had caught her attention.

Julia whirled around, clutching the gown against her front. "Thank you. I can do the rest."

Carolyn's shock rapidly turned to contrition. "I'm sorry. I didn't mean to react . . . It's not so bad, really—just a surprise." She looked mortified. "Damn, I'm just making it worse."

Julia felt sorry for her. "It's okay," she said, "really."

Sudden understanding lit Carolyn's eyes. "That's why you had to have the dress altered for Alex's wedding. It wasn't that you didn't like it—you couldn't wear it."

"Yes." Her confirmation invited no further confidences, and Carolyn soon left her alone.

She found her clothes neatly unpacked in one of the bedroom closets and exchanged the gown for a pair of slacks and an oversized top she could work on over the cast. She looked longingly at Kurt's big bed, but settled for the couch in the sitting room. That was where Kurt found her an hour later. She half opened her eyes and gazed at him vacantly a moment before slowly sitting up.

Kurt smiled. "You don't have to get up."

Julia pushed hair out of her face and glanced at her watch. "I should go tuck Nick in."

"I already did." Kurt was carrying a present. "He fell asleep during the middle of my pirate story. I guess he finds his old man dull."

Dull? Not a word she would ever use to describe Kurt.

"What are you smiling at?" he demanded, eyebrows raised in wounded innocence. "All the times you've fallen asleep on me, too? A guy could develop a real problem with his ego around you two." He sat down next to her and handed her the package.

"What is it?"

"Open it."

Curious, she removed the paper and lifted the top of the thin box. She gave a small "ooh" of wonder, carefully lifting out the painting inside. "A Mary Cassatt." In awe, she examined one of the artist's familiar mother-child images.

Familiar only because she'd seen prints of it in books. "I can't accept this. It must have cost a fortune."

"I want you to have it," he insisted. "Your work reminds me of hers."

That raised old questions about the paintings of hers he'd bought, but she wasn't ready to go there yet. "Thank you. It's beautiful." She shifted uncomfortably. "I don't know what to say, especially since I didn't think to get you anything. Is there something in particular you would like?" she added lamely.

He considered, and after a moment, his mouth quirked up. "And would you give me whatever I wished for?"

The amused glint in his eyes made her hesitate. "That would depend at least in part on whether I could," she hedged.

"Oh, I rather think you could manage it." He made her wait, and the glint turned positively wicked. "I was thinking that another baby would be nice, eventually."

She blinked, shocked, then laughed a bit nervously, treating it as a joke even though she couldn't tell if he meant it to be. "That would raise a few eyebrows, given our history, if we *had* to get married."

"We did have to get married," he pointed out.

"Why did you buy so many of my paintings?" she blurted out.

He hesitated. "You're very observant; haven't you figured it out by now?"

She gave a small shrug. "I guess you must like my work."

"That's certainly part of it."

She held her breath, ruing the impulse that had prompted the question in the first place.

"The other part," Kurt continued, "is that I was fascinated by something of you I saw in them. Something from that place you try your damnedest to keep well hidden from the world."

"Well," Julia said brightly, rising from the couch and heading for the small kitchen, "I should be flattered that you saw so much in my work."

"You're running away again," Kurt said bluntly.

"No. Just getting a drink of water. Would you like some?" She found a glass and filled it.

"You're afraid."

She took a sip, buying time to compose herself. Then, carefully she set the glass aside and turned to face him. "All right, yes, I am afraid. I entered into a desperate agreement to marry a man so I could be sure to keep my son. And right now I don't know what I've gotten myself into. I'm not even sure what kind of marriage you envision for us."

He watched her steadily. "As I said from the start, I want a real marriage. A future together for all of us."

"So that you can have Nick."

"And you." He rose and walked toward her with perfect masculine grace and purpose.

Julia swallowed hard. "I know you expect sex, but—"

"This is not just about sex and you know it." He raised a hand and gently ran it down the side of her face to her chin. "But I'll take it," he added huskily, not giving her a chance to utter any of the "buts" she had stockpiled. "For now." He lifted her chin and lowered his mouth to hers.

She'd understood perfectly this part, at least, of their deal when she agreed to it, and she expected to fulfill her end. But it was happening too fast! Her injury was supposed to be a barrier, allowing her time to prepare herself mentally. It wasn't so much the physical act that worried her—he'd always had the bewildering and embarrassing ability to reduce her to a hormonal puddle with little effort. Already, heat was building and being guided by his hands as he thoroughly explored each curve, each bone, in a slow descent down her back. His mouth was hot and hungry on hers, demanding her response and, after she gave up a useless attempt to remain detached, getting it.

Yes, it would be no hardship to endure physical intimacy with Kurt.

It was the emotional intimacy that threatened to follow that scared her silly. She would be a fool not to recognize the increased risk of the latter from engaging in the former.

Even as the warning formed in one dim corner of her brain, she was dragged deeper into the hot pleasure.

She tried to adjust the position of the hard cast between them. He used a more direct approach to overcoming the obstacle by simply cupping her buttocks and hitching her tightly up against him. Julia gasped and froze in reaction to both the hard evidence of his arousal and a simultaneous jolt of pain from her injured arm.

Kurt felt her flinch and stilled. "Are you all right?" he said against the top of her head. "Did I hurt you?" With effort he loosened his hold, allowing her to ease out of his embrace while every nerve ending in his body protested. Unfortunately, the small distance was enough to jerk her out of the hot current that had been sweeping them toward the big bed in the next room with far more ease than he'd expected.

She stared at him, breathing hard.

"Julia?" He reached for her, breaking the spell, and she eluded him.

She shook her head, put up a hand to stop him. "No. I'm fine." But her normally fluid voice sounded hoarse. She cleared her throat, glanced at her injured arm as if only then remembering it. "I—ah . . ." She gulped another deep breath, looked back at him and then away again. "It hurts some when it gets bumped," she explained, tentatively touching her arm above the cast. "The cast doesn't actually cover the break."

"I'm sorry. I'll make sure it doesn't happen again."

"I think it would be best if we waited a while." She stepped behind the couch. "Just until I get the cast off in a week or two. Then we'll have only the sling to contend with."

He didn't say anything, just watched as she drew on her normal composure. He could almost visualize her mentally scurrying around, stitching up all the rents he'd made in it.

"I'll wait you out," he said finally. "No matter how high you build that wall around you, I'll be right here every time you look out."

She blinked in surprise. "I don't know what you're talking about. It's just my arm."

He studied her in silence, determined to halt her retreat, and finally said softly, "I know about your family, Julia. How you were left alone when you were only sixteen years old. It's a horror no child should experience."

"No—please . . ." She raised an imploring hand. He ignored it.

"It must be hard to love and trust again."

"I have that with Nick," she said, her distress a palpable thing.

Kurt came around the couch and took her good hand. It trembled in his. "Nick is a boy. Soon he'll be a man. You'll have to let him go. Then what?"

"I don't need it."

"If you don't, you won't really be alive. Just an imitation of a flesh-and-blood person."

She hesitated, then pulled her hand back. "I need time."

Her beautiful voice quivered, and Kurt decided to relent. For now. They had time.

"I'll be right next door tonight if you need anything. Oh, and Julia, just for the record . . ." He paused on the threshold and looked back at her. "I've wanted you for my own from the moment I saw you plunge into the water after that little girl. Before Nick was more than a dream."

It was a long time before she stopped shaking. And even longer before she dared examine the question flickering temptingly at the edge of her mind: Could she . . . ? It would be so easy to love this man. Perhaps the more pertinent question was whether she could stop herself from loving him.

She raised her good hand to her temple. It was too risky, too complicated. There were too many problems, too many grudges standing between them. It wasn't safe to love him. He would end up tearing her apart.

Utterly exhausted, but wanting to check on Nick before she went to bed, Julia set off down the corridor leading to the children's dorm. The doors she passed led to storage areas and unused servants' quarters. Marcus stepped out of one, startling her.

"Marcus!" She put a hand to her heart. "You gave me such a fright! What on earth are you doing up here?"

"Waiting for you." He gave her a lopsided grin that didn't quite reach his beautiful dark eyes. "You know, you still sound so very British at times."

"Why lurk about in a back hallway?" she asked, eyeing him suspiciously. He looked nervous. "Why didn't you just come to Kurt's room?"

His expression turned grim. "They're guarding you. Or maybe holding you prisoner."

"Who? What are you talking about?" she asked with some exasperation.

"Kurt and his hired goon. They won't let me near you."

She assumed he was referring to Sam's earlier interruption in the downstairs hallway, and sighed at Marcus's increasingly tedious penchant for drama. "I think you're exaggerating. In any event, you've found me. So what is it?"

"I have to warn you that if you go through with this—"

"*If*, Marcus?" She stared at him in impatient disbelief. "I already have!"

He gritted his teeth. "I saw you at the altar. Everyone did. You came close to walking out on him, and I was ready to cheer you on."

Julia inwardly winced. Had it been that obvious?

"You can still leave," he continued urgently, "before you end up with more than a broken arm. I'll help you get back to London, or somewhere else safe. He won't expect it now."

Curiosity sharpened her gaze as Marcus came close to pleading with her. He was desperate. Why should he care so much?

Regretting her impatience, she tried to make him understand. "I don't want to run. What kind of life would that be for Nick? And what makes you think an ocean would stop Kurt?"

"You've fallen for him," he said flatly. "You don't want to leave him."

"Maybe I don't. Maybe I want to try to make it work."

He made a feeble attempt at a smile, but it came out more like a sneer. "I appreciate the sentiment, but it's wasted on Weston. You still don't get him. He doesn't love you. To him you're the enemy. He probably wants your face"—he reached out and gave her cheek a feather-light caress—"and your body, until he gets tired of them. But mainly, he wants to defeat you. To own you and Nick. And now he does."

Julia pulled away from him, disgusted that he would say such things to her now.

"I can see you don't believe me," Marcus observed. "You think I'm overreacting. So then, I assume you don't know that he bought up your mortgage?"

"What do you mean? The bank still owns it. Nothing has changed except the extension."

"Oh, yes, darling, it has. I was curious when your bank agreed to the extension, so I made a few inquiries of my own." Marcus had the look of a player holding a trump card. "Turns out Kurt bought up your note two months ago. He left the administration of it with the bank, obviously so you wouldn't find out. And now, by marrying you, he's managed to tie up the last loose end. Now he owns you, Nick, and your land."

Julia suddenly felt ill as the pieces fell into place. *Tell the bank about the spill. Ask them for an extension.* Kurt had known all along the lender would agree to it because he *was* the lender.

"Even if he did buy up the mortgage, that hardly means he owns the land."

"Technically, no. But depending on the language of the extension you signed, he may have a purchase option, or who knows what else, written in there. That's really the reason I wanted to talk to you alone. Meet me tomorrow morning at your place and we can look over the papers, see what's actually in them. Then we can plan what to do."

That was the last thing she needed now. "I don't know,"

she said tonelessly. "I'll have to let you know in the morning." She glanced up at him. "Thanks, Marcus, for telling me."

Marcus looked at her intently. "What are you going to do now?"

"Go tuck Nick in." She knew that wasn't what he meant, but in truth she was too upset to think straight. Why had Kurt bought her loan on the sly? She couldn't think of a single reason she would like. The possibilities ranged from bad to worse, from added leverage in the custody battle to stealing her land outright. The outrage she felt was nothing compared to the crushing sense of disappointment and betrayal.

"If you tell him you're meeting me, he won't let you come," Marcus warned, giving her a pitying look. "You're hardly more than a beautiful bird in a cage here."

In the dimly lit hallway outside Kurt's study, Julia stopped with her hand poised on the door. Her mouth hardened as she recognized Kurt's voice raised in frustration. *"Why isn't he cooperating with the police? Has anyone bothered to tell him what the penalty is for illegally dumping toxic wastes?"*

It took her a few more seconds to identify Sam Livingston from his more subdued response. *"He says he worked alone, that he didn't target Julia's property, and that it was just a convenient place to dump his load."*

"Bull. That doesn't explain why the drums were pried open."

"He claims some of them popped open when he pushed them off the truck."

"Bull," Kurt repeated. *"He's more afraid of whoever hired him than he is of the police."*

Julia leaned closer to the door. So, the rogue hauler was in custody. Apparently Kurt was keeping quite a lot from her—damn his black soul! Their voices dropped. Even with her ear pressed to the door, she couldn't catch much. Sam seemed to be moving around the room. Her own name kept popping up, and "Marcus" and "trust," until finally he must have turned toward the door, because she heard him say quite clearly and urgently, *"You've got to ask Julia about the trust. There must be papers somewhere, and if there is a connection . . ."*

What trust? Kurt had asked her about a trust once, and she'd set him straight then that she was no trust-funder. The educational trust her grandmother March had set up years ago ended upon her graduation from college. Anyway, what would Marcus have to do with it?

"No," Kurt's voice interrupted Julia's racing thoughts. *"Not yet. You saw her in the chapel. If there's money there and she knew about it, do you think for one minute she would have walked down that aisle?"*

After a moment's silence, Kurt went on. *"We'd probably be in the mother of all custody trials about now. Besides, we don't know that Marcus ever had anything to do with Julia's trust."*

"Maybe not. But we do know Mrs. March made Charles Fuller trustee and he later turned his practice over to Marcus. It's not a huge leap."

"No, unfortunately not," Kurt agreed, then muttered a curse. *"Look, I know you're eager to break this thing open—so am I—but we've got to play it cautiously."*

"Why? Because you're afraid of losing Julia or because of a potential scandal involving the Fullers?"

"Both."

Julia barely heard the last. She stared blindly at the door, her mind traveling down a dark tunnel to her past. A bearded young man, beautiful enough to be a movie star, standing in the high tropical sun, bringing news of the trust Mary March had created to provide for her grandchildren's education.

If Charles Fuller was Grandmother's lawyer, then that means Marcus . . .

How had she failed to notice the resemblance? It had been right there in front of her all these years.

The murmur of voices inside the study broke her paralysis.

Stiffly she pushed away from the door, abandoning her mission, and stumbled away down the hall.

It was 8:00 A.M., barely dawn, when Julia placed a call to Charles Fuller using the cottage number Marcus had given her years ago, and which she had dutifully copied down in her address book but had never used. She didn't really expect to reach him there at this time of year—it was simply a place to start—so she was surprised when a man's voice answered on the third ring.

"Mr. Fuller?"

"Who is this?" came the curt response.

"Julia Griffin. Marcus's . . . friend." She nearly choked on the word. "I'm sorry to bother you this early." Outside, the first gray light stained the sky. "We met—"

"Yes. Julia!" He cut off her explanation in a considerably warmer tone. "What a nice surprise. No need to apologize; I was up. I hear congratulations are in order." His voice dropped in good-natured reproach. "Although I have to admit I am disappointed things didn't work out between you and my son. But enough on that."

"Actually, I didn't really expect you'd still be up north this time of year."

"Usually we're not, but I had a few matters that needed attending to. What can I do for you?" he asked. "If you're looking for Marcus, he isn't here."

"No. It's you I want to talk to."

"Well, anything I can do . . ."

Did he sound a bit wary under all that hearty good-old-boy solicitude? And where was the dementia Marcus had been embarrassed about? She decided to plunge right in. "Were you the trustee of a trust my grandmother, Mary March, set up for me about fifteen years ago?"

Silence met her question, but he didn't hang up, so she asked another. "Was Marcus—did he deliver a letter about the trust to my father in the Bahamas?"

After a considerable silence, she heard him heave a sigh.

''Mrs. Weston, I think you have questions we should address in person. Would it be possible to meet at your cottage today? I won't be here after tomorrow.''

''We could meet at the diner, around eleven?''

''I think it best if we met at your cottage. It would be more private. Call me when you arrive and we can arrange a time.''

She agreed. Before he hung up, Charles Fuller added, ''You may find it difficult to believe right now, but for what it's worth, my son cares a great deal about you.''

Marcus watched the red Subaru race down the long drive in a billow of snow until it disappeared around the corner. Then he stood and stretched muscles stiff from his vigil at the window in the garage apartment. Conveniently, Sam Livingston had vacated the apartment and stayed in Belle House last night. Marcus noted the time—8:15 A.M.—and yawned as he punched in a number on his cell phone. His plan was working. He'd flushed her from the nest.

''She's on her way,'' Marcus said.

''Good. Now, no more shilly-shallying around. This doesn't affect just you anymore. You've dragged us all into this mess, and I expect you to fix it.''

''I *know,* Dad,'' Marcus answered sullenly.

''One more thing: she knows about the trust.''

Chapter 28

When Julia turned up missing later in the morning, at first Kurt thought she might have left him. Livingston informed those gathered around the breakfast table that she'd gone to Cherry Beach. "I assumed you knew," he said to Kurt. "She said there was something important she had to find."

"Did she take Nick?" Kurt asked tightly.

"He's upstairs with Mom and Andrew," Carolyn put in across the table.

Kurt's shoulders eased a fraction of an inch. She did mean to return, then. "What car did she take?" he asked Livingston, standing abruptly.

"Is it safe for her to go there?" Alex asked worriedly. All eyes turned to him expectantly.

Kurt uttered a rare profanity, effectively answering that question for all of them.

Livingston shook his head, obviously upset. "I'm sorry. She said it was okay because the police had the man who dumped the chemicals in custody."

Kurt froze. "She said what?" As Livingston repeated exactly what Julia had told him, Kurt wondered how much else she'd overheard last night. "Where's Marcus?"

His sudden change of subject baffled the others. Rob looked at him curiously. "He left for Chicago a little while ago."

Okay, a quick in and out. Julia carefully scanned the cottage and surrounding inlet from the safety of the car. *Grab the box and go.* She took a minute to screw up her nerve before cutting the engine. The police had one man in custody, but two men had come into the woods after her, and there was no guarantee the same men were responsible for both incidents.

Nothing looked out of the ordinary. The inlet stretched silently in all directions—a frozen white tundra covered by a gray December sky. Not even a breeze disturbed the unusual stillness. Julia shivered and unclenched stiff fingers from the steering wheel.

She hadn't intended to be doing this alone. In the wee hours of the night, when she'd finally stopped trying to make sense of what she overheard outside Kurt's office, and began to think about what she ought to do, she'd remembered the box. Her plan had been to stop at the lodge and have Ted come over with her to retrieve it. Unfortunately, it had slipped her mind that they wouldn't be back until this evening.

The metallic creak and slam of the car door as she got out echoed harshly across the frozen silence. Julia paused, her gaze darting nervously about the inlet, finding nothing. Still, it didn't feel right. She shivered again.

She could almost feel the dark monster watching. Waiting.

Stop it! She couldn't let herself sink back into the past. No one knew she was here. Even if, God forbid, she had become some creep's target, he wouldn't expect her to show up now. And she'd be damned if she would sneak around her own home, her haven, like some scared little bunny. She wanted answers, and if they were here, she meant to get them.

She quickly crossed the yard to the cottage. The phone

was ringing when she opened the door. She let the machine get it.

"Julia, are you there? If you are, pick up."

She scowled as Kurt's deep voice filled the living room. He had a lot of explaining to do, but not now. She needed to find the box her grandfather had left her. Maybe then.

"What the hell are you trying to do?" he demanded over the machine.

Julia suddenly realized that *he* was angry with *her!* Of all the . . . !

"Get out of there now. It may not be safe." His voice softened. *"Look, I know you overheard us talking about the toxic-waste hauler last night. You're upset that I haven't told you everything. You're probably wondering if there's anything else I've kept from you. . . ."*

"Like the fact that you now own my mortgage?" Julia muttered to herself, detouring to her file drawer to find the loan extension papers. Might as well take them, too.

". . . but damn it! You should have come and talked to me, not run off half-cocked. If I've made any mistake, it's been trying to protect you and make things easier. I know how hard all this has been for you."

Julia felt something give in the vicinity of her heart. She clenched her teeth against it. What was the matter with her? He'd been shamelessly manipulating her, stacking the deck against her to an extent that she now suspected was far beyond anything she'd seen. And to think he'd almost gotten to her last night. Again. For a moment she'd yearned to give their marriage a real shot, despite the fact that the very notion scared her silly.

"We can talk about this later. Right now, get out of there. Go to Sid's and wait for me. I'm on my way." The machine cut off.

Julia grabbed the manila loan file and was headed for the attic when the phone rang again. This time Alex came on, swearing mightily at getting the machine. She lit into Julia anyway. *"You've really done it this time. What's the matter with you? How could you walk out the morning after your wedding?''* Astonished, Julia stopped dead on the stairs. *''Everyone is wondering what's going on between you two. Kurt is beside himself with worry. You made a fool of him in front of all these people. I pried the whole story out of him about what you overheard last night, and I'll just bet you've worked yourself up into a righteous lather. That's a lot less risky than giving him a chance to explain because, God forbid, maybe he could.''* Before hanging up, she added, *''What on earth are you doing there, anyway? Who knows if it's safe?''*

It hadn't occurred to Julia that her absence would cause such a stir. It hurt that Alex was taking Kurt's side, especially without hearing hers. Maybe it had been cowardly and foolish to leave without first talking to Kurt, but damn it, it was his fault in the first place that she had learned about Marcus's connection to the trust the way she had. And neither understood that Marcus's involvement in her life went far deeper than what they saw on the surface, far beyond the trust itself.

Marcus Fuller. Julia felt a wave of revulsion gathering strength and fought to keep a clear head. *Don't think about it. Just get the box.*

She raced up the stairs to the cramped attic. It was a junk bin. For years Seth had used it as a catchall, and later she had, too. Boxes of Nick's outgrown clothes meant for Goodwill were jumbled in front of older stacks of boat-rigging hardware, furniture, and mystery boxes. She had long intended to sort through the mess, but there was always some more immediate need.

She started working her way across the attic, lifting smaller boxes with her good arm and pushing others aside as best she could. To anyone else, the job of locating a particular box in the mess might have looked hopeless, but Julia knew the box she was looking for would be near the juncture between her things and Seth's.

After a few minutes, she found it near the attic window: a medium-sized brown file box with ''For Julia'' scrawled in her grandfather's hand across the top. Before his death, he'd given it to Susan for safekeeping, and she'd delivered it to Julia after his funeral. At the time, she'd given it a cursory look. But when she found it filled mostly with family memorabilia and nothing pertaining to his estate, she'd put it aside.

Now she held her breath as she lifted the top. If Seth had kept anything pertaining to her trust, this was where it would most likely be.

Ignoring scrapbooks and loose snapshots, she thumbed through manila files tucked in the back containing her various school and medical records, until she came to one labeled "March Trust." Her hand shook as she flipped it open.

At first she couldn't make sense of what she saw. The first few pages appeared to be yearly accounts of a trust, except that there appeared to be a lot of money, and all of the dates were after her grandmother's death. Then she came to a letter to her grandfather, stuck in toward the end. It was from Mary March shortly before her death and clearly written in anticipation of that event. The letter built on an earlier telephone conversation and was thus sketchy, but one passage in particular caught her attention:

Julia appears to be a headstrong girl, much like her mother. I would strongly prefer that she not know of my bequest ahead of time. I have made my wishes known to Charles Fuller and trust that you will honor them as well. By that time she should have the maturity to manage her finances. And, too, that will protect her from falling prey to unscrupulous men. In the interim she is to receive no income after her graduation from college. As I explained on the phone, at age thirty-two, she may begin drawing interest . . .

Julia slowly reread the letter. Her grandmother had left her a small fortune. Apparently, she would soon be eligible to begin drawing a modest yearly income from the trust.

Had she known sooner, she could have borrowed against her future income and financed a solid defense to Kurt's bid for custody.

For a moment she felt a peculiar sense of relief that she hadn't known about the money, but it wasn't something she had time to analyze now. She pushed it aside for later and quickly worked her way through the remainder of the thin file. After that, there were only yearly statements documenting the growth of the fund—unremarkable but for one thing.

Her eyes climbed back to the top of a yearly statement dated several months before Seth's death. The name sprang out at her.

Marcus A. Fuller, Trustee

All the rage she had been holding in check rushed over her as each piece of the puzzle clicked into place. Marcus had lied to her. He not only knew of the business relationship between his father and the Marches, he handled the March trust—her trust!—and had for years, even before her grandfather's death, probably from the time he took over his father's law practice. He would have known exactly who she was from that very first chance meeting at Belle House years ago. He'd known when he went to great lengths to befriend her, spending years, she saw now, demonstrating his loyalty, years chipping away at her reticence.

He'd used her. He'd deliberately intruded in her life a second time. Perhaps to assuage his guilt. Perhaps to work off his sins. His reasons didn't matter to her. He had tainted her new life. It revolted her to think she had willingly spent even one minute in his company. Her father and brother were dead because of him. He may not have pulled the trigger, may not even have meant to hurt them, but his deceit and greed had brought hell down on their heads. Her mouth drew into a tight line. She would never forgive him for that. Never!

She closed the file and slipped it into her tote bag, shaking as much from her violent emotions as from the frigid attic air.

The first thing she intended to do was get Marcus removed as trustee. She would gladly expose his evil to the world if that's what it took. Shout it from the rooftops—

She sensed someone watching her even before she heard the whisper of movement on the stairs behind her. She whirled around in time to see the door at the foot of the attic stairs swing closed. The click of the lock pierced the silence, metallic and unreal.

Heart racing, she stumbled down the half flight of stairs and pounded on the door.

"Kurt?" she called out, hoping against hope that it was Kurt, that he was paying her back for leaving the way she had. But she knew with sick certainty that it wasn't. "Marcus?" she tried.

The front door banged distantly. She tested the attic door, put her uninjured shoulder into it, but it didn't budge. A phone rang in the distance. Not hers. It stopped.

Quickly, she ran back up the stairs and waded through the clutter to the only window in the attic. Blood pounded in her ears. Her throat clenched with the effort to keep a lid on the nameless fear. Nameless but familiar. Her nightmare pursuing her relentlessly through time.

The small window afforded a view only to the north, toward Deer Cove. She couldn't see the parking area or the inlet road. A car sputtered to life on the other side of the cottage. She felt a spurt of hope. Maybe her jailer was leaving. Maybe she could find a way out before he returned. Maybe he wouldn't return at all. . . .

Her relief was cut short when the red Subaru she had borrowed came around the house. Oh, God, she'd left the keys in it. The car bumped across the yard to the edge of the woods near the back trail. She spied another vehicle parked next to it, an ancient utility truck, barely visible through the trees.

A man got out of the Subaru. He walked toward the rear of the truck, opened the hatch door, and picked something up before starting toward the cottage.

Julia strained to see. Questions buzzed wildly in her head. *Who? Why? What now?* He carried what looked like a plastic milk jug, except it was filled with a clear liquid. She didn't recognize him. From above she stared down at the top of scruffy ginger hair. There was something furtive about the way he moved, like a night creature not really comfortable in broad daylight. Something about him seemed familiar. . . .

He looked up at the window. Their eyes locked.

Julia gasped and jerked away from those eyes. Inhuman, dead eyes. She couldn't breathe. The attic shrank around her, the clutter suddenly suffocating.

She remembered those eyes.

"She's not at the diner," Sheriff Dan Farley reported to Kurt by phone. "I'll send someone by her place to see if she's there. She's probably fine, but no sense taking any chances."

The good sheriff's stock took a major jump in Kurt's estimation. He'd half expected Farley to refuse him any help at all. "Thanks." He paused, then added, "I owe you."

Kurt stomped on the accelerator and the car jumped forward. He was making better time than expected. The snow that would have slowed Julia had stopped, and there was little traffic on a Sunday morning to hold him up. Farley was likely right, Kurt told himself. She was probably perfectly safe. And when he found her and reassured himself on that score, he just might strangle her himself.

Julia wrapped one end of an old cotton docking line around her waist and secured it with a sailor's double half-hitch. Then she threaded the other end through a wooden boat block she'd attached to an attic beam. The pulley would reduce the load on the half-rotted line—enough to keep it from breaking, she hoped. And it would reduce the burden on her good arm. She needed to finish and get out while he was still occupied downstairs. He'd made another trip back and forth to the truck. Now she could hear him rummaging around through her things.

Working fast, adrenaline pumping, she used the tools she'd salvaged from an old footlocker to chip away at the windowpane, using clothing to muffle the noise. If he heard her, it would be all over. She would be at his mercy again, just as she'd been last summer after the music festival. Only this time Kurt wasn't here to stop him. This time . . .

Hysteria misted her vision as childhood horrors pushed up from the depths. She breathed hard to clear her head. She only had herself. Her own wits. She couldn't let the past sabotage her. The stakes were too high.

Nick—*No, don't think about Nick.*

A sob caught in her throat, raw and primitive. But the thought of Nick gave her new determination. She would get through this. She had to.

She left her tote bag, with its evidence of the trust, behind a box. Then she shoved a trunk into place below the window, climbed up on it, and wriggled feetfirst through the opening. Even without her jacket it was not easy to squeeze through because of the cast. She had a scary moment when the line stretched and finally held. But after that, once she got her feet into place against the side of the cottage, it was a fast scramble to the ground.

She left the rope dangling against the side of the cottage. She couldn't afford to waste time hiding it. Cradling her arm against her body, she raced for the woods.

The itchy feeling between her shoulders began to fade when she got past the first line of trees. But the snow was less packed here, the going slower. Every dozen steps or so she broke through the crusty surface and stumbled. And it had begun to snow again. She was leaving footprints. Easy to track.

She changed course and broke free of the woods. She could make better time on the road. The best she could hope for was that he hadn't missed her yet. She needed time to get to the phone in the lodge. Just a few more minutes. She concentrated on keeping her feet moving and shut out the protesting throb of her injured arm and, most of all, her terror.

Marcus turned the rented Explorer onto the inlet road, drove around to the back of the old lady's house, and stopped. His foot drummed a fast beat against the floorboard as he peered into the trees. "Come on," he muttered. "Where are you, you dumb ox?" Thank God all the neighbors were gone, he thought. It made things a lot easier.

He released his pent-up breath in a rush when he spotted the burly dark-haired figure emerging from behind the building. His mouth relaxed into an impatient sneer as he watched Eddie's lumbering approach. It was hard to imagine that Eddie and Deek had sprung from the same bitch. Even beyond the obvious difference in size and coloring, they were nothing alike. Eddie was slow-moving and thinking, the exact opposite of Deek's quick cunning. But both looked exactly like what they were: trailer-park trash.

Marcus had reservations about involving Eddie, but Deek had insisted on a lookout. Oh, well, the big lug may be no genius, but that, too, had been useful in the past.

Eddie stopped a few feet short of the car and silently eyed Marcus.

"Well, get in," Marcus snapped.

Eddie shook his head. "Deek said to stay here."

Marcus clenched his teeth. Whatever Deek said, Eddie did. "Right, you were to stay here until Deek was done," he said with exaggerated slowness, as if to a child. "By now he is, and it's time to get out of here."

If Eddie felt the insult, he didn't show it. He also didn't budge. "It ain't done. Deek's waiting for you. He said he weren't doin' it until you got there."

"That son of a bitch!"

"So what are you guys doing in there, anyway?" Eddie shifted uncomfortably from one foot to the other but stuck out his chin. "Because I ain't takin' another rap and watch you and Deek walk. I did ten years in that hellhole for you."

Marcus didn't waste any more time on Eddie. He jammed the gearshift into drive and floored the accelerator, causing the SUV to fishtail across the narrow ruts. Deek would take care of Eddie. He always did.

Chapter 29

The black SUV appeared suddenly, speeding toward her down the narrow track. Julia scrambled over the snowbank and backed away, ready to flee across the dunes. The vehicle skidded to a stop a few feet from her, and the door sprang open.

Marcus. Her step faltered. She'd almost forgotten. Disoriented, it took her a moment to make the connection—he'd asked her to meet him at the cottage this morning.

"Julia!" His surprise at her appearance was evident as he took in her dirty jeans and ripped sweatshirt.

For an instant she regarded him, wavering, revolted by what she saw. *Fool!* She couldn't afford to be picky at a time like this. She needed his help.

"Marcus! We've got to get out of here." She scrambled back to the road. "There's a man at my house. We have to call the police!" She cast an apprehensive glance up the road.

Marcus took her good arm. "Hold on. Slow down—"

"There's no time. Where's your cell phone?" Not waiting for his answer, she tried to tug him toward the vehicle. "Come on!"

"Take it easy. Tell me what's going on."

"Marcus," Julia implored desperately, "we've got to get out of here. Now!" She shot another quick glance over her shoulder, and her heart jumped into overdrive.

"Oh, God—look!" Her tormentor had come into view around the bend in the road and was jogging toward them, gun in hand. "Come on!" When still he didn't budge, she let go of him and started to flee on her own. But Marcus's hand snaked out and caught her arm in a vise grip, bringing her to a jarring halt. She watched in horror as the armed thug bore down on them.

"Too late," Marcus said, sounding strangely calm under the circumstances. A dreadful suspicion took shape.

The vile creature puffed to a halt in front of them. Pale-blue eyes flicked her a glance before coming to rest on Marcus. "She got out the attic window." Julia recognized the raspy voice as that of both the anonymous caller and the man in the woods.

Marcus's eyes narrowed on him. "If you'd stuck to the plan, she wouldn't have."

"You?" Julia choked out, staring at Marcus in horror, not wanting to believe it even now.

"Yeah, me," he admitted grimly. "I didn't want it to come to this, Julia. I did everything I could to avoid it. For years, I tried to get you to go back to England—hell, anywhere."

Julia knew then with terrifying clarity that they meant to kill her. That was the "plan" to which Marcus referred. "Then why?"

He glanced nervously up the inlet road. "Let's move this little confessional back to the cottage, shall we?" Already he was dragging her toward the Explorer. "I believe you've already met my associate, Deek, here, last summer? He can be a bit vicious when he's crossed, so I'd advise you to be on your best behavior."

He pushed her into the front passenger seat and then hurried around to the driver's seat. His "associate," Deek, sat behind her. She could feel his pale gaze on the back of her head—feral, without conscience, she recognized instinctively. She was his target. His prey.

The monster is loose, bringing death and destruction to all who stand in its path.

Julia closed her eyes and clung to the remnants of her sanity. She thought of Nick. Of Kurt. As long as she breathed, there was hope.

Marcus parked out of sight, next to the other two cars. He dragged her along to the cottage. Deek followed behind. She listened to the crunching sounds their boots made against the snow, and thought it odd that she would notice such an insignificant detail now.

"I never wanted to hurt you," Marcus said, abruptly breaking the silence. "Christ, I was willing to marry you to keep it from coming to this."

Julia seized on his misgivings. "Then why?" She dug in her heels on the front porch, forcing him to stop.

He looked at her in surprise. "Money, of course."

Of course. What else? But actually to hear him say it. She stared at him, finally seeing him for what he was: a man utterly without principle or morals, a man consumed by greed. "Deer Cove?"

"No, that was just the icing."

"The trust, then."

"So you do know. How did you find out?"

"I found some papers in the attic."

"She was looking through a box up there when I locked her in," Deek volunteered.

"Excellent." He nodded to Deek. "Get it."

Deek hesitated, his pale eyes slits across his face as he assessed the risk of leaving her in Marcus's hands. Marcus pulled a gun out of his jacket pocket with one hand and waved Deek away with the other. Julia was relieved when Deek disappeared inside. She suspected that he hadn't obeyed Marcus so much as reached his own decision on the matter.

"I've looked for those trust papers for years," Marcus

said, "even before that old coot grandfather of yours died. Never could find them."

Julia stared at him as another horrifying suspicion took shape. "My grandfather?" Only a whisper could pass through her constricted throat. "Did you—?"

"What? Put him out of his misery?" he said impatiently. "He was dying anyway. He insisted on telling you about the trust before he croaked."

Sickened, she turned away from him. Fury erupted in the next breath, building until she thought it would burst out through her skin. Was this the monster she'd lived in fear of all these years? This weak, dissolute son of Satan who casually used and discarded people like so much debris in his greedy path?

Long practice enabled her to don the appearance of self-control when she turned to face him. "Why now after five years?"

"I always knew that someday you might find the trust papers yourself and ask questions. Or remember me from the Bahamas. Kurt's presence increased the odds of both. The longer you were around the Westons, the greater the chance someone would discover you were the Marches' granddaughter and mention their connection to my father. Or Kurt would mention my drug arrest in the Bahamas and that would ring some bells. But why right now?" His face twisted into a hard mask of hatred. "Because your dear husband started digging around in my past. Because he bought up your loan. Because I can't stand the bastard and you married him!"

"You'll never get away with it."

"Sure, I will. In a few minutes there will be no evidence the trust ever existed. You had the only remaining documentation."

"There must be court records—"

He smiled smugly. "Not anymore, thanks to a brief but highly productive fling I had with a court clerk."

"There's your father."

This time he laughed at her. "Dear old Dad? He cooked

the books on your trust for years. Small-time stuff. I simply pushed the envelope. He doesn't approve of that, but he's completely behind the damage control. A matter of the family name and all."

Julia shrugged indifferently. "Actually, the trust is of little interest to me. What I really meant is that you won't get away with murdering me. You'll be the first person Kurt suspects. He's been warning me about you for months." Her mind raced, weighing the consequences of revealing more. She didn't want to put Kurt in danger. Nor did she want to hasten her own end. But perhaps she could convince Marcus that his plan could not succeed. And there was something else she'd noticed: the longer he talked, the less vigilant he appeared.

Julia glanced through the front door, looking for Deek. It should take him a while to find her tote bag. She hoped. Because Deek, she recognized instinctively, would be impossible to manipulate. She took a breath and gambled. "In fact, Kurt is on his way here now."

Marcus merely smiled. "Oh, I'm counting on that. If he wasn't, I would have made sure of it." He raised an elegant brow at her stunned expression. "Does that really surprise you?"

"It makes me think you're living in some warped fantasy world. Killing me is one thing, but you'll never get away with killing Kurt."

"Don't be dense. We're not going to kill him. He's our patsy."

"How?"

"Come on. You're a bright girl. Who's always the number one suspect when a wife is killed?" When she refused to answer, he answered for her. "The husband, of course."

"That's ridiculous. No one would believe that of Kurt. But you, Marcus, in a heartbeat."

An angry flush crept up his face. "Consider the facts. The two of you have been fighting a very public battle over Nick. For years you kept his son from him. He forced you to marry him." When she shook her head in denial, he reminded her with a sardonic smile, "There are about forty witnesses to the fact that you didn't do it eagerly. On top of all that, since Kurt came to Cherry Beach you've had several mishaps that will, in hindsight, look like attempts to eliminate a troublesome former lover, or gather information about her. The police will either think he did it himself or hired someone to do it for him."

"That was all you, then." Stunned by the scope of his scheme, she had to work to keep her voice level. "You set him up."

"Actually, that was an unexpected benefit," he admitted. "At the time, I was mostly trying to scare you into going back to London. The toxics were to force you into the land deal I had set up for you. The break-in was to search for the trust papers—we took advantage of the paparazzi."

He was enjoying himself. The anticipation of victory glowed in his beautiful eyes.

"In a way, I'm sorry things didn't work out between us," he continued. "I really thought we would have made a good team. Aside from the fact that we look very good together, I've always thought we were a lot alike."

He must be mad! How had she so completely misjudged him all these years?

At her look, his mouth gave a cynical twist. "We're not as different as you would like to think. We've both had to fight to get what we want in life. We didn't have it all handed to us like the Westons. Neither one of us really needs other people. We certainly don't trust them. We're not the type to delude ourselves with some kind of romantic fantasy."

While he talked, the gun dipped lower until it pointed to the porch deck in front of her feet. Time was running out. It was now or never.

She lunged for the gun in Marcus's hand. She had the advantage of surprise, and for a moment it seemed as if she could wrench it away with her good arm. But he recovered quickly and landed a blow to the side of her head that sent her staggering backward. Only her death grip on the metal barrel kept her on her feet. In desperation, she used the only weapon she had. She raised her injured arm high and brought the cast smashing down on Marcus's wrist.

He screamed and let go of the gun.

Shaking, she fumbled with it. Pain radiated down her injured arm. She wondered vaguely if she'd rebroken it. In the split second it took to turn and run, she glimpsed movement behind her, hurtling at her. The force of the blow knocked her off her feet. Blinding light exploded behind her eyes before blackness folded its arms around her and dragged her into oblivion.

"Why the hell did you hit her so hard? We need her to sign those papers." Marcus grimaced as he used his handkerchief to dab at the blood welling from the gash on his wrist. The sight made his stomach turn. Christ, he'd probably need stitches.

Deek squatted over Julia's unconscious form, examining the angry welt forming on the side of her face. Without looking up, he replied, "I didn't hit her. She fell against the railing."

Unmollified, Marcus persisted peevishly, "If you'd stuck to the plan and taken care of her right away, we'd be out of here by now. Why did you wait?"

Deek's calmly detached gaze shifted to Marcus. "Insurance."

"What the hell is that supposed to mean?"

"Mine won't be the only bloody hands."

Marcus was too shrewd to miss Deek's implied threat, though he felt reasonably confident he could keep him in line. As long as he controlled the flow of money, he controlled Deek. Still, once Deek had served his purpose, he would have to consider taking out his own insurance policy—something more permanent. He couldn't afford to leave behind any loose ends.

He regarded his old confederate. On the surface, their association might appear incongruous; they were, quite obviously, from different worlds, and in the ordinary course of affairs would never have met. But drugs had a way of blurring class boundaries. It had been a profitable convergence of resources and talents: Deek had access to drugs, Marcus to a wealthy clientele. And Deek had proved to be unburdened by anything as inconvenient as a conscience—a quality Marcus appreciated. They'd had quite a nice little operation going until they tried to move up the food chain. But a close call with a Caribbean drug lord, followed by a short stint in a steamy, roach-infested Bahamian jail, convinced him that there must be an easier way to make his fortune. Upon their release, he'd largely parted company with Deek. And Eddie had spent ten years locked away.

"Help me get her inside," Deek said, hooking his arms under Julia's.

"I think you're wasting your time," Sheriff Farley said as Kurt slid back into his car in front of the diner. "My deputy said the whole inlet is deserted. And we haven't seen any sign of a red Subaru, either. She probably stopped along the way and you passed her up."

Maybe. Except that he'd watched for the red car and hadn't seen it. So where was she? She should have reached the cottage an hour ago. Unless something—or someone—had intervened. The inlet seemed the logical place to start looking.

By the time he reached the turnoff, it was snowing again—big, thick flakes that filled the ruts in the dirt track and slowed him to a crawl. If he'd been going any faster, he might not have seen the large, thickset man materialize out of the woods next to Mrs. Hornig's cottage. Kurt stopped the car and watched the man approach.

Chapter 30

"How long is she going to be out?" From his post at the window, Marcus spared a brief glance over his shoulder at Julia's prone figure on the couch.

With a noncommittal shrug that grated on Marcus's nerves, Deek got up and disappeared into the kitchen. Marcus heard him rummaging around in the cupboards. A minute later he reappeared with a bottle of ammonia and a washcloth.

"We've got to get out of here. We're sitting ducks." Marcus's gaze darted nervously across the inlet.

"Eddie will call if anyone comes."

Their voices floated at the edge of Julia's consciousness. Instinctively, she shied away from that place.

"You sure we can get out the back way?"

"That's the way I came," Deek rasped. "The snow will cover our tracks." He raised Julia's head and stuck the ammonia-drenched cloth against her nose until she came to, coughing and gagging. "Get more gas from my truck," Deek ordered Marcus, leaving Julia to sputter the rest of the way back to life on her own. "Leave the trunk open so the fumes don't build up."

"But . . ."

Deek leveled pale eyes on him. "Unless you'd rather . . . ?"

Marcus followed Deek's glance to Julia. She had managed to sit up on the couch.

"No. That's what I'm paying you for." He stomped out under Deek's knowing smirk.

Julia shuddered when Deek turned his foxlike face and those soulless eyes on her. He pulled some papers out of an inner pocket of his camouflage jacket.

"Sign it," he ordered, thrusting the document and a pen at her.

"What is it?"

"Your will."

The paper swam before her eyes. She tried to ignore the pain in her head and force herself to concentrate on the paper. "Isn't that going to be rather obvious, if I suddenly leave everything to Marcus?"

"It only makes him your . . . what-d'ya-call-it—executive."

"I won't sign it." She felt cold and sick, and her head hurt more than her arm, but she figured she didn't have anything to lose if they were going to kill her anyway.

He studied her dispassionately. "You think you got nothing to lose. You're wrong. If you sign, I leave your boy alone. If you don't . . ." He left the unmistakable threat hanging.

Julia took the pen and scrawled her name on the line he indicated, and again on a copy he handed her. Satisfied, Deek stuffed the papers inside his jacket. Without another word, he pulled her from the couch, pushed her into one of the kitchen chairs, and tied her to it.

Leaning in close enough that she nearly gagged from the sour smell wafting off him, he warned with deceptive softness, "I'm going to go see what's takin' Pretty Boy so long. If you value that kid of yours, don't move."

* * *

Outside, Marcus slammed the rear hatch of Deek's truck. "Enjoy the fumes," he muttered spitefully. "May you light up a fag and blow yourself to smithereens."

The notion gave him pause. Maybe he could increase the odds of that happening.

He pried open the rusty door again and considered the single remaining gallon of gasoline sitting amid the compartment's squalor. Simply pouring it over everything would be too obvious. But a slow leak . . .

When he finished, he closed the hatch again and turned back toward the cottage.

"You son of a bitch," a low voice snarled in his ear at the same time a large arm cinched around his neck from behind. "I ought to blow your head off right now. One move and I will."

Deek burst back inside within such a short span of time that Julia knew he couldn't have gone far. In rapid, economical movements, he untied the rope that bound her to the chair, and jerked her to her feet. It was the first sign of excitement she had seen him exhibit.

"Move!" he hissed, roughly pushing her ahead of him outside onto the porch.

She stumbled. His arm hooked around her neck, jerking her back against his chest. Then he hauled her backward until his back was against the side of the cottage and she was in front of him. Cold metal pressed against her temple.

Seconds ticked by, during which the only sound was the rapid hiss of his breath in her ear, and the chatter of her own teeth. Then she saw Marcus, with Kurt behind him, cautiously turn the corner of the cottage.

If the sight on the porch surprised Kurt, he gave no sign of it. Other than a brief flash of recognition when he saw Deek, Kurt's face remained coldly expressionless. Julia's heart lurched hopefully at the sight of him. He looked strong and capable, and she'd never felt so glad—or guilty—to see anyone in her life.

With the barrel of his handgun, Kurt prodded Marcus up the porch stairs, using him as a human shield the same way Deek was using her. "Call him off, Marcus," Kurt ordered.

"Drop the gun, Deek!" Marcus demanded. "He's going to kill me if you don't!"

"He probably will anyway," Deek responded mildly.

"Deek, please! Drop the damn gun! We haven't done anything wrong. Just a little mix-up." Julia could see the wheels turning as Marcus worked on a new spin.

"He won't be able to pay you if he's dead," Kurt pointed out to Deek.

"Or if I let you win." Deek clutched her closer. Excitement hummed through him like an electric current. He flexed his hips against her bottom and she recoiled, sickened. He yanked her back. "Looks like we got us a Mexican standoff."

"Deek, wait!" Marcus yelled.

"Shut up!" Deek snarled at him. "Now, the way I see it, the question is, are you as willing to shoot through your pretty wife here as I am to shoot through that piece of shit you got?" For emphasis, he slowly removed his gun from Julia's head and aimed it at Marcus.

"No! You work for me!" Marcus shrieked.

"Because," Deek went on after Kurt coolly silenced Marcus by cutting off his air supply, "you have to shoot through her to get to me."

"Kurt—Don't listen to him!" Julia cried out before Deek's arm choked her.

Slowly, deliberately, Kurt tossed his handgun to the porch. Then he shoved Marcus forward, sending him stumbling to his knees.

"Now the other one." Deek nodded toward the gun Kurt had taken from Marcus. It was stuck in the waistband of his jeans.

When Kurt complied, Marcus grabbed up both guns, and Deek released Julia. On wobbly legs she crossed the porch and buried herself in Kurt's arms. It felt good to be there.

For a moment she closed her eyes and let herself hide from the cruel reality of their plight.

"I'm sorry, Kurt. I've done this to you. And Nick." A sob caught in her throat.

"We're not finished yet," he whispered.

Across the porch, Deek tried to use a cell phone. After a few seconds, he pocketed it.

"Just follow my direction and trust me," Kurt whispered in her ear.

"I think your brother screwed us over. I knew we shouldn't have trusted him." Marcus glared at Deek. "And I'm beginning to wonder about you."

"Shut up! His battery must be dead. He called before to warn about the cop." Deek's eyes narrowed to slits as he gazed out over the inlet. "Okay. We make it look like a murder-suicide. Give me Weston's gun."

"No! I want him alive," Marcus objected. "I want to wake up every day knowing the highlight of the once mighty Kurt Weston's day will be lifting weights with the brothers."

"Stop pissing in my ear. He can identify us."

"They won't believe him."

"Listen, dick-head . . ." He jerked Marcus into a huddle. It ended abruptly with Marcus reluctantly handing over Kurt's gun.

Deek's pale eyes zeroed in on Kurt. "How did you know something was going down before you got here?"

"I didn't. I was just being cautious. Julia should have arrived here before me, but the sheriff said she hadn't."

Kurt's answer seemed to satisfy Deek. He nodded toward Marcus. "You move, he shoots you." Then he picked up two of the three gallons of clear liquid sitting by the door—gasoline, Julia guessed by the smell—and disappeared inside the cottage.

Marcus leaned against the porch railing a safe distance away and lit a cigarette. "How the mighty have fallen." He smiled at Kurt. "I guess a guy can't even believe his own PR anymore. Kurt Weston really doesn't walk on water."

Kurt shrugged, refusing the bait, and to her surprise said, "Can you spare one of those?"

"Sure. What the hell. Last request and all." Kurt caught the pack and lighter Marcus tossed over. "Thought you gave them up after about two weeks in high school."

"I'm a closet smoker. Mind if we sit?" Kurt indicated the bench by the door. Marcus nodded.

Julia gratefully collapsed onto it. Kurt moved the jug of gas away from her feet and sat next to her. He took a token drag on the cigarette, appearing relaxed and unthreatening. Julia wondered what he was up to. She knew he didn't smoke, but she was having a hard time clearing the cobwebs from her throbbing head.

"I can't tell you how interesting it is to see you like this," Marcus gloated at Kurt, his good humor restored now that the danger had passed. "You were always the golden boy. Never would have thought you'd give up this easily."

"Don't kid yourself; you're in no better shape here than we are."

Marcus snorted. "I'm the one holding the gun."

"A few minutes ago your goon was eager to decorate this porch with your brains."

"A bluff. He has a paycheck to earn. He'll behave."

Kurt's mouth curved into a derisive sneer. "You're out of your league, Fuller. I've known men like your partner before. They're wolves—cunning, ruthless. They'd screw over their own mothers if it suited their purpose. By now your partner knows this latest scam of yours is tanking faster than the *Edmund Fitzgerald.* He's already looking to save his own skin, and the best way to do that is to get rid of all the witnesses—including you. You're probably his new fall guy."

"Shut up."

"Why else would he insist you give him my gun? He wants all the bullets to come from your gun and mine. No one will ever know there was a second perp—"

"Shut up!"

"Let alone a third. By the way, Eddie doesn't seem particularly loyal to you, either. Something about owing you one."

At Marcus's look of astonishment, Kurt shrugged. "I lied. Eddie's phone wasn't dead. Listen."

In the silence, Julia heard the sweetest sound imaginable: the distant wail of police sirens. They were still many precious minutes away. Yet suddenly, their chances didn't look quite so bad.

"You son of a bitch!" Marcus ran for the cottage door next to them. Julia could feel the muscles in Kurt's thigh tense, ready to spring. But before Marcus got there, Deek burst out with Kurt's gun drawn.

"Cops. Everyone inside," he ordered.

"I'm out of here," Marcus declared. "Do it and call me."

"No," Deek rasped. "You stay to the end."

Marcus looked suspiciously at the gun in Deek's hand. "Then what the hell do I need you for?" he demanded in that careless, reckless way of his that Julia had sometimes glimpsed.

For a moment, time seemed to slow to a snail's pace. Marcus unexpectedly turned his gun on Deek; several loud cracks split the silence of the inlet. On Marcus's chest, framed by his open jacket, a plume of crimson blossomed brilliantly against his white cotton shirt. His eyes widened in surprise.

Then, abruptly, time lurched forward. In one quick motion, Kurt kicked over the gasoline and shoved Julia inside the cottage. She had a last glimpse of Marcus, eyes glazing over as his legs folded underneath him.

Chapter 31

"Down!" Kurt yelled, diving inside after Julia and catching her up to roll toward safety. Behind them a wall of flames sprang up across the threshold of the cottage, blocking it off.

Boom! Boom! Shots ricocheted through the living room, breaking glass and splintering furniture. Flames licked hungrily over gas-drenched floors, sending up clouds of black smoke.

"Up!" Kurt choked out. "He'll get us if we go out the back."

They scrambled up the stairs. Smoke was already filling the second floor.

"The attic," Julia gasped.

They collapsed on the other side of the door, coughing and gasping. It was better here, but Julia guessed they had only minutes at most before the entire cottage went up. Kurt must have been thinking the same thing, because he pushed himself weakly to his feet and reached out a hand. "Come on. Get to the window."

He stumbled on the first step and would have gone down

had she not rushed to prop him up. She wrapped her good arm around his waist and touched wet cloth.

He'd been hit!

She helped him the rest of the way over to the attic window and eased him down to the floor. In the light, she got her first good look at him. What she saw made her dizzy. Blood, lots of it. It soaked the right side of his shirt and his jeans. She lifted his shirt and stared in horror at the gushing wound in his side.

"I'm okay," Kurt gasped, abruptly bringing Julia back to her senses. "See if you can spot Deek. But keep your head down."

"You're not okay." She struggled to keep her voice even, the panic out. "You've been shot." She grabbed a bunch of Nick's old cloth diapers.

Kurt tried to push her hand away, a feeble attempt that indicated just how quickly he was weakening. "There's no time!"

"I've got to stop the blood!" she insisted.

She worked quickly, padding the wound with diapers and cinching his belt over it as tightly as she could to apply pressure. Even though the attic was fast becoming a furnace, Kurt was turning an alarming shade of gray and was beginning to shake with cold. Time was running out. Smoke poured through the attic floor. All that kept them alive was the flow of fresh air from the window.

Frantically, she scanned the yard. Where was Deek? And what was taking Dan so long? She couldn't even hear the sirens anymore over the roar of the fire.

"Leave," Kurt said weakly.

"No." She yanked up the rope she'd used earlier and began to loop it around him under his arms.

"Nick—" he murmured.

An explosion rocked the cottage. It took her an instant to realize that it came from outside, not inside.

"Kurt," she stammered incredulously, looking out the window. "His truck blew up!"

He didn't respond. "Kurt!" Julia cried, dropping down beside him.

His eyes were closed and he was still, barely breathing. Frantically she ran her hands over his face, his arms, but he didn't respond.

"Oh, God, no," she sobbed. "Please don't do this. He hasn't done anything. *Please* don't take another person I love." Tears streamed down her face. "Damn it! Does everyone I care about have to die before you're satisfied?" she wailed at the heavens.

She felt the faint pressure of his hand and looked down into gray eyes. "Leave," he strained to whisper. "Nick . . ."

"Julia!" The shout came from the window, and a second later Dan's face appeared. "Thank God," he said, seeing her.

"Oh, Dan!" Julia cried. "Kurt's badly hurt."

Chapter 32

"Mrs. Weston . . . ?" The doctor's voice penetrated Julia's concentration. Automatically, her glance jumped over the dozen or so people gathered in the small waiting room, to Pat Weston. She was vaguely surprised to see how large their number had grown.

News travels fast in a small town. Friends and relatives had been streaming in throughout the long afternoon. By the time Julia was released from the emergency room, Chloe and Frank had already hurried over. Pat, Alex, and Rob arrived an hour later. More had come as word spread. Carolyn waited with Nick and Andrew a few blocks away at Kurt's house.

Sheriff Dan Farley stood near the door, waiting for answers, quietly consulting with his deputies as they came and went. He wanted to know what had happened and to whom the second body belonged. It was burned too badly even to identify as male or female. He'd tried to question Julia earlier. She'd put him off with the excuse that her throat hurt from the smoke—which it did—although that wasn't the real reason she didn't want to talk yet.

Every fiber of her being was distilled down to sustaining

Kurt's hold on life, willing him not to die. To defy fate. Or God. Or whatever perverse force it was that robbed her of those she loved. Because she did love him. The irony was that it had taken the threat of losing him for her finally to admit it. Somewhere along the way it had sneaked up on her. Or maybe it had been there all along. In the end, hiding from it had not lessened the agony she was in now.

She had assured Dan there was no longer any danger. He was frustrated by her lack of cooperation. Julia didn't care. "Leave her alone," Alex had objected to his questions. "Can't you see she's in shock?" Dan had backed off but lurked nearby, biding his time.

Now, in the expectant hush of the surgeon's entry, Pat met Julia's gaze with a faint glimmer of humor despite the worry etched on her face. "I think he means you, dear."

"Mrs. Weston?" The doctor swung around as she rose on shaky legs. His eyes skimmed over her shapeless hospital scrubs, the cast on her arm, to her face, and lingered there a moment before he seemed to recollect himself. "Your husband is asking for you. He's still in recovery, but I think it would do him good to see that you're in one piece."

"Is he . . . ?" Her throat clenched on the words.

"He's going to be fine." Around the room there was a collective sigh of relief as tremulous smiles replaced worry.

Julia couldn't quite believe it. "But he looked so bad."

"As I sent word out earlier, the most serious problem is loss of blood," the doctor explained patiently. "He's lucky—the tissue damage is relatively minor. He'll have to stay here a few days, but he'll be fine."

Julia's knees started trembling. "Easy." The doctor extended a steadying hand. "I think you could use some rest, too."

"I'll see to that," Alex promised.

The doctor took her to the recovery room. Kurt was the only patient there. His eyes were closed, his face pale, but his breathing was regular and his color better than it had been when he'd come in. The doctor left her there with a warning not to stay long. Uncertainly Julia stopped at the foot of the gurney, staring at the alarming array of plastic tubing.

"You don't look so hot," Kurt rasped softly.

She looked into smoky gray eyes. "Ditto." The smile she tried for slipped, and tears blurred his features. She'd been holding herself in tightly for hours. She couldn't keep it together any longer. "Oh, Kurt, I'm sorry," she whispered hoarsely, moving to his side to take the hand he held out. "This is all my fault. If I hadn't gone off like that . . ." Her face crumpled and the tears began to fall. She sagged down onto the chair beside him, resting her head on their entwined hands while great shuddering sobs racked her hunched shoulders.

"They would only have tried something else," he murmured.

"But you wouldn't—"

"Shh. We beat 'em. It's over."

But once released, her emotions were not easily restrained. When she finally looked up, she gave him an embarrassed smile. "Look at me; you've been shot and I'm the one crying. And I'm monopolizing your time when there are a whole lot of people waiting to see you, your mother and Rob for starters."

Kurt shook his head, the movement barely discernible. "Later. Want to sleep," he mumbled. His eyes drifted closed a moment, then opened again, and he gave her a faint smile. "Didn't want you thinking I'd made you a widow after only one day."

Julia laughed through fresh tears. "No, I can see that I'm not." She squeezed his hand.

"You're stuck with me," he warned. "Just hope you don't expect every day to be as stimulating as the first."

"No, I can live without it, too," Julia agreed.

"Does the press know?"

"Yes. They're camped outside the front door."

Kurt's eyes drifted closed. "Did you talk to . . . sheriff?"

"Not yet. I couldn't while you were—"

"Good. Wait."

"Okay." He let go of her hand and she stood. "I'll tell your mother and Rob to wait a while before they come in." She paused at the foot of the gurney, looking back at this man who had somehow managed to get through all her defenses. It made no sense. She didn't want to love him. But she did. And she didn't know what she would do about it.

His eyes were on her again, fighting back the fog. "The monsters are dead, Julia. We won."

By Tuesday, newspapers were casting the entire incident as a robbery gone bad, the lone suspect still unidentified, his body burned beyond recognition in an explosion triggered by a buildup of gasoline fumes in his truck. Marcus Fuller was buried by his grieving parents on Thursday, the day after Christmas—an unfortunate victim caught in the wrong place at the wrong time. That was the version Julia and Kurt worked out with Sam Livingston and sold to Sheriff Dan Farley. The three agreed there was nothing to be gained by revealing Marcus's involvement, and much to lose. No longer a media innocent, Julia had quickly realized how much worse the media circus would grow if they got wind of the full story. Deek's crime and death would have warranted barely a footnote in the national papers but for the Weston connection. But Marcus was part of Rob's branch of the Weston clan and supposedly her former fiancé. If his crimes came to light, the story would rival the O. J. or von Bülow affairs. The press would never leave them alone.

So they told Sheriff Farley about the meeting Marcus had set up with Julia at the cottage that morning, to explain how he happened to be there, and gave a general description of the mystery suspect, but no name. If Dan suspected there was more to the story than they were telling, for his own reasons he chose not to inquire too rigorously. For once, his penchant for seizing the easiest solution worked in their favor. He was satisfied to put the matter to rest, see the backsides of the reporters, and tuck the village back into its usual winter slumber.

Julia did not attend Marcus's funeral. Nor did Pat or Carolyn. Julia sensed that somehow, they'd figured out Marcus had not been an innocent victim. Nick, Andrew, and all three women moved into Kurt's home in the village while he was in the hospital.

Only Sam and Rob were told the whole story. They met with Julia and Kurt in Kurt's hospital room two days after Marcus's funeral. Kurt was scheduled to be released the next day, and not a minute too soon by his way of thinking. When Julia arrived, Sam was already there, conferring with her husband over the small table he'd finagled from a doting nurse. Kurt had on sweatpants and a T-shirt and sat in front of a laptop computer. Julia frowned but didn't bother to say anything. From the beginning, he'd refused to rest quietly in bed. More often than not when she stopped in, she found him bent over blueprints or reports, with Chloe dancing attendance. It didn't seem to have done him any harm. Only an occasional grimace when he moved too quickly belied his injury. Otherwise, he looked like a remarkably fit and disturbingly handsome man.

Sam offered her a chair at the table, and Julia turned her attention to him, interested to hear the latest news. He had not been idle in the intervening days. Armed with Marcus's confession to her and the trust documents that she'd had the presence of mind to heave out the attic window before the entire cottage went up in flames, he'd continued his investigation. While they waited for Rob, Sam began to piece events together. To begin with, he thought it likely Marcus had begun looting Julia's trust soon after taking control of his father's law practice. Rob was to get Marcus's records from Charles Fuller, which would shed more light on it.

"But how could he have gotten away with it for so long?" Julia asked.

"It's a private trust," Sam explained. "There would be no automatic outside audits. At first he may have intended to return enough of the funds to make it look okay before your thirty-second birthday, which we know from your grandmother's letter was the date you were to learn of the trust and begin receiving income from it. Your grandfather apparently threw a wrench into Marcus's plan by insisting you be told before he died. That would have been about five and a half years ago. At that point Marcus was probably in so deep he couldn't make it right.''

''Or never had any intention of doing so,'' Kurt said flatly. He suspected that Marcus might simply have seen a golden opportunity to embezzle the whole thing.

''Either way,'' Sam continued, ''he couldn't take the chance that once you learned of the trust you might insist on an outside audit, which would expose his fraud. With your grandmother gone, Seth Griffin was the only person who stood in Marcus's way, and he was dying. Whether Marcus went to Gull Inlet intending to kill him, we'll never know. But the opportunity and means presented itself, and he took it. All he had to do was mix a fatal amount of the morphine Seth had for pain into his beer. You were right at the time, Julia. Your grandfather didn't intend to kill the dog. He didn't know the beer Marcus gave him was drugged.''

''Murphy was found outside,'' Julia remembered. ''Marcus must have let him out.''

''Right. And once Seth lost consciousness, Marcus had a chance to look for the trust file.''

''But it wasn't there,'' Julia said quietly.

''Where was it?'' Kurt asked.

''At the lodge. Seth had gathered various records of mine and family mementos he wanted me to have and given them to Susan, to make sure I got them.''

''The box you threw out the attic window,'' Kurt said.

Julia nodded. She'd heaved it out of the burning cottage along with the trust papers Deek had not found. It was extraordinary that the one thing she had managed to save from the fire was that connection to the past. That and her precious photo albums of Nick. She'd taken them along to Belle House to show Kurt's mother. Otherwise they'd now be ashes like everything else. Her eyes misted at the memory of what she'd found Christmas day when she'd gone with Susan and Ted to view the damage. All that remained was a charred hulk. There'd been nothing left to salvage from the cottage, though fortunately her studio had survived unscathed.

"Why didn't he burn the cottage down back then?" she wondered out loud.

"He wouldn't have known if the evidence was really destroyed or if it was a time bomb lurking in some safe-deposit box," Kurt noted.

Sam nodded. "He probably intended to return and look again, but you came almost immediately. I imagine he was fit to be tied waiting for you to ask about your trust. Then, when you showed up at Belle House with Alex and Kip, he must have thought he was done for."

"Until he realized I didn't know him from Adam and our meeting was pure coincidence. But then we met again by chance back in Cherry Beach."

"I doubt if there were any more coincidences after Belle House," Sam said. "He was likely keeping tabs on you from then on."

"He did work hard to befriend me," Julia agreed with a grimace of self-disgust over his eventual success. "And to get me to move back to London."

"And to discourage you from telling me about Nick," Kurt added.

"Everything he did to all of us—you, Nick, my grandfather . . ." *Daddy. Jack.* Julia's voice wavered and she paused to steady it. "It was all because of the trust."

Kurt also thought Marcus probably had taken a perverse delight in having a relationship with Julia after he had failed with her. And Nick must have been the icing on the cake. How the son of a bitch must have loved keeping his son from him. The ultimate payback for a sewer-full of imaginary injuries.

Thank God he'd gone to Julia's exhibit in Chicago. Thank God he'd gone ahead with the project here. Kurt's gaze fell on the discolored shadow marking the side of her face, visible in spite of the makeup she'd used to hide it. *Thank God they got out of there alive.*

"He also had his eye on your land," Sam said. "Knowing Marcus, it must have driven him nuts watching you sitting there on that prime chunk of undeveloped real estate."

"Oh, it did, once he learned about Deer Cove."

"And that's when he came up with that suspect loan agreement I saw," Kurt said.

"Yes, after I refused to sell."

Sam leaned forward in his chair. "Let me guess. You took the papers to your lawyer and Marcus found out."

"Yes, and they were taken from McGinn's office."

"Probably Deek's work. Marcus wouldn't want another lawyer scrutinizing the document if there was something shady about it."

"It all fits," Kurt murmured.

Julia rose and wandered several feet to the window. Kurt's gaze followed her. Despite her surface calm, he could tell she was still raw, understandably so, given everything she'd been through: the loss of her home; all the ugly truths she was having to face, particularly about her grandfather's death.

"It must have blown him away when the bank agreed to extend your loan," he said.

"When *you* extended my loan," Julia corrected.

"Okay, when *I* instructed the bank to extend your loan." They needed to talk. Alone. And they'd had frustratingly little chance of that so far. After that first day, when he was still groggy from the anesthetic, he hadn't managed to be alone with her again.

"Marcus said the authorities would automatically suspect you for all my 'mishaps' because of our custody battle," she said softly. "When all along, it was Deek and his brother." She looked over at him. "I don't understand why this Eddie had a change of heart at the last minute and warned you about Deek and Marcus."

"It wasn't so much a change of heart—Eddie wasn't really part of it. Deek kept him in the dark about why he needed a lookout. Eddie said he assumed it was a robbery and didn't want anything to do with it but was afraid of Deek. When I drove up, he recognized me—he's been working construction for us—and decided to bail on them. Thank God he did, or the outcome might have been very different."

"He didn't seem to mind shooting at me in the woods," Julia said bluntly. "Or jumping us after the music festival." She still wasn't convinced Eddie should get off scot-free.

Sam spoke up. "Deek told him they'd been hired to scare off trespassers. He wasn't trying to hit you. Although Deek may have been." At her look of skepticism, Sam gave a wry smile. "I know, it sounds like bull. But if you talked to him you'd see that he is—I guess *simple* is the word I'm looking for. He couldn't make up a story like that. His brother exploited him. Always had."

"Have they traced Deek's truck?" Kurt asked Sam.

"Not to Deek. He was a real pro. The truck was stolen. Odds are, with his body burned so badly and nothing to compare DNA to, it's unlikely they'll ever identify him."

Kurt shrugged. "Even if they do, it won't matter. Eddie won't talk, because he's scared to death of going back to prison. Besides, he wasn't there to see what happened."

"So what exactly made Deek's truck explode?" Julia asked.

"Some of the gas must have spilled inside the truck," Sam said. "The State Police expert concluded that fumes from spilled gasoline were ignited after Deek got inside, either by a spark from an electrical short, or he may have lit up a cigarette."

"Marcus set it up," Kurt announced. Both Julia and Sam looked at him in astonishment. "It didn't occur to me until later what he'd done. When I first spotted him he was fiddling with one of the containers, and put that one back inside the truck. He even checked to make sure the windows were closed." His mouth twisted into a wry smile. "I had other, more immediate problems on my mind, so I didn't think much about it then."

Sam looked skeptical. "It would have been a long shot."

"It worked."

"Spectacularly," Julia agreed. "So even before you went to work on Marcus trying to undermine his trust in Deek, he'd already decided Deek had to go. Except he planned to do it after Deek eliminated us."

"Apparently so."

They talked about it until Rob arrived, trying to make sense of much that would ultimately remain unknown, including who else, if anyone, may have been involved with Marcus in trying to buy or cheat Julia out of Deer Cove. Over the past few days, Julia had observed Rob's normal buttoned-down look begin to fray at the edges as he learned more and more about his cousin's villainy. Now he looked positively haggard when he slumped into a chair, and she wondered if it wouldn't have been kinder to leave him in the dark.

"Well, I talked to Uncle Charles about the trust," he told them.

"And?" Kurt prompted.

"At first he claimed the trust had been dissolved years ago. It was only when I showed him the trust papers Julia saved that he came around. We talked a while. He finally saw reason." Rob's grim demeanor hinted that he'd needed to apply considerable pressure to achieve his goal. "He's agreed to make good on the trust out of Marcus's estate, as long as we don't go public. There won't be enough to replace what he took, but it's something, anyway. As you can imagine, my revelations came as quite a shock to poor Uncle Charles. It's not the sort of thing a parent wants to hear about a child he's just buried."

Julia's wrath toward "poor Uncle Charles" flared at the sight of Rob's guilt. "Don't beat yourself up over it, Rob." Anger edged her voice, making it sound more clipped than usual. "Charles knew exactly what his son was up to."

A stunned silence followed, during which three pairs of eyes mixed with varying shades of disbelief locked on her.

"Marcus was eager to talk when he thought I would be taking his secrets to my grave. He said his father not only knew he'd embezzled money from the trust, but that Charles himself had done the same for years, though on a smaller scale. Even more damning, Marcus said his father knew of and approved his so-called damage control. I took that to mean that Charles knew of Marcus's plan to kill me and frame Kurt for my murder."

Julia sent Rob a look of apology. "I'm sorry, Rob, but I have every reason to think that, in this instance, at least, what Marcus said is true. You see, before I even left Belle House, I called Charles to ask about the trust. He, too, asked to meet me at the cottage that morning to discuss it. In fact, he was quite insistent that our meeting take place there rather than in town."

As she talked, Rob's look of disbelief gave way to one of bitter awakening. Her heart went out to him. But much as she regretted destroying his illusions about his uncle, she suddenly understood that Kurt was right: Rob needed to know the truth. Like his son, Charles Fuller was a wolf in sheep's clothing. And they were the most dangerous kind because the danger was hidden, insidious.

Kurt rose to his feet, his face taut. "I'm going to kill him."

"Don't bother." Wearily Rob rubbed his brow. "He has some kind of liver disease. Word is that he doesn't have long." He slumped back and shook his head morosely. "There were always rumors about Uncle Charles—sly innuendoes about shady deals. But he could be such a great guy."

"Charming as hell," Kurt agreed sarcastically, "when he wished to be."

Reluctantly Rob offered up a course of action that would open the door to the kind of lurid publicity that was anathema to his social set. "Maybe we should go public, tell the authorities."

Kurt glanced questioningly at Julia. "It's your call. Personally, I'd like to rake him over the coals."

Slowly Julia shook her head. "I vote no. I'm no lawyer, but it sounds like a weak case, anyway. He'd probably get off, and in the meantime the press would turn our lives into a circus.''

Sam nodded. ''I'm afraid Julia might be right. With Marcus dead, all we have is her statement about what he said his father knew. Even that might be inadmissible hearsay.''

''That's it, then,'' Kurt said, settling the matter.

Julia slipped out to keep an appointment with Susan at the clinic next door. When she returned half an hour later, she was pleased to find Kurt alone. She needed to talk to him about her plans before his release. She had spent the past few days facing some hard truths about her life—ironically, prompted in no small part by what Marcus had said about their being a lot alike. Difficult though it would be, she knew what she had to do.

Kurt glanced up from a heap of papers strewn across the table. His gaze traveled over her and settled on her arm. ''You got your cast off.''

''Susan thought I'd be better off without it.'' She touched the sling that still protected her arm, making a face at it. ''But I'm stuck with this for a few more weeks.''

''In other words, she thought it in your best interest to disarm you.''

Julia perched on the edge of the hospital bed. ''That may have been part of it,'' she admitted with a wry answering grin that gradually died as more sobering memories rushed in. The horror was still fresh.

''I'm proud of the way you fought them,'' Kurt said, guessing the direction of her thoughts. ''Even when you were hurt and didn't think we had much of a chance, you didn't give up.''

''I wasn't going to let Marcus win if I could possibly prevent it.'' *Not this time.*

''This time?''

Julia glanced up to find herself the object of Kurt's puzzled scrutiny, only then realizing she'd spoken the last aloud. This was one piece of the puzzle she hadn't shared with any of them. Marcus's earlier intrusion into her childhood remained hidden. It really had no bearing on present events. No relevance whatsoever, except to her. For a moment, though, she was tempted to tell Kurt. His eyes invited her trust. But the moment passed. *Soon,* she thought.

Shrugging, she said lightly, "He manipulated all of us for a long time." She wasn't sure whether Kurt looked disappointed or she only imagined it, but he nodded and let it pass. She was left to wonder again whether he knew more than he let on.

"Mom said you went out to see the cottage," he was saying. "Julia, I'm sorry about your home. If I'd been able to come up with any other plan . . ." His face expressed his profound regret.

"Kurt, please!" She reached a beseeching hand toward him. "You have nothing to apologize for. I loved that cottage, but I'd have done the same thing if I'd thought of it. You saved my life! It is I who should be on my knees thanking you."

"It isn't your gratitude I want. Although the knees bit raises some interesting possibilities." He sobered. "I want to know whether you meant what you said in the attic."

She was surprised he'd heard her wild lament to the gods, much less remembered, but she didn't pretend not to know what he meant. "Yes."

"Then marry me."

Julia smiled faintly. "I thought I already had."

"For real. Not that pretense you were planning to suffer through for a year."

Julia looked away. This wasn't going at all the way she'd planned. "Kurt, I—"

"No!" His hand cut the air. "Don't say anything until you find the guts to give me the only answer that makes sense."

Julia raised pleading eyes to his. "Kurt, please, it's not that easy. You're asking me to stop thinking and go with my emotions." She shrugged helplessly. "That's not the way I am."

"On the contrary, I'm asking you to follow your head and your heart instead of letting your life be ruled by a blind emotional reaction to tragic events that happened a very long time ago. I think that's exactly what you've been doing all these years—running from life."

She began to utter the automatic denial that sprang to her lips, then bit it back when she caught a knowing look that said he saw right through her. She stared at him with troubled eyes. He'd always had a disturbing ability to see into her hidden places. Was he right? Had she spent her entire adult life on the run from her past? From life? These were some of the very questions she'd been asking herself these past few days.

He came over and sat on the opposite side of the hospital bed. "To live is to risk," he continued more gently. "I can't change that, but I can promise to always love you. Always, Julia. It requires a leap of faith. Make it for me and Nick and, mostly, for you."

She felt as if she were teetering on the edge of a vast cliff. Behind her lay a desert—safe, known, barren—while before her lay a lush valley, spread out across the horizon like a forbidden feast. Far below, Kurt held out his arms for her. But if she leaped, would he catch her? And if he did, would he eventually tire of the weight of her love and cast it aside?

A brisk knock broke the silence, and Chloe breezed in. "Here's the project file you wanted," she announced, depositing a briefcase on the table and tossing a "Hi, Julia," over her shoulder. "I threw in your personal mail, too, Kurt."

The interruption gave Julia the chance to pull herself together and recall why she was there. She rose, tempted to take the coward's way out and tell him her plans via a note, when Chloe turned to her.

"I've got something for you, too." Chloe dug through her shoulder bag and came up with a white envelope. She handed it across the hospital bed.

Recognizing the airline logo, Julia quickly stuffed it out of sight in her bag. "Thanks. And thanks, too, for lining up a housekeeper,'' she added, trying to turn Chloe in another direction. It didn't work.

''Because of the fire, the travel agency didn't know where to send your ticket,'' Chloe continued undeterred. ''I said I'd get it to you.''

''Ticket?'' Kurt asked.

Julia repressed a groan. ''That's what I came back to talk to you about.''

Chloe's gaze shot from Kurt to Julia, her mouth forming a silent ''Oh'' as she deciphered the cause of the sudden tension between them. Grimacing apologetically, she made a diplomatic withdrawal from the room. ''I think I'll just grab a cup of coffee from the cafeteria.''

''Where?'' Kurt asked when the door closed softly behind Chloe.

''I'm flying into Nassau, then catching a charter to the out islands.''

''When?''

''Tomorrow morning.''

Silence fell heavily between them, so thick Julia thought she could chew it more easily than she could breathe it. Unable to stand it any longer, she plunged in: ''It's just for a few days—a week at the most. Your mother has agreed to stay with Nick, and the Clearys are available as backup.''

''When were you going to drop the news on me? It doesn't get much more last-minute than this.'' Suspicion sharpened his gaze. ''Or were you planning on sending a postcard?''

Julia flinched at how close to the truth he'd hit. ''All the arrangements were last-minute because I didn't want to leave until I knew you were better.''

''How considerate.''

When he didn't say more, she went on. ''I've been doing a lot of thinking over the last few days about us—about everything—and I realized this is something I have to do.''

''Why? Because you need to work on your tan? Or because you realize you crossed a line back there in that attic and need to run away again?''

So that was it. He thought she was running away from

him. Of course he would think that. Wasn't that exactly what she'd done over and over again?

"I'm not running away. Not this time. If I were, the Bahamas is the last place on earth I'd choose to run to. For me, this is turning around and facing my demons." She glanced past him out the window. "I've spent most of my life pretending I had no childhood, because memories from the one I had were horrific. It never really worked, of course. You've seen the nightmares." She looked back at him. "Kurt, I have to go back. I've been looking through that box my grandfather left for me. This is something I need to do. I'm doing it for all of us."

"What do you expect to find there? If it's some sort of miraculous closure . . ."

For a moment she allowed herself to think about giving in and not going. It would be such a relief. Couldn't he see she dreaded going back? But if she didn't go, the past would always be there, in their way. She would never be free to love him until she reclaimed at least a small part of that trusting, well-loved girl she'd left behind, forgotten, until she'd seen her again in Seth's pictures. Crazy or not, she couldn't shake the conviction that her past held the key to their future together.

"No, not closure. That's probably impossible." She willed him to understand, and wait, this one last time. "But I don't think I can move forward until I at least acknowledge my past."

Every instinct told Kurt to not let her go, not let her walk away again. Of course, he could stop it. All he had to do was invoke their prenuptial contract. But at what cost?

"I hope you find what you're looking for."

Coda

Chapter 33

Sun glinted off the side of the small jet as it descended down the fifteen-mile length of Elizabeth Harbour on its approach to the tiny airstrip. Minutes later it taxied to a stop, the hatch swung open, and Kurt climbed out. He squinted through shimmering waves of heat rising off the deserted tarmac, searching in the direction of a small building that evidently passed as the airport terminal, until he spotted her walking toward him from a lone taxi.

She stopped a couple of feet away, hesitated there the briefest moment, then closed the distance and gave him a quick hug before stepping back.

"You look better," she said, her eyes roving over him. "Thank you for coming."

Kurt lifted a brow. "Did you think I wouldn't?"

"It had crossed my mind."

In short order his luggage was transferred to the taxi, and after a brief consultation with the Westco pilot, they were on their way. The driver, donning his tour-guide hat, immediately launched into a colorful dissertation on passing points of interest, which gave Kurt a chance to study Julia. She'd gone native. Despite the heat, she looked cool and comfortable in a cotton sarong and sleeveless cotton top. It suited her. In the five days since he'd seen her, the bruise on her face had faded, replaced by a sun-kissed tropical glow that made her eyes more vividly sea green. Island eyes. The only reminder of their ordeal was the white sling she still wore.

"When did you get in?" he asked during a rare break in the driver's spiel. He knew she'd been in the Abaco islands to the north; she'd called every day. He also knew, from news clippings Sam had dug up, that her brother and father had died in a bloodbath off a small cay there.

"Yesterday. I caught the morning mail run down." Small clapboard cottages dressed in colorful pastel shades slipped past the windows as they came into George Town, capital of the Exuma Islands.

"Would you like to stretch your legs?" she asked.

They sent the taxi ahead with Kurt's luggage. As they strolled toward the center of the small town, she peppered him with questions about Nick. The streets were as deserted as the airport had been.

"It's a sleepy backwater compared to the glitz of Nassau," she said, reading his thoughts. "It's pretty much always like this except when the mail boat comes in. Or during Regatta."

In the center of town, several women plaited straw and sold their wares and food in the shade of an enormous fig tree. Kurt bought a straw tote bag and filled it with conch fritters, grouper sandwiches, and coconut tarts. They found a place to sit, and he nodded back toward the group of women under the tree. "So is everyone on this island related?"

She smiled. "I gather you've noticed that every other person's last name is Rolle."

"Hard to miss." He'd also noticed that the women knew Julia by name and treated her with the easy familiarity they might use with one of their own.

"I love these things." She popped a conch fritter into her mouth and moaned in bliss. "The majority of the islanders are descendants of slaves brought from Africa to work on island plantations," she explained. "An Englishman, Lord Rolle, had one of the larger spreads. Back then, slaves commonly went by the last name of their master. It's not a pretty story. But I like to think that in the end the African Rolles had the last laugh, because cotton proved unprofitable and they inherited this little bit of paradise."

"How did they make their living?" he asked, enjoying the interlude, the sound of her voice.

"Fishing, farming. The same as now, for the most part, I expect."

They talked about the island, its history, its emergence as a sailing mecca—the sorts of things friendly acquaintances might talk about. Anything but the matter that had brought them together on this distant island.

Julia felt Kurt watching her, patiently biding his time, not pushing for the answers she knew he wanted. For now. She checked her watch and stood. "Why don't I show you where we're staying?" Her eyes skimmed over the twill slacks and short-sleeved gray polo shirt he wore. "You can change into something cooler and then we can ride a few miles farther up the island."

"Sounds good. You have a car stashed away somewhere?"

"No. A motorcycle." Julia frowned at him questioningly. "But you'll have to drive the thing because of my arm. Are you well enough? Can you handle it—with me on the back?"

He grinned. "I think I can handle the two of you."

They passed a church perched atop a bluff, its bright-blue trim cheery against a white clapboard background. He paused to check it out.

"St. Andrew's church," she supplied. "That's Lake Victoria behind it."

"Pretty. It would appear that even God resisted those pesky English carpetbaggers and went native."

"So it would seem," Julia agreed softly.

Something in her voice drew Kurt's attention. She appeared to be almost steeling herself as she contemplated the church. "Do we have time to take a look around?"

"No! I—" She said sharply. "Maybe tomorrow. We should get going if you want to see more of the island before sunset.'' But her earlier light mood was gone, and Kurt wondered what memories the place held for her.

The small screened-in cabana she took him to overlooked Elizabeth Harbour just north of town. Its simple floor plan consisted of a combined living-kitchen area on one side and two bedrooms on the other.

''Nice.'' Kurt glanced around the interior. ''How did you find it?''

''I know the owner.''

Kurt waited patiently until she elaborated.

''It belongs to my father's former partner. He has a boat charter coming in tomorrow, so you'll probably meet him.''

She led him to the front bedroom. It was immediately clear from the absence of her personal things that she had taken up residence in the other bedroom.

''I thought you would enjoy being on the ocean side.'' She didn't look at him. ''When you're ready, I'll—ah—be outside.''

Kurt had just returned from a slow run along the beach the next morning when a perfunctory knock on the lanai door preceded the entrance of a startlingly handsome Latino man. ''Manny!'' Fresh from the shower, Julia padded past Kurt in her white terry cloth robe, wet hair dripping, straight into Manny's enthusiastic embrace. ''I didn't expect you until later.'' Her broad smile said that she would be pleased to see him anytime.

''We had a good wind so we decided to press on. I didn't want you to be alone when you—'' He left the thought dangling as his eyes locked with Kurt's. ''But I see you are not.''

Julia pulled back, including Kurt in their circle. ''Manny, this is Kurt Weston, the man I told you about.''

''Husband,'' Kurt corrected coolly.

Puzzled, Julia looked from Kurt to Manny trying to fathom why both men were acting aloof. *Jealous,* she realized in the next breath. The answer caught her midway between surprise and amusement. Kurt thought Manny was poaching on his property. Poaching *her*. His Latin-heartthrob looks were still landing him in hot water.

Ignoring the tension, Julia explained to Kurt, "Manny was my father's partner in a sailboat charter business. He and his wife now operate their own charter business between here and Marsh Harbour." She glanced at Manny. "Speaking of spouses, did Elena come with you?"

Manny dragged his gaze back to her and gave a sheepish nod. "She's in the village stocking up on provisions for a picnic lunch. Which is why I have disturbed you so early—we're taking our guests over to Stocking Island for the day and wanted you to join us. Your husband, too, of course," he added.

Stocking Island, a long, thin barrier island a mile offshore, formed the eastern boundary of Elizabeth Harbour, and boasted some of the best shelling beaches in the Bahamas. For Julia, it was a trip down memory lane.

"Penny for your thoughts." Kurt tossed borrowed snorkeling gear onto a towel and sank down on the sand next to her, letting the high southern sun dry the ocean from his skin.

Julia glanced up, making no effort to shake off the ghosts that hovered close around her. They'd been with her ever since she'd stepped aboard *Discovery* for the short jump over from George Town. Just as they had when she'd talked Manny into taking her back to the other place. Ground zero, as she'd come to think of that small cay. The place where it had all ended—or begun, she supposed, depending on how one thought about it.

But here, there were only bittersweet memories, no monsters.

"My mother loved shells." In her good hand she held up a fragile shell with a delicate pink pearl interior for Kurt to see. "This was one of her favorites. I don't remember its name.'' She placed it on a neat pile in front of her. Her gaze settled out over brilliant tropical water.

''We came out here a few times, just the two of us, before my little brother was born. Those were good times.'' She smiled sadly. ''All these years, I've forgotten the good times. I threw them out with the bad.''

Kurt reached out and gently stroked her cheek, wiping away a tear that had slipped out, but saying nothing to interrupt the flow of words.

''My parents lived big. Loved big. Manny reminded me of that.'' Her mouth twisted into a smile that fell short. ''They would have been appalled at the way I've lived my life.''

She looked at him, shaking her head helplessly. ''Oh, Kurt, I've messed up royally. You were right about me—I am a coward. I've worked so hard to avoid the bad things that I've missed the good. If it weren't for Nick, my life would be a waste.''

''No. I was wrong. You're one of the bravest people I know. That I'm still alive proves it.''

She waved that off. ''I mean emotionally. I've always played it safe. I had to stay in control, not get too attached. And that meant I couldn't give us a chance. I hardened my heart against you.'' She looked intently at Kurt. ''But you have to believe that I did send you that note when I learned I was pregnant. I at least did that much.''

''I know. You convinced me of that the night we were snowbound together.'' He paused. ''I've given it some thought, and I think Marcus must have intercepted it. Probably using Vanessa. He knew you were coming to Belle House, and Vanessa was conveniently in place to hustle you out of there and grab your letter before I arrived.''

Julia sighed. ''That makes sense. Marcus discouraged my going to see you from the first.''

''With good reason. He didn't want me anywhere around meddling in his schemes.''

She wondered what would have happened if Kurt had

gotten her note. "None of that excuses the fact that I did nothing more to make sure you knew."

"What should you have done? You thought I'd left you twisting alone in the wind."

"Don't make excuses for me. The truth is that I was more relieved than disappointed when you didn't respond to my note. I didn't want to push it. It was better—*safer*—to believe you were a bum and let it go at that."

"Why?"

"I think you know."

"Humor me."

Irritation flickered on her face for making her say it. "Because you were what I feared most. You threatened my safe little world. Made me think about things that were off limits. And you knew it. You read me like a book."

"And now?"

"You still scare the starch out of me." She gave him a grudging smile. "A little voice is still whispering, 'Run! Run! As fast as you can.' "

He grinned. "Is that little voice saying anything else?"

Her eyes misted. "Yes," she whispered. "It's saying, 'Too late.' " Down the beach, Elena and a deckhand toted coolers containing lunch across the sand to the half-dozen guests wandering the beach or snorkeling in the shallows. Julia stood. "I think the writing was on the wall from the second Nick decided to fall in love with you."

She glanced toward Elena, brushing the sand off her shorts with her good arm. "I'd better lend a hand."

His exasperated gaze followed her progress across the sand.

An open book? Like hell! That last bit about Nick muddied everything else she'd said. Did she mean it was too late because of her own feelings for him, or because of Nick's? Or both?

For a few moments, he'd hoped that she was working up to saying exactly what he wanted to hear. That *she* loved him, independently of Nick. Enough to want to spend the rest of her life with him. He sighed in disgust. God, he was pathetic. Of course she was doing this for Nick. Everything she did was for Nick. But she was his now. He'd won. That much was clear. And that was all that really mattered. Almost.

"He has a good heart."

Julia dragged her attention back to Elena and the lunch they were setting out on a makeshift table. She smothered a smile as she contemplated Manny's wife. Short, plump, and nut brown, she did not in the least match Julia's imaginary picture of the woman who would finally snare the Latin heartthrob.

"Your husband," Elena clarified, her eyes following the earlier path of Julia's gaze down the beach to where Kurt was helping Manny beach a sailboard. "He is a good man, no?"

Julia's expression turned thoughtful as she looked at Kurt. "Yes, I believe he is."

"I am glad. Maybe that will help ease Manny's conscience."

"Ease Manny's conscience? I don't understand."

Elena paused, scrutinizing Julia before she answered. "Manny blames himself for not doing more to save your father and brother." She spoke slowly, choosing her words with care. "He has felt guilty all these years that he survived. I know this because I was the nurse on duty in Marsh Harbour the day the authorities brought him in for treatment. That is how we met."

Julia was stunned to hear Elena attribute to Manny thoughts that had haunted her for years. "But there was nothing he could do! It was a massacre."

"It is not rational, I know. But you three were all the family he had. Suddenly Evan and Jack were dead. You were badly injured and then gone to the States with your grandfather. We fixed up his body easy enough, but it has taken much longer to heal his heart."

"I had no idea," Julia said softly. "I didn't even know he'd been hurt."

"Nothing as serious as your injuries. That is why he was not airlifted over to Nassau with you. Which is my good fortune." She smiled, dispelling some of the gloom. "It is good that you have made a family of your own. Manny worried about you. You know he kept in touch with your grandfather until his death?"

Julia nodded. A letter had come several months after Seth's death.

"And I am glad to see you well settled, because now I don't have to worry about you stealing my Manny away."

Elena grinned teasingly when Julia raised an eyebrow. "Oh, Manny told me how you used to follow him around with puppy-dog eyes. All the young girls still do. I have to beat them off with a stick. But none of them have grown up to look like you." She sighed. "It is sometimes tedious to be married to such a beautiful man."

"I expect so," Julia commiserated, stifling a smile.

Across the beach, Kurt and Manny were engaged in a private conversation of their own. Judging by their serious expressions, it wasn't about sailing. Eventually, they shook hands, holding on a bit longer than necessary.

"You're not leaving the island right away are you? Manny was not sure of your plans."

Julia shook her head, watching the men. "Not today. There's one more thing I have to do. Soon, though." She had to get back to Nick.

On the bluff behind St. Andrew's church, dappled sunlight filtered through rustling trees to dance across the small cemetery and the two figures standing on the far edge. Kurt glanced at Julia's face, still and expressionless as she stared down at the three simple crosses. They'd gone for a walk after returning from Stocking Island and she'd led him here, to these three graves with their markers identifying them as Julia's family. "Would you like some time alone?" he asked.

The softly spoken question brought Julia back from the edge of the abyss. "No." Her hand trembled as she reached for his arm. It was easier with him here. His presence helped to repel the darkness. "There are things I need to tell you."

She drew a ragged breath, struggling to stay on course. It was time to say good-bye and finally put aside the old fears. She had allowed them to control her life for too long.

"I'm ready to listen for as long as you want to talk." He took her hand from his arm and enfolded it in his hand, sending warmth flowing back into her. "But you need to sit down before you topple over." They found a bench close to the edge of the bluff and she sat. He chose to lean against a nearby tree.

For a time she was silent. Below them, the rippled surface of Lake Victoria glittered like diamonds in the late-afternoon sun. Moving. Alive.

"The last time I was here was after my mother's funeral," she began. "We'd sailed up-island from the Caribbean when my mother became pregnant with my brother . . . Jack. We came because she wanted to settle down someplace and my father had been offered a job with a charter operation here. I was almost twelve then." She spoke without emotion, keeping her distance.

"Before that we'd moved around quite a bit—St. Kitts, Martinique, a few of the other British and French islands—anywhere my parents could pick up an odd job teaching or tutoring or piloting a yacht. It was pretty much hand-to-mouth. I expect expenses were modest because we lived aboard *Discovery*—the schooner we went over to the island on today. My father had restored it. My parents were essentially disaffected idealists. Hippies. They met in the Peace Corps. I didn't understand until much later how unusual our lifestyle was.

"For a few months life here was perfect. My father had a steady job. For the first time we lived in a real house. The islanders were friendly." She drew a slow breath. "But a few months after Jack was born, my mother died. Some kind of infection. My grandmother March blamed it on poor medical care and my father."

Julia's eyes grew luminous. "My dad took it hard. Eventually, he lost his job. But every now and then the charter company would send him customers who wanted a boat with a crew. He and Manny would take them out on *Discovery.* They did pretty well during the season."

"Who took care of your brother?"

Julia looked at Kurt blankly, as if she'd forgotten he was there.

"Your father must have been gone a lot—who took care of the baby?" he repeated.

"A woman from the village watched him while I was in school. I had him the rest of the time."

"What about your father?"

She looked away. "My mom's death was hard on him."

"It must have been hard on you, too."

"Jack kept me too busy to think much about it. But every time my father looked at Jack, he couldn't help remembering."

And when he looked at you, Kurt speculated. Sam had found a picture of her mother. Julia bore a striking resemblance to her.

"About a year later, my father moved us all up to Marsh Harbour in the Abaco Islands. At that time the Abacos were considered the sailing center of the Bahamas. He thought he and Manny would do better from there. He was right. The charter business grew. Jack was thriving."

Abruptly Julia rose from the bench and took a few steps to the edge of the bluff. She looked out over Lake Victoria, trying to summon the strength to speak of the unspeakable. It created a gulf between them that she knew she had to breach if they were to have a shot at a real marriage. But she had kept the horror locked away for so many years.

It repelled her. It threatened to suck her into insanity.

Kurt watched and waited and shoved his hands into his pockets to keep from reaching out to her, wishing he could protect her from her monsters. He was too damn late for that. But she was a strong woman. She could confront them on her own. "What happened?" he prodded gently.

She drew in a shuddering breath, not seeming to notice him move to the bench that she'd vacated, where he could see her face.

"A young man came to our house one day," she began haltingly, letting it play through her mind. "I was almost sixteen. Jack was four. He was on spring break from college in the states and came to deliver a letter to my father. It was the off-season, otherwise my father wouldn't have been home. He delivered the letter and left. I assumed that was that. But he returned later wanting to arrange a boat charter for a few days. He wanted to sail up to a small cay not far to the north where some friends were waiting, then continue up-island and make the hop over to the Florida coast, where they would disembark. Because of the season, *Discovery* was idle and my father agreed to the plan, provided Jack and I could come too because the woman who took care of Jack was away.

"When we arrived at White Sand Cay, the man left, saying he would return with his friends the next morning. The cay is small, only about a mile long with just a few secluded cottages and a dirt airstrip. The next day, a small airplane landed. My father discovered that the man and his friends were trying to run drugs back to the States. Apparently, they thought a sailboat like *Discovery* would provide a good cover and fool the authorities. But they mistook the real danger, and we ended up caught in the middle of a war with the local drug lord."

Julia's gaze grew distant, her breathing faster, as the past sucked her in.

"My father was frantic to get us away from there. As soon as we were under way, he put in a call to the authorities over the radio. He was angry and worried. It scared me. We had nearly cleared the point of the cay when one of those big cigarette boats roared around it from the opposite direction. There were several men on board. They had guns."

Julia's eyes filled with tears. "Manny had the helm. Daddy had his rifle. It all happened so fast. As soon as they got close enough, they started shooting at us. They sprayed the boat. Daddy shouted at Jack and me to go overboard. He wanted us to swim for shore.

"I couldn't move." Her voice shook with bitter agony. "I just stood there and let those monsters shoot us. I watched Daddy get hit. He fell backward into the cockpit. Jack screamed. There was blood everywhere. On all of us."

Tears streamed unnoticed down her face. Her voice was choked with them. "I don't remember jumping in. I only remember being in the water, hanging on to Jack. Then Manny was there and got us to shore. And then there was a helicopter. But it was too late. Jack was dead. Daddy was dead."

She saw Jack's little body lying pale and lifeless next to her on the sand. Hot new agony twisted her features. Eyes closed, she didn't recognize the keening moan as coming from her.

Strong arms gathered her against a warm chest, enveloping her in a safe cocoon. "I'm sorry, Julia. Christ, I am so sorry."

Just breathe. Everything is all right now. It's over. They're together. She repeated the familiar words, but felt the difference. Warmth seeped back into her center where once there would have been only empty cold. She didn't have to face it alone anymore.

Slowly, shuddering, she let go and buried her face against Kurt's chest. For a long time he held her close, rocking gently until she cried herself out.

Unsteadily she eased away and made a futile, embarrassed swipe over the wet shoulder of his shirt. "I've ruined your shirt."

"It'll wash out."

He walked her to the bench and gathered her back against his chest, circling his arms around her waist. "It's not your fault that Jack died."

The soft words stirred the hair on top of her head. His

deft ability to locate and extract that single thread of agony from all the others—the one that had tortured her the most over the years—hardly surprised her.

"He was my responsibility. I was the closest thing to a mother he had."

"You were a frightened child who did amazingly well under horrifying circumstances." His arms tightened as if he wanted to shake some sense into her. "It's not your fault that you lived and Jack died."

"I should have moved right away when my father yelled. If I'd gotten him into the water sooner . . ."

"No, it would have made no difference. Listen to me—over on the island, Manny said that you and Jack were both hit again in the water. For years, that man has carried around the guilt that your bodies actually shielded him as he pulled you to shore."

"Manny talked to you about it?" She turned and looked up at him. Manny had seemed as reluctant as she to relive it aloud when they revisited the cay together.

"Not much. He thought I should hear it from you. But something you said has him concerned that you might blame yourself for Jack's death. He just wanted to set the record straight: the fatal bullet struck Jack after you were in the water. The only thing that prevented those butchers from killing all of you was the arrival of the police helicopter."

Julia mulled it over. She could remember little of what happened after they'd gone overboard, other than a few images seared into her psyche: the horrible pain, Manny pulling them to shore, Jack in her arms, then his lifeless little body on the sand. But the rest? She had no clear memory of whether they'd been shot in the water. And only a vague memory of the police helicopter that had chased the monsters away.

"He said he'd never seen anyone more brave or determined than you were," Kurt continued. "You hung on to your brother all the way to shore, fighting for him even though you were badly wounded, too."

For a long moment, neither spoke.

"They were monsters," she whispered. "And they got away with it."

"They were never caught?"

"No. At least not for that." Her hair brushed Kurt's chin as she shook her head. "The helicopter couldn't follow their boat." *Because it had to take me to the hospital.* "The police had a short list of suspects with little hard proof. But I learned from the police chief up in Marsh Harbour that during the following years they all ended up in jail or murdered by rivals. The local drug lord was deported and later killed in South America by members of his own cartel."

"Live by the sword, die by the sword," Kurt murmured. "At least all the scum were taken out of circulation."

"Not all."

Kurt frowned, then understood. "The college student."

"It was Marcus Fuller." She heard him suck in his breath in surprise. She turned and faced him. "I didn't mention it earlier, because his name meant nothing to me until years later."

"But you didn't . . . ?" Uncharacteristically, Kurt hesitated, shock plain on his face.

"Recognize him?" she finished. "No, I didn't. Even with his conspicuous beauty." Her voice hardened with bitterness. "It's a tribute to my success in blocking out most of that time. When I finally met the man responsible for annihilating my family, I didn't even recognize him."

"When did you figure it out?"

"Not until after our wedding, when I overheard you talking to Sam about the trust. That's when it all clicked. That's why I went back to the cottage the next morning. I figured my grandfather would have kept a file on the trust, and that's where the answers would be."

"But Marcus evidently recognized you when you first showed up at Belle House."

"He looked at me like I was a ghost." Julia's face tightened at the memory. Another clue missed. "It must have been a huge shock seeing me after having just murdered my grandfather, but he played me like Freud. I didn't trust him at first. I sure didn't want him hanging around. But he persevered and figured out what I wanted in a friend and made himself into that friend.'' With the disturbing clarity of hindsight, she recognized that her conditions had been pathetic, few, and ridiculously easy to satisfy: no crowding, no prying, no romantic overtures.

A friend? Her brow furrowed in self-disgust. She had a more intimate relationship with Sid at the diner. She glanced up to find Kurt lost in his own thoughts.

''I should have seen it,'' he mused. ''I knew he'd gotten into trouble down here with drugs. His parents hushed it up, and he was never tried. It never even made the papers.''

''Do you think Deek and Eddie were the friends waiting on the cay? It didn't occur to me to ask the officer up in Marsh Harbour.''

''I'd bet my last dollar on it. Eddie was willing to sell Marcus out because he'd taken the fall for something Marcus and Deek did a long time ago.''

''The officer in Marsh Harbour said they eventually had to let Marcus go because they couldn't tie him to the drugs.''

''I'm sure Marcus made certain of that. Eddie was the designated fall guy.''

They sat in silence, watching the falling sun paint the sky in vivid hues. Julia felt drained and a little awkward, but mostly relieved to have her past finally out in the open. No more living in shadows.

On the way back, they stopped for a snack at the local watering hole, the only place showing signs of life in the growing dusk. When they stepped outside, twilight had blackened into night. Strains of a guitar drifted across the inky water, soon joined by a rather good tenor. Julia tilted her head to listen. ''Manny.'' She smiled. She would recognize his voice anywhere. It was one of the good memories she decided she would keep. ''We should stop by for a minute to say good-bye.''

They found Manny and Elena on *Discovery*'s deck with a few of their charter guests, relaxing over drinks in the cockpit. "Stay," Manny insisted, and Elena pushed tall glasses of some potent island concoction into their hands.

"Come on, Julia." Manny's liquid eyes sought her out where she lounged beside Kurt on the cabin trunk. "Sing a duet with me. That one your mother liked," he urged, already strumming the opening strains of "What a Wonderful World." "For old times' sake."

Julia thought she could see ghosts again, and her eyes misted. She blinked to clear them and smiled. "You go first, Slick," she agreed huskily, teasing him with the old nickname.

Elena snorted loudly. " 'Slick,' huh? It fits."

Manny rolled his eyes, muttered something about women never forgetting, and began to sing in his best gravelly Satchmo imitation.

Their voices mingled and carried out into the still blackness beyond the glow of the schooner's lanterns. When the last notes faded, a chorus of appreciative whistles and nautical bells echoed back from the darkness. At the urging of everyone aboard, they sang another before she and Kurt exchanged more farewells and plans for some future visit and, finally, took their leave.

Chapter 34

There was a whisper of movement in the dark lanai behind him before she spoke. "Kurt?"

He turned from his contemplation of surf and sky and froze, feeling as if he'd just taken a sucker punch to his tender side. She stood in the dim glow of light spilling out from the living room behind her, a modern Aphrodite adorned in a creamy, silky slip of lingerie that conjured up the sudden, hot vision of white satin bedsheets. Occupied. If that weren't bad enough, when she stepped out onto the lanai a breeze molded it against her stomach and thighs, leaving blessed little to his imagination. The second thing he noticed was that she wasn't wearing the sling.

"I thought you'd gone to bed," he said stiffly.

"I heard you leave."

He shrugged, trying to keep his eyes on her face and away from all those provocative shadows and long, exposed legs. "I took a walk."

He had a lot to mull over and hadn't been tired enough to sleep, knowing she would be only a few feet away on the other side of a very thin wall. Not after seeing so many barriers fall today. And now it was going to be impossible, he thought, watching her.

"You should get some sleep," he said finally. "It's been a rough day for you."

His voice sounded strangely abrupt. She peered into the dark, trying to read his expression. She stood uncertainly, feeling ridiculous and exposed in the satin chemise and wishing she'd kept her clothes on.

She swallowed hard. "I don't want to be alone tonight."

Her statement elicited a short, incredulous laugh from him. He strode across the porch to her, not stopping until he stood close in front of her, close enough that she could now sense the tension radiating off him in waves. His hot, frustrated gaze swept over her, then returned to linger on her chest. It made her shiver and feel suddenly overheated at the same time.

"Do you think I can lie next to you and hold you all night long and not make love to you? Because I can't. The one time I did manage it—barely—I succeeded only because I was still angry at you and because our son happened to be sleeping about two inches away." He leaned in closer and said softly, "I'm not angry anymore." He didn't need to point out that the other part of the equation was absent, too.

Julia raised a finger to his lips to silence him. "Kurt, we're married. I agreed that we would sleep together. If you're well enough . . . ?" She'd noted earlier on the beach that his stitches were gone and the wound was healing well.

"Oh, I'm ready, but are you sure? Today was hard for you."

"It's past time. Tomorrow we'll be going home. It will be easier here."

He stared at her a long moment, visibly holding back. At length, he pulled her gently into his arms. "I gave you a chance," he muttered as his mouth came down on hers.

The kiss made her light-headed. She gasped the next instant when he swung her up in his arms and carried her in a few swift strides through the cabana to his room. He deposited her on the bed and immediately reached for the bottom of his polo shirt.

Having made up his mind, he evidently wasn't going to give her a chance to change hers. Her heart was in her throat as he peeled off the shirt and shucked his shorts. The sight of all those hard planes and muscles made her feel ridiculously dizzy. Then, inexplicably, with thumbs hooked inside the waistband of his briefs, he stopped.

She raised questioning eyes to his. He was looking at a point on the wall above her head, his mouth set. "Why are you doing this?"

She stared at him in confusion. "Why am I doing what?"

"Why are you now willing—even eager—to go forward with this marriage?" He assumed an air almost of indifference, but his gray eyes settled on her. "Is it solely because of Nick? Before you answer, rest assured that it will not change anything, either way, and I will never bother you about it again. I just want to be straight on it."

She wasn't fooled for an instant by his seeming indifference. She was an old hand at that game. Her answer mattered—a lot—although pride wouldn't allow him to show it.

Absurdly, considering the complete emotional striptease she'd already done in front of him today, a part of her still instinctively wanted to back away, to play it safe. The old, familiar fear curled through her stomach. But she forced herself to meet and hold his gaze, feeling her way along. "I can't deny that I would never have agreed to marry you if I didn't think you were good for Nick. I love how you are with him. But I don't love you because of him."

Kurt looked away, disappointment palpable in the slump of his shoulders. She went on in the same slow, steady voice, never taking her eyes off him. "It's not because of Nick that I feel ridiculously weak in the knees when I look at you." That brought his eyes back to her, and the spark of hope in them made her heart thump painfully. "And it has nothing to do with Nick that when you're nearby I have a difficult time keeping my eyes off you, or that I love talking to you about so many things and constantly find myself wondering what you would think about something or other. And it has nothing to do with Nick that I wanted you at my side today when I finally confronted my demons."

She continued in a choked whisper past the lump in her throat, watching him through a haze of tears welling in her eyes, "And it's not because of Nick that I find—much to my surprise and in spite of the frightful risks involved—that I love you . . . desperately. And if you don't come over here—"

He did, pulling her up from the bed into his arms before she could complete the sentence. With raw emotion, his lips burned a trail from the top of her head down to her mouth, fusing there until Julia turned her head away.

"Wait!" She held him off with a shaky hand against his chest, struggling to clear her head. "Turnabout is fair play." She hated having to ask, hating feeling vulnerable. "Are you doing this because of Nick or because you want me? And not as some trophy wife."

He gave an incredulous snort, staring at her as if she'd gone mad. "You really need to ask?"

"Humor me," she insisted, as he had earlier on the beach.

"Okay, for the record . . ." He raked a hand through his hair in evident frustration, but on his face, amusement and happiness mingled with a look of warm indulgence that said he would give her the world if she asked. "I think I began to love you when I watched you dive into frigid water to save a little girl's life. I didn't realize it at the time, because I was scared and angry that you would do something that foolhardy." He shrugged. "Later, loving you seemed more a curse than a blessing, but it was always there. At first, only the sense that you might return my feelings if you'd let yourself kept me coming back. You are the only reason I decided to proceed with the Lost Harbor Bay project after we'd mothballed it." He gave a rueful grimace. "I needed an excuse to be near you to properly launch my siege against your considerable defenses. Then, later there was Nick."

He cupped her face gently in his hands, and his voice

vibrated with emotion. "But believe me, I have never loved you more . . ." His gaze dropped to her mouth, and he trailed a line of kisses along the length of her jaw from ear to mouth. ". . . than I do at this moment."

He lingered, exploring her willing mouth, while his hands flowed down the satin-covered length of her back in a slow exploration that reversed course when they reached the bare skin of her thighs, and then began a more intimate return journey north underneath.

She started and nearly bit his tongue when his large hands rose from her thighs to cover her bare bottom. "Wait!"

"What is it?" He pulled away just enough to peer into her face. They were both trembling and breathing rapidly. She dropped her forehead against his shoulder.

After a moment, she lifted her head, breathing more evenly. "Sorry. It's nothing. Just wedding-night jitters."

"We've made love before," he pointed out patiently. "It was the one thing we got right."

"Those were one-night stands. This is different. I don't want to mess it up."

"You won't."

He maneuvered her backward to the bed and then, unexpectedly, turned her around so she went down face first. She sent him a questioning look over her shoulder. "What . . . ?"

"Relax, darlin'," he growled in her ear as his hands closed over her rib cage and pushed her gently down into the mattress, taking care not to hurt her arm. "You're about to discover that there's more than one pair of talented hands in this family."

Within seconds, Julia blissfully agreed. Starting with her head and neck, Kurt skillfully massaged and stroked every inch of skin from her scalp to her toes, careful to take it really easy on her injured arm. He spent so much time on each limb and everything in between that she forgot to be nervous and gradually slid into a state of limp, mindless arousal. Slowly, seamlessly, the massage shifted from the sensual to the sublimely erotic. Somewhere along the way that she lacked the clarity to pinpoint, she found herself on her back, divested of the chemise.

"What are you doing to me?" she moaned, vaguely wondering if she ought not to be a bit embarrassed to be sprawled naked across Kurt's bed, shamelessly reveling in the utterly hedonistic things he was doing to her. But the notion evaporated as quickly as it took shape, unable to compete with the pleasure Kurt's wandering mouth and hands were generating.

"Well, right now, I'm stimulating certain incredibly beautiful erogenous zones that make you love and admire your husband and want to make mad, passionate love to him all night long."

"I think it's working."

"You think so?"

"Ah-huh." She reached for him and was bewildered when he evaded her arms.

"Not yet." He gave her a smugly masculine grin. "You haven't quite convinced me."

She was subjected to more of the exquisite torture until she burned so hot she didn't think she could take anymore and moaned her frustration. "Kurt . . . Please . . . !" And finally, he had mercy on her.

At first their lovemaking was gentle and tender, with Kurt taking care not to hurt her arm, and Julia taking care not to hurt his wound, but soon raging needs took over and pushed them spiraling into oblivion. Afterward, they lay with limbs entwined, savoring the soft ocean breeze wafting over their heated skin, sometimes talking softly and sometimes simply listening to the hypnotic rush of surf. She told him more about her childhood, focusing on the good things, and found that it was easier this time. He told her a little about his vastly different upbringing. Eventually, they got around to the question that had nagged him since she'd left Cherry Beach.

"Did you find what you were looking for here?"

"Some, I guess," Julia said, running her hands through the light dusting of hair on his chest. "I can't turn back the clock. I'll never forget the horror. But maybe now I can remember some of the good things.'' She smiled up at him, through eyes that were suspiciously bright, and whispered, ''And there were so very many of them.''

Kurt didn't say anything. He didn't need to. The love and compassion in his touch eased the old hurt more than any words could.

After a minute, she continued more steadily, ''I figured out that I wanted a real marriage with you. Merely surviving isn't enough anymore. You made me see that.''

He pulled her even more tightly to him. ''I thought I'd lost you when you left to come down here. I'd done everything I could think of to tie you to me.''

''There's one thing I've wondered about,'' Julia said later. ''Why didn't you tell me about the trust before we were married?''

Beneath her arm, Kurt's chest rose and fell on a long sigh. ''I was afraid you'd eventually get around to asking that. Partly, I was trying to protect you until I knew more. But the less noble part is that I was doing everything I could to stack the deck against you. I wanted you to give up and marry me, and I didn't think you would if it turned out you had a pile of money available to finance a court battle.'' He came up on an elbow to peer down at her. ''Was I right?''

Frowning, Julia tugged the sheet up under her arms and rolled over onto her back. ''I don't know,'' she said pensively. ''Marcus insisted all along that every move you made was aimed at taking Nick away from me. Of course, the more I got to know you, the less I believed him, but I could never completely discount him when the stakes were so high.'' She turned onto her side and trailed her fingertips across the stubble on his jaw, her eyes seeking forgiveness.

''Then I'm glad I didn't tell you.''

She smiled. ''I wish we didn't have to go home tomorrow.''

He pulled her close, kissing the tip of her nose. ''I was

thinking that maybe my mother and the Clearys could handle Nick just fine without us for another day or two. We have a lot to make up for."

Julia smiled. "Yes, so many years."

Epilogue

Wordlessly Kurt led the way across low dunes, away from the noisy gathering at the lodge. Amused, curious, and simply enjoying the feel of sun-warmed sand under her bare feet after the long winter, Julia let him tow her along in his wake. She hadn't bothered to protest when Kurt pulled her away from a lively debate among several teachers on the relative merits of *West Side Story* versus *Oklahoma!* for next year's high school musical.

"Are you going to tell me what was so all-fired important for me to see that we left, without our son, in the middle of Ted and Susan's party?" Julia asked mildly. She stopped to push her sunglasses up on top of her head so that she could get a better look at him.

"It isn't in the middle—everyone is about to leave anyway." Kurt neatly sidestepped her question and continued to tug her along toward the beach. "As for Nick, I told Susan we had some business to attend to, and Annie agreed to watch him."

"Business?" Julia questioned skeptically. They had reached the beach and she noted the presence of *Witchcraft*'s dinghy conveniently ready to go at the water's edge. She'd been set up! Not that she minded, exactly. She hid a smile and eyed him disapprovingly.

"And I suppose this business is aboard *Witchcraft?*" She glanced out at the sailboat bobbing gently at its mooring. The three of them, her new little family, had sailed the ketch down from Harbor Springs the weekend before. Although Julia doubted she would ever love to sail the way she once did, she hadn't been about to let them go without her, either.

Kurt grinned unrepentantly. "Can't pull anything over on you smart girls."

She groaned. "Kurt! Susan will know exactly what kind of 'business' we're up to."

"So?"

"Not to mention that we have a big new bed in our brand-new cottage not ten minutes' walk from here," she grumbled. Nevertheless, she let him assist her into the dinghy, and her stomach did an anticipatory flip-flop when his large hand rested on her hip longer than was really necessary to get the job done.

As Kurt shoved off and hopped in, her gaze sought out their new home, partially visible across the dunes. She missed the old cottage, but loved the new, nearly finished beauty that had risen from the ashes. For the time being, they were to make their home here. As for the future, Kurt was considering moving Westco's main office to nearby Traverse City. Recently, the firm had been awarded the contract to construct a new civic center there, and most of their other projects were spread out across the country. To Julia, it didn't matter a great deal either way. She could take her work anywhere. But home was wherever her two special men were.

"Now honey," Kurt was saying, a devilish grin playing around the corners of his mouth as he rowed, "you know how seriously I take your education."

Julia rolled her eyes. Ever since she'd owned up to her general lack of experience in matters of the flesh, Kurt had declared it his duty to further her education.

"And I think," he continued, his eyes drinking her up

from bare feet all the way up to the answering smile she couldn't quite suppress, "that it's about time we conduct a little . . . ah . . . field work." The last bit of improvisation was accompanied by a pleased smirk.

"Just what did you have in mind, sailor?" Julia drawled in a voice like dark honey. "A broad reach? Or maybe a close haul?" Deliberately turning the tables, she slithered forward a few inches on the hard seat and slipped open the next button on his shirt as he rowed the last few feet to the side of *Witchcraft*.

"I had in mind more serious research belowdeck." He wasted no time climbing aboard and hauling her up after him.

She gave him an arch smile when she took in the bottle of champagne and glasses waiting in a nook next to the freshly made bunk.

"My, my, you have been a busy sailor boy," she teased in that sexy silk-and-honey voice that both delighted and amazed Kurt. How far she had come from that shut-off woman she'd been when they first met. And how close she had come to eluding him.

He blinked at the moisture in his eyes and jerked her into a fierce embrace that didn't end until she was beneath him on the bunk. "I must be the luckiest jerk on the face of the planet."

"No, I am," Julia declared with equal fervor. "I love you, Kurt Weston. You brought me back to life. You helped me open a door I thought was closed forever." Her eyes filled until tears began to flow. She swiped at them impatiently. "You must think I'm crazy. I never used to cry. But with you, I'm a fountain."

"I'm willing to overlook it," he said, kissing her. "Because I have the most loving, courageous, talented—"

"Don't say it!" she warned.

". . . headstrong, aggravating. Oh, yeah, and did I mention gorgeous and sexy?"

Julia groaned.

". . . trophy wife of any Weston yet."

She swatted his back, the only place she could reach given that he had her pretty much pinned to the bunk.

"Ouch! Feisty, too," he had the gall to complain. "Anyway, despite that serious drawback," he teased, then, cradling her face in his hands and looking into her eyes, promised, "I will love you . . . always, Julia."

Always. She liked the sound of that.

Discover the Magic of Romance With

Kat Martin

__The Secret

0-8217-6798-4 **$6.99**US/**$8.99**CAN

Kat Rollins moved to Montana looking to change her life, not find another man like Chance McLain, with a sexy smile and empty heart. Chance can't ignore the desire he feels for her—or the suspicion that somebody wants her to leave Lost Peak . . .

__Dream

0-8217-6568-X **$6.99**US/**$8.99**CAN

Genny Austin is convinced that her nightmares are visions of another life she lived long ago. Jack Brennan is having nightmares, too, but his are real. In the shadows of dreams lurks a terrible truth, and only by unlocking the past will Genny be free to love at last . . .

__Silent Rose

0-8217-6281-8 **$6.99**US/**$8.50**CAN

When best-selling author Devon James checks into a bed-and-breakfast in Connecticut, she only hopes to put the spark back into her relationship with her fiancé. But what she experiences at the Stafford Inn changes her life forever . . .

Call toll free **1-888-345-BOOK** to order by phone or use this coupon to order by mail.

Name______________________________

Address______________________________

City ____________ State__________ Zip____________

Please send me the books I have checked above.

I am enclosing $__________

Plus postage and handling* $__________

Sales tax (in New York and Tennessee only) $__________

Total amount enclosed $__________

*Add $2.50 for the first book and $.50 for each additional book.

Send check or money order (no cash or CODs) to: **Kensington Publishing Corp., Dept. C.O., 850 Third Avenue, New York, NY 10022**

Prices and numbers subject to change without notice. All orders subject to availability. Visit our website at **www.kensingtonbooks.com.**